THE BOY FROM THE SEA

GARRETT CARR

The Boy from the Sea

Alfred A. Knopf
New York
2025

A BORZOI BOOK

FIRST U.S. HARDCOVER EDITION PUBLISHED BY ALFRED A. KNOPF 2025

Published by Alfred A. Knopf, a division of Penguin Random House LLC,
1745 Broadway, New York, NY 10019. Originally published in Great Britain
by Picador, an imprint of Pan Macmillan, in 2025.

Knopf, Borzoi Books, and the colophon are registered trademarks of
Penguin Random House LLC.

Library of Congress Control Number: 2024952789
ISBN: 9780593802885 (hardcover)
ISBN: 9780593802892 (eBook)

penguinrandomhouse.com | aaknopf.com

Printed in the United States of America

2   4   6   8   9   7   5   3   1

The authorized representative in the EU for product safety and compliance
is Penguin Random House Ireland, Morrison Chambers, 32 Nassau Street,
Dublin D02 YH68, Ireland, https://eu-contact.penguin.ie.

For my sons

1.

WE WERE A HARDY PEOPLE, raised facing the Atlantic. A few thousand men, women and children clinging to the coast and trying to stay dry. Our town wasn't just a town, it was a logic and a fate. We knew there were more pleasant and forgiving places, we saw them on television, but they seemed meek in comparison. Each evening seagulls wheeled above returning trawlers and the sun sank fiery orange into the sea, giving us an understanding of our place on the round earth. We liked this feeling, we savoured it, but we didn't go on about it. Atlantic winds had whipped away our words until we learned to do without them. Although our town's situation was dramatic it was no postcard, and we were focused on practicalities. The presence of the sea might've invested some people with spirituality, but not us. We weren't given to spirituality and if we had superstitious feelings we stayed quiet about them.

Donegal Bay was murky and yielded nothing easily, but we had two strong countermeasures: we knew what we wanted and we knew how to work. Our ambitions were to pay off our mortgages, be a car's first owner, dig up the stones at the front and get a decent lawn down. Some of us, after the dinner, spoke quietly of conservatories or getting an extension. We were willing to toil for these things and toil was available in our town; we could get a berth and fish or work in the processing plants or drive the lorries taking our catches across the country and beyond.

We were also working for our children. We all wanted a few acres close by to put them on when they were grown, although a site for a house was the least of what we passed to them. We'd watch them toughen, enjoying their slow discovery of the industrialized bay we had landed them into. We liked having big families but there was always a chance one or two might turn out delicate, the sort who'd one day look up at us, dismayed by the bleak outlook and the isolation, crying, 'Do we have to live here?' We'd explain this was a unique, distinguished place and hopefully they'd come around. But in truth we shared something of their restlessness. We weren't actually sure we were living in the best way, or that this was the best place to be doing it. Perhaps achieving our goals would bring no real satisfaction and so much toil would be the death of us. Deep down we were hoping that our children might find their way to better lives.

This psychology might explain the fuss, the almighty fuss, when the baby arrived. Any fresh baby represented possibility but here was one with no parents, no history, a child who was entirely future. Deep yearnings were activated when he landed among us. Suddenly, somehow, there the baby was, in the arms of a man whose expression was blank, like he was himself nothing, solely his role: carrier of the child. It was Mossy Shovlin, we all knew him. Usually he was sitting on the wall of the diamond, the car park by the pier, and he wasn't the sort to bother anyone. He had walked up the shore path, from where he lived with his parents and siblings, but today somehow he held a baby. A Friday morning this was, an overcast, ugly sky with rain building. There was the strong smell of fish and damp nets, the pier was busy with clattering forklifts and hundreds of seagulls were screeching from the roofs of our houses and shops. The baby wasn't crying exactly, but making yelps and squirming, wrapped in an old towel and a woolly sweater. The sensible move would have been to take the baby to the clinic but Mossy walked past the clinic and past the garda station too. Women came out of the shops, stretched out their hands and said, 'Give us that child here.' Mossy brought the baby tight to him, bent forwards and showed them his back until the women fell silent and followed him instead. Soon Mossy picked up more followers: children on their way to school, the not-working men and John Cotter who was out buying the newspaper. Everyone was impressed with Mossy; his new sense of propriety, his dignity. By the time he was on the steep brae to the chapel a dozen people were trailing him, all thinking he was bringing the baby to the priest. But no, he walked past the chapel too. Mossy didn't stop until he got to our branch of the Ulster Bank. The building obviously held some special authority in his mind, it did have tall windows, railings all around and big stone steps. Mossy ascended the steps then turned to face the crowd. 'The tide brought the child in,' he said, 'he was laid in a barrel.'

Attempts were made to get sense out of him. 'Who's he belonging to?' asked Justine O'Donnell.

'He's a gift from the sea,' said Mossy.

Our town's dominant religion required us to believe in miracles, but we didn't.

'Go to the stony beach if you think I'm lying,' said Mossy.

The stony beach was beyond the edge of town, near St Catherine's Well and the Ships' Graveyard. It was a nook in the coast, just the length of a lorry and trailer, composed of round grey stones, seaweed and rubbish; twists of frayed rope, chucks of polystyrene and orange spherical floats broken from nets. Currents in Donegal Bay had their own patterns, the tide deposited junk on this stretch while in the next inlet it did the opposite, picking the stones clean twice a day. Flotsam was always washing up on the stony beach so Mossy, as he walked by, had paid no mind to the half-barrel heaving on low swells sixty feet out. The barrel was blue and made of tough plastic, the sort we used for exporting salted fish. It was sawn in half lengthways and the way it floated had caused Mossy to stop. 'It was quare steady in the water,' he said, 'only for that I'd have gone by.' He shook his head at the realization. 'I could've easily gone by.'

Mossy had stepped off the path and walked to the tideline. From both its draught and its even keel he could tell the half-barrel was ballasted. Water lapped near his feet as he watched; it would take half an hour for the barrel to drift in but Mossy had no big plans for the day, just a session of sitting on the diamond wall. In a while Mossy saw movement and a flash of silver inside the barrel and that was when he pulled off his shoes and socks and went in. The barrel was lined with tinfoil, probably some notion of insulation, and the ballast proved to be a small concrete slab with a blanket folded over it. On top of that was the baby, pink, eyes wide to the grey sky, well wrapped. Most of us would have stared in shock but Mossy had the kind of mind capable of instant acceptance, an undervalued ability. He reached in and picked up the baby.

"The barrel's still there if you don't believe me,' said Mossy from the bank steps. 'Go and look.'

Later the doctor declared the baby healthy enough, considering, and just a few days old. The district nurse offered to take him home until the next move was decided. She was pleased to have charge of the baby; the whole town was chatting about him and he was likely to get a full page in the *Donegal Democrat*. The idea that the baby came in on the tide was madness, yet it was the only explanation going and we were gripped. Shyly, some of us approached the district nurse's driveway, watching the windows of her house, and feeling ridiculous. We were glad when others arrived to feel ridiculous too. It was evening when the nurse started letting people in, four at a time, and soon her place resembled a wake house, cars parked up on the verges all around and lots of us coming and going, speaking quietly. We brought gifts: soft toys, rattles and woolly hats knitted that afternoon in a frenzy. Four by four we were ushered in to stand before the sofa where one of the nurse's teenage daughters was reclined with the baby, contented and snoozing in his new white babygro. 'He takes the bottle great, not a bit of bother,' said the district nurse. 'He's a wee dote.'

The baby had startling black hair but there was no talk of fairies or spirit children in our town, you'd go to Galway if you were after that kind of thing. The baby was just another human child, but all the same we felt shaken by mysteries and wanted to give our regards. The nurse and her daughters kept vigil over the baby all night. The woman next door placed a lit candle in her window and soon half the town was at it, pinpoints of light quivering on windowsills in every street. On Sunday people who hadn't come near the chapel in years returned and the masses were full. Fishermen, the not-working men and the other men from the town who normally stood down at the back came and knelt in pews with the old, the women and the pious. If a baby was abandoned in a hospital car park or other common location the priest would've been sure to give out, going on about teen pregnancy and blaming television and the Rolling Stones. Instead, that Sunday he led us into contemplation. He spoke of Moses found floating in a basket. Hughie Devlin turned to his wife and was heard to whisper, 'Didn't I tell you this whole thing reminded me of something?'

The district nurse had her job and the daughters had school so she started lending the baby out to spend a night with other families around town. A fisherman named Ambrose Bonnar got to hear of this and drove straight to the nurse's place. Standing at her door, Ambrose said, 'Our boy is clear off the cot now but we still have it and the other tackle.' Ambrose was willing to take the baby away right then. He pointed with his thumb towards the back of his car. 'I've got a basket for him,' he said. 'Very comfortable.'

The nurse was surprised to have a man asking after the baby. This was 1973. 'Has Christine agreed?' she asked.

'The wife's great with a baby,' said Ambrose.

The nurse hesitated. 'And how are you with a baby yourself?' she asked.

Ambrose stood straighter. 'Even better than her,' he said.

False immodesty; many of us used this style of presentation but Ambrose was particularly committed to it.

'It'll only be for tonight,' said the district nurse. 'The McGinleys want him tomorrow. The Church Lane McGinleys that is. The Crochna Road McGinleys haven't asked, though I'd say they will.'

When Ambrose arrived home Christine was in the kitchen area with their two-year-old, Declan, and her sister Phyllis. Phyllis lived a short walk up the lane and called to her sister daily.

She was in her spot, the high stool near the back door with an ashtray on her knee. The Bonnar bungalow was small; the living area and kitchen area were one room, separated only by the transition from lino to carpet tiles. Christine was in her usual tea-and-cigarette position, the armchair by the washing machine. The chair gave her a grandmotherish air, although she was only in her early thirties. The sisters smoked Silk Cut Red, which had tinted their fingers yellow; Ambrose was a Benson & Hedges man. Declan was in his playpen and laughed when he heard Ambrose entering the house and calling out, 'Someone here wants to meet you all!'

Declan's mood changed when he saw the visitor in his father's arms. He dropped the lump of plastic he was gnawing on, gripped the bars, pulled himself to his feet and stared. 'Why?' he said. A few months previously 'why' had been his first word, as if he knew he was going to need it.

Phyllis put it differently. 'What kind of madness is this?'

Christine looked at her husband and waited for an explanation. Ambrose offered none, just sat at the table in a pleased sort of way, putting the baby facing out on his knee. Triggered by his upright position, the baby opened his eyes. They were like two raisins, they reflected no light. He gazed in the direction of the toddler in the pen, then in the direction of Phyllis Lyons and finally at Christine Bonnar née Lyons. He remained neutral about all of them.

'When are you handing him back?' Phyllis asked Ambrose.

Declan grunted. 'Why?' he said again. No one noticed his excellent enunciation; all were fixated on the baby.

'A fine specimen of a child, isn't he?' Ambrose said to everyone. 'Look at the hair on him!'

'Spanish father I'd say,' said Phyllis, 'there was a boat of them in last year.'

'Whisht,' said Ambrose.

'I'm thinking of the mother,' said Christine, 'she's probably alone somewhere now. Sick, frightened.'

'Sure, didn't the child float up the bay?' said Ambrose, glibly.

'Even you've more sense than that,' said Phyllis.

By this time some of us were getting over the spell of the child and the mystery of his arrival, we were rediscovering our common sense. There were surely plainer explanations than the supernatural or that he had drifted up the bay. Not all of us felt able to air our good sense publicly yet as some of us were still enthralled, but Phyllis had avoided that problem by being openly cynical from day one. 'Who's going to change the filthy nappies?' she asked.

'I can handle a nappy,' said Ambrose, 'when need be.'

'Don't you do a thing with the child,' Phyllis told her sister. Phyllis was four years older than Christine and always ordered her about. When Christine found a husband Phyllis had adapted, learning to order him around too. Her position on the stool helped her dominate, not because it was tall but because it was uncomfortable and near the back door. Locating herself there kept her hosts destabilized as she seemed permanently on the cusp of leaving. Why argue with someone on their way out the door? By constantly seeming about to leave Phyllis got her way often, and would still be there an hour later as well. She'd delay all afternoon now, over this baby.

Christine dragged on her cigarette. 'What's his name?' she said.

'There's no name on him,' said Phyllis, 'he's no need of one.'

'Every child needs a name!' said Ambrose. 'We should give him one.'

'By what right?' said Phyllis.

Declan made another grunt of agreement and it drew his father's attention. 'What do you think would make a good name?' Ambrose said to his child, in the jokey voice he put on when broaching something important to him.

Somehow Declan knew he was being misused; he slapped the bars of his pen and said, 'Why?'

'What did you say? Martin, was it?' said Ambrose. He turned the baby to face him and stood up, holding the baby at arm's length to reassess him. 'No, I don't think he's a Martin. There's a softness about him.'

'Why?' said Declan, tears forming in his eyes.

'Brendan? Brendan, you say?' said Ambrose and as he gazed at the baby an enchantment spread over his face, creases opening until he looked five years younger. Ambrose had always thought Brendan a beautiful name. 'Brendan, the boy from the sea.'

Christine smiled, she liked to see Ambrose enjoying himself and had always appreciated his originality. But Phyllis studied him coldly: what kind of man comes home with a stray baby? He was surely up to something. From his playpen, Declan was also watching closely. He was barely verbal so his instincts were raw and sharp and he saw what was happening, seeing further even than Phyllis. This baby wasn't going anywhere, this baby was going to stay. The world as he knew it had ended.

Some history must now be gone into. You'll want to know how Ambrose came to live in our town and how he came to belong. Ambrose was born and raised on Arranmore, an island not far off County Donegal's coast. The island is only a fifty-mile stretch around the coast from our town, but that was enough to make Ambrose a blow-in. Pure fisherman though, he'd gotten his start young, a quiet child who was transformed when he began seine-netting for mackerel in the island's rocky inlets. Mackerel fishing was a community task and young Ambrose found he had talent for organizing the other children and later the adults too. When still only eleven or twelve Ambrose was held in enough esteem to be let roar orders at everyone. He'd set some islanders throwing stones into the water to scare fish toward the mesh, and position three or four families to handle the net. Once full, the net was dragged onto the strand and everyone fell upon it, grabbing the flopping fish, giving them a good knock on the head and throwing them into boxes. Ambrose went at this work lustily, loving the primal satisfaction of landing a catch and the sense of self-worth that resulted. Across Arranmore men and women would greet him on the road saying, 'I'm told you did great work today,' or 'I hear you did well.' They all said he was a natural-born fisherman.

In his teens Ambrose, a brother and two cousins formed a four-man crew to cast nets from a twenty-footer. They worked like demons and weren't afraid of hail or pitch-black nights. They were the island's most successful crew and well known on the mainland where they'd sell their catch. Other crews started to fit their boats with outboard motors or adapted van engines, installing them mid-vessel to drive a prop, but Ambrose had his crew stick with oars. A boyish notion of manhood had him completely and he felt no need for an engine between him and the sea, he was a natural element himself.

Ambrose's brothers and sisters were migrating in a steady

stream and everyone could see Ambrose would leave too. He
had a simple aspiration, to work on bigger boats, trawlers, so one
day he divided the last take with the crew and they went home
without him. Ambrose travelled to a fishing town at the opposite
corner of Ireland, Dunmore East, County Waterford, where he
took berths on trawlers and became a feature of the pubs when
ashore. Ambrose fished and caroused about the place for three
years until a dissatisfaction grew in him again. Now he wouldn't
be happy until he was a skipper, with his own crew under him,
and he couldn't imagine it happening there. Waterford's fishermen annoyed him, they were tame and too fond of priests. He
was deckhand on a trawler and only three hours out one day
when they heard that President Kennedy was killed in America.
With great solemnity, the skipper said they were returning to
port as a 'mark of respect'. Mark of respect! And the sea heaving
with fish! It was the most demented thing Ambrose ever encoun-
tered. Words were had.

Ambrose was only really happy working with Tommy
O'Gara. Tommy was another young Donegal man looking
around the country before settling. He was from our town and
we knew his parents well, the O'Garas of Three Mile Cross,
lovely people. Not to be confused with the O'Garas who ran the
post office, although they were lovely people too. Most trawlermen played cards during downtime but Tommy and Ambrose
got into chess, going in together to order a magnetized set from
a catalogue. While Waterford men banged down their playing
cards and roared in exaltation or complaint, Tommy and
Ambrose played chess peaceably, passing only occasional
remarks, compliments or light mockery. Making a moderately
good move Ambrose always said, 'That's you now, doomed.'

Fishing, they agreed, would be their lives and in search of more experience they travelled on to Cork. They often fished together out of Castletownbere over the next few years.

There were other experiences to be sought and during his travels Ambrose had his fair share of dalliances with women. Ireland's shop girls and barmaids found him original at least and they'd lean in to a fumble happily enough and go a bit further down over time. He and the girls were young and this was before contraception so things were simpler, so simple some of us went a year or two unsure if we were technically virgins or not. Sexual education tended to consist of watching cows or goats going at it so it was a good thing the country had plenty of livestock. Sex was still an undeveloped, pawing sort of thing and its language was all about prohibition rather than options. Sex talk from a woman was only to raise alerts with a breathy whisper or a hiss. 'We don't want an accident.' 'That's your limit now.' 'Go on then so but off to the side there.'

Soon Ambrose and Tommy began to find Cork crews irritating too. The two Donegal men could stand side by side repairing a net in contented silence for an hour at a time but Cork ones always had to be chatting. 'And even with that,' said Tommy, 'they like to leave you feeling they've kept something from you.'

They weren't as bad as Connemara men though, as Ambrose discovered when he fished out of Galway City the following year. They were crippled by superstition. A big, strong fisherman might arrive at the pier before set-off and he'd be fretting like a child because he had met a red-haired woman on the road, or he had accidently packed an odd number of socks, or a blackbird had chirped at him three times, or some other nonsense.

After Galway, Ambrose worked a few seasons going for razor

clams out of Dublin. He didn't like Dubliners either, they thought
Donegal was in Northern Ireland and put no effort into understanding his accent. By now Ambrose had his skipper's ticket but
was hankering for something more: ownership of his own vessel.
He told no one about this aspiration until the afternoon he spotted Tommy on the pier. He hadn't seen him in a year and he
almost ran to him. He didn't of course, but almost. They leaned
together on a wall and smoked and talked for ages. Ambrose
complained about his new crew but Tommy had grown more
tolerant over the years. 'You shouldn't expect to meet the finest
men of any given town on a deck,' said Tommy.

Ambrose was unsettled. He had always believed fishing
attracted the finest men.

'I know your problem,' said Tommy, 'you want to be closer to
home, on more familiar rocks. And to be honest I'm the same.
Let's do it then, let's go back to Donegal.'

So they did, not to Arranmore but to Tommy's town, our
town, Killybegs. Ambrose settled in quickly, he liked our familiar
pace and even the cast of our faces was homely for him. Here he
could make the next step. He was only in town a week when he
visited the boatyard. Our yard was the full shebang, steel sheets
and oak trees went in one end and, some months later, a boat
came out the other, through its big double doors and directly
onto the bay. Ambrose had no appointment, he just walked up
to the first man he saw and said, 'Can I stick my name down for
a boat?' This was unorthodox but did no harm. Soon the Sea
Fisheries Board agreed a hire purchase deal with Ambrose,
lining him up for a £30,000 fifty-six-footer. These were big numbers for a young man. Fifty-footers were more standard those
days but Tommy persuaded Ambrose to go bigger, ordering the

kind of trawler he too was investing in. Six feet mightn't sound much but draught and beam went up proportionally and you got a more robust vessel, taking an engine of over a hundred horse-power. 'English boats travel days to get to our waters,' said Tommy. 'Meanwhile our fleet always stays within sight of shore. We need to go further, beyond the horizon, that's where the money is.'

Ambrose and Tommy saved up for the latest wheelhouse equipment and, while awaiting the construction of their own vessels, they worked on boats where they'd learn to use it. We were getting smarter, investing in new equipment that meant fishing was less about chance and instinct. Some boat owners travelled to Sweden, returning with new nets and techniques. Once a genuine living Swede was shipped over and put up in Marie Cotter's bed and breakfast so he could spend a week walking up and down the pier telling everybody what they were doing wrong. Ambrose didn't mind as the Swede went about it in a chirpy sort of way that he enjoyed. Assisted by new echo sounders boats could now come home with seventy or eighty cran of herring. Getting heavy trawls aboard was becoming a problem for the smaller boats, the bags so full the fish could get crushed against the hull and the load lose buoyancy, causing the vessel to lurch. If the sea was heavy things could get dicey. One day a fifty-footer Ambrose was working pitched so sharply he was lifted clean into the air, head first in an arc with an ultimate destination overboard. Death brushed against trawlermen about twice a week but Ambrose always said this was his closest pass. The next thing he felt was Tommy grabbing him by the collar and then the shock through his legs as he was planted back on deck. 'That's no day for a swim,' said Tommy.

One thing making Ambrose different from us was that he believed in luck; we weren't ourselves given to superstition. It seemed everything had aligned to keep him from going in the water that day and Ambrose felt intensely lucky. Back late in the evening, he was exhausted but still electrified. Tommy and the rest of the crew were home to their beds but Ambrose slapped a palmful of Brylcreem into his hair and went to the dance hall. The next part of his life was about to begin.

Christine Lyons had struggled to get the hair up that evening, grunting and jabbing the back of her neck with clips, sitting on the edge of her bed, the wardrobe open so to use the oval mirror inside the door. She couldn't set the hair by herself but Phyllis wasn't moving from her room next door. 'Ach, please?' said Christine.

The wall between them was thin and as children they learned to talk through it, keeping each other company when their father sent one to her room, usually Christine. Even now they maintained the habit, quietly speaking to each other through the wall at night and first thing in the morning. 'Will you not leave it a while?' said Phyllis, both pleading and chastising. 'It's only been two days.'

'No, I'm off out,' said Christine. 'Now will you come here and help me with this?'

Christine heard her sister leave her room but she didn't come through her door. She thought Phyllis might've gone to make a report to their father. Eunan Lyons was in his sixties and a severe kind of man. He worked hard lobstering but at home expected, and got, everything done for him: he had never folded a shirt, cleaned a cup or prepared a meal of any sort. Christine started grappling with her hair again, she'd feel better equipped to argue with him if her hair was up, no one could outsmart her when the hair was up. But Phyllis hadn't gone to their father, she had paused in the hallway a few seconds to put fear into her sister, and she now entered the room, although looking annoyed about it. Without nicety, she took her sister's hair in both hands and lifted it, wrapped a hairband around the end and rolled it up. 'Them ones in the town will be delighted to see you,' she said. 'It'll give them something to natter about.'

The Lyons lived about a mile out of town and said such things, as if the half-hour walk to the diamond gave them a lofty perspective. The mile was only part of it, their father had instilled in them the idea they were different. Many of us lived inter-dependently, with neighbours, cousins and through marriage, but that wasn't Eunan Lyons's style at all, he believed only imme-diate family mattered. He sold his lobsters in the town, married a woman from the town, his daughters went to school in the town but he was determined not to belong to the town. This contrariness and self-reliance was bred into him through gener-ations of slog, dark moods and the lack of opportunities. His grandfather had claimed to remember the Famine and some-times Eunan thought he did too.

When the hair was erected Christine blasted hairspray into the air above, the cloud descending to give the beehive a hard shell. 'How do I look?' she said.

'You're more Aunty Brigit than Brigitte Bardot,' said Phyllis.

The Lyons lived up an old bog lane, off the main road west, just beyond a steep sharp corner we called the bad bend. Christine had walked the road to town for school every day, coming to know every pothole, and since leaving school she walked the road thousands more times for jobs in fish-processing plants, the

THE BOY FROM THE SEA

Ship Inn, and, most recently, in Conway's shoe shop. Conway's suited her best, the satisfaction of an ordered storeroom and the pleasing stiffness of new treated leather. You'd also meet a better class of man in a shoe shop. When knelt down to do a fitting Christine might place a man's socked foot on her leg, just above the knee, casual like, almost feasibly just for convenience. She did this a few times before finally accepting that men from our town weren't able to take hints.

The Foresters' Hall smelled of hairspray, tea and the fish scales under our nails. The showband were into their first set. The hall was only half-full but four bouncers were on duty as fights often broke out when boat crews arrived. Some daughters weren't allowed to attend dances due to these brawls but Eunan no longer imposed such rules; Phyllis had taken up his objections so fully they were now her own, while Christine earned money for herself and couldn't be stopped. All the same, we were surprised to see Christine arrive that night. Inside the door she shed her long dark coat and the turquoise sheen of her dress was suddenly there and brash and almost shocking. Christine went to the women's side, smiling hello to people in a determined manner. She bought a cup of tea at the urn and took up a position alone, watching the band. She was very still. Across the way the men spoke in huddles, all hunched and wearing more-or-less the same suit. They looked like bank robbers as they glanced over at the women. There was no alcohol at these dos but some men got pints into themselves before arriving. Tonight Christine ignored the men completely, not a glance. She held one arm angled away from her and in her long fingers, the way a starlet might hold a cigarette, was the teacup on its saucer. Live music attracted some old ones and a few married couples and they mingled as they pleased on both sides of the hall. Their presence might've been the reason Ambrose, when he walked in, misread the arrangement and walked straight over to the women's side. He was also lured by the brightness of Christine's dress. Ambrose was wearing his winter woolly pullover but you couldn't have told him he looked ridiculous as he was impervious to that sort of thing. Later they'd remember the showband was playing 'Strangers in the Night' as he approached Christine, but it was actually 'Crystal Chandeliers'. Ambrose didn't ask her to dance as he wasn't one for dancing.

'Hello,' he said. Big grin on him, you might've taken him for simple-minded. 'Fine evening.'

'So who are you?' Christine asked him. She knew well but wasn't letting on.

'Ambrose Bonnar,' he said. 'Pleased to meet you.'

They shook hands.

'I've my own boat,' said Ambrose. Although done with contemporary flourishes his courtship style was essentially what a woman might've got in the Stone Age.

Christine made sure not to smile. 'Well for you,' she said.

'Or I will when she's built,' he said. 'There's a waiting list, but I'll have her in a year or so.'

By making it clear he wanted to impress her, Ambrose had handed Christine the role of being hard to impress, and therefore put her in command. She decided to keep hold of this position. Ambrose glanced around and didn't seem to know what to do with his arms, but he was enjoying himself, still giddy with luck. He asked, 'Would you take a Kit Kat?'

'No, you're all right,' said Christine. Her expression was neutral but she kept her gaze on him. Ambrose was very ruddy, like he was never under a roof in his life, but get past that and he wasn't bad-looking. Christine knew a lot of women would've liked to be in her flats now, the consensus said Ambrose was a good catch. It had taken a while to recognize this due to his rough demeanour and the fact that he had taken up the caravan behind Big Jimmy's cottage, which was usually rented by drunks and drifters. Yes, he'd need domestication, but he worked hard, got on with everyone and would soon be the youngest boat owner in town. Ambrose also had the wide capabilities of an island man; aside from fishing, he could strip an engine, lay a brick, cut a tidy run of turf, drive a lorry and bone a chicken. Some of his skills were heading out of style but the range indicated confidence and a good brain. Being an outsider did him no harm either, it gave him an air of possibility. Arriving fresh and unburdened, Ambrose seemed like a man with a better-than-average chance of doing well. A woman needed a bit of hope.

'Would you believe I made more than five pounds out the bay the day?' said Ambrose.

Christine decided to test him with the truth. 'Would you believe my mammy's only dead, we buried her two days back, and here I am at a dance?'

Ambrose's hesitation was minuscule, if there at all. 'I believe it because I see it,' he said.

'I'll be given hell for it,' said Christine.

Ambrose considered this. 'Then we'd better make it worth the while.'

Just then the double doors were barged open by a bunch of boys in uniform. The band lost their places and took a few chords to recover. An Irish navy corvette had docked for supplies and it looked like half the crew were out on the town.

Grinning, they cut across the floor in triangular formation, scoping out the men, the women, and the tea and biscuits. They were delighted with themselves, in their white hats, and their assertiveness was an affront to the local men. You could actually see agitation pass along the crowd, like an electric charge leaping man to man.

'There's going to be a fight,' said Christine. She pressed her cup on Ambrose. 'How about you get tea for us and we'll find seats with a view.'

After the dance Ambrose walked Christine home, not quite to her door but all the way to the bad bend. There they stopped and had a mighty shift under the stars.

One afternoon a month later Ambrose met Christine's father for the first time. She warned him about Eunan, saying he was judgemental and argumentative and sure to be difficult but Ambrose still walked in confident, the father was a lobster-pot man and Ambrose was sure they'd find plenty to chat about. The Lyons's front room was the living area but the dining table was in there too, while the kitchen was down the hallway at the back of the house. Collected by Christine's mother, various vases and figurines were dotted about the front room, including many along the mantelpiece, although the fireplace hadn't been used since her death, an embroidered picture in a frame now concealed it. Eunan was sat at the dining table and didn't arise for the visitor. His disposition was tense.

'Fine place,' said Ambrose, sitting down opposite him and patting the tabletop with his palm. He grinned all about him before settling on Eunan. 'Working the day?' he asked.

Eunan eyed Ambrose suspiciously. 'Yes,' said Eunan. 'A man has to be of use.'

'You're damn right!' said Ambrose, delighted to have the matter put so deftly. He looked to Christine, who was perched on the footstool by her father's armchair. 'Isn't he damn right?' he said.

Christine nodded encouragingly. Ambrose was doing well.

Eunan narrowed his eyes further. The truth was that Eunan needed glasses, but he wasn't going to admit it for another two years. To him Ambrose was mostly just a ruddy, talkative shape at the other end of the table.

'Any big lobsters in it?' Ambrose asked him.

Eunan didn't like people knowing his business. There was a long pause before he said, 'Big enough.'

Phyllis came in to serve tea, pouring it for her father first. Ambrose looked down at the cup, which was on a saucer and ridiculously small and delicate. The cup threw Ambrose off, he suddenly felt out of place. He looked to Christine for assistance, but she didn't understand. Still looking at her Ambrose found himself saying, 'The biggest thing I ever hauled was a sunfish.'

He had spoken very quietly. 'A what?' said Eunan.

Ambrose turned to him. 'A sunfish,' he said. 'Have you ever seen one of those creatures?'

Eunan gave nothing away, just made a slight move of the head, and Ambrose continued. 'This one was bigger than a tractor's back tyre,' he said. 'It came up in our net. Water spouting from its mouth and its eye roving around. We all jumped across deck to free it. Massive it was, huge.' Ambrose's words fell away again as he became caught up in the memory. That day he had experienced an awe so intense it permanently marked him. He had known enormous fish were passing beneath them all the time but he had never looked one in the eye before. 'Huge,' he said a couple more times at the Lyons's table, his voice almost a whisper.

Eunan interrupted loudly: 'Would you not just carve up the creature?' he said. 'It sounds like there'd be a lot of dinners got from it.'

Ambrose paused. 'No, we didn't,' he said carefully, 'we didn't want it aboard, it was the width of the deck.'

Christine thought the sunfish story was great. 'That's amazing,' she said, gazing at Ambrose.

It didn't much matter what Ambrose said that afternoon, Eunan would've taken a dislike to him anyway. Eunan was against anything without set purpose and complete predictability and a human tended to fail on these requirements. He was against surprises, he hadn't allowed a telephone in the house for many years as you never knew when it might ring on you. He mocked anything frivolous: placemats, dessert, having a lie-in, suffering from your nerves. 'Get away out of that!' he'd shout at cream cakes and people with hay fever. To him harsh words weren't a bad thing, they were just a little sandpaper, giving a person a hard-wearing exterior. 'I was often spoken to harshly and it's done me no harm,' he'd say and no one dared disagree.

Eunan loathed anyone making a display of themselves and didn't approve when, a year later, Ambrose took delivery of his trawler and named it the *Christine Dawn*. 'Ambrose's boat should just be called *Ambrose's Boat*,' he said. 'That's what we'll be calling it under this roof.'

Nor did he like when they got married and Christine took Ambrose's name, she seemed too eager to drop Lyons.

Nonetheless, Eunan gave them the site for a house. He owned the two acres along one side of the bog lane to his place and gave them the lower section, down closer to the main road. 'It'll do you,' he said.

Ambrose was not delighted to build three hundred yards from his father-in-law but a free site was a free site and the old man only had a limited number of years in him surely. The plot was nothing only windswept banks of heather, but it was elevated with a view of the bay and horizon that was wide and splendid. They got a mortgage and built a two-bedroom bungalow in the high-Donegal style of the era: excessively large windows; concrete render that would look better when painted or pebble-dashed but would do grand until you had the money, and a section of irregular cladding, like crazy paving, on the wall near the front door. The latter element had no structural purpose, it was just there to look modern for a few years and then look terrible for decades. The house sat on open heath, twenty steps from the lane, no garden, nothing to indicate the site boundaries. The driveway was created by the JCB digger when it pulled off the lane to dig the foundations, Ambrose getting the operator to go back and forth a few times until the clay was pressed down nicely.

Ambrose was making a small but steady living with the *Christine Dawn*. She was a lively boat, dry and good in any weather. He went to sea happy but wasn't one of these men glad to be away from the wife, he rarely went to the pub after a trip out, preferring to get home. Now he and Christine had shelter and a livelihood we expected a child, but a few years went by with no sign. If there were difficulties they were got over as three or four years into the marriage an eight-pounder was landed and christened Declan. Christine and Ambrose were wild for the boy and there was at last one living person Eunan approved of without reservation. Motherhood helped Christine connect with women from the town, something she had never quite done before. Asking about their men at sea tended to gag them with stoicism but their children got them chatting. We could see Christine becoming more her own person. Now when we met her we asked after Declan, not Eunan. Phyllis remained in thrall to their father but there was reasonable satisfaction on the lane: two sisters in two houses, one child, a father, a mother and a grandfather. That was the scene when the new baby arrived, the boy from the sea.

2.

AMBROSE FELT A SLEEPING BABY bestowed a specific hush on a house: warm and tangible, you could lean in to it. In their bedroom he draped a towel over the lampshade to make the light soft. Declan had been moved into the other room to free up the cot and Ambrose laid down the swaddled baby. 'Look at you,' whispered Ambrose and he reached over to the bedside locker, switched the radio on low and the shipping forecast emerged faintly, its repetition a kind of lullaby.

Christine needed a while to get Declan settled in the strange bed. Afterwards she came to the door and stood in the frame, watching Ambrose as he watched the baby. She decided not to disturb the moment, slipping away to the kitchen and lifting a bag of groceries to bring to the Lyons. About twice a week Phyllis rang Christine and asked her to 'nip to the town' for supplies. Christine knew the requests were Phyllis's way of reminding her of her original family, reminding her that she had other responsibilities, but she didn't complain, it was a small contribution.

A thin layer of drizzle coated her hair in the short time it took to reach the Lyons's bungalow. It was of concrete, built in the 1950s, and gave a strong impression of weight and mass, with unpainted stone-chip render, thick wavy asbestos roof tiles, coated in moss, and steel-frame windows divided into small panels. Atlantic storms never damaged this house; the glass panels were too small, the tiles too heavy. She opened the front door while tapping on it with her knuckle and deposited the bag of groceries on the carpet. Phyllis appeared in the doorway to the front room and said, 'Come in.'

Christine hesitated, she preferred a quick handover but Phyllis had already ducked away. Since finding her own life Christine noticed herself shrinking every time she entered her father's house. The shrinking was physical, a downward pinch on her shoulders, but also mental, a sense of inhibition, a choking of the personality. She had realized she must've been shrunken all those years without knowing it, the decades she lived under those heavy slates.

The Lyons's front room was lit by a single but intensely bright bulb hanging from the middle of the ceiling. The light was cast cleanly downward by a thick lampshade, giving the room an interrogatory atmosphere. Christine stayed by the door, not wanting to step into the cone of light. Normally her father would be sitting at the dining table, waited on by Phyllis, or in his armchair watching television, so it was disconcerting to find him standing at the far wall. 'You've a guest,' he said.

'It's just for the night,' said Christine.

'We were never people for charity, giving or taking,' said Eunan.

'Just one night,' said Christine.

A framed photograph sat on the television cabinet, Declan as a baby. But that didn't mean Eunan wanted other people's offspring about the place. His pride in his grandson was mostly of a procreative nature, it was good to see oneself extend into the future.

'Ambrose has lots of brothers and sisters,' said Phyllis, standing in the shadows by the dresser. 'A man raised like that always wants a big family for himself.'

'Ach, you and your theories,' said Christine.

'Wait 'til you see,' said Phyllis, 'he'll start dropping hints about keeping the child and then mope when he doesn't get his way. You should get that child back to the nurse first thing in the morning.'

This was the limit of Phyllis's world, thought Christine, the man of the house would want things and the woman had to scamper around fulfilling those wishes, or else contrive ways to block them without direct confrontation. Phyllis simply couldn't imagine that Christine might do something because she had wants of her own. 'I'd better head back down,' she said.

'Did you bring the ham for Daddy's sandwiches?' asked Phyllis.

'You didn't ask for ham,' said Christine.

Phyllis looked away along the floor, let down again.

'I'll go to the shop in the morning,' said Christine.

Christine walked home, her arms folded tight to herself and tapping a forefinger against her jacket, wanting a cigarette. The heaving bay was invisible in the night but it charged the air, a low white noise emitting from all points west. At home she found Ambrose stretched across the two-seater in the living area, smiling up at her with a gentle contentment, the presence of the baby had him in great form. Her husband had always maintained an innocent positivity about the world, a characteristic that sometimes infuriated Christine, although she could admire it too. She took the cigarette from between his fingers, had a long drag and looked down on him. 'Enjoying yourself?' she said.

The next afternoon the phone rang and Ambrose answered, it was the district nurse. He listened then put his hand over the mouthpiece and said to Christine, 'The McGinleys can't take the baby after all, so she's asking if we can hang on to him another night?'

Without hesitation Christine said, 'We'll have him surely.'

The McGinleys' change of mind was a sign that our enchantment with the baby was fading. We were always inclined towards plain realism, and would've gotten there eventually ourselves, but got there faster due to Phyllis. She had pointed out a few hard truths around the town. That morning she had gone into the post office and found a small crowd of us standing around talking about the baby. We tended to adopt a solemn tone for these conversations, and some of us had just taken a pilgrimage to the stony beach to look at the barrel. Sally Keeney had her hand up to her own throat, a poise of reverence. 'It's beautiful, just sitting there,' she said.

Phyllis butted in and asked, 'Is it true the barrel is lined in tinfoil? Like for a Christmas turkey!'

Sally wasn't pleased but everyone else looked at each other to confirm it was okay to laugh, then did laugh. Until then we always said the barrel was lined in silver sheets, knowing it was tinfoil really but never acknowledging this publicly. Now it was acknowledged and the crib's magic was reduced.

Next, in the butcher's, Phyllis questioned the barrel's location: thirty feet beyond the tideline and next to the path. Mossy could've dragged it up certainly, but why so far? Those present admitted this was a good question. Furthermore, the barrel was raised on a pile of stones. There was no reason for Mossy to build this heap, all he needed do was lift the baby and head for town.

Conversations continued among us and soon another version of events took shape, a more likely version. Someone, the mother presumably, had wanted to leave the baby safe but also get away unseen. The stony beach made sense, it was secluded but workers and youngsters heading for school were guaranteed to pass that way and see right into the barrel as it was placed by the path. We began to realize the barrel hadn't drifted in and the boy wasn't from the sea, he was just another abandoned child, Mossy just happened to be the first person going by. Mossy's family went at him for the truth but he clammed up. 'Could Mossy be the father?' Manus McManus wondered aloud with the other customers at the counter of the Ship Inn. This was contemplated a moment before there was general laughter. 'Mossy's next shift will be his first!'

Talk converged around a girl who had been staying in the terrace behind the fire station. Those houses had broken windows, peeling paint and yards thick with four-foot weeds. Some of the not-working men lived in them, along with dropouts who'd stay a fortnight and kip anywhere. The girl had come and gone from the terrace a few times over recent months and picked up work in a processing plant, but there was confusion about her name. Colette? Catherine? Someone said Christabel which sounded unlikely but peculiar sorts flopped along the terrace. We knew she was no longer in town and the girls who had been working the belts near her were convinced she had been pregnant.

First we had associated the baby with the Atlantic and fresh air but now he was tainted by the back street, rising damp and drifters with secrets. The district nurse said the baby wasn't such a dote after all, he had vomited on her uniform and given her dirty looks. She rang the Bonnars and asked Ambrose to keep him a third night. Again, he put his hand over the mouthpiece and looked to Christine. She gazed at his open expression and hopeful eyes and she nodded silently.

That evening Ambrose again placed the sleeping baby in the cot. He then lay back on the bed listening to his breathing and the wind against the slates. Ambrose knew he should go to the kitchen but he felt a reckoning coming and his instinct was to avoid it, he was of the sort who prefer to live in an ongoing flow rather than deal with negotiated decision points. When he heard Christine approach, Ambrose closed his eyes and pressed his head into the pillow. She came in, looked at the baby then sat on the bed. Christine didn't engage with her husband's pretence of sleep, she just spoke. 'Tell me what you're thinking.'

Sounds simple, but Ambrose wasn't well equipped for it. This wasn't for lack of words, he had plenty of words in both English and Irish, what he lacked was the ability to see himself from the outside, to understand himself with perspective. He wasn't the only one, we all had bills to pay and no time to sit around thinking about ourselves like we were fascinating conundrums. Ambrose came from a long line of men and women who were the same, with no facility for and not much interest in analysing their own ways.

Christine said, 'You know this baby isn't any of the ones we lost?'

Ambrose's face crunched up. It could've been pain, it could've been mirth. 'Ah, now,' he said, 'I'm not a complete fool.'

'And you know his real mammy might come looking for him?' said Christine.

'I know,' said Ambrose and he opened his eyes.

'She could show up any day,' said Christine.

'But who'll take care of him until then?' he said. And then more carefully, 'Who'll take care of him if she doesn't?'

Christine didn't reply. She had learned to deal with Ambrose's rhetoric within a fortnight of knowing him, just look at him until he supplied his own answer. Usually this took five seconds but tonight twenty-five were required. Christine waited while a series of expressions ebbed and flowed across his face. Eventually he said, 'I was thinking we might.'

Only a few days later the Bonnars' adoption application was submitted, going by post to Dublin along with supportive letters from the priest and garda sergeant. Then they waited. Christine didn't care what her father thought but was worried about Phyllis so she didn't tell either of the Lyons about the application, the thought of her sister's reproachful face stopped her. Instead, Christine reminded herself that the application mightn't even succeed, there was no need to go on about it. Most of us would agree with Christine on this policy, we knew it was best not to talk about a thing until it was certain, but Ambrose was a ferociously optimistic person and hard to suppress when excited. He couldn't help but chat about the application in town and one evening Phyllis marched down the lane and through the Bonnars' back door. Christine had just mopped the lino, leaving a scent of fake lemon and a wet sheen, but Phyllis walked across the floor regardless and Christine knew she had heard about the application.

'True, is it?' demanded Phyllis.

'Yes, it is,' admitted Christine.

'A baby that's nothing to do with us!' said Phyllis. 'A child that could've come out of anywhere!'

Christine held her hands together, sorry to have hurt her sister but saying nothing.

'You can tell Daddy yourself!' said Phyllis. 'I'm not doing it for you!'

Christine grimaced. Her sister's idea of hell was having to tell their father something that would displease him. Christine decided right then that she'd tell him and do it proudly, high time somebody stood up to him. Her stance straightened in a way that would've been imperceptible to most people, but Phyllis saw it.

'Have you no respect for him at all?' she said, shocked at the display.

Christine's gaze was firm.

'And what about me?' said Phyllis.

Christine softened at that. 'Ach, of course, Phyl. I want you to be happy,' she said.

'So you keep secrets from me?' said Phyllis in a low voice, weak with abandonment. Phyllis knew the baby would take all her sister's attention, she'd vanish back into the obsessions of motherhood, just as when Declan arrived, but at least Declan was family, whereas Christine was going to unnatural extremes for this other child.

'We don't even know yet if they'll let us have him,' said Christine.

'Oh, they will all right,' said Phyllis and she got strident again. She could find anger easily by telling herself she was fighting on her father's behalf rather than her own. 'You'll beg and beg until you get him. You're desperate for any excuse to stay away from Daddy. You'd rather look after someone else's child than help me look after your own father.'

'No, no,' said Christine but she felt sick inside, caught.

Phyllis turned and went, leaving the back door open. If Christine had run after her right then their estrangement could've been avoided, but she didn't. She let her sister go.

It was a sudden mistrust of her own motivations that had pinned Christine to the spot. She felt a rising nausea, you needed good reasons to adopt a child. A necessity occurred to her; there was a test she had to conduct right away.

Christine could hear Declan playing in his room but no sound emerged from the room she and her husband shared with the baby. She went in, trepidation causing her to walk on her toes. The baby was asleep in his cot, curled around like an ear. He smelled like softened toffee and talcum powder. Christine gazed at him and was relieved that she didn't have to feel around inside herself, the tug she experienced was immediate and strong. She leaned close and looked at his face, it was strange to do so without the usual impulse to find connection, seeking traces of herself or her husband. There was none of that and it made this baby seem a complete individual, unique, and a boy who'd need help to achieve belonging. She reached in and picked him up with great ease. Love grew from shared experience and Christine was sure that she and this child were going to share a lot of experience. Christine put the baby to her shoulder and felt a kind of interlocking. 'No bother,' she said.

The adoption board took only ten minutes to decide on the Bonnar application. They'd normally take great interest in a baby's religion but there were no clues to it in this case. Ambrose's dangerous job was mentioned but they decided it wasn't so dangerous as to prohibit adoption. That was it, papers were stamped. The board didn't see adoption as an event with span, something

33

they'd keep an eye on, they had just stepped in and swept up. Things were simpler in those days. So the baby stayed with the Bonnars, his new parents fell for him completely and a certain satisfaction moved through the town. Most of us didn't enquire after the details, respecting the Bonnars' privacy the way we'd want ours respected if we ever took in a baby found in a barrel. If some nosy or troublemaking person started asking how the child had become a Bonnar we'd just say it was 'arranged' and change the subject. We considered this wording response enough to many mysteries: it was arranged. A child needed rearing and Christine and Ambrose were up for it and we observed, understood and accepted this with a nod and even admiration. Some, of course, liked to predict trouble, saying a romantic notion had swept them up and they'd soon regret taking in the child. We gave them no heed.

The Bonnars named their new son Brendan. They had no adoption party but one evening Tommy O'Gara arrived at their door. 'Come in!' said Ambrose, delighted to see him, and Christine fussed about the table in the kitchen area, clearing a place, their pleasure at his visit all the stronger for being unplanned. Just showing up was often our way, we didn't want people feeling they ought to have a meal ready. It would've been considered rude to tell someone you were coming. Tommy brought a teddy bear for the child, exactly the same bear he brought when Declan was born. He had a box of them in his garage that he had picked up at a discount as people were guaranteed to have babies. Not that Tommy was tight with money, he was just sensible.

Ambrose pulled Declan from his bed so Tommy could have a look at him. Declan stood in his paisley pyjamas, too sleepy to complain, eyes cast down from the lights. 'Aren't you the hardy lad?' exclaimed Tommy, knowing what was required. Christine put Declan back to bed then risked waking Brendan by fetching him from the cot. 'Give us a go of him,' said Tommy, making a cradle of his arms and crunching down so Christine could give him the baby. 'Will you look?' he said, straightening up. 'Perfect, like a blue sky.'

Brendan slept in the crook of Tommy's arm as they sat at the kitchen table. Tommy refused a drink but took tea and a slice of buttered brack. Neither Ambrose nor Christine brought up the baby's origins and Tommy went along with this without difficulty, chatting like he arrived by the usual channel. Ambrose loved him for this, we were a discreet people but Tommy was a particularly fine diplomat. If there was a trophy for not mentioning things Tommy would've won it, then kept it at the back of his wardrobe and never mentioned it. He smiled down at the baby and gave him great compliments, he had no wife or children himself but had a good way with youngsters. For many years, each December, Tommy put on a fake beard and red suit and played Santy for the national school. He'd give a great performance although the children would've known him by his distinct teeth: crooked and yellow, they seemed to belong in the head of a much older man.

'I've a proposal for you,' Tommy said to Ambrose, speaking slowly, a touch embarrassed to be raising business, not wanting them to think this was the reason for the visit. He needn't have worried, the Bonnars had sense and understood that life and work ran together. Ambrose smiled, drawing him out. 'If you're up for it,' continued Tommy carefully. 'We could pair up.' He gestured a line in the air between them.

'Well, Tommy, I thought you'd never ask,' said Ambrose and he went into a big laugh. Tommy smiled until he was done. This was often their way, Ambrose finding great amusement in things and Tommy gazing at him, with a certain fondness, and waiting patiently until he was let pick up the subject again. 'It'll be a substantial cash investment,' said Tommy, emphasizing the statement with a move of the head. 'New net and fittings.'

'More fish in less time,' said Ambrose, thinking beyond the gear and straight to the results.

Pair trawling would mean towing a single net between them, moving in parallel and taking turns to fill their boxes. It was more efficient and seemed a good move as Ireland had just joined the European Economic Community and the seas were getting busy. Now when our fleet got out the bay their radios would crackle with Dutch and French voices. Most boat owners had been against joining Europe and opening our waters. A crowd of them hired a minibus and went down to Dublin to picket the government. That all the protestors fitted in a minibus tells you the problem, and they were up against thousands and thousands of farmers, all gagging for the EEC. So the competition from foreign trawlers was fierce and pairing was a smart move for Ambrose and Tommy, maybe essential.

Pleased at the thought of the pairing, Christine settled back in her chair. Now this was progress, they might start putting money in the bank at last. She had needed something to look forward to. Phyllis was staying away from their house and never rang any more. The estrangement was constantly playing on Christine's mind, it could set her biting her nails. She had witnessed such grudges before, Phyllis took against various people in the past and punished them with silence, a technique inherited from Eunan. Tonight Tommy's proposal lifted her mood: let Phyllis be like that if she wanted, bitter and always blaming. Christine decided to look to the future.

'We'll have that drink after all then?' said Ambrose, ready to seal the arrangement.

'My only question is what happens when we disagree on things, which marks to go after or where to sell,' said Tommy. 'There's bound to be a bit of that.'

'We're usually of a mind,' said Ambrose and he took on an airy tone. 'Many's a time I was working a stretch and looked around to see you steaming in behind me. I'd nearly say I was followed.'

Tommy smiled but remained on topic. Many paired trawlers were controlled by a single owner, but neither Ambrose nor Tommy wanted to be boss of the other. 'We could divide areas of responsibility?' said Tommy. 'I'll have charge of some things, you'll have charge of others.'

'We'd both know a good plan when we hear it, whether from our own mouth or not,' said Ambrose. 'We'll be fine day by day.'

Tommy was known for his note-taking, many dealers had experienced the chill of seeing him record their commitments, although ultimately we respected this approach. Tommy liked everything clear, ordered and free of vagaries, and we decided he was wise. He never normally had difficulty drawing up a list and had brought a notepad and pen with him to the Bonnar house tonight, yet the idea of taking notes now seemed indecent to him. It wasn't because of the welcome Tommy was given, it was because of Brendan, still asleep in the crook of his arm. Making notes in his presence would feel shallow, almost shameful, and ridiculous given the open-ended commitment Ambrose and Christine were making to the unknown of this child. Tommy kept records to try to keep order, but Brendan Bonnar seemed to mock the idea of order, or rather he seemed to evoke a higher order that was elusive but with far greater importance. Tommy wasn't the only one to feel this way. Although we had snapped out of our trance about the baby many of us still felt something profoundly settling, comforting, in how Brendan had found harbour among us. We didn't talk about him much any more, but we still thought of him. We were thinking of Brendan more than we let on.

Tommy's notepad remained in his pocket. 'It's just that I'd be afraid of rows,' he said meekly.

'Sure, just take turns with decisions if you're minded differently,' suggested Christine.

'That's it!' said Ambrose. 'We'll try it for a few runs anyway.'

It was a big financial outlay just to try something, but Tommy allowed himself to be carried along. They'd go on trust. He inclined his head agreeably and said, 'We'll have a drink then so.'

There was much chat in town about the pairing, we recognized a pleasing balance and liked to comment upon it, the way we'd remark on a fine stretch of road surface or a married couple who were equally good-looking. We approved of the matching aft winches fitted to the *Christine Dawn* and the *Warrior*, liking the symmetry. We knew there was less symmetry in Ambrose and Tommy's skippering styles, but hopefully they'd be fine. Tommy's diplomacy extended to his crew, he referred to them as 'associates', which we had found amusing before coming around to it, and he never raised his voice. Ambrose, on the other hand, was very pally with his crew but under pressure could get sweary and shouty. But both men had retained steady three-man teams and this reflected well on them. The early risers among us got to see their crews loading ice one cold morning, preparing to trawl together for the first time. Christine drove Ambrose to the pier with the sleeping boys loaded in the back, Brendan snug in his basket and Declan laid out asleep under a blanket. Christine wasn't often on the pier so she got out of the car and said hello to everyone. Ambrose was in great form, bouncing from man to man, shaking everyone's hand and not giving out to Stevie Shine although he was clearly hungover. The pairing and the presence of his sons had inflamed Ambrose's pride. He wanted to lift the baby and show him off but Christine wouldn't let him be disturbed, so instead Ambrose got his crew to come over and admire the child through the car window. Tim O'Boyce had to be cajoled over. He had little fondness for youngsters, even his own. Tim was as bald as a coot but had a big grey moustache that hung down concealing his lips, as if to say to the wife and anyone else, *I've no interest in kissing, don't even try it.* With a rolled cigarette sticking out of his moustache Tim looked at the baby for the minimum time required not to be offensive. 'A child,' he said.

Ambrose kissed Christine on the cheek and said goodbye. 'Mind yourself,' he said.

The trawlers set off, steaming to the mouth of the bay where herring overwintered – our boats weren't steam-driven of course, this was just how we termed it. The *Dawn* was mostly black and varnish on the wood, while the *Warrior* was blue and white and had a shelter deck. Living with his parents kept Tommy's overheads low and meant he could afford such extras. The trawlers were close enough together that each man on Tommy's boat could be identified despite all wearing the same orange oilskin trousers, bib and matching jacket. 'Would you lookit,' said Stevie Shine from the port rail, 'Tommy got his boys matching gear.'

'I see that,' laughed Ambrose, leaning out of a wheelhouse window on one arm, the other stretched to the wheel, keeping the *Dawn* right with his fingertips. 'He thinks he's their mammy.'

Stevie Shine was youngest aboard and had gotten his start from Ambrose only the year before. He'd still whistle in amazement when he saw a giant jellyfish suspended in the water and he'd still vomit over the side three times in the first hour out. They made him prepare breakfast anyway, the newest always cooked.

'Try porridge,' said Joseph McBride wisely. 'Porridge is best for sickness.'

Everything Joseph McBride said was said wisely. He had a neat beard, glasses and, a rare thing among our fishermen, he smoked a pipe. All this gave him an *air*, not quite of authority, something more philosophical. He'd seen a lot of the world working freighters before coming home to fishing. He had the most experience and was on the biggest percentage.

Tim O'Boyce would complain no matter what breakfast he was given, although he'd still shovel it in under his moustache. He was physically impressive but prone to sullen moods and not every skipper would tolerate him. Two fingers were gone from his left hand.

In his youth Ambrose found marks by shining a light into the water; this caused fish to jump and herring would be easily known by their white bellies. But now everyone used sonar to identify good chances and this morning there was an extra clue, a few boats trawling back and forth along the horizon, close

THE BOY FROM THE SEA

together and clearly on to fish. Gulls flapped over each stern, their cries just about audible from the *Dawn*. Everything was civil so far, just the odd bit of banter on the airwaves. Each man aboard the *Dawn* sensed the temperature dip as they hit the lip of the Atlantic. Stevie stamped his feet against the deck despite three pairs of socks. The swells coming at them became broader and more solid, each lump of water feeling like it had come fifty miles specially to elevate the *Dawn* and the *Warrior* and put them down again. At the wheel, Ambrose whistled a tune, feeling joy pass up along his legs as he braced, warming his whole body. Most people lived invisibly, lost in the midst of towns and dense populations, but at sea Ambrose could use his coordinates and find himself on the entire globe, minuscule but definitely there, real. Imagining himself on the revolving earth gave him great contentment. He felt he could power onwards, keep inside the morning, until he was across the ocean.

Tommy didn't bother with the radio, he slid down his window, leaned out and gestured for the *Dawn* to draw closer. Soon they were rising and falling in synchronicity and Ambrose could see Tommy's yellow teeth and a light in his eye. Joseph McBride appeared in the galley, which was one step down behind the wheelhouse. He was uncoiling the transfer line, silently offering to make the throw, but Ambrose wanted the first time to be his. 'Take the wheel,' he said.

The transfer line was a length of orange rope with a hard plastic buoy at one end. It would be flung to the *Warrior* then used to tow the net across for sharing. Ambrose went to stern, letting the weighted end pendulum from his hand, getting a feel for it. There was no shame in needing a couple of tries to get a transfer buoy to splash down close enough to be hooked from another deck, but Ambrose felt a superstitious pulse go through him. The first throw was like an opening ceremony and he wanted success, it would be a good omen. Ambrose's belief in luck had only hardened over the years. Why wouldn't it? He'd had so much good fortune: meeting Christine and now beginning this other sort of pairing with Tommy. He had one fine boy and, out of nowhere, another son to be brother to the first. Ambrose thought himself blessed.

He tensed his knees and stood with his boots apart, moving with the swells. Stevie stood behind him, watching intently, and Tim emerged from the hold, unable to conceal his interest. Eighty feet away the crew of the *Warrior* were also expectant, ready to whoop or mock. Tommy himself stood with the grappling hook in an opening of the shelter deck, ready to snag the line if Ambrose got it close enough. Ambrose swung the buoy wide, then wider and sent it into full and fast revolutions, making a disc in the air and producing a fine swishing sound. Gradually he brought the gear above his head until it was spinning horizontally. Ambrose looked like a cowboy with a lasso as he let rope ride through his hand, widening the circle, building speed. He felt some irregularity hit the spins and decided to let go that instant before he lost control. The buoy arched away, the rope uncoiling and whipping after it.

Ambrose watched its trajectory and his pleasure grew while the buoy went into descent. The *Warrior*'s crew scattered as the buoy came down directly on their aft deck, bounced but stayed aboard, jamming itself into rails. The *Warrior*'s crew cheered and ran to secure it. They'd soon be trawling.

'There's how it's done, lads!' shouted Ambrose, turning to his crew.

Stevie was lying on his back, shocked, a trickle of blood in his hair. Tim was kneeling beside him and looking up angrily at Ambrose. The spinning buoy had glanced off Stevie's head just before release. Ambrose stared a moment then said, 'You'll be all right!' He knelt and pulled Stevie up into a sitting position; sometimes you had to override a problem with sheer will. Stevie was dazed but he'd be grand. 'A good douse of Dettol and a bandage will sort you out,' said Ambrose.

Ambrose decided he'd not believe in omens after all.

3.

WE GOT OVER THE CHRISTMAS and the season turned. When we met on the road or by the shops we'd remark upon the returning house martins or the likelihood of rain. We'd also remark on new houses, weighing up the pros and cons of their sites, their orientations and wondering at their likely cost. Though interest rates were high new builds kept appearing, bigger and bigger. 'One mansion after another!' Big Jimmy would say to whoever was giving him a lift into town. He considered anything with two storeys a mansion but some new houses on the hills overlooking the water could truly be described that way: fine big places with smooth driveways and heavy gates, we were amazed by the numbers of dormers and the wide expanses of glass. These houses belonged to the owners of our largest boats and processing plants. We'd do a sideways dip of our heads and say, 'So-and-so's place is looking well,' or, 'So-and-so is obviously doing all right.' The houses were impossible to ignore but after our initial observations we'd run low on words. We didn't have a name for this new tribe of wealthy people among us, we had no history with terms like 'middle class' or the like. Nonetheless, such houses made it difficult to pretend we didn't live within social stratifications and in time certain turns of phrase became our version of class, phrases putting every family into a category. For a start you either *had money* or a *want of money*. Most of us were covered by *want of money*, within one of two subcategories: some families having the *usual want* while others had a *terrible want*. The latter were families completely wrecked by poverty and other scourges, some living in an area we called the high lanes, beyond the abattoir, in flat-roofed places no bigger than cabins. 'The so-and-sos have a terrible want of money,' we'd say, with a shudder. Within the families that *had money* we developed subcategories too. *Making money* meant a high income but a breadwinner who was still hard at it. These families could live in a new build and go to foreign countries on holiday. 'They're making money,' we'd say, with a touch of admiration. Others had already built up big businesses or assets and could relax, they had their *money made*. 'They've got their money made,' we'd say, with a touch of contempt.

The pairing of the *Christine Dawn* and the *Warrior* was doing well, keep it up and Ambrose and Tommy would soon attain *making money* status. When others couldn't see a profit and stayed home Ambrose and Tommy would head out, paying little heed to holidays or the sabbath. They had no clashes although Ambrose was frequently amused by Tommy's dry managerial manner. He'd always check that Ambrose made his boat repayments on time, saying it was important that they both gained a reputation as a good investment. Tommy referred to fishing as a business. 'And businesses have to expand,' he said one afternoon as they were coming back up the bay from a trip, his voice cutting through the static on the *Dawn*'s radio. Both their crews had retired to their bunks below and Ambrose and Tommy were talking over the radio quietly, like a married couple driving home from a night out, not wanting to disturb the children asleep in the back. They left long silences between observations and didn't bother with 'over' or 'standby', just speaking when a notion took them.

At the *Dawn*'s wheel, Ambrose smiled at Tommy's comment. He could picture Tommy at his wheel gazing up at the huge new houses overlooking the bay. Ambrose had been surprised to discover that Tommy knew who lived in each and what they had paid for the site. Ambrose didn't mind such houses himself, he wasn't ambitious that way, other people's wealth didn't bother him, no more than looking at millionaires in the American programmes on telly. 'Look what's in front of us,' said Ambrose. 'We're doing well, earning steadily.' Today they were bringing home so much fish they had filled their holds and then piled more directly on the decks of the *Dawn* and the *Warrior*. Good job the bay was calm or the excess would've spilled over the sides.

The radio hissed and Tommy's voice emerged again. 'Going steady is going backwards in this economy,' he said.

But all Ambrose wanted was more than his father had accrued and he was there already. The children influenced Ambrose's values too, especially Brendan. Taking in the boy had altered him, gave him a sense of completion and achievement you'd normally only see in a satisfied retiree. Saving one boy from an orphanage was a small mark on the world but Ambrose would be happy enough if it was the biggest mark he'd ever make.

After offloading, Ambrose went straight home, smelling of fish and diesel. He stepped into the kitchen hoping, as ever, that Christine and her sister would've made up and Phyllis would be back on her stool. He was disappointed again. Clothes were scattered about and Declan's muddy boot prints looked as if they had been on the lino for days. Phyllis wouldn't have allowed this, she'd have shamed Christine into housework. Bowls from dinner were still on the table, crusted with mush. The boys must've been in their bed and cot and Christine was stretched out asleep on the two-seater, looking like she had collapsed from exhaustion. She opened her eyes at his arrival but didn't move. Ambrose crouched next to her and said softly, 'Do you want me to go talk to your sister for you? This can't go on surely.'

'The situation is her doing, not mine,' said Christine, and she closed her eyes again.

It wasn't as if Phyllis and Christine never spoke, they might exchange a few flat words in the queue in Hegarty's, but we suspected this was mostly so each could demonstrate – to us, to each other – that they were the person most wronged. One afternoon in the dry cleaner's Christine tried, in a rather aggressive manner, to get Phyllis to hold Brendan. 'He's only a harmless child,' she said.

Phyllis looked away and hurried out the door saying, 'I've to get things for Daddy.'

Nobody interfered, we weren't the sorts to interfere, although we all agreed it was awful sad to see Christine and Phyllis harden this way. We had seen it in other families: resentment becomes part of a personality, fuses into position and can never be reset. It might sound unlikely that two sisters living on the same lane could go on like that for nearly a year but consider the Cassidy brothers of Abbernadoorny. They hadn't spoken in ten years and they lived in the same house.

So with nowhere else to go, Phyllis was spending more time with her father, serving his wants. It wasn't sufficient explanation to say Eunan had Phyllis so oppressed that she couldn't imagine a different life, she was devoted to her martyrdom and didn't want Eunan doing things for himself as she'd lose her sense of purpose. Her father would always make sure she had plenty of purpose. Knowingly or not, he had preserved his inabilities so he'd always require looking after. He had refused to learn to drive so Phyllis had to taxi him about. Once a week he'd insist on being taken to the Ship Inn where he'd remain standing at the counter for a gin and tonic, rejecting the lemon as he didn't trust citrus. Phyllis would hover at his elbow, taking a gin and tonic too but not enjoying it. 'How are you, Mr Lyons?' we'd say, clearing a stretch of counter for him. 'I have my strength,' he'd say.

This response changed quite suddenly during the summer when, one evening, Eunan said instead, 'I'm on the way out, thank God!' We later concluded this was because he was gradually retiring from lobstering. Eunan was seldom seen on the bay any more and never having had anything as frivolous as a hobby he didn't know what to do with himself. When he later sold his yawl, life became a particularly intense annoyance to him. 'I'm over and done with!' he'd say, as if willing to drop dead right there.

Eunan's new fondness for death didn't affect his appetite. He may've stopped working but he still ate like he was perched on a stern board, lifting food from a pail and jamming it into his mouth so to have strength for the next lobster pot. Eunan never saw a meal he couldn't eat in under three minutes, getting it in so fast and loudly you'd think there was a goat in his chair. He had warm feelings for butter, which he'd smear thickly on bread, but mostly saw food as raw fuel. Phyllis didn't eat with her father much, she'd just serve him and retreat down the hallway to the kitchen as listening to him chew was very off-putting. One day during lunch Phyllis heard him shout, 'I'm done!' She returned to clear the table but Eunan was still eating his mash and fish. She realized that he had just paused to announce that he was finished with living, just like he did in the Ship Inn, out loud but to himself. 'Over and done with,' he said, before taking another mouthful.

'Something's going to crack with the Lyons,' we said as we imagined Eunan stalking about the house all day every day, going on about death and demanding another cup of tea.

Christine wouldn't admit it to anyone, not even herself, but she had found liberation in the split with her sister. She didn't miss the fusty atmosphere of the Lyons's house or the arbitrary tasks Phyllis assigned her. She threw herself into her new life. There's a certain picture you might've picked up from the films: a fisherman's wife waiting by a shore, standing on a hillside between clumps of rushes, with her arms folded, gazing out to sea, the Atlantic breeze making her hair lift and wave. A pretty notion maybe, but Christine wouldn't have been that sort, she had too much to be getting on with. 'I'm non-stop with these children,' she'd say when we saw her on the main street but she'd be smiling about it. Her interests began extending further too, into the wider world. Christine hadn't paid attention to languages in school but now she borrowed Linguaphone cassette tapes from another mammy and began learning a few words of Italian. Pair trawling was profitable and she wanted to visit Florence. She started buying a newspaper every day and forming opinions on politics. These things were important, this was the world she'd send her children into some day and even if they stayed in Donegal the world was guaranteed to crowd in on them at some point.

Christine always had the boys with her, Brendan in the push-chair and Declan trotting alongside. They were well turned out, a credit to her. Normally we'd only make a big deal of a baby the once, then forget about them until we were pressing a pound into their hand at their First Communion, but we'd halt on the street for Brendan. Even men took an interest. First, we'd slip in a general affirmation of Christine's saintliness. 'You're very good,' we'd say to her, or the like. It must be admitted that we wouldn't pay much attention to Declan although he'd be looking on. We'd lean down to the pushchair, pat Brendan's little hand, and say something encouraging but we'd only ever get a blank look in return. Brendan had a stillness about him, with a flat, unsmiling expression that didn't vary. He wasn't one for blinking. His self-containment was unusual for a one-year-old, and he was still that way aged two. His look could've been called contemplative or just vacant, opinion was divided.

One morning Christine and the boys were sheltering from the rain in Melly's. The café overlooked the pier, a canteen for the forklift drivers and boat crews. The only decoration were a few posters illustrating species of fish. Christine put a plate of chips before Declan, used her teeth to open two sachets of tomato sauce and squeezed them all over, that was how he liked it. She had barely withdrawn her fingers before Declan went at the chips savagely, he was all hands and teeth, no notion of cut-lery. Christine angled the other way, lifted Brendan from the pushchair and plonked him in the highchair. She put another plate of chips in front of him, opened a sachet of brown sauce and squeezed a little on the side. Brendan took a chip and raised it high, like the priest with his chalice, then dipped it in the brown sauce and nibbled the tip with great delectation. Brendan was only halfway down his second chip when Declan had already finished, crumbs of his chips lying sprayed across the table. Then Declan began to snatch at Brendan's chips. Christine let him away with it, no one doubted her ferocious love for her sons but that didn't mean she attended to every issue arising, she was the sort to let them get on with things. She was leaning the other way and reading the headlines in the *Irish Independent*.

Brendan looked at Declan's grabbing fingers then gazed up at his red face as he stuffed himself, watching his big brother with a wide-eyed fixity. At that moment, at last, Brendan gave something away. His face, normally so unreadable, became full of emotion, the boy's inner world shining through: he was gazing at Declan with complete awe and admiration.

The season turned. A king wave hit the *St Colette* taking most of her gear but the lads were safe, thank God. A draw was organized by the local Mentally Handicapped Association and Sheila Gallagher won a hamper. Marie Cotter died of heart disease and there was a big turnout for the funeral, reflecting our high regard for her. Declan Bonnar started school.

At home Declan mostly ignored Brendan or domineered over him, eating his rusks and stealing his Dinkies, yet when he started school Brendan missed the defining factor of his brother's presence. On his toes at the front window he'd be sad as he watched

Declan disappear down the lane with his school bag. Soon, however, Brendan understood the benefit; he'd have his mammy to himself all day.

She'd be at housework first thing. Some mornings she didn't say much but when in good form she'd chat or lilt a song. Brendan didn't really listen to her words, only her voice, and when she went off to another room he'd arise and go after it. Around ten o'clock she'd announce, 'We'll have a cup of tea.' The tea was for her but she'd give Brendan a Kimberley biscuit. He'd twist the top off and eat it, a brown slab that adhered to the roof of his mouth, dry but satisfying, then bite into its mallowy centre, the large granules of sugar crunching loudly in his head. He enjoyed that. Next they'd normally go into town but one day when the better weather arrived Christine said, 'We'll stroll up to the bogland, will we? I haven't been in years.'

Brendan didn't know what or where she meant, but his eyes brightened enthusiastically. He'd go anywhere his mammy wanted.

The bogland stretched for a few acres across the top of their hill and walking to it meant going up the lane past the Lyons's bungalow. They walked by on the far side, staying close to the forestry plantation. Donegal County Council owned the land that side of the lane and had recently planted it with hundreds of spruce trees. They were still only four feet tall; a low, mean forest, ignored by crows. As they went by Brendan tried to look at the trees and not towards the Lyons's house. The child was becoming vaguely aware of his life's shape, beginning to feel the limitations, smelling them in the breeze, hearing them in the clipped phrases exchanged over his head but mostly through the sensation that there was trouble in his family. He wasn't yet three but Brendan sensed something difficult, intolerant, radiating from that house. He almost succeeded in keeping his eyes averted all the way but then some compulsion made him glance at the house and he had a feeling he couldn't express: a twist of fear, deeper than his pool of words.

His mammy, on the other hand, stared resolutely ahead until they were beyond the Lyons's place, she didn't waver.

Further on the lane wore away to black soil. The bogland was all heath and turf banks, at least a mile from any other house and overlooking the bay. From there the sea was vast and the horizon so far that only on the coldest, sharpest days was it not lost to atmospheric haze. Eunan hadn't cut his turf measures in a decade, the ridges' definition was slowly softening. The chocolate brown peat was topped in a green mesh of sphagnum moss, and when Brendan pressed down on it tiny mites danced around his hand. The openness and isolation got him animated and talkative, scuttling about, fuelled on fresh air. Christine chased him and he ran fast, small and light, a constant tinkle of laughter emerging. Christine identified plants for him, using the real names or names she invented. Brendan picked and studied a tiny bog flower, holding it an inch from his eyes, then dropped it to startle himself, a tiny plant suddenly replaced by the whole sea. He said, 'Up here it's like the world has forgot us.'

This seemed a sad thought to Christine but when she looked over he had a big smile on him.

Through her front window, Phyllis happened to see Christine and Brendan on the lane when they were walking back home. She had just put Eunan's lunch before him and he was tearing into a fried side of whiting. Standing back from the net curtains, Phyllis watched them go by. She hadn't been up to the bogland in a long time although she remembered well how, as children, she and Christine went often with their mammy. Just then Phyllis became aware of a weakness in her legs, like there wasn't enough blood in them, but she regained her strength by deciding Christine had deliberately gone by so she'd see her, see her with that child. Cynical, yes, but Phyllis was at least partly right, Christine thought it might happen and thought it with satisfaction. Walking on the far side of the lane kept Christine away from the house but also meant that she and Brendan were visible through the windows for longer.

Phyllis felt a surge of anger at the child, then felt ashamed of it. The whole thing got her in a mood and she did something unusual, sitting down with her father while he ate lunch. He noted the change but passed no remarks. She watched as he poured milk on his potatoes and mashed them down with his fork before shovelling the results into his loose mouth. Phyllis said, 'How do you think we'd be living if Mammy was still with us?'

Eunan raised his head and gazed towards the mantelpiece, seeming to contemplate his daughter's words while his mouth worked on. Eventually he said, 'Much the same, I expect.' He lowered his head to the plate and took another fork-load.

'I think I'd be different if I'd had her a bit longer,' said Phyllis, thoughtful in a way that requested some thoughtfulness in return. Her mother's death had left a void in Phyllis, but that is a common story, her specific problem was that she rarely spoke of it, instead memorializing the void within herself, until it had grown hard and become heavily defended. There it sat, likely to echo for ever. 'I could've learned from her ways,' she said.

Eunan grunted. 'She kept the house well.'

'Not like that,' said Phyllis, her voice rising. 'I mean, she was good with people, she might've given me advice.'

Eunan looked at her. 'I'll give you all the advice you need,' he said.

Phyllis held still a while, looking at him, then got up and went back down the hallway to the kitchen.

Soon Christine and Brendan were making regular bogland visits. A bit of drizzle didn't stop them and one day they headed up in their orange macs. As they were passing the Lyons's place the front door opened and Phyllis was standing there, watching them. She said hello and Christine said hello but she squeezed Brendan's hand tightly in her own and kept walking. Phyllis stood regarding them as they went by, against the dark trees, their hoods up, the brightest smears of colour anywhere on the lane. With surreptitious glances from under her hood, Christine tried to read her sister's expression. There was no clue there, but standing in her open doorway surely had meaning, was it a kind of reaching out? Maybe. Christine stopped and faced Phyllis, Brendan's hand still in hers, and, in the simple act of stopping, Christine felt an unlocking inside, and a release. Phyllis said, 'Come in a minute.'

Christine was happy to go in, she was surprised by how happy. Brendan was small for his age so she picked him up as the two steps to the Lyons's door were very high and she kept him in her arms as she walked after her sister. Phyllis led her to the front room and there stood Eunan, obviously waiting to address her. Christine's happiness dissipated and she felt foolish, tricked. She should've known nothing good could happen in this house.

'Ambrose is out the bay, is he?' said Eunan.

'He is,' said Christine. Brendan wriggled in her arms but she didn't put him down.

'Making money, is he?' said Eunan.

'Yes, he is,' said Christine, with defiance. The Lyons hadn't thought Ambrose would do well, but he was doing well, he and Tommy sometimes filled the auction hall with their catch alone. She settled Brendan by turning back and forth a few degrees on her hips. He lowered his head onto her shoulder and gazed unblinkingly towards the window, grey sky reflected in his wide eyes. Christine wasn't offered tea, instead Phyllis settled in one of the dining chairs and said, 'I saw Tommy O'Gara on the pier yesterday, making a good study of those foreign boats.'

We all saw them, two pairs of Norwegian trawlers in selling their catches. They were the first of a new generation: ninety foot long and holding two thousand boxes. 'Town men are happiest looking at boats,' said Christine. 'Commenting on cranes and winches and the like.'

'I can imagine Tommy commanding one of those big boats,' said Phyllis.

'Can you now?' asked Christine.

Phyllis looked away. She'd never admit to fancying a man, but she might let a notion slip and we could make conjectures. It would've been good to see her with a husband to pass the evenings with but it was getting hard to imagine at that stage. With a great fastidiousness, Phyllis had built her life around her father. 'They're all just boats to me anyway,' said Phyllis, withdrawing airily, knowing she had misstepped. 'I've no interest in them. I don't even like the sea.'

'It's sad you not liking the sea, given as it's always in front of you,' said Christine, nodding towards the view.

'I'm too busy to look out the window,' said Phyllis, pointedly not looking out the window. 'And the forestry is getting taller. I'll be happy enough when those things reach the sky.'

The Bonnars were near the bottom of the lane, away from the County Council's spruce plantation, but it was directly opposite the Lyons. You might've expected them to object to the inevitable loss of their sea view as the trees grew tall but Phyllis and Eunan weren't sentimental about that sort of thing. Eunan no longer needed the bay, they could drain it, and scenery was irrelevant. A window was merely a cheap source of light and a way to see who was knocking so you wouldn't get a shock when you opened the door.

'Neither of you could ever hold to a topic,' said Eunan.

Phyllis put her hands together, chastened, while Christine said, 'What is the topic?'

'Her car has broken down,' said Eunan.

It wasn't broken down, it needed new tyres, brake pads and a rear spring. Eunan preferred to stay in ignorance of a car's workings.

'We need two hundred pounds to keep the car running,' Phyllis said to Christine, 'and we don't think it's too much to ask, given how little else you do for us.'

So this was it. Christine squeezed Brendan in her arms, causing him to whimper. 'That's all you wanted?' she asked.

Phyllis nodded firmly.

'I'll write a cheque and stick it through the letterbox,' said Christine, already turning to go.

Christine's disappointment became bitterness as she led

Brendan along the lane, but surely by now she and Ambrose could be described as *making money* and making money had its pleasures. She looked forward to writing a cheque for them, a big cheque with her name on it, *Bonnar*.

4.

THE SEASON TURNED. THE VOCATIONAL school had its first public exams and the students did well. The *Ros Finn* went up on rocks and two of the crew were treated for hypothermia. Johnny the Matchbox won good money on the sweepstakes and we all despaired as he was sure to waste it.

One morning through the living-room window Christine saw Tommy O'Gara pulling up to the house so she went and opened the front door to him. The air was full of silent teeming rain, Tommy was standing under a golf umbrella and wearing a shirt and suit jacket. 'I'll not keep you,' he said, unwilling to come in. 'Ambrose is out the bay, is he?' His offhand delivery suggested that Tommy was confirming something he already knew.

'Yes, but not fishing,' said Christine. 'He's taken the boat to Arranmore.'

'Arranmore?' said Tommy, who could imagine no reason for such a trip.

'There was a phone call,' said Christine. 'The roof was lifted off his grandfather's old place in a big wind two days back. Ambrose wants to save the range out of it. He can't bear it going to rust.'

'Think of the fuel he's burning!' said Tommy. 'Would he not borrow a van and head over on the ferry?'

'Joseph went with him,' said Christine in her husband's defence. Surely if Joseph McBride was involved then it wasn't so foolish.

'He's some charmer,' Tommy said with an edge of anger. 'He wanted to show off the trawler, let his family and old pals get a look, and make a big event of salvaging the range. It'll give those islanders something to talk about, it'll keep them going for years.'

Christine thought there was cruelty in that and was dismayed by this turn in Tommy. 'Ambrose was very fond of the grand-father,' she replied, 'and he says the range'll be a great heirloom for our boys. He told me you weren't to fish for a couple of days.'

'That's right,' said Tommy, 'but I've a meeting with the Fish-eries Board set up for this morning. I wanted Ambrose to come in on it, but he won't be back, will he?'

'Not until tomorrow,' she said. 'Too bad he didn't know about it.'

Tommy didn't tell Christine that Ambrose knew well about the meeting. The plan, Tommy thought, was they'd attend together and discuss financing an expansion. He had advised Ambrose to shave and iron his shirt.

Just then Brendan appeared at Christine's legs, put a hand to her lower back to grip her skirt and began slowly twisting on one foot, gazing up at their visitor. Tommy looked at him and sud-denly felt bad about how he'd spoken. Brendan could affect us like that. Most said it was because we remembered his tough start, left abandoned and defenceless, it reminded us of our own vulnerabilities and gave us perspective. Just looking at Brendan could cause you to reassess your priorities. A few people went further and claimed Brendan had an 'aura' that compelled a person to examine their way of being. Most of us rejected such mad talk, we weren't given to superstition, but they'd go on insisting.

Tommy reached into his pocket to give the boy fifty pence, then said goodbye and drove off, taking the bad bend too fast. He still felt guilty about his comportment with Christine later, as he sat in his car outside the fisheries office. He'd never actually apologize but he'd be extra jovial in their next few encounters; this was how we indicated we were sorry for something we'd said or done: by acting oddly the next time we met you. Tommy wasn't surprised that Ambrose had skedaddled before a meeting with the board, it wouldn't be his scene at all. Christine handled their money, Ambrose preferred lively chat and grand gestures to contracts and pinning down a detail. Taking in a boy found in a barrel was his biggest gesture but bringing his trawler to fetch a family heirloom ranked high as well. It was probably one of those government-issue ranges, thin steel and legs that always went wonky. Steaming fifty miles to salvage an old range! Insanity. Tommy got out of the car, lifted his folders and went inside, exactly on time.

Christine was also unhappy about the conversation, not due to Tommy's tone but the discovery that Ambrose had made an error of some kind. She over-boiled Brendan's egg. He didn't complain but watched her quietly as she stood with her back to him, drumming her fingers on the draining board. There was another knock on the door and Christine felt a tightening throughout her body. It was Phyllis's knock and she'd be after cash. Paying for the car repairs had just been the start, Phyllis was now knocking for twenty or forty pounds every week or so. Christine opened the door and Phyllis was standing in her long coat. She only appeared at the front door these days, a choice that sent a strong cold message, and she never stepped inside. All the same, Christine was so unsettled by Tommy's visit that she told her about it, and how Ambrose was missing some sort of meeting.

'What's he at instead that's so important?' asked Phyllis.

Christine hesitated before saying, 'He's out on the boat.'

'Well, at least he's making money,' said Phyllis.

'Yes,' said Christine weakly, she'd walked into it.

'Speaking of money,' said Phyllis.

The season turned and we remarked on the black week on the roads, over a dozen car accidents across Donegal. A careering gull smashed through the Breslins' front window. Jackie Meehan fell from a mast and was concussed. Brendan Bonnar started school.

Every morning Brendan and Declan trudged to the bottom of the lane and away to be educated. There was no question of getting walked or driven to school, they didn't even get walked to the door, we raised our children to be able to look after themselves. The road had no pavement so they'd take the bad bend on the wide side and if a van or car came shooting round they'd leap across the ditch and cling to the wooden fence until it had gone by, the driver catching a glimpse of their impassive faces in the rain. The route wasn't exactly rural, the land was hard-worked: the spruce plantation, a factory and an electronics workshop stood along the road between the Bonnar place and town, but there was also a field with a donkey and a one-hundred-year-old cottage that could've been on a Bord Fáilte advert but for its corrugated roof and the HiAce van decomposing outside. Once they reached town Declan would leave Brendan behind, pacing ahead and falling in with other boys his size on their way across the diamond, striding along, copying the way their fathers walked down the pier or across the floors of processing plants. Their goal was to impersonate them until it was no longer an impersonation, until they became the very thing. Ten minutes later, feeling rejected and lonesome, Brendan would appear trailing after, identifiable from a distance by his wedge of black hair and the way he meandered, pausing to examine the dead fish that had spilled from lorries and lay in gutters. The school bag would be half off him, the straps in the crooks of his elbows rather than over his shoulders. At school, Brendan didn't take to the reading, writing or sums but seemed to derive some entertainment from working with Marla, a coloured clay teachers handed about daily. 'There's no harm in him,' his teacher would say in the staffroom.

Breaktime clustering goes on in school yards, alike types coming together. For boys like Declan it was immediate, they'd sight each other across the yard, recognize something elemental in each other's attitude and within seconds be climbing trees together. Then there were the wary children, wary and recognizing wariness in others, Brendan was one of these. They came together too but slowly along the yard's boundary or by the front steps, Brendan winning trust by giving away his lemon curd sandwiches. When in pairs they tended to lean side by side on the playground wall rather than face each other, poking at moss growing between the bricks and talking about good hiding places. When five or six of them huddled together they'd look conspiratorial and a tougher boy might charge in and scatter them, but they were only ever at some innocent study: admiring a big scab or stroking a particularly smooth stone they'd found.

Declan might've been the sort to enjoy harassing wary ones but he didn't as he didn't want to go near Brendan. He wouldn't, couldn't, let go of the idea that Brendan was an interloper in his family. When Brendan had been put sharing his bedroom Declan drew a crayon line between their beds, down the middle of the carpet, and he still renewed it regularly. At school Declan didn't refer to Brendan as his brother and corrected anyone who did. 'What'll we call him then?' said Pat Ward one day in the schoolyard shelters. He wasn't belonging to the coal dealer Wards, but the Straoughter Wards, the ones with the freckly faces.

'Don't call him anything,' said Declan. He was a gruff boy, quick to shout, and not used to getting contradicted by any other six-year-old.

'Suppose we have to, what'll we call that boy who lives in your house? Should we call him, *that boy who lives in your house?*'

Declan shoved Pat to the ground and stood over him. Declan's expression could've been rage or terror, his face was certainly a bright red. Pat started crying so Declan ran off. They'd be pals again in a while, but Pat would remember never to mention Brendan.

Threat of a scrap may have helped, but in time Declan found not referring to Brendan meant the boys and girls in his class didn't either. Evasion, Declan was learning, was a great way to handle problems. His teacher Miss Roper was unaware of his family story as she had moved recently from a town in Cavan – hence her foreign-sounding name – and once, in front of the whole class, she asked Declan if he had a brother or sister and he dared to say, 'No, Miss.'

Her attention moved off and Pat Ward turned around to look at him, smiling. 'Good one,' he whispered.

Declan got away with this until a January day of heavy snow which made the high roads impassable and meant some children couldn't get near school. You may be sure the Bonnar boys were sent, a glacier would need to be laid across town for Christine to concede; but Brendan's teacher was absent so her youngsters were distributed among other classes, each child sent to sit with a sibling. And so Brendan ended up inside the door of Declan's classroom.

'Who do you belong with?' Miss Roper asked him.

Every child except Declan turned around to gawp at Brendan and he looked very small and timid standing there alone. He raised his hand and pointed to the back of Declan's head. Miss Roper couldn't identify who he was pointing at and besides, she wouldn't accept a silent gesture as an answer, she was still new to Donegal. 'Speak up,' she said.

Brendan did speak, and the way he did surprised everyone. You wouldn't have thought such a small frame could've produced the determined voice. 'I'm Declan's brother,' he said.

Declan's face darkened and he became hunched, arms dropping straight by his sides. A humiliation was born in Declan at that moment and embarked on its own life. He couldn't help but look up to see if his state had been noticed. There was Pat Ward leering back at him, his freckles particularly abrasive right then.

Back at the Bonnar house that afternoon Brendan was playing in the snow while Christine was inside at the sink peeling potatoes from the twelve-stone sack they got delivered monthly. Ambrose was in the kitchen area too, in a chair, leaning in to

67

the radio on the counter and listening to the news. Gathering himself to the radio was a style Ambrose picked up from his father, dating back to a time when broadcasts were recognized as a kind of sustenance by men on lonely headlands. They liked to get close to the source, as if to drink from it. Declan walked into the kitchen and said to his parents, 'Why'd you take in that Brendan?'

Christine was startled by the aggression in his voice, he sounded like a sour old man, but Ambrose didn't notice it. He just glanced at his son to deliver a line he had used often to escape the topic: 'Did your aunty put you up to this?'

'No!' said Declan. 'It's me, I want to know.'

Ambrose went quiet, he'd need a new line.

'The boy's capable of his own thoughts,' Christine said to Ambrose. She let a spud plop into the cold basin, placed the knife on the draining board and turned to Declan. 'Brendan was alone and needed looking after,' she said. 'Me and your father had learned all about looking after boys, thanks to you. We reckoned we'd enough love for him too. And we do.'

It was all true and Ambrose was impressed at how Christine had put her finger on it, although even she had only limited success today. Declan continued the interrogation. 'Why'd you make his birthday the same day as mine?'

'I told you he'd get mad about that some day,' said Christine, turning away to the potatoes again, leaving Ambrose on his own. He could see he made a bad move with the birthday, they'd divide them the following year but the damage was already done. So this was having a family: you might mean well but hurt them anyway, they had reactions and felt disappointments you couldn't predict. Ambrose looked at the radio, preferring that relationship, the radio never demanded explanations. He spoke slowly. 'It was your birthday just a week before Brendan arrived and the nurse told us he was a few days old so I figured we'd stick your birthdays together for, you know . . . handiness.'

Declan began squirming on his feet, his discontent taking physical form. He made little fists.

The sight just made Ambrose smile. 'You're only small fellas yet,' he said blithely, 'one cake is enough for you both. Isn't that right, Christine?'

She'd not be drawn. A potato plopped into the basin of water and she went straight after another.

'I want my own room,' said Declan.

'When we get the extension built,' said Ambrose.

'I want it today!' said Declan.

Ambrose was so shocked that he laughed. A child demanding things, he never saw the like. It was as if some mid-sized town was accidently given a seat in NATO and was now vetoing everything and ruining the meetings. 'For years I shared a bed with my brother,' he said, 'with three of my brothers, all of us in a row!'

Declan's eyes were raging and he bared his baby teeth in frustration. If you'd picked him up by the ankle he would've remained rod-straight. A sharp hiss emerged from him as he turned and pitched out of the room.

Declan went to the bedroom, today filled with winter's cold blue light. Two single beds were against opposite walls and, in between, toys were scattered across the brown carpet. He stood a while looking at the toys before selecting Brendan's cuddly octopus. Holding it against his chest, Declan wriggled under his bed and lying on his back, breathing in the dust, he felt some of the comfort of a burrowing animal. One by one Declan pulled each leg from the octopus, there was a *toc toc* as the stitches popped.

Afterwards, lying under the bed among the toy's innards, Declan felt sinful and low. He picked at bits of stuffing that clung to his jumper, gathered all the ripped pieces and packed them into his pockets. Then he emerged from under the bed and slipped away from the house. A boggy slope rose out the back and Declan crouched down among the rushes near the top, swept away the snow then pawed at the soil. By the time he'd scraped open a hollow his fingers were red with cold and black muck was compacted under his nails. He put the toy's remains in and covered them up, then slunk back to the house. Presumably Brendan missed the octopus, but it wouldn't have occupied him too much. Any childhood is full of losses.

It was Christine who noticed the destroyed toy a few weeks later and guessed what had happened. She talked to Ambrose about it that evening. He was once again by the radio and she was in her new tea-and-cigarette position, her chair was now by the range. The range hummed with warmth and the smell of turf and occasionally emitted a puff of smoke. She said that Declan's intransigence was a worry in a boy so young. 'It's out of jealousy,' she said.

'What's he got to be jealous of?' said Ambrose flippantly.

'He wants your attention,' said Christine. 'You have to treat them the same.'

'I do!' said Ambrose.

Christine looked at him sternly, but there wasn't much to say. Ambrose loved his sons equally, that was clear, but Brendan had him captivated in a distinct way. Perhaps it was because

Declan was merely natural whereas Brendan's arrival felt magic-
al and fated, the boy seemed to cast a special light. Christine
had seen it reflected on her husband's face and maybe Declan
had too.

Ambrose turned away, leaning in towards the radio again.
'Don't worry about the boys,' he said, 'they'll be grand.'

A note on our use of the word 'grand' is here required. It might
sound like a relative of good or great but in our usage it was
something different. 'Grand' was how we acknowledged that
something wasn't good or great while also saying nothing could
be done and there was no point going on about it. Ambrose
relied on the word a lot at sea. 'It'll be grand,' he'd say as the gear
strained. 'It'll be grand,' he'd say when the crew expressed concern over the ten-year-old engine. He was the same at home. 'It'll
be grand,' he'd say, scraping a dot of mould from a slice of white
bread before sticking it in the toaster. 'It was grand,' he'd say
when Christine asked him about his childhood. Ambrose said it
again one evening after hearing Tommy was investing in a bigger
boat and putting the *Warrior* up for sale. He went home, sat
down heavily at the kitchen table, looked off into nothing and
said, 'It'll be grand.'

On the day Tommy was due back with his new trawler
Ambrose couldn't rest easy on his seat, jumping up every few
minutes and going to the window to examine the choppy grey
bay. Then there she was, rolling home, gleaming white and king-
fisher blue and ninety-five foot long. Ambrose was mesmerized.
From his window she was the size of a thumb at the end of an
outstretched arm but her silence felt strange given the heavy
seas, bow rising high twice a minute, followed by a huge but

soundless crash. *Warrior II* was Dutch built, with a well-flared bow and a beautiful sweep to her steel hull, extenuated by the superstructure's forward rake. It was a well-timed purchase; Irish negotiators had gotten the European Community to double our quotas, it wouldn't make much difference to small boats, like the *Dawn*, but the *Warrior II* could meet these quotas and more, not a single fish anywhere in our waters could relax. Ambrose felt a thrill for Tommy but something spiky had appeared within him too. There'd be no more pairing with the *Dawn*. Tommy could go much further out on the *Warrior II*, to the slope of the shelf if he wanted. Ambrose startled himself when another possibility occurred to him, Tommy could go to Rockall. Rockall was a pinnacle of pure granite sitting alone in the North Atlantic, two hundred miles from the nearest land. It was the size of a four-storey building but, apart from seabirds, uninhabited. Ambrose had never been anywhere near it and, although Rockall was daily listed in the shipping forecast, it was like a mythical place in his imagination, too splendid to be true. Suddenly it was real, completely within reach of his friend Tommy. Rockall's waters held fish but that wasn't the allure for Ambrose. Reliability, singularity and plain strength, these qualities appealed to Ambrose and Rockall represented them perfectly.

'He's coming in,' Ambrose said to Christine.

She turned and saw Ambrose pulling his cap on, signifying an intention to go and be on the pier when the *Warrior II* came alongside. Many of us would be there, we took great interest in new boats. 'Ach, are you sure you want to?' said Christine.

'Why wouldn't I?' said Ambrose in a challenging manner.

Christine paused before saying, 'Go on then.'

Ambrose got in the car. He wasn't normally the sort to pick up something expressed in a roundabout way but his wife's hesitation played on his mind as he drove into town and on to the pier. Before the arms of the pier, which were supported by piles, there was a half-acre of concrete on rockfill and he brought his speed down as he crossed it. A net was laid out awaiting repair, two large wooden spools left sat on their ends so they wouldn't roll. Seagulls stalked about, fighting over spilled fish. A dozen cars were parked up ahead and a crowd building although the *Warrior II* was still a mile out. Ambrose slowed further, just a tap above stalling, and pictured himself among the crowd as the vessel manoeuvred alongside. Everyone would be stirred up and voicing admiration. When a crewman tosses the mooring rope more men than necessary would run to catch it. Tommy would glance over from the bridge and see Ambrose looking back at him. Tommy would raise his hand, Ambrose would raise—

Ambrose turned the car sharply and exited the pier, shaky with adrenaline, like he had just avoided a collision. The picture's positivity had hit Ambrose hard because he knew it was false. He didn't head home, but drove a short distance along the bay road, did a U-turn and parked by the sea wall. He'd watch from there and still be able to say he attended the arrival. The tide was in, and the *Warrior II* loomed above the crowd as Tommy swung the stern around. Some might find a trawler's bow the most compelling aspect; tourists tended to photograph our boats head on, but we knew better. Bows were all the same, a boat's true magnificence was to stern with the working gear, that was where you learned about capacity, style, what kind of a beast she was. Ambrose had read the spec, he knew we were commenting on the mighty-looking power block and double-reach crane, she was capable of purse-seining should Tommy fancy it, but mostly we were taken by the sheer mass of metal. *Warrior II* was one of Ireland's first all-steel trawlers. There was no roaring or cheering, we weren't given to that sort of thing, but there was an intense regard. 'Tommy's done well,' we said.

When Ambrose had seen enough he started the car and did another U-turn so to get away without going by the pier. Only then did he see three other cars had parked along the wall behind him, in each sat one man and each was skipper of a small boat like his, all there watching the *Warrior II*. No man acknowledged any other as Ambrose drove by.

Ambrose wanted to call off the next trip and it would've been easy done as prices weren't great and the cost of fuel was high due to ructions in the Middle East, but it would mean ringing each of his crew and he couldn't face that either, so he was in his gear and on the pier at 3 a.m. *Warrior II* smelled strongly of fresh paint and had her halogen floods left on, light bouncing off the deck's zinc coating hurt Ambrose's eyes. The *Christine Dawn* was moored in a line so Ambrose had to cross three other decks before stepping aboard. Joseph McBride was arranging the tyre fenders. Stevie Shine was pressing cartons of milk into the ice tub, using them to conceal two cans of Tennent's. Tim O'Boyce was oiling the engine and giving out about something, he was taking the pairing's break-up very badly.

Ambrose thought he should make a speech but wasn't in humour, so he just said, 'How's it going?' to everyone and didn't stop for an answer. The *Dawn* was the outside boat so they could leave immediately but Ambrose felt furtive as they pulled away. He tried to counter the feeling by pressing the engine harder. The *Dawn*'s keel was set in a way that made her lively, the bow rising when the throttle was up. Normally this sensation improved Ambrose's mood but now it wasn't enough. As they left the shelter of the harbour solid air broke over the *Dawn* and poured through every crevice, blowing everything clear, and Ambrose raised their speed further; it was four hours' steaming to the Stags of Broadhaven. He wanted to get out there, he longed to be in the sea's authority.

A full moon shone through the cloud and the deck's spotlight picked out the foamy crests around them. Each man aboard found a place to be alone and get a bit of peace. Ambrose at the wheel, Joseph to stern with his pipe. Stevie was in the galley and had left the radio off so it seemed quiet – the engine's blare was a sound these men no longer registered. Tim was in his bunk consulting a tabloid or perhaps he had reached for one of his sexy paperbacks, kept above his bunk on a shelf he called the 'fisherman's friend'. The books all had helpful-looking ladies on the cover and titles like *The French Mistress*, or *Night in Versailles*. France still had erotic appeal in those days. Stevie brought Ambrose a mug of tea and Ambrose was relieved he delivered it without making any banal observations about the conditions. Ambrose knew well he had sneaked some lager aboard but decided to say nothing this time. He didn't feel like talking.

In dawn's light they shot the net and began a north-westerly trawl. The sounder wasn't making any promises but Ambrose had the Decca location memorized, having been successful here before. Rain began to pellet the deck and windows of the wheelhouse and galley. The crew sat at the galley's fitted table and Ambrose stood in the door to the wheelhouse, one foot each side of the sill, bracing and unbracing his knees with the swells. Everyone was subdued as they ate sausages wrapped in white bread with a good squirt of tomato ketchup.

'I'm thinking of going to England,' said Stevie. He didn't say any part in particular, we tended to speak of England in a non-specific way, with little sense of its length and breadth.

'There's plenty of work in it,' said Tim.

Joseph nodded wisely, meaning he nodded once while holding his pipe.

'England,' said Ambrose dismissively. 'There's people stabbed and murdered in it every evening.'

They drifted back into silence as the sea grew. Ambrose wouldn't admit it but, statistically, you could stand almost anywhere in England and be safer than on the deck of a trawler. All his brothers and sisters lived over there and not one was ever stabbed or murdered. When Ambrose was young, many men, his father included, took jobs in England half the year, coming back in spring to work the land, but now Donegal migrants didn't return. It had become permanent relocation and women were at it too. People seemed to vanish over there, his siblings still called Donegal home but truth was they rarely visited. The brothers often said Ambrose should come over too, they'd set him up with work, but the thought left him sad and cold. He couldn't go to one of those landlocked towns, disappear into the crowd, become just another Irishman in England. To us, the physical relocation meant less than the mighty internal change that had to precede it: the person you had to become to be the kind of person who goes to England. Like giving up the drink or finding God, it tended to happen in a sudden, sharp change in personality. 'Haven't seen so-and-so in a while,' we'd say. 'Ah, they're away to England,' we'd be told. It was as if they had undergone transfiguration. Birmingham, Manchester, Swindon, it didn't much matter, we didn't even ask.

Three hours later they hauled the net. Excited gulls cried and dive-bombed, but the winch was humming happily, telling Ambrose the catch was small. When the purse was dumped on deck they could see it barely covered their fuel. Herring, but in low numbers, some mackerel, dogfish, their stomachs coughed up by the change in pressure, and something they had started seeing in recent years: crushed plastic bottles. There was no worse sight than plastic bottles sitting on a scrappy catch. Ambrose and his crew stood in the needles of rain, smoke from the stack enveloping them from time to time, it stank but at least warmed their faces. Ambrose would've liked to retreat to the wheelhouse and think things through but wasn't given the chance. 'We'll go again?' enquired Stevie.

Ambrose looked around. The Stags, tall pyramids of rock a couple of miles offshore, were faintly visible in the watery haze, as were other fishing boats. Iceland had got a two-hundred-mile exclusion zone lately, which meant more boats heading for Ireland and all those Ambrose could see were foreign. A French vessel was out in deep water, using a fine mesh probably. They scooped up everything as there was nothing their agents couldn't sell; the French ate anything with an eye in it. A massive Russian was stationed three miles off, with smaller boats all about her. They'd trawl back and forth in parallel, loading the mother ship in turns, until they cleared the seabed completely. Both operations were obviously on to fish but no way could Ambrose bring the *Dawn* near those marks, their lines would get cut right through.

'We'll take her south,' said Ambrose. 'Swing closer to the Stags.'

'Not too close though,' said Joseph, at the pipe.

Joseph took the wheel so Ambrose could have a turn at the gear. He wanted to be out on deck with his hands and mind busy but was unable to lose himself in the work as Tim was in bad form, moaning about everything: the rain, the rolls, the wife. 'We're supposed to be saving for an extension,' he said. 'The wife will eat the head off me if I don't put something aside for that. And I don't even want another room, I'm happy enough to go sit in the car when we've a row.'

Once they were trawling again they sorted the previous catch, lowered the boxes to the hold and iced them. It didn't take long and they retreated to the galley. Ambrose stood in the doorway again. Stevie made tea and sat at the table with Tim, who was rolling a cigarette. He had learned to do this mostly with one hand on account of his missing fingers.

'You never did tell us how you lost the fingers,' said Ambrose. It was the first time he had spoken in ten minutes and there was an edge to his voice, even Joseph at the wheel heard it.

'You know well enough,' said Tim, paused with the cigarette paper an inch from his lip.

'Caught under a line, sure,' said Ambrose. 'But you know, the details. You normally add plenty of detail to your woes.'

Tim cast his eyes down and focused on the cigarette. A plate skated along the table but he didn't place it on the rubber mat, just let it slide back and forth. Ambrose was silent a while and it seemed they had gotten past the situation until he added suddenly, 'A man can get plenty done with just a couple of fingers, it's if the thumb goes that he's in trouble. You're grateful, I'd say are you, to have kept the thumb?'

Stevie made a nervous giggle. 'Ah now, skipper,' he said, 'grateful is hardly the word when a man loses fingers.'

Tim still said nothing. He struck a match to light the cigarette, the flame was his statement.

Stevie placed his hand on the loose plate and said, 'Time to haul, is it?'

It was another bad catch, the day was a failure. Ambrose went straight to the wheelhouse and decided to stay there from now on. Something rolled in his stomach, like a fish flopping over, he didn't have a word for the feeling but others might've recognized it as stress. Apart from his own family's needs, he was supposed to provide a livelihood for the crew. He would've been relieved to replace Tim and unconcerned about Stevie but feared losing Joseph to another boat. He pushed down the Plexiglas and spoke to the crew on deck. 'We'll go by the Stags again but in a bit,' he said. 'I saw a big flock of gulls sitting on the water over there.'

'Following birds, are we?' asked Joseph, from him the question sounded like a philosophical enquiry.

Ambrose made a sidelong dip of the head, a gesture that admitted cons as well as pros to the plan. 'That's how the old men did it,' he said.

'Fuck's sake,' said Tim, loud enough.

The rain was a dense drizzle, concealing the Stags although they were close and something of their gravity could be read in the sea. Gulls wheeled out of the fog and sure enough one had a fish in its beak.

'We should find another spot,' Stevie shouted to everyone. 'That gull's away with half the shoal.'

Nobody laughed. Ambrose turned hard to port and the *Dawn*, unburdened by much catch, danced into the turn. He would've preferred a good weight of water under the hull, pushback from the Stags made the currents unpredictable, but when he switched on the sounder the screen was full of dense bars. 'It's black with fish down there!' he shouted.

They shot the net, Ambrose throttled up and aimed for open water. Stevie cheered at the speed in which the net wound away while Joseph grinned into the rain, pipe clamped in his teeth. Ambrose knew the gear intimately and could feel the net gathering, like a driver knowing their car boot is loaded. They had motored an hour when the whole vessel lurched and halted. Each man fell forward, Ambrose lost a tooth against the wheel and Tim's favourite mug got smashed. It was like they had struck another vessel, but they hadn't. 'You've snagged us,' roared Tim. 'We're snagged, you fucking eejit.'

Keeping his mouth clamped shut and gulping blood, Ambrose scrambled to stern and looked out. The net's steel cables were as taut as guitar strings. The *Dawn* was stopped dead, which felt like going backwards when lifted by big water. He pursed his lips, spat blood and said, 'Yous relax while I steer us loose. Stevie, come up and find my tooth.'

Ambrose wasn't completely lacking in vanity, before anything else he got his tooth, shoved it up into his gum and bit down on a rubber spacer so the root would take. From the wheelhouse he ran the winch. It whined but lacked the might to pull the net free, instead the stern was sucked to the waterline and a swell came over. Ambrose opened up the engine and reoriented the *Dawn* thirty degrees one way then the other, trying to wriggle free. He sensed the hull's planking stretch and contort in this tug of war with the sea floor. The crew had fastened all hatches and were sitting tight in the galley. 'You have to give up the net,' shouted Tim. 'Cut it loose.'

Ambrose spat out the spacer. 'Stick on the kettle,' he called back.

He was unwilling to lose the net, not for the fish in it but the cost of the net itself, upwards of three thousand pounds. He imagined the rocks below, malicious, holding the net and enjoying themselves – Ambrose could feel very victimized sometimes. He needed to piss and could've gotten Joseph to take the wheel but he wanted the net free first, he'd have a great slash then. He drove the *Dawn* almost broadside to the swells, the cables tugging her under and the deck awash. The end of a bulwark plank sprang loose. Ambrose could hear Tim swearing and suddenly Joseph was at his side. 'You don't want to risk the boat over this,' he advised. 'The other net's in good shape, we'll be trawling inside an hour.'

'Nets cost money,' said Ambrose.

'I'm cutting it loose,' roared Tim from the galley.

'Don't you move!'

Frustration was like a heat rising in him, Ambrose felt his urine boiling in his bladder. He heard a heavy rattle from behind him in the galley and knew it was the spare bolts knocking together as Tim slid the toolbox from under the bench. 'Tell Tim not to go near the hacksaw, he's not to use it!'

'It's smart to be ready,' said Joseph. 'We may have to act fast.'

The 'we' stung Ambrose. Heat filled his fingertips as he made a big move, spinning the wheel to bring the *Dawn* around. Tension fell from the towlines and the boards, the whole boat relieved to drop the fight. Near empty, the *Dawn* surfed with the swell for a full three seconds before the propeller cut water again. Ambrose opened the throttle further. 'Ah, here,' said Joseph.

Ambrose was going to get a run of speed and snap the net free. Below, the gear twisted and the catch was mashed into paste but the net could be saved. Joseph stepped away and braced himself in the doorway. Stevie locked his legs around the table post and dabbed at his stomach and forehead, young enough to remember how to bless himself. Next to him, Tim was impassive, smoking a roll-up, refusing to brace out of sheer belligerence.

The snap was coming, coming, then it hit. Stevie slid along the bench into Tim but Tim didn't budge. Ambrose slapped on the hydraulics, giving the winch full power. The *Dawn*'s bow lifted high, the Atlantic floor pulling on the cables. The winch barrel got hot and the lubricant ran thinner than water. There was a bang and a wrench and the sound of wood ripping as the *Dawn* shuddered her whole length. The winch stopped dead and the bow fell. Stevie jumped up to see what had happened and his shoulders dropped. Ambrose couldn't bring himself to look but listened as Stevie described the situation: the winch was still bolted firmly to its decking, but the section of decking had lifted, six or seven lengths torn up, and screws wrenched out. 'I think we're going home,' said Stevie.

It was a hard blow, there'd be the cost of the repair and the sea days lost, plus they'd have to cut the net loose and leave it on the sea floor. 'The biggest disaster of a trip I was ever on,' said Tim, picking up the hacksaw.

Ambrose closed his eyes and put his forehead to the wheel.

5.

WE WEREN'T THE SORTS TO judge people on one mistake, or
even several. If a mistake demanded recognition, if it was as big
and brash as a hole in the ground, we'd remark on it while trying
to be non-accusatory. 'A mistake was made,' we'd say. We were
sympathetic when a crane driver reversed into one of the
Keeneys' gateway pillars, smashing their decorative eagle. 'That
road by the Keeney place is terrible narrow,' we said. Jack Boyle
was up in court and fined three pounds for driving with a defect-
ive handbrake. 'Cars aren't so well built any more,' we said. This
was our manner, our policy, we had to live together after all, we
had to live with ourselves. But money had no such concerns.
Money was vindictive. We all heard about the accident on the
Dawn, nobody wanted to blame Ambrose but all of us knew the
Bonnars would have to take care. They were stuck with a large
mortgage and the interest rate was high and getting higher. The
rates were merciless.

Over the following months Christine found that the cash
amounts she had to guard were shrinking, twenty pounds was a
significant amount, then ten. One day she realized she was
thinking about money all the time, it had begun to dominate
her life. Want of money eventually forced a meeting between
Christine and Phyllis. Christine left a note asking to meet in

Melly's Café, figuring it was neutral ground. Phyllis was already there with a pot of tea when Christine arrived. It was quiet that morning, just a few forklift drivers and fish agents eating beans and chips. Christine sat opposite her but neither was willing to pour the tea so it stayed there between them, teabags stewing in the stainless-steel pot.

'How's himself?' said Christine.

'Same,' said Phyllis.

The door swung wide as someone exited and it took an age to swing closed again. They heard the scream of gulls, lorries going by and the thud of fish boxes being stacked and dragged into the auction house.

'I can't afford to pass money to you any more,' said Christine.

Phyllis had foreseen this. 'And how am I supposed to get on?' she said immediately. 'His pension is next to nothing.'

'You could get some hours in one of the factories,' said Christine.

'And how would he manage by himself?' asked Phyllis.

'He's not as helpless as all that,' said Christine. 'He'll make himself tea if left alone with the kettle long enough. I saw him make toast once, though he later denied it. Wouldn't it be good for you too, to have some independence?'

Phyllis glanced around the café, as if for help, as if to absent herself, like she was getting propositioned by some dirty old fellow on the bus.

'If you don't want a job you could always sign on for un-employment benefit,' said Christine.

Phyllis's nostrils flared. 'I could not!' she said. 'I am employed. Have you ever seen anyone busier than me? The dole!'

Phyllis's horror might've got you thinking she never considered applying for benefits, but she had. The dole office was down the back lane by the launderette and Phyllis was seen visiting. She had stayed in her car until the street was clear, slipped in and closed the door quietly behind her. Inside she stayed within inches of the door, gripping her handbag. It was a long room with no chairs. The walls were the same colour as hospital toilets and completely bare; no posters with helpful advice or information on entitlements. There were no entitlements in those days, only dispensations. Most of the light came from fluorescent tubes as the windows were barely translucent, sheets of weathered Perspex as dense as lunchbox lids. Against one wall was a wooden counter and opposite was a single hatch through which Phyllis heard a ring binder click shut. Then the top of a woman's head appeared and Phyllis held her breath, but the woman's attention was focused downward as she dated documents. If Mrs Dolan knew Phyllis was standing there she gave no sign. Even when someone was at the hatch she tended to assist them without looking them in the eye. This wasn't seen as rude but as correct propriety and appreciated by all of us. Mrs Dolan also knew not to have a radio going or to stick up tinsel at Christmas, a dole office should be a place of reflection. Dark wood and well-worn floors, it felt like the inside of a confessional box and this was suitable. We would lean in the hatch and whisper to Mrs Dolan's inclined head, admitting our shortcomings, our failures, our needs.

Phyllis didn't get that far, seconds after arriving she had turned and fled.

'This is a fine state of affairs,' said Phyllis in Melly's and Christine prepared herself, that phrase always preceded terrible acrimony. 'He can't help but treat me like a skivvy, but he doesn't know any better,' said Phyllis. 'But you . . . you'd take in a boy abandoned on stones while ignoring your own flesh and blood. Well, I'm here to remind you that Eunan's our father and he's still with us, just up the lane.'

Christine took hold of the teapot and poured carefully, guiltily.

'Ha!' said Phyllis, loud and triumphant. The girls behind the counter looked over. Phyllis lowered her voice and said, 'If I'm to be left alone with him then I'll do it my way.'

'All right,' said Christine, 'that's all right then so.'

The tea was as black as oil and without steam, neither of them drank it.

So it was Christine who took on a job, not in a processing plant but a few afternoons cleaning in the hotel. Cash kept going up the lane, but the conversation had exposed a nerve in Phyllis that heightened her frustration and made her want other things too. Money was a help, but surely the Bonnars should be making themselves more useful generally. She acted on this belief the following summer at the blessing of the boats, an annual occasion that took place in low season when most of the fleet was in. Hundreds of us attended. As little girls Phyllis and Christine, in Sunday clothes and hair plaited with ribbon, had always attended with their parents. They would walk into town for it, Eunan striding ahead. In later years Christine decided the event was an embarrassment and refused to go, but Phyllis continued to accompany her parents, having come to believe there was dignity in duty. She wasn't so sure any more.

Over breakfast her father announced his desire to attend the blessing and while he got in his jacket Phyllis went ahead to the car and pushed the front passenger seat all the way back, making space for his long legs. She noticed her father turn at an angle before coming down the two front steps, going at them sideways. He'd soon need a walking stick. That'll be another drama, Phyllis thought, when it's time to raise that subject. Eunan positioned himself alongside the car then slid in. He didn't do up his seat belt as he didn't believe in them. Phyllis put her thumb and forefinger to the key in the ignition but, before turning it, paused. This was the exact point at which Phyllis decided she wasn't going, she wouldn't accompany her father to the blessing of the boats. She started the car but drove only twenty seconds to her sister's bungalow and stopped. Eunan said nothing but looked at her questioningly, his eyes made large in his glasses.

'I'll not be long,' she said.

He didn't protest, just faced forward and went into waiting mode.

Phyllis knocked and Christine opened the front door. She had a damp towel in her hand, the air in the house was moist as a jungle and tasted of Persil Automatic. 'Daddy wants to go to the blessing of the boats,' said Phyllis and she held out her car keys. 'It's your turn.'

Ignoring the keys, Christine turned to hang the towel on the radiator just inside the door. It was important to hold the towel taut, taking care the back half didn't buckle in the gap between radiator and wall. If she allowed that it would be longer drying and damp would get in the plaster. She took great care over the job.

Phyllis shook the keys.

Christine looked over and gazed at Phyllis a while, then

extended her open palm. Phyllis dropped the keys into her hand and, without another word, left for home.

'Right,' said Christine. She turned around and there was Brendan, watching. The boys were aged seven and nine by then. She told Brendan they were going to the blessing of the boats and he should wash his face, then she stepped outside looking for Declan. In those days children tended to pass the time outside of their houses instead of inside them, a healthier way to be surely. She found Declan sitting inside a fish crate, using a stone to pound six-inch nails into a breezeblock. She led him inside and told him to put on his good jacket. Ambrose was watching the telly. He felt no need to witness his trawler being blessed but when Christine handed him his cap he stood and put it on.

In front of the house Brendan stepped up beside Declan and touched his arm. 'We're going to the blessing of the boats,' he said, excited and eager to share the day with his older brother. Brendan loved going about with him, even though Declan was usually sullen and unresponsive. Declan didn't respond this time either, just huffed like everything was an extraordinary annoyance and shoved his hands in his pockets.

Outside, Ambrose got in the back of the car and Brendan slid in next to him, leaving plenty of room for Declan, but Declan wouldn't accept an arrangement that had Brendan sitting between him and his father. He went around to the other door. 'Ah now,' said Ambrose but he shifted into the middle and Declan got in next to him. That was the way of the boy, his parents were used to it.

Christine got in the front and started the engine. Eunan made no remark about the new arrangement. Either daughter was fine, it made no difference.

A big crowd of us were at the pier, ambling about and awaiting the bishop. There was much greeting and chat and the
shrieks of our babies mingled with the cries of gulls standing on
the roof of the auction house. We saw the *Dawn* among the
other fifty-six-footers, moored in rows extending perpendicu-
larly from the pier and all starting to look quaint next to the
massive blue, red, green and white steel vessels moored on the
other side of the pier. The jumble of masts and antennae looked
well with long strings of bunting. Our children sat in rows inside
trawler rails; legs dangling off the sides and their faces coloured
with the sticky crust left by ice lollies. As soon as Christine got
parked Eunan was out of his seat and walking ahead, carving his
way through the crowd, looking for a place with a good view. The
Bonnars trailed after.

To her surprise, Christine felt glad to be there, she so rarely
did this, walk in town with her entire set, and pride fountained
within her. She was pleased even with her father up ahead, dig-
nified as he cut a path through the crowd. He could be a bastard
but he'd had a hard life. She looked at the young girls milling
about in pairs or trios, putting a hand up to conceal their
mouths as they whispered this minute's concerns. When that
age Christine wouldn't have believed she'd still be in our town
as an adult, she planned on being a thousand miles away. Yet,
here she was and enjoying it: the sense of community, the famil-
iarity of the ritual. She and Ambrose paused here and there to
make remarks with other couples, exchanging compliments on
their youngsters' robust health or rapid growth. The Bonnar
boys stood quietly as we studied them, assessing them like cattle
at a mart. Some of us went so far as to clasp their shoulders and
give them testing little shakes. Ambrose and Tommy were still

great pals but it was no harm that the *Warrior II* was off getting lengthened as the sight of her could get Ambrose in bad form. Instead he was chatting away, putting everyone at their ease. Ambrose was a hand-shaker, he was known for this, but with so many about he was reserving his handshakes for men with whom he once had a strong disagreement. Christine looked up at him slyly as he talked, reminded that, in general, she was pleased with him. His hair was greying and he wasn't so light on his feet any more but Ambrose still said surprising things a few times a week, worked hard and never went near gaming machines. Nor did he drink to excess, something respected by everyone, especially those who drank to excess. Ambrose still had his outsider's neutrality too, something he was smart enough to value and maintain. He never engaged in gossip, even when speaking with Christine on their own Ambrose tended to take the most optimistic soundings from anyone's behaviour, not seeking hidden motivations. She wasn't sure if this was policy or if it just never occurred to him, either way it was mostly a good thing. And there were her boys, an even greater source of pride, she was glad she'd put them in their best shirts. They were both walking up the pier a little ahead of her, either side of Ambrose. Declan was broadening fast, he was ruddy, just like his father, with dark eyebrows that amplified his angry expression when in a temper. He was best on his own, when he'd sometimes entertain her with witty remarks and was willing to do housework, sweeping around the range and putting on a wash. Brendan was too much the daydreamer to be useful in that way. Although Brendan had black hair his eyebrows were vanishingly light, giving his face an open, innocent quality. He was still young enough to reach for his father's hand, which was exactly what he did right then. Declan immediately noticed and Christine saw his face pinch. Until recently he would've taken Ambrose's other hand, not to be left out, and might've even contrived to tug him away from Brendan, but maybe Declan felt too old for hand-holding now. Instead he upped his pace to walk alongside his grandfather. Christine had noticed Declan developing a bond with Eunan.

Eunan identified a spot where they'd get the best view of Ambrose's boat and aimed that way, expecting the crowd to open for him and sure enough we did. The Bonnars gathered beside him, Ambrose steering the boys to the edge and telling them not to be falling in the water. We couldn't see the bishop for the fleet but the sound of a puttering outboard was enough for our voices to drop and for smokers to stamp out their cigarettes. 'Here he is now,' said one of the McCafferty girls and the bishop appeared from around a hull. He was standing in the bow of a clinker, his vestments filling and falling in the breeze and his collar blown back over his shoulder. He had left the mitre off, no way would he get away with the mitre. The clinker belonged to Ed Curran, of the Altcor Currans, with the son studying medicine, not to be confused with the Bugnago Currans, with the son in prison. Ed was hunched at the back with the outboard, the white hair he normally kept combed over his bald head was whipping about in a long stream. Joe McGee of the Fishermen's Association was also aboard, in his suit and with light glinting off the oil in his hair. The outboard was ticking over as they moved along the fleet and the bishop splashed holy water on each bow with a shiny sprinkler he had for the job. We couldn't hear his incantations but could see his lips going. A breeze picked up and ruffled the bay and although the rocking was slight the bishop decided he couldn't do the job standing and so sat on the forward bench and gave his blessings from there. This reduced the theatre of the event and there was muttering in the crowd, some travelled thirty miles to be presented with a bishop on his backside. Eunan was among the grumblers.

'Ach, Daddy, he's over seventy years of age,' said Christine.

'I'm over seventy and you'll not see me make a show of myself like that,' said Eunan.

When the bishop got to the *Dawn* Ambrose placed a hand on a shoulder of each son, glad to be there after all. It was a moment deserving regard.

'He didn't give her much of a splash,' said Eunan.

The bishop's boat moved on and we did too, trying to keep him in sight. Ambrose and Christine went with the crowd but the bishop was reduced in Eunan's estimation and he walked with a resentful slowness. Declan hung back with his grandfather causing Brendan to hang back too, hoping for brotherly attention. 'If I'd four more pence I could buy a Mars Bar,' he said to Declan.

'Get lost,' said Declan.

When the bishop reached the shelter of the larger vessels we could hear his words and conditions were stable enough for him to get back on his feet. We were happy and all would be forgiven, although not by Eunan who'd boycott future blessings until there was a new bishop. When the last trawler was done the bishop's boat disappeared back towards the slipway and we lit cigarettes and dispersed. Christine and Ambrose found Eunan and Declan at the town end of the pier. 'Where's Brendan?' said Christine.

'Is he not with you?' said Eunan.

Christine put her hand to her mouth. Declan jumped up on a bollard and looked up and down the pier, feeling a sudden weight of responsibility and far more forcefully than he would've expected. Ambrose spun around but couldn't see Brendan so he ran to the edge and looked along the water. Some may not believe a boy could fall off a busy pier without being noticed, but Ambrose knew better. He had been among four crew on the deck of the *Ard Ronan* one day out of Castletownbere, up to their knees in white fish; sorting, gutting and boxing. They were working intently, heads down. There were swells but nothing unusual and the rain was light and it might've been a full minute before they realized one of their number was missing – certainly no more than a minute, they later assured each other. Ambrose stared at the space where their mate had stood, needing seconds to comprehend the meaning of the uninterrupted horizon. Had he stumbled, fainted, slipped on blood? They'd never know, but his body washed up a week later and Ambrose was left with a deep understanding of something: the sea could claim you silently; we lived and worked on the edge of a vast appetite, put a foot too close and you'd be gone before getting a yelp out, you'd leave nothing behind but your last breath.

Ambrose ran up the pier shouting, others picked up the situation and called it forwards. 'Brendan Bonnar is gone over!' In an emergency even our heaviest fishermen could spring like deer and they sprang now to the ladders. Our speed, our worry, would've been the same for any child, but there was surely a distinct feeling among us right then: communal and propulsive. This was Brendan Bonnar, who had come among us in a way that, nobody denied, was at least a little mysterious. Who we always watched with extra interest. We didn't go on about it, but this was the boy who caused us, for a while at least, to feel a helpless wonder that we had never forgotten.

Ambrose slid down a ladder until his feet were in the water and he looked through the pier's shadowy underside. A system of concrete piles held it up, horizontal, vertical and diagonal; and the black water, with a skin of oil, slapped against them. No sign of Brendan. With so much of the fleet tied up anyone falling would likely hit a deck, but a small boy could slip between hull and pier. Ambrose saw other men dropping onto decks and scanning the water, he could hear shouting and the outboard motor as Ed Curran turned around. Ambrose wasn't one for prayer but his thoughts flitted to God, he spoke to him quietly but firmly. 'If you've taken Brendan from me I'll murder that bishop on you,' he said. 'I'll stab him in his neck.'

There was a voice from above. Mick Cannon was at the top of the ladder. 'He's okay, Ambrose,' he said. He pointed not along the pier but out over Ambrose's head. 'I see him, he's safe.'

The fear lasted less than thirty seconds, but long enough for Ambrose to have become wound so tight that his body now sagged utterly, slack and useless. He wasn't able to climb the ladder yet, his arms only fit to drape over a rung and keep him on. He watched the clinker emerge from beyond a trawler with Ed, Joe, the bishop and, at the bow, Brendan. He had a flat expression on his face and wasn't wet or hurt. Ed called to Ambrose, 'He'd climbed down a ladder and was reaching out to us, we took him for fear he'd fall in.'

'Take him to the slip,' said Ambrose.

With a terrible exhaustion Ambrose hung for a while then

climbed the ladder and stood on the pier, dirty water oozing from his good shoes. We waited around him, leaving plenty of room and not annoying him with words. There were tears in Mick Cannon's eyes but he had always been soft. When Ambrose moved we all moved, forming a silent procession to where Brendan had been left on the slipway. Five or six women were standing around giving out to him and Christine was bent over so her face was just an inch from his, gripping his upper arms hard and roaring.

That day was the start of something. Brendan began taking long walks, going missing for hours. Nothing wrong with children wandering, we had no playground and you couldn't have them under your feet all day, so it was good they made their own entertainment. Declan was often roaming the town with the two Sharkey boys and no harm was done mostly. But Brendan's style was very different, he was always alone and his range was much wider: distant lanes, remote bogland or far along the shore. We came to call his walks 'hunts', it felt right. His parents tried to keep him home but they had lots to do and Brendan could always find opportunities to get away on a hunt. Along the tracks Brendan might get distracted like any child, stopping to examine a stump or a dead sheep, but the sheer distances he covered proved a strong will was at work. We all knew his face and would stop if we happened across him wandering too far from home. He'd be awkward with us, glancing about, holding his hands together behind his back. Ask him where he was for and he'd say, 'Only up this road,' or 'Beyond,' indicating onwards with a dip of his head. He had a way of looking off to the side and speaking with a sigh that made you feel you were distracting him from important things that he'd not explain as you'd be too thick to understand. 'That boy's an awful worry for Christine,' Phyllis would say in the shop or the clinic waiting room, neglecting to mention that she could be a bit of a worry for Christine herself. It was true that Christine was getting lines about the eyes and didn't seem so easy-going. It was most likely the want of money that had her anxious, but some people, not just Phyllis, insisted on blaming Brendan. 'They were brave to take the boy on,' they said. 'No idea of his stock, no idea what his time in the barrel might've done. It's no surprise he's turning out wild.'

Childless people would confidently agree but parents might take a gulp of their pint or tea or whatever they had before them and say nothing. These were the parents of troubled ones, children who were perhaps older, grown and out of the house, but still a trial, needing patience and money. Perhaps too uneasy with people, too fond of the drink or imbalanced in some way that worked against them. These parents knew you can never tell how a child will turn out, naturally yours or not. They had learned, fundamentally, every child comes in from the sea, washes up against the ankles of their parents, arms outstretched, ready to be shaped by them but with some disposition already in place, deep-set and never quite knowable.

One warm Sunday the following spring Declan and the two Sharkey boys were exploring the yards of the processing plants. Tall sliding doors on each end made the plants look like aircraft hangars. The air smelled of machine lubricants and fish. Not rotting fish, rot is the smell of breakdown, this smell had layered up over years and was stable: rich and salty, sharpening under sunlight. Run a finger over any surface and they'd disrupt a layer of dried fish scales that came away like confetti. The plants were closed for the weekend and the boys were at liberty to climb towers of crates, roll each other around in barrels or break things. Each activity was decided by Declan, he was boss. His ability to exude disdain got him this role, a skill he was honing through living with Brendan. He knew to reserve part of himself, he was able to ignore what another boy was doing even if, secretly, he thought it was interesting and wanted to do it too.

They approached a stack of blue plastic barrels, laid horizontally, by the wall of Gallagher's fish plant. The barrels were held in place by a wedge and removing it was sure to make them avalanche enjoyably. Declan was about to pull out the wedge when they heard movement in the thicket beyond the chicken-wire fence. A figure emerged, Brendan, on one of his hunts. He wasn't so interested in the yards, preferring the half-wild, overgrown patches behind the processing plants, zones of ragwort, bramble and young sycamore. The fishing industry's junk lay among the roots; shredded conveyor belts and piles of old nets that had fused into solid masses. Now Brendan was holding a length of chain set into a permanent U shape by rust. He held it up. 'Look what I found,' he said.

Were the Sharkeys alone they'd have called Brendan mental but Declan was his brother or something so they looked to him. Declan was already walking away. 'Come on,' he called to them, not glancing back.

Brendan sank back into the undergrowth.

The encounter left Declan troubled; roaming aimlessly was something Brendan did and Declan realized he had been doing it too. He decided to stop, he'd never roam again. This decision, although his own, upset him and sent him looking for his father. He walked to the pier, not passing through any more yards though he knew the Sharkeys, tagging behind, wanted to. The *Dawn* was tied up and Ambrose was greasing the blocks and sheaves on the derrick, preparing to head out. Declan climbed down the ladder and stepped aboard. The Sharkeys didn't follow him down there, a sense of the primacy of family and the way a vessel represented it made them hang back on the pier, and ignored by Declan, they soon sloped off, feeling mistreated although not so much that they wouldn't follow him around again.

Even Ambrose could be disconcerted by Declan's controlled manner and he suddenly felt unhappy about the state of the deck. 'It's high time I got her repainted,' he said in a jovial way. Had Brendan been there Declan would've started competing for Ambrose's attention and gotten talkative, but alone he didn't feel the need. He just stood there. 'This is a good bit of kit,' said Ambrose, giving one of the crane's levers a tap so it hopped in its slot. 'I could start it up if you'd like a go?'

Declan shook his head, deck equipment held no thrill for him, it all seemed stained with shortage and unease. Most days his parents talked about what was owing to the shop or the ESB. By now, aged ten, Declan had learned that fishing was a precarious livelihood. Instead, he stepped into the galley and his father followed him, wiping his hands on his trousers. Ambrose was grinning and his eyebrows were raised in an expression that was almost submissive. 'Stevie-boy hasn't bought our supplies yet so I've no biscuit to offer you,' he said. 'But here—' He opened the bag of sugar on the table, a teaspoon was permanently stood inside, he lifted it out heaped with sugar and offered it to his son.

'I don't do that any more,' said Declan.

Presumably the boys were growing at steady paces but Ambrose only noticed their development in jumps and he was suddenly struck by the adult frankness in Declan's stance, thumbs hooked in the pockets of his jeans. 'Oh,' said Ambrose and he looked at the sugar and put it in his own mouth instead, sealing his lips so every granule stayed in as he pulled the spoon out. 'Good energy in it,' he said.

It didn't show, but Declan loved the galley. Everything was hard-edged and full of function although also required tending and intimate understanding. It all fascinated him, the two-ring cooker and the dented but sturdy grill; the handwritten list of frequencies taped to the radio; the gas bottle under the counter held in place with an old tyre tube and, screwed to the wall, a wooden rack holding mugs with their handles sticking out. There was domesticity, the men cooked and ate right here, but it was manly domesticity, without fuss or excessive hygiene. This was no place for mammies. One thing in common with the kitchen at home was a tall white bottle of Fairy Liquid by the sink, but the *Dawn*'s bottle was covered in black fingerprints. Declan saw his dad do it at home so knew the crew would squirt pools of it into their cupped hand and use it to wash themselves, even their faces. This was men's Fairy Liquid.

Ambrose sat at the table and reclaimed half a cigarette from the ashtray. He was rolling his own these days, to economize. 'Any idea where your brother is?' he asked.

'He's not my brother,' said Declan.

Ambrose laughed and extinguished his match by shaking it rapidly. 'You'll be great pals one day, wait 'til you see,' he said.

Declan gazed around the galley again and Ambrose had a

sensation so foreign he could've barely named it: embarrassment. He hated the battered grill and that gas bottle was surely a liability.

'She'll not get us to Rockall,' said Ambrose, with a wistful tone of admission, 'but we get far enough.'

'What's Rockall?' asked Declan.

'A legendary place,' said Ambrose and he felt a romantic mood take him, overriding any embarrassment with ease. He knew he'd be able to charm his son with a bit of sea lore, he had done it many times previously. Such stories did no harm and might broaden Declan's horizons. 'It's a small island, a single rock where the seabed raises a knuckle,' said Ambrose. 'It sits halfway between here and Iceland, the most remote dot on the planet.' Caught up in the vision himself, Ambrose looked to the north-west although there was nothing to see from the bench but streaks down the plywood walls.

'Good for fishing, is it?' asked Declan.

'Yes, but it's more than that,' said Ambrose, making an expansive gesture with his hands. 'Rockall is beyond all hassle.'

That thought made Declan look to the north-west as well. 'Have you been there?' he asked.

'Oh no, no,' said Ambrose, smiling and shaking his head. Declan wasn't a boy who was eager to please, but he was eager to find his father impressive. Indulging his son and perhaps himself too Ambrose raised an index finger in a way that signified possibility. 'Maybe some day,' he said.

After a while Declan went home but his visit left Ambrose feeling intensely motivated. He went around slapping grease on the *Dawn*'s moving parts and ordered the hold, wanting to head out as soon as all the crew were aboard. Joseph appeared first and had just stepped on deck when Ambrose said, 'I've made a decision. I'm going for a bigger boat, the minute we get back I'm walking into the bank and laying it all down.'

Joseph drew on his pipe, removed it from his mouth and said, 'You have to make an appointment.'

So it was a few days after returning that Ambrose spent an age in the bathroom cleaning under his nails. He didn't mention the appointment to Christine, he wanted to surprise her or, if declined the loan, he wanted the option of telling her in his own time, or not at all. A good walk helped a man get his mind in order so Ambrose walked to the bank. When he arrived an army convoy, three jeeps and an armoured car were pulling away with the cash truck. Ambrose enjoyed the sight, it was a good omen: the manager knew he'd need a load of extra cash today. Ambrose strode up the steps and almost went straight into the manager's office, one of the staff had to point out that others were waiting. They were stood along a counter totting up figures and, unlike Ambrose, had uneasy expressions. Tank McHugh was doing sums and getting exasperated by the pen's short chain. Ambrose didn't need to do anything last-minute; in a folder he had letters from the BIM and a business plan Tommy had helped him draw up.

Wilbur Kane met Ambrose at the office door and welcomed him in. His glasses looked the part but Wilbur was young for the role. Ambrose preferred his predecessor, a cheery red-faced fellow who had a sideline as a cattle dealer and enjoyed telling people he couldn't type. He was gone a year, heart attack. Ambrose gazed at the objects on Wilbur's desk. The computer looked like a sounder screen but with a keyboard attached. Next to it was a shiny plaything with five spheres, the size of marbles, hanging in a row inside a cube-shaped frame. A Newton's cradle was the height of office chic in those days, making a great gift for a bank manager uncle with no obvious passions. That was how this one ended up on Wilbur's desk. He had another two at home. 'We'll sit here instead, sure,' said Wilbur, directing Ambrose to the coffee table and two less formal seats, although Wilbur couldn't help but remain formal even when sat in one. 'I hope your sons are well?' he said.

'They're healthy,' said Ambrose, preparing for an allusion to be made about his goodness, especially now Brendan was turning out difficult. They were an offering Ambrose could've normally done without yet he missed the custom today when Wilbur didn't partake. 'Glad to hear it,' was all he said, without much interest.

'I hear you're giving out loans for new boats,' said Ambrose.

'Those are big loans,' said Wilbur and he paused, looking at Ambrose with significance, as if expecting him to say he didn't want the loan then, being as they were big. The optimism took another knock.

'Tommy O'Gara is advising me,' said Ambrose. 'He'll keep me right.'

'Mr O'Gara knows what he's doing,' said Wilbur.

Ambrose wanted to get a laugh from this man, he'd feel confident again if he did that. 'I taught Tommy everything he knows,' he said, smiling.

Wilbur did smile, but not the sort of smile Ambrose was after. 'Not *everything* surely?' he said.

'No, not everything,' admitted Ambrose.

'There's a problem in this town,' said Wilbur, 'people aren't straight with one another. It's for good reasons, we live and work side by side so we're eager to keep everything peaceful; we never want to meddle, cause a row. But this means nobody will tell you what you're doing wrong, even when it's obvious. Mr Bonnar, I'm not going to waste your time or mislead you by omission, I'll tell you right out: you won't get a loan from a bank due to missed repayments. That's the reality of lending in the current climate.'

'Missed repayments?' said Ambrose, sinking back into his seat. 'But I haven't.'

'Not on your boat, on your house,' said Wilbur.

Ambrose thought for three seconds. 'Ah,' he said.

Soon Ambrose was out on the street again but knew not to go directly home. We saw him walking to the pier and when he spotted one of us he raised a hand in a stiff greeting that also communicated an unwillingness to talk. A family of tourists were nosing about the pier and had stopped to photograph the *Christine Dawn*. Ambrose didn't want to be irritated with questions so waited until they left before descending to the deck. He heated water in a pot and used it to clean down the kitchen then threw more water on the aft deck and scrubbed it too, the suds escaping through drain holes in the side. People on the pier heard him swearing a couple of times. He didn't stop for a cup of tea or a cigarette but went straight into hosing and then brushing down the mid- and foredeck, his arms, his whole upper body, going like a machine. When all that was done he decided to risk going home.

Ambrose stepped into the living room, Christine and the boys registered his arrival but didn't acknowledge him as they were watching *The Incredible Hulk* with great concentration. A foolish man was riling Banner up, even hitting him a slap. 'You wouldn't like me when I'm angry,' said Banner but this dope kept at him. Christine was watching from the two-seater, sharing it with her ashtray. Brendan was sitting in his usual telly spot, on the carpet tiles by her legs, leaning against one of the seat's wooden arms. Declan was on the matching single-seater, knees up to his chest, gripped to the point of real fear. A curious aspect of Declan's personality was his susceptibility to television. Banner started transforming into the Hulk: turning green, roaring and bursting out of his clothes. 'Terrible waste of a good shirt,' said Christine.

Ambrose folded his arms, the movement in their peripheral vision reminding everyone he was there. 'Where were you?' Christine asked, eyes still on the screen.

The Hulk picked the man up and chucked him through a wall.

'Working on the boat,' said Ambrose.

Nobody said anything for half a minute. In slow motion the foolish man was thrown about some more.

'I got talking to Wilbur Kane,' said Ambrose.

'I used to sell him shoes,' said Christine.

'He says we've missed payments on the house.'

'Lots of people do,' she said and she looked at him. 'Was he complaining? Don't mind him. No bank'll foreclose over a few thousand. Half Donegal will be out on the roads if they do that. We'll get caught up.'

Ambrose was silent. The man was groaning under chunks of plasterboard. The Hulk heard police sirens approaching and bounded away, heading for the hills.

'I needed the money to help out Phyl and Daddy,' said Christine.

'I thought that was it,' said Ambrose. He lifted the ashtray and sat down beside her as the adverts came on.

'Does it matter?' asked Christine.

'No, it doesn't,' said Ambrose. 'What's for the dinner?'

6.

THE SEASON TURNED. THE FUNFAIR came and went, our children went back to school and we got over the Christmas. There were frosts, washing hung stiff on our lines and we had to mind black ice on the roads. The milkman left deliveries by our front steps but by the time we got to them little birds would've pecked holes in the tops, wanting the fat. Noreen Coyle's pipes burst and ruined her carpets. Kathleen Cunningham was in and out of hospital for tests. We all remarked upon another rise in the interest rates. 'It's beyond ridiculous,' we said, although it was probably worst for those saying nothing. Daniel McGuinness, of Drimbarty, had all his furniture taken by debt collectors and didn't let on to anyone for three months.

So far the 1980s weren't treating many of us well. Any money about was pooling around fewer and fewer people, while others lived in want. Our determination to build homes for ourselves remained strong but many projects fell victim to the economy and houses stood unfinished on the roadsides. Money might run out halfway through the build leaving four breezeblock walls, with voids for windows and doors, a kind of constructed ruin that would sit for years doing nothing but holding on to the planning permission. Even when we got a house completed we couldn't rest easy, then we had twenty-five years battling to keep it off the bank. Getting a site, getting a house built, getting to live and die in it, these were our obsessions.

No wonder our children were touched, and you could see it in the amount of work they put into constructing dens. Plenty of materials were available in our town: pallets, barrels, crates. Watch from a distance as a bunch of youngsters built a den and you might've thought they were enjoying themselves. But no, their minds were full of the responsibilities of making and maintaining a home, concerns absorbed from their parents.

One day Declan, aged eleven, had the urge to embark on a project and he had no bother getting the two Sharkeys to climb the fence into the net factory with him and steal lengths of rope. He was even able to persuade them to lift a pallet and lug it half a mile. They brought the gear to the spruce plantation near his house. It was a good site, overlooking the road but hidden, the trees now tall enough to provide concealment. At Declan's urging, they dug out a load of earth so the den would have a flat base then went roving for more materials. It was when faced with carrying a fourth pallet all the way back that the Sharkeys' enthusiasm faltered. Now they said the site was too well hidden, if other boys couldn't see it why build it? The best part, surely, of a den was defending it against interlopers. 'What are we going to do once it's finished?' they asked.

'We can just be in it,' said Declan.

The Sharkeys looked at each other.

'I'll get a gas stove and a few bowls and the like,' said Declan. 'We could have feasts.'

The Sharkeys laughed and headed home, abandoning Declan. The rejection didn't trouble him – Declan never had much faith in other people. Showing great perseverance, Declan handled the last pallet alone, placing it on one end and revolving it again and again, a square wheel, all the way to the plantation. There he tied the pallets together to make a floor and walls and nailed a plastic sheet over the top, letting it hang down the front like a tent flap. Declan slipped inside and just sat. Sat for a long time, feeling the contentment of shelter. The sound was comforting, a silence which was in fact a constant low fuzz, like being inside a shell. It gave him a sense of security and he didn't leave until hungry.

Declan emerged from the trees and went into the Lyons's house. It was by now established that if Christine was working a shift in the hotel the boys would get their dinner from Phyllis. It was good to see a bit of cooperation on the lane, although forced by want of money. Brendan arrived at the house too, back from a long hunt along the shore to the Ships' Graveyard then up around the back of the town. Phyllis sent them to lay the table: a white sliced pan was placed in the middle, along with a catering-size squeezy bottle of ketchup and a shaker of salt. Pepper only came out at Christmas. The boys said hello to Eunan, in his armchair watching television. When Brendan went to the kitchen to get the butter Eunan beckoned Declan over and slipped him a mint. Fox's Glacier Mints rated low as sweets but Declan was pleased with anything that reaffirmed the true bond between the old man and his actual grandson.

Eunan took the head of the table, Phyllis brought in plates of potatoes and whiting and everyone began to eat. Phyllis normally couldn't help but show more interest in Declan but today was different, she directed her first question at Brendan: 'So, where were you this afternoon?'

'Nowhere much,' said Brendan, looking down, perhaps made wary by her attention. He took a mouthful of fish.

'One of your hunts?' she asked.

Brendan went *yom, yom* like he was enjoying the food too much to register her words.

'You were seen on the high lanes,' prodded Phyllis.

'Just strolling,' he said, casting his eyes down and eyebrows up, a face to say his day was of no consequence or interest.

'Strolling!' said Eunan, mocking both the activity and the fancy word for it.

'You were seen coming out of Biddy Donoghue's cottage,' said Phyllis. She kept her eyes on Brendan but spoke to her father. 'You went to a few dances with Biddy when you were young, didn't you, Daddy?'

'Gaaah,' said Eunan, the fish in his gullet giving the sound a particular timbre. 'She's half-mental.'

'What business could you have with her?' Phyllis asked Brendan.

'It's not a business,' said Brendan.

Phyllis angled her head to one side. 'What is *it* then?' she said.

What indeed. Brendan had visited with Biddy several times in recent weeks, mostly because she welcomed him although the stopped-clock feel of her cottage appealed to him too, nothing had changed since long before he existed. Going into Biddy's cottage felt like slipping out of the world and he was never in a hurry to return. 'We talk and she gives me a cup of tea,' he said.

'Having tea with a child!' said Eunan, and he laughed in a long wheeze. His speedy eating had made his face quite red.

'I don't mind tea,' said Brendan, mildly objecting.

'Do you get any cake off her?' said Declan and Brendan shook his head. Biddy wasn't the sort to have cake, a slice of white bread with a sprinkle of sugar maybe.

'Some sad things have happened to her,' said Brendan.

'She should keep them to herself, like the rest of us,' said Phyllis.

'Her children are in Canada and never visit,' said Brendan.

Eunan's wheeze was cut off by a grunt. 'Keep your children close, that's what I say,' he said. 'Otherwise, what's the point having them?'

Phyllis looked at him, then she put down her cutlery and pushed her plate away. Eunan got back to his potatoes. The boys said no more and concentrated on their food. When Phyllis eventually looked at her father again he had stopped eating and placed both hands in his lap. 'Finished?' she asked.

'Yes,' he said.

There was still fish on his plate so she kept looking at him, unsure. Eunan was always against wasting food, as his daughters well knew. His expression was strange, like he was remembering something humiliating. Neither would be like him, humiliation or remembering. The boys were eating away, oblivious.

'Aren't you going to your armchair to watch the news?' Phyllis asked him.

'No, I'm fine here,' he said.

Slowly, like it might be a trap, Phyllis lifted his plate and hers and carried them to the kitchen. Declan raised his head, saw Eunan's face and stopped eating, his jaw falling slack. 'Do you feel okay?' he asked.

'Fine,' said Eunan, but he definitely looked uncomfortable.

Five minutes went by, Phyllis started at the dishes in the kitchen while the boys finished their dinners, mopping their plates with a few slices of bread. All the while Eunan remained sitting at the head of the table, not speaking, either gripping the edge with his hands or resting them in his lap, palms up. 'Do you want anything?' Declan asked him once, then twice.

Eunan's lips made the shapes for, *I'm fine*.

Phyllis returned and stood studying Eunan with her hands on her hips. He was developing cataracts but something new was happening in the milkiness. She leaned closer and as her shadow fell over him one of his pupils contracted and the other expanded. She lunged to catch him as he fell from the chair. He'd had a stroke.

Phyllis drove after the ambulance to Letterkenny General. Eunan was unconscious on arrival and placed on a drip, attached to a heart monitor, and later a feeding tube was inserted. Phyllis kept vigil all night. She realized her father had been aware the stroke was happening but said nothing as he hadn't wanted to make a show of himself. Christine and Ambrose arrived in the morning, Declan had fought to come with them but it was a school day. Ambrose was washed and changed but unshaven and bleary from three days out. Christine was so disturbed by the sight of her father laid prone she remained against the ward's far wall a while before approaching him. They had brought home-made cards from the boys, drawn on folded letter paper. Declan had written 'Get well soon!' across the front and drawn a lobster with a cleaver through it. There were no words on the front of Brendan's card and the picture was hard to interpret; swirling lines and circles produced solely with black biro. It might've been a bunch of flowers or a fruit tree or perhaps the spinning planets of a foreign solar system. 'What's this?' demanded Phyllis.

'Brendan's card,' said Christine.

'Looks like something you'd put on a grave.'

'He's sensitive,' said Christine.

'That's one way of putting it,' said Phyllis. 'I'm not leaving this here for Daddy to see when he wakens, it'll put him back in a coma.' She opened the card. Inside in his tiny handwriting Brendan had written, 'Hopefully things will improve.'

'You girls go get a bite to eat,' said Ambrose, 'I'll keep an eye on himself.'

Phyllis was the sort who responds to difficulties with self-denial, she hadn't eaten in fifteen hours but still she delayed.

'Don't worry,' said Ambrose, smiling, 'I won't pull any tubes.'

Phyllis allowed her sister to lead her away.

Eunan's bed was at the end of the ward with a view over the car park and towards distant blue mountains. Ambrose looked at them a while and opened the window a few inches, reaching out to feel the damp air. Beside him Eunan lay unconscious and Ambrose sat down and took the opportunity to take him in fully: the peeling scalp, the veins of salty blood and the thin, dry breaths, like you'd hear if you put your ear to a lizard. Nothing would adhere to his chest, the nurses had to pile on the medical tape as the monitor's electrodes kept falling off. Ambrose had never looked at Eunan this steadily before, never sat so close to him. He leaned forward and whispered, 'How about letting yourself go finally? Let those girls be free.'

Downstairs, every table in the canteen was taken but it was still quiet, as the customers spoke only in whispers. Phyllis gazed at the tabletop, the sugar bowl and shakers, all made from the same stainless steel as the kidney dishes and forceps at use elsewhere in the building. She was exhausted and longing to be taken care of. Christine poured her tea, added her milk and half a sugar. When Phyllis spoke her words came out as a wail. 'You're the only person in the whole wide world who knows how I take my tea.'

Christine placed her hand over her sister's and Phyllis allowed it. They sat like that a while, saying nothing. 'Don't worry about Daddy,' Christine said eventually. 'He'll be back home inside a week.'

Phyllis sniffed. 'Gives me the chance to defrost the freezer, I suppose.'

'Yes, you should keep busy,' said Christine.

'And I could air out his room properly,' she added, thinking.

'There you go,' said Christine.

Phyllis was suddenly gripped by possibilities. 'It badly needs painted,' she said.

'Now you're talking,' said Christine.

Eunan remained unconscious and Phyllis sat with him each day. She was advised to play music or read to him from books but Eunan didn't like music and was against books so Phyllis tried reading aloud from local newspapers. An article in the *Donegal Democrat* complaining about potholes in the roads did cause his eyelids to flicker, but there was no lasting change. On the eighth day his heart rate slowed dangerously so he was moved to intensive care. Phyllis overheard a nurse saying he was surely on his way out.

At home if Christine was working Ambrose did the dinners, bad news for the boys as he was fond of fried liver and convinced everyone ought to be, dishing it up with boiled potatoes that he refused to peel no matter how grey the skins. That was his entire repertoire, almost. One evening when Eunan had been in hospital two weeks, Ambrose returned with a plastic bag full of crab toes, raised it exuberantly and told Declan to stick on a big pot of water. Although called toes they were actually the arm and claw of the crab and these ones were big, the weight of a snooker ball in your palm. 'Mick Cannon was disgusted at the prices going in the auction hall so elected to give them away instead,' said Ambrose.

When Christine returned she found Ambrose at the cooker with a boy each side of him, all looking into the bubbling pot. Brendan, who was small for a nine-year-old, was standing on the low stool. 'Tonight we eat like kings,' Ambrose told her.

'Go get Phyl,' Christine said to Declan. 'She might be up for this.'

Being alone in the house every night was at first distressing for Phyllis, then just peculiar and now she had begun to appreciate the peace and quiet. The television sat switched off, the doors closed over the screen. Having Eunan's room painted set something off in her and she kept asking J. J. Brown back again. The hallway was done and her own room in a pale blue she saw in *Homes & Gardens*. She could spend ten minutes simply walking from room to room, loving the freshness. She had ordered in a cosy yellow for the front room and put up matching curtains with a flower pattern, an old-fashioned scheme that looked well in their 1950s bungalow. Phyllis had a good eye for colour and balance, a thing not widely known although some of us had remarked upon the elegant flower arrangements she made for the mother's grave. When Declan arrived he found her standing in the hallway, basking in the transformation.

She went with him back down the lane. The Bonnar windows ran with condensation and she remarked on this to Declan to lessen the keenness of the moment as she stepped through the back door. The kitchen smelled of rock pools on a hot day and everyone was on their feet. Phyllis felt excitement in the air, she knew the Bonnar house wasn't this way every evening but it still felt like she was getting to a party that had been happening without her for years. Christine placed her hand on her upper arm for a second and Ambrose said, 'Come in! Welcome!'

The toes had simmered five minutes so Ambrose dumped the whole pot in the unplugged sink, where they clattered and crashed like coins, filling it to the rim. Juice had seeped from the severed ends and solidified in the hot water to create fatty white plumes. When the sink had drained he plunged his bare arm in and gave the toes a rattling swirl, knocking off the last of the water.

Phyllis's stool was in its usual place and she approached it but Ambrose saw and said, 'Ah now, have a seat at the table.'

She did as she was told.

Ambrose turned to the boys. 'Declan, bring in the extra chair, will you? And Brendan, get the hammer.'

It wasn't often the boys operated as a team but this was one such occasion.

Using both hands together and not minding the hot shells, Ambrose scooped the crab toes back into the dry pot. Declan looked in at them. 'Would be nice if we'd some chopped parsley to toss in there,' he said.

Everyone stared at him.

'For presentation,' he explained. Declan had started watching cookery programmes on the telly. 'How do you serve them?' he asked.

'Serve!' laughed Ambrose.

Ambrose carried the pot across the room and dumped the toes onto the middle of the table where they made a heap eight inches tall. The family sat around, took a toe each and a turn with the hammer, smacking the shell then peeling back the broken pieces. There were no plates and only Phyllis used a fork, the others hoking out the tender white meat with their fingers. Any conversation was solely about the food: appreciative comments on how the meat flaked or its buttery texture at the claw tips. The tabletop hopped as the hammer came down. The boys were soon skilled at making clean breaks, leaving no bits of shell in the meat. Everyone's pace picked up, Phyllis dropped the fork and went at the feast with her hands too. Empty shells were thrown back in the pot, which was sitting on the floor, and it resounded like a bell as they hit the inside.

Ambrose was in great form: he decided if he was to be skipper of a fifty-six-footer for ever then so be it. Many had far less luck. He had a home, a good-looking wife, two healthy sons and God, or whoever, was finally claiming his father-in-law. Ambrose was the man he was and Christine was the woman she was and he was satisfied with them both so he could, with no great difficulty, also be satisfied with where their personalities had landed them. They were obviously not the types to end up with a Norwegian hundred-footer and a five-bedroom place with a garage. He remembered the tourists by the *Christine Dawn* after his rejection in the bank. 'Beautiful boat,' they were saying and they were right, the *Dawn* was the last of our fleet composed entirely of wood. Ambrose appreciated tradition. Privately, he felt he had more soul than most fishermen: a good red sunset on the bay, a white wave crashing over deck, a blue shark thrashing in the purse, such things stirred him in ways that, he suspected, were beyond most fishermen. Many talked about the ocean like it was a factory floor, men such as Tommy. So let him stay cosy and fish via consoles if that made him happy, Ambrose lived for the raw encounter with the ocean. He was a hunter, a provider, like the first men who fished this coast with spears or whatever they managed with in those times. Ambrose felt kinship with Mick Cannon, who'd rather feed some friends than queue in the auction house to get a few measly pounds from a dealer. Maybe Mick didn't have a great head for business but he had dignity and decent instincts and Ambrose believed those were finer things, they were the finest things a man could have.

Declan had stopped eating and was watching the others. 'I wish Grandad was here,' he said.

Christine patted his hand. 'It looks like he might slip away from us,' she replied, with as much pity as could be expressed with a mouthful of crab.

Still concentrating on his food, Ambrose said, 'He's very ill, but remember he had a long life.'

'Daddy could never abide crab anyway,' added Phyllis.

All this upset Declan more. His voice went high, almost panicked. 'I want Grandad to be here,' he said. 'He's good to me!'

Christine swallowed. 'Ach, I know. You miss him, it's not easy.'

'Don't we all miss him sure?' said Ambrose, his arm going like a darts player as he aimed another empty shell for the pot.

'We'll have to manage without him somehow,' said Phyllis as the pot rang.

Declan pushed away from the table, the chair's legs vibrating noisily along the lino. 'Grandad should be here!' he shouted. 'It's him who should be in the fifth chair!'

Even from the midst of the feast Phyllis was alert to an insult. 'You mean instead of me?'

'No, instead of him!' Declan leapt to his feet and pointed at Brendan. 'This b-word shouldn't be living here at all.'

Ambrose jumped up but Christine stayed him with her hand. His sharp move hadn't scared Declan, who glared back at him boldly. 'Don't talk about your brother like that,' said Ambrose.

Declan looked at his father and calmly said, 'Piss off.'

There was trouble. Ambrose paced about shouting at Declan, Christine adding angry comments from her chair by the range, and Brendan retreated to the bedroom.

Phyllis headed home. It had all been too much for one evening. She was glad to close her front door, her own quiet house was a relief. Phyllis paused in the hallway to enjoy the smell of paint.

A week went by. We were hit with a night of thunder and the electricity went for hours, a good thing we all kept plenty of candles stored beneath our sinks. Our under-fifteens won the Donegal title. We enquired after Eunan Lyons but there was no change.

Until one morning there was; Phyllis was in the hospital canteen with a *Woman's Way* when a nurse told her that his eyes had opened. Chastising herself for not being present, Phyllis dashed to his bedside. It wasn't clear if he recognized her but Eunan was something close to conscious. Phyllis sat and smiled at him weakly. She felt a pressure on her legs, then upper body and arms, spreading everywhere, as if she was lowering herself into a bath. In a few seconds she realized what it was: completeness returning to her, going all the way to her fingers and toes. It was devastating.

In just a few days Eunan was sitting up and his appetite returned with a wallop. His first full sentence was to give out about snoring in the ward. He was forever wanting something fetched or adjusted and the nurses were glad when Phyllis arrived as they'd get a break. Eunan looked like he had aged a decade, his face had drooped and his hair had thinned, but he started daily exercises and kept at them with resolve. He needed help in and out of bed but was soon walking about with a four-footed stick. 'It's miraculous,' said the physiotherapist.

Eunan would never again talk fondly of death, he was now determined to stay alive. 'Years in me yet,' he'd say. 'Years!'

One evening as Phyllis was leaving the hospital a doctor bid her sit down with him in reception. She perched on the chair edge, already worried. He grinned, pleased to have good news. 'I'm recommending your father for discharge,' he said.

Phyllis pulled her handbag to her body, her fingers tightening around it, she had known this was coming yet wasn't prepared. She thought about negotiating or complaining or just explaining that she wanted, needed, more time. The doctor seemed a nice man, the type to be understanding. He had smooth hands and his cuffs were ironed although one had a small blue ink stain. She could've gotten that out for him. 'Another week or two of physio-therapy would do wonders for my father,' said Phyllis.

'Discharge tomorrow,' said the doctor. 'You're the carer, right?'

'Tomorrow,' said Phyllis.

The doctor pushed on. 'He's in control of his bladder and bowels but you should get support bars by the toilet and maybe a commode in his room for the nights. There's a touch of facial palsy, very little, but watch him during meals. We don't want him choking, do we! We'll give you a leaflet showing the lift holds you'll need to use.'

Phyllis squeezed her handbag, already bulging with many, many leaflets. Every visit she'd pick up more to compensate for the fact that she didn't read them. She chided herself internally, what was she doing every evening? Was she half-mental? The doctor was saying something, he looked concerned, she tried to concentrate . . . 'You are the carer, right?'

'Yes, I am,' said Phyllis quickly.

'Good,' he said, 'I'm sure you'll be fine. It's obvious how well you understand his needs, all the nurses mention your patience. Remember, your father will get frustrated at his new limitations, not only physical but cerebral too. We think there's some loss of vocabulary, an effect of the stroke. Have you noticed?'

She hadn't. 'Maybe a little,' she said.

'Staff here say his communications can be basic. It might sound like he's barking orders at you.'

Phyllis said nothing.

The following afternoon it was raining hard and Phyllis sat at her dining table, lights off despite the dull, waiting. She had her head in her hands so she heard the ambulance before seeing it, rain striking the roof so loudly it could've been gravel. The driver parked then came around to swing open the rear door, lower the steps and help Eunan down. The nurse who had travelled in the back with him had an irritated look on her face and refused to step out. Holding an umbrella, Phyllis approached to accept the handover. Eunan was supplied with a tripod walking stick, each end tipped with rubber, but still found it difficult to negotiate the lane's rough stones. Phyllis took hold of his arm and the contact caused Eunan to look at her. 'There you are,' he said, satisfied.

The two steps up to the door were a challenge, Phyllis watched as he slowly raised his foot and held on to him as he creaked after it. He got through the door without mishap and inched carefully down the hall, stopping occasionally to check the way was clear before beginning the journey again. She saw him register the changes to the front room but he made no comment, walls had to be a colour and yellow was good as any. Phyllis hung back in the doorway. Eventually Eunan arrived at his armchair and he turned to her, his face sickly pale against the bright background. 'Tea,' he said.

Without noticing Phyllis's lack of response, Eunan addressed himself to the armchair. Bending his knees, he lowered himself one way, stopped, stood straight again. He tried the other way but couldn't manage that either. The stroke had taken some of his face's expressivity but a building realization was visible. Next, he tried placing all his weight on the walking stick, thinking he might drop straight into the chair from standing, but again he stopped, it was too risky. Eunan stood looking at Phyllis. She looked back at him.

7.

THE SEASON TURNED WITH DAYS of heavy drizzle, great blocks of it coming in from the Atlantic and straddling the town. 'It's like living inside a cloud,' we remarked. Susan McGee had a hip replacement. An uncharted rock ended the working days of the *Ard Barra*. Tank McHugh was caught stealing a steak from a shop in Donegal Town. A killer whale was seen out the bay. There was angry talk about Sally Keeney's extension as it overlooked her neighbours and she hadn't got planning permission. Eunan Lyons was out of hospital and being cared for by his daughter Phyllis.

We didn't see Phyllis in town much any more, maybe in the aisle at Hegarty's selecting the usual things, something robotic about her as she paid at the counter. 'Poor Phyllis puts up with a lot,' we'd say, after she was gone. Eunan could dress himself, which was a relief, and getting down on the bed, a big soft target, he managed but Phyllis had to lift him off in the morning and get him both in and out of his chair, reaching under his arms and holding his shoulder blades, his flesh so slack she couldn't help but picture his skeleton. Within a month she had more physical contact with her father than in the entire forty-five years previous.

One evening Phyllis decided to try something new; rather than lift Eunan from his armchair and help him to the dining table she'd leave him there for dinner, he could eat off the big tray. He wouldn't like it, but she deserved a break. It had taken Phyllis a long while to notice a change in herself: she didn't feel so dominated by her father any more. The stroke had withered him; his voice warbled, the severity was gone from his face, he had even lost height. Phyllis had realized that she might have an option or two. She walked into the front room and, making airy sounds as if distracted, put the tray across the arms. Like the tray on a baby's highchair, it didn't touch his lap. Eunan looked at it, confused then affronted. 'No,' he said.

Pretending not to hear him, Phyllis went to the kitchen and fetched his dinner. She felt a tingle of sin: she knew what she was doing was wrong; proven by the fact that she wouldn't be doing it if anyone was here as witness. When she returned her father was looking pleased, he had removed the tray and placed it on the floor. Phyllis put the dinner on the dresser and sat the tray across his chair again. 'This way you can watch television while you eat,' she said with a forced liveliness, 'you'll enjoy that.'

While she turned and reached for the dinner plate he put the tray aside again.

'Now, now, Daddy,' chided Phyllis, putting the tray back and drumming her fingers on it, as if to affix it. Eunan snarled and threw his arms up; Phyllis jumped back and the tray flipped in the air. It knocked a Belleek china figurine from the mantelpiece, a woman in a gown, delighted with herself, daintily lifting the hem over her ankle. The figurine hit the fireplace's tile surround and broke in three. Eunan looked at the pieces and made a low whimper, probably remembering how his wife had liked it. Phyllis looked at the broken figurine and had a revelation: she wouldn't miss it, she was glad it was broken, one less footery thing to dust.

THE BOY FROM THE SEA

There were a few other things around here she'd like smashed. 'Oh, aren't you a terror?' she said to her father.

Eunan knitted his fingers together, looking at the mess he had made. He swallowed, the flesh of his neck quivering.

Phyllis dropped into a dining chair, smiled angrily and said, 'An absolute terror!'

Eunan looked up then leaned away from her, frightened by her face.

Her voice became shrill. 'But you were always a terror, weren't you, Daddy?'

Eunan raised his shoulder as if to shield himself.

'A terror,' she said, quietly now, leaning back in her chair.

We all have badness in us, so it's as well we've got guilt to keep us from going awry completely. Phyllis did indeed feel very guilty later, after Eunan was in his bed. She put on her reading glasses, placed the lamp with the hundred-watt bulb on the dining table and arrayed the china pieces. It was a calm night; the only sound was the tick of the carriage clock. She touched the pieces, the contrast of the glaze's smoothness and the sharp breaks upsetting her fingertips. Phyllis sat and glued the figurine back together. She remembered being a girl and the formal tone men from the town used when speaking with her father, a distinction that had made her proud. Yes, he had sometimes brooded darkly for days, but he always made sure there was food on the table and heating oil in the tank. Yes, he had often given out ferociously, but he never raised a hand to any of them. Yes, he once confined Christine, aged eight, to her room for half a day, jamming a chair under the door handle, but he hadn't stopped Phyllis going into her own room although he knew well they spoke to each other through the wall.

Phyllis repaired the figurine, but there was no way to replace the tiny flakes of glaze, thin as eggshell, that were missing. It was obvious she was once dropped.

And so life in the Lyons's house developed a certain rhythm. Phyllis would operate contentedly for weeks at a time, all seeming well. When the boys came up for their dinner she fussed over them, spoke pleasantly to Brendan and allowed Declan to do little jobs in the kitchen, like chop carrots or make tea for his grandfather. But eventually she'd become overstretched and unhappy, overwhelmed by the knowledge that this was it, this was all she was going to get out of life. A few days in advance of the badness there would be warning signs and Eunan learned to spot them: a suddenness to her movements, pauses before she responded to him and a flatness in her voice. Eunan became watchful of Phyllis's mood, reading her fluctuations was an exercise that kept his brain sharp. The doctor had told him to do daily mental workouts, although he hadn't meant like this.

All his life Eunan was against visitors to the house but he now longed for them, glad even to see the district nurse, though he wasn't able to answer the door. One afternoon when he was in his armchair the doorbell rang. It set off a whole sequence of pre-recorded gongs, sounding like a cathedral, Phyllis was very aspirational when selecting the effect. She was in the dining chair nearest the window reading *Homes & Gardens* and Eunan looked to her keenly. The presumption riled her. 'I'm not expecting anyone,' she said, 'are you?'

He turned away and said nothing.

Phyllis stretched out, tilting her chair on its two back legs so she could see through the net curtains to the front steps. Bella Power was at the door. Phyllis was curious to know what she wanted but found she could resist knowing so to indulge in something more appealing. She gasped cartoonishly. 'It's the Grim Reaper himself!' she said. 'Oh, he's a sight! Standing there, scythe and all. I wonder would it be me or you he's after?' She dropped the chair's front legs to the carpet again and eyed her father. 'Will I let him in to find out?'

Eunan jolted in his chair as the gongs went another time, reverberating around the house.

'I'll not,' said Phyllis as they faded. 'Being as we're having such a nice time, just the two of us.'

She picked up her magazine again and didn't leave her chair.

Bella Power gave up, got back in her car and drove away unfulfilled. She had hoped to discuss Brendan's activities. Brendan was only ten years old and his ways were getting stranger. Traipsing about was one thing, but his hunts now also involved visiting people and not just Biddy Donoghue. Greg Dorrian was a regular and Mary Pat Kennedy, and her totally batty. He was seen going into Ignatius Deeney's place, which was a worry as he was prone to fits. Brendan seemed to be drawn to the oddballs, the old and the isolated, or perhaps it was more that they were drawn to him. Bella herself saw Johnny the Matchbox invite Brendan into his terrace house and, alarmed, she followed him inside, not knocking but bursting in the door like she thought she'd be breaking up a criminal act. All she found was Johnny showing the boy his collection of matchboxes, over four hundred of them arranged on the table. They looked up at Bella in surprise.

Bella caught up with Phyllis a few days later, by the milk and butter in Hegarty's, and told her there was a lot of talk over Brendan and these visits. She claimed it was an agenda item during the last meeting of the local branch of the Irish Countrywoman's Association. 'What can he be at?' Bella kept asking. Phyllis didn't like family issues being the subject of town discussion and her resentment of the boy was again inflamed. Brandishing a litre of milk, Phyllis got by without giving in to her questions.

One evening Brendan didn't appear for his dinner so Phyllis rang Christine in the hotel and insisted she come up right away. When Christine arrived Phyllis was pacing around while Eunan and Declan were eating at the dining table. Brendan's meal was sitting cold and Phyllis's too was untouched. 'I can't eat with the aggravation,' she said.

Christine went and stood looking out the window at the spruce trees and Phyllis stood by her. 'Could Biddy or Ignatius be giving Brendan a meal?' wondered Christine.

Phyllis shook her head and said, 'They live off nothing but soda bread and the Complan the district nurse pours into them.'

'Did you see him on the road after school?' Christine asked Declan over her shoulder.

'I'm not his minder,' said Declan and Christine turned to give out to him but what she saw made her stop: Declan was leaning over the table, his head almost touching his grandfather's, and pressing down on Eunan's fish with the flat of his knife, exposing the bones. Eunan hadn't the motor skills to pick them out, so Declan was removing each for him, using his thumb and forefinger and flicking them away. It was the most tender thing Christine ever saw him at.

Brendan didn't appear but Ambrose did. 'Yous can relax,' he

said as he came into the room. 'He's in with the Cunninghams, they gave me a ring.'

'Which Cunninghams?' demanded Phyllis.

'Kathleen and her crew,' said Ambrose.

Kathleen had taken brain tumours; we'd seen the weight come off her, the hair thinning and her teeth become pronounced, bigger in receding gums. There was a scene one mass when she rose from her seat and walked out, supported by her husband, while the host was blessed. She never returned to the chapel and by now went nowhere at all, confined to bed. 'Turns out Brendan sits with her the odd time,' said Ambrose.

'And you'd no idea?' said Phyllis sharply.

Ambrose released a breath loudly; he didn't deserve this lashing. 'Not specifically, no,' he said.

'*Not specifically*,' said Phyllis, unsatisfied. 'And what is she getting out of it?'

'She finds him a comfort,' said Ambrose. 'There's some around town who believe the boy's special, on account of the way he first appeared.'

'Abandoned in the weather by a dropout?' said Phyllis.

Ambrose ignored that. 'People like to tell Brendan what's troubling them,' he said, 'and, from what I hear, he may give them a blessing of some sort.'

'A blessing!' said Phyllis.

'Apparently,' said Ambrose.

Declan was listening. 'Do they pay him?' he asked.

Ambrose shook his head. 'He just puts a hand on their shoulder and says a couple of nice things. It's innocent enough, I think.'

Ambrose looked to Christine: if she said it was okay then it was okay. Phyllis gave up on Ambrose and addressed Christine too. 'We have to put a stop to his madness,' she said. 'He should be home, off the roads. He's got no qualifications for giving blessings.'

'What I have to do is get back to work,' said Christine and she walked out.

Phyllis followed her onto the lane and stopped her by the car. 'It's yourself I'm really worried about,' she said. 'That boy's a lot to put up with, it's not fair on you.'

Christine stood by the car's open door and studied her sister. In their youth Phyllis had often displayed a protective instinct over her, although it was usually misguided, oppressive in fact. She was now using similar words but, Christine decided, her sister was at something different. Phyllis had never wanted Brendan about the place, she just couldn't accept him, not fully, and she'd always make a problem of him. It was an unkind way to be, so in order to get along with her Christine was going to have to believe her sister couldn't help it. She didn't want another rift, they were only getting over the last. Patience was required. Christine had deep reserves of patience to call upon as, ultimately, she knew she had escaped while Phyllis hadn't. 'People seem to think Brendan is some terrible burden,' said Christine, 'but honestly he's the least of my chores.'

She drove away, while her sister stood in the lane gazing after her.

Our hotel was on the main street, near the pier. Christine's tasks were like those at home but multiplied: thirty times the bedding needing ten times the detergent, a triple-sized laundry basket and she was twice the age of even the oldest girls she worked with. Christine preferred the laundry room, which she ran alone, but duties might force her to pair up with one of the teenagers. This evening she had to show a new girl about: Debbie Pringle, of the Largynagreana Pringles. This Pringle was slow-moving and unresponsive but Christine reserved judgement, your teens weren't easy. The reception had three big mirrors and Christine showed her how to clean them with newspaper so as not to leave streaks. All the girls now used newspaper for mirrors thanks to Christine's example, something giving her a touch of professional pride, although it could annoy her too, sadden her even, that years of marriage and raising children had made her better at cleaning than anything else.

Debbie seemed suspicious of the idea of using newspaper, even when shown evidence of success. Next Christine mixed a paste of vinegar, salt and baking soda to do the brass panels behind the reception desk. She got up on a footstool to apply it then wipe it off. 'See?' she said, the brass now gleaming.

'It's like witchcraft,' said Debbie. Christine laughed but was cut short when she turned and saw Debbie's frightened expression.

Next they did the rooms upstairs. The en-suite was empty and the bathroom made a good location for a cigarette. Debbie didn't smoke so she sat on the bath's rim and picked at her nails while Christine stood on the toilet seat and had a Silk Cut Red with her head out the skylight. 'Have you any plans?' she asked.

'I'll see what the other girls are doing,' replied Debbie.

'I'm not talking about where you're going tonight,' said Christine, 'I mean plans for the future, for your life.'

Debbie obviously wasn't used to this line of enquiry, she thought for a long ten seconds before saying, 'I'll see what the other girls are doing.'

Christine said no more. She got to her toes and stretched her neck to take in the scene. Spotlights on moored trawlers were reflected in long white verticals on the black water. Nearer, street lights made the wet roads shine. People were walking along, hunched against the rain, and they all, most likely, had problems of some sort. She and Brendan, as she had predicted, shared many experiences, yet in some vital way the boy was remote from her and the love had brought a lot of worry. Declan's belligerence was difficult but she felt she mostly knew how to steer him and would make sure he was settled eventually, but with Brendan there was no obvious route. She definitely didn't want him thinking life was washing other people's bedding or breaking even on fish, but these were the only examples she and Ambrose were offering. Christine knew many mothers would bar their child from walking the lanes and giving blessings to the infirm but if she didn't know what was best for Brendan should she really stop him trying to find out for himself? Perhaps Brendan was doing the right thing. Even if not, it was certainly his own thing.

When Christine returned Ambrose was having a pre-trip nap on top of the bedspread. She lay down beside him and he grunted awake. They had low voices they used when talking about the boys, it was a small house. She put her chin on his shoulder and said, 'We'll leave him go. Brendan's a good boy, let him find his way.'

'Agreed,' said Ambrose.

They slept.

But Phyllis couldn't sleep. Her sister obviously wasn't going to put a stop to Brendan's behaviour so she resolved to do it instead. Some day Christine would thank her, that's what she told herself.

You might've thought Phyllis had enough to deal with already but having enough to deal with can make certain people ignore the whole pile and deal with other things instead. Plus, Phyllis had a particular susceptibility to agitation those days, she may've even sought it. Blessings indeed! She decided to recruit Declan, knowing it wouldn't take much to stir up his jealousy. She'd tell him that everyone was talking about Brendan, he'd hate that. She'd hint that Ambrose seemed pleased with Brendan's role in the town, he'd hate that even more.

Next thing we noticed was Declan walking home from school with Brendan each afternoon. He hadn't done this in years and we could see how happy it made Brendan, he'd be nattering to him all the way along the main street, Declan's long stride meaning every fourth or fifth step Brendan had to skip to keep up. We were pleased too, until we deduced that Declan was only doing it to keep Brendan from wandering off and calling to people. The effort worked; Brendan stopped the visits immediately when offered the chance to walk home with his brother instead.

On weekends Phyllis made additional plans to break up Brendan's 'cult', as she called it. Our town had a small cinema and on Saturdays she gave the boys enough money for tickets and two packets of Opal Fruits. She'd pick up the boys afterwards and bring them straight home. Brendan wasn't taken in by cinema, too crude, too loud, but was glad to do anything alongside his brother. Declan, on the other hand, was overwhelmed every time by the drama and raw emotion. He cried at the end of *E.T.*, although our town's general consensus was that the creature was better off in space. Declan's reaction to *Superman III* was even more dramatic. When Superman got into bad form and turned evil Declan wet himself. He said nothing, put his coat on his lap and stayed in his seat until it looked like the final scene, then hurried out. Brendan scuttled close behind Declan, shielding him with his body to help ensure nobody would see. They got to the car safely but Phyllis caught a whiff and saw his damp trousers. 'At your size!' she said and later reported it to his mammy.

'It's a difficult age,' said Christine.

The season turned. The house martins went off again. We voted four to one against letting abortion into the country. The Anti-Gaming Machines lobby held a meeting in the hall to get support for their campaign. Declan started in the vocational school. Guarded and bad-tempered, he turned thirteen. Muted and inscrutable, Brendan turned eleven. It seemed every age was a difficult age.

A person's forties could be hard going too and one afternoon Phyllis finally broke. It was painful, but a relief.

Christine was washing the dishes and Declan was at the table with his schoolbooks when she came in and took her place on the stool. 'I haven't been sleeping well at all,' she said, her head hanging.

'Ach,' said Christine. 'Dr Quinn will do you some tablets, I'd say.'

Phyllis looked up at her. 'It would be a great help if you'd come up some night and do his bedtime,' she said.

Christine turned back to the sink.

'Please,' said Phyllis, which wasn't like her.

Christine was glad she was at the dishes when her sister arrived, there was no harm illustrating how busy she was. She dropped a few cups back into the soapy water to extend the job. Her sister's request mightn't have sounded much, but Christine felt she had to defend her life. Even one night was a danger, caring for Eunan Lyons would be like a bogland sinkhole, get too close and she'd be sucked under. She could imagine it, suspended for ever in the tarry black and invisible to the world. 'I've this house to keep and the hotel job and these ones to feed and educate,' said Christine, referencing Declan with a dip of her head.

At that moment Declan did appear very focused, he was drawing the AC/DC logo on the back cover of his science book.

Phyllis said nothing, but it wasn't a resentful silence, she seemed worn down completely. Her chin sank until she was looking at the floor.

'Why don't you put him to bed earlier?' suggested Christine. 'Get him down for nine then come watch telly with me. The BBC have this programme called *Crimewatch*, getting the public to help solve crimes. It's like *Garda Patrol* only with proper reconstructions; big robberies and even murders. You'll enjoy it.'

The Lyons had just the two Irish television stations, meaning limited choice and during the breaks an onslaught of GAA players endorsing brands of cattle feed and fluke worm treatment. But the Bonnars' tall aerial picked up the BBC which had no adverts at all and, some might argue, a better standard of programming. Phyllis would've loved to watch *Crimewatch* but duty forbade it, she shook her head solemnly. Eunan's life was restricted enough without losing an hour a day as well. Anyway, the problem wasn't time, it was helping him change into his pyjamas night after night: the loose crinkles between his legs, the deathly angles of his pelvic bones, the grey penis and pubic hair. The district nurse said it would help to remember that he changed her many times when she was a child, but surely the nurse knew, surely the whole town knew, Eunan had never changed a child in his life. Phyllis began to tremble.

'What's wrong?' said Christine, taking two steps towards her. Phyllis opened and closed her hands, revealing her palms and hiding them again. 'I'm mean to him sometimes,' Phyllis said eventually.

'Ach, you are not,' said Christine.

'I made him watch *The Late Late* on Friday even though *The Guns of Navarone* was on the other side.'

'Don't worry,' said Christine, 'he probably didn't know it was on.'

'He did know!' said Phyllis. 'Didn't I make a point of telling him!'

Christine was surprised by this.

Phyllis continued, 'I give out when he drops things. I ignore him for hours on end. I don't buy the batch loaf he likes. This morning he wanted marmalade and I let on we'd no marmalade. But we did have marmalade, of course we had marmalade.' Her voice broke and she cried, 'We always have marmalade!'

Exhausted by her confession and red around the eyes, Phyllis looked at Christine and awaited judgement.

Christine gazed at her steadily. Then she said, 'He can take it.'

Silence hung between the sisters. Christine pulled out the plug, watched the water swirl away, then put on the kettle.

Phyllis had hardly registered that Declan was listening. Although he had started at the vocational school she still saw him as a child with limited understanding, so she was shocked when he spoke up and made an offer. 'I can go look after Grandad in the evenings,' he said, 'change him for bed, whatever he needs.'

Christine gazed at him, delighted and proud, leaning against the counter to take him in fully. She looked at her sister and said, 'There you go now.'

So Declan started going to the Lyons's place most evenings about nine. That was when the television news started and his grandfather never missed it. Declan would pull over a dining chair and they'd watch it together. Eunan's voice was croaky but he'd still manage to rage at reports of state failure: butter mountains, milk lakes and the like. 'A bunch of women could run the place better,' he'd say, gripping the arms of his chair and hoisting himself forwards in angry excitement. But sometimes Eunan didn't seem able to follow detail and Declan suspected his bouts of complaining were triggered by the reporter's cues, not by a grasp of events. 'See this crowd of animals,' he said one evening as Declan arrived, 'rioting over a football game.'

Declan looked at the report, footage of men marching filled the screen. It was the Middle East and they were holding automatic weapons.

'I don't think it's over football,' said Declan.

'Hooligans,' said Eunan. He had his opinion now and that was that. Even the footage that followed, a helicopter firing rockets into a building, didn't cause him to reassess. Declan looked at his grandfather, the pictures flickered on the surface of his eyes but didn't sink in.

Declan liked being there. At home his father's attention was constantly roving to Brendan, at least that was how it felt, but the connection he had with his grandfather and this house was Declan's alone. He didn't sit with Eunan the entire time. He might go to the kitchen and one evening, leaning in the back door, he smoked his first cigarette. He took to studying the cook-books which had belonged to the grandmother he never met, her handwritten notes still clear in the margins. She had written out recipes, copied down on loose pages and stuck inside the covers, the tape now brittle. Adjustments were made over the years, measures scored out and replaced, additional steps added. Declan asked his mammy if they could have one of the cook-books for their house, but Christine shook her head. Her mother's cookbooks repelled her, loaded with bad associations. Processed food filled the Bonnar fridge and freezer.

One night Declan found some leftover mashed potato in the Lyons's fridge and took a notion. He knew his aunty wouldn't like anyone interfering with her kitchen domain so he scooped out just a small amount, too little to be noticed. He whipped it with cream, egg and pepper and shaped two small cakes. These he coated in flour and fried in butter. Sitting side by side in front of the television Declan and his grandfather ate one potato cake each, holding them in their hands. Eunan couldn't manage a compliment but his noises were positive. Declan smiled. 'It's time for your bed,' he said.

Every night at around ten Declan would hoist his grandfather from his seat. Eunan had rejected the institutional tripod and demanded a traditional wooden stick, with a lumpen end for a grip and, with a constant rasp to his breath, he used it on his trek to the toilet. He hadn't the coordination to brush his teeth prop-erly and never let Phyllis do it, however, after some cajoling, he did allow Declan. Then the trek to the bedroom would begin, where Phyllis always left the bed ready, five blankets folded over and pyjamas laid out. Declan would remove Eunan's glasses and place them on the bedside locker while Eunan lowered himself onto the bed. He could raise his arms without difficulty but hadn't a hope with buttons. The waxy flesh on Eunan's chest and stomach didn't sag, he was too thin, but it seemed to want to slide from him. Declan wasn't troubled by his grandfather's body, he had taken to assessing himself in the mirror lately and was satisfied with what he saw. In fact, the contrast between his body and his grandfather's gave him a sense of his own vitality, all the more for seeing close up how it would eventually fail.

Eunan would lie looking at the ceiling as his grandson said goodnight and shut the door, assuming Eunan was closing his eyes. What nobody knew, what Eunan himself might've forgotten by morning, was that he lay awake as much as an hour, listening to the house creak. Easterlies sounded as they did all his life, as did rain against glass, and these sounds could send Eunan back decades, not into memories, he had few, but unlocking sensations held in the body, experiences, states of being. Feeling the blanket rasp under his chin made him a child again, past and present interlocking like his fingers interlocked across his chest. He could see his parents' faces but not hear their voices. Every night he wished he had asked Declan to leave the door ajar and a light on in the hallway, but the following night he'd always forget to ask.

Meanwhile, down the lane *Crimewatch UK* was everything Phyllis had dreamed. It was broadcast live and people would be ringing in with information right there, behind the presenters you'd see police constables at desks answering phones. Christine and Phyllis observed the crime reconstructions and listened to the descriptions of brutality with fixed expressions, like watching *Crimewatch* was a paying job they had to get on with. Brendan watched with them but Ambrose would clear out of the

GARRETT CARR

room. While watching telly there was an intense togetherness about the sisters and Ambrose couldn't find a place in it, perhaps because it returned them to a time before he wedged himself into their lives. Side by side on the two-seater, they were girls again, although they had outgrown the fits of laughter that used to overcome them and instead now had great focus and a wish to witness, from a safe distance, the worst human behaviour. Photofits of scowling muggers would appear on screen and Phyllis would say, with a sort of energized dread, 'He looks a bad article.' The only light moment in *Crimewatch UK* was at the end when the presenter, after getting viewers wound up all evening, would tell them not to be anxious. 'Don't worry yourself,' he'd say, 'all in all, not many get murdered' (or words to that effect).

Christine and Phyllis were glad he told the audience not to worry, it was probably good for children and old people, but they didn't want mollycoddling themselves. They understood reality: most of us won't get murdered but some of us will and there's no point pretending otherwise. Phyllis's sole complaint was that *Crimewatch* focused too much on England. 'You'd think they'd put up an Irish murder the odd time,' she said.

'We don't pay the TV licence fee, so we're on our own,' said Christine.

A Third World War was a big fear in those days and there was a special week of programmes about nuclear war and how shocking it would be. No way would Christine and Phyllis miss a minute of that, every evening they sat together for the collapse of civilization, their faces cast hard with enthralment. The programmes had staged footage of nuclear attacks and how society would crumble in the aftermath: people wailing, running around in hysterics and fighting over the last tin of Spam in Sheffield.

Phyllis and Christine sat through our extinction, sipping cups of tea, gripped.

'You'd be better off having a bomb hit you square on rather than survive to go through all that,' said Christine, eyes locked on the screen during one dramatization, 'but they'll have no reason to drop a bomb here. Donegal will be ignored again.'

'Yes, it'll be nuclear winter for us,' said Phyllis bitterly, 'we'll be expected to put up with it.'

After such evenings Phyllis would return home refreshed. The breaks helped her a lot and in time she became less aggravated by Brendan's activities, yet Declan remained so and his meanness sharpened further with his adolescence. The vocational school got out later than the primary so he could no longer escort Brendan home. This was a frustration for Declan as, loose on the road, Brendan had started at the visits again and giving his blessings, picking up a couple of new fans too. Friday was the main day for these activities so one Friday afternoon Declan slipped out of school early, jogged up to the primary and waited at the gate. Despite years of antagonism from Declan, poor Brendan still grasped at anything looking like brotherhood. Declan could already anticipate his gormless face when he saw him by the gate, happy to walk home with him again.

At last bell youngsters emerged from the school building onto the yard, Declan spotted Brendan and raised his hand in greeting. Our primary school didn't have a uniform but the children were nonetheless a very consistent troop of brown jumpers and dark blue parka jackets. Most boys' school bags were red with either Man United or Liverpool printed on them and when clear of the building they used them to clout each other. Still at the clouting, they poured out the gate but Brendan could no longer be seen among them. Declan waited. Dirt on the road swirled as the bin lorry rattled past, chased by school children. The dirt rose again as a Gallagher lorry rumbled by in the other direction, chased by the same children. Eventually Declan had to concede that Brendan had slipped away from him, gone over the back wall probably. He was surprised by a sensation of emptiness, loss. He started for home thinking that maybe this feeling was loneliness but he soon shook it off and got irritated instead. On the main street Declan stopped, thought for a moment, then turned around and went up Butcher's Lane. First he tried Biddy's then Johnny's but Brendan wasn't with either so he went to the Cunninghams' place. Their driveway was always full of cars as their children were grown up and working but still living at home or visiting constantly. He wound his way between the cars and found Kathleen's husband down on his knees scrubbing the front steps. He was going at it hard and mumbling to himself. Declan stopped silently, awkward, but before he could back away Mr Cunningham looked up from the chore, smiled and stood, his knee bones clicking. 'You're Brendan's brother,' he said.

Declan took a long hard pause. 'Is he here?' he said.

'Not today,' Mr Cunningham replied, 'but tell him to visit again, Kathleen's always glad to see him and the blessings give her a boost.'

Declan was defeated, he could think of nowhere else to seek Brendan and Mr Cunningham's attitude had his thoughts in a tangle. He could only head home.

Inside the Bonnars' door Declan saw Brendan's school bag abandoned on the floor. 'Brendan?' he shouted.

Christine appeared and stood in the doorway to the kitchen,

looking at him strangely. Declan never called out for Brendan, it might've been the first time ever. 'I think he's up in Phyl's,' she said.

Declan went straight back out and up the lane. It started to spit rain. Crows were hopping along the ditch stabbing at worms. Declan had a bad feeling and broke into a run when he realized Phyllis's car was away. The door would be unlocked but instinct drove him to the window first, he wanted to know what was going on in there. The window was high but he kicked up the wall, lifting his weight on the sill to see into the front room. Eunan was in his armchair, seated forwards, hands on top of his stick, eyes closed and head bowed, not like his grandfather at all, a pose of supplication. Brendan was standing before him, he was speaking and he had a hand on Eunan's shoulder.

Declan rushed through the front door, down the hallway and into the room. Forewarned by the noise, Brendan had stepped away and Eunan had fallen back in his armchair, the back cushion was beginning to compress under his weight. Declan stood, breathing hard, staring at Brendan then his grandfather. 'How long is this going on?' he demanded.

Eunan lifted a hand from his stick and made rapid gestures with it; he was obviously embarrassed but the gestures had no other meaning Declan could understand. Finally Eunan made a hook with a finger, motioning for Declan to bring his ear close. Declan did so, hoping to hear an apology for the treachery. 'Be good to your brother,' said Eunan.

8.

If Eunan could get carried away by Brendan and his blessings then any of us could, and, sure enough, we did. Many of us wanted a try. A last snag was our discretion, we didn't like a show, but the only chance most of us would get for a blessing was on the road as it was the only place we'd see him. Once it became acceptable to take a blessing in public the whole thing really took off. We'd approach Brendan, halt, offer our shoulders and whisper our request. Young and old partook and any location was fine; we might be out the front of Melly's, down near the pier or on the road to the bad bend. Brendan would stop, place his hand upon us and say something like, 'Hopefully things'll work out for you.' It was a job of seconds, none of the slow pace or sonorous prayer you'd get from the monks in Rossnowlagh. What Brendan did was spiritual but not quite Christian. The priest was concerned by this boy moving in on his territory but knew speaking against him in the chapel would only increase his attractiveness. Instead he invited Brendan to become an altar boy, an attempt to co-opt his appeal, but Brendan was still a wary lad who'd squirm on the spot if you tried holding him in conversation, perhaps he blessed people because it was easier than talking to them. He'd never put himself on stage in the chapel, Brendan didn't like a show either.

Both Brendan's touch and his words to us were non-assertive and brief and this was just right for our sensibility: he knew what we needed, and how to give it to us. If we were questioned later by a doubtful person we'd usually just say, 'It can't do any harm, can it?' But that was a dodge, a way of avoiding what we couldn't put words on. The truth was that many experienced something profound when Brendan blessed us; in his touch we understood our insignificance, we were barrels adrift at sea, yet we also felt a benevolent force might be at work, a helpful current, and that was a comfort. So we sought a blessing from him and a week later we might seek another.

By way of contrast, look what went on in the rest of the country around the same time. There was much excitement when somebody, in the easy country far south, claimed to have seen a statue of the Virgin Mary in their village shrine begin to breathe, her chest heaving in and out for several minutes. Word of the moving statue spread fast. There were lots of open-air shrines to the Virgin around Ireland and soon other people claimed to have seen their statues moving too; raising her hands, speaking or weeping. Each county succumbed one by one. No need for a degree in psychology to see what was going on: jobs were scarce and the youth were emigrating as fast as we could raise them, add in the cost of living and the threat of nuclear war and it's no surprise Ireland was grasping for miracles. Perhaps we were too, but elsewhere in the country people made a big show of it; hundreds attending vigils at shrines, praying and watching far into the night. They were filmed and the footage was displayed on the TV news every evening. We watched in disgust. There were plenty of holy statues in Donegal but they didn't move and they said nothing. 'Our statues just aren't excitable,' we said but really of course it was us, we weren't as excitable as people only fifty miles away, not as excitable as the people across the bay.

We trusted Brendan's discretion and soon, if there was time and a little privacy, some people began to tell him their troubles, just a few whispered phrases. He'd listen but not comment, which was appreciated, just absorbing our worries and then reaching out with a blessing and kind words. A moment later we'd step away a little lighter.

When Christine heard about this it occurred to her that maybe her father was confiding in Brendan too. She bought a big bottle of 7up and poured him a glass when he arrived home from school. Christine began with a broad enquiry. 'I don't want to know exactly who's saying what,' she said, sitting down at the table with him. 'Just, you know, roughly, what sorts of things do they go on about?'

'Normal things,' said Brendan, sounding bored. The non-answer wasn't because he was secretive or concerned about confidentiality, nor was it indifference, although it sounded that way. Brendan was an empathetic lad but still too young to have a complete understanding of all he was hearing.

'Same with the old people?' she asked carefully.

'Just normal things,' confirmed Brendan on an exhale.

Christine was gripping her hands together under the table. 'How about Daddy?' she asked. 'Does he have regrets?'

'The blessing is all he wants,' Brendan told her. 'He never talks about anything at all. He likes me to say, "May you live another century yet."'

'That's it?'

'Then he says, "Thank you."'

A change of a sort, but Christine had hoped for more. 'Does he ever mention Mammy?' she asked.

'No.'

'Does he ever mention Phyllis?'

'No.'

'Does he ever mention me?'

'No,' said Brendan.

Christine was in bad form for a few days after that.

She finally got to witness this part of Brendan's life thanks to Big Jimmy. He worked at this and that and was well into his fifties by then, always with cap on head, in his grimy shirt, suit jacket and braces. Christine knew him because he'd sometimes sit in the hotel reception to look at the tourists. She and Brendan met him outside the butcher's with a bag of sausages in his hand. He gave her a big smile and a salute, then took in the boy. Jimmy's expression was frozen for the next four seconds: chin forward, mouth hung open in pre-speech, bad eye squinting but the good one round and lively. 'It's the boy from the sea, is it?' he said.

'Some people call me that,' said Brendan.

Big Jimmy was delighted. 'Give us a blessing, will you?' he said, stooping to offer his shoulder and removing his cap. He was bald but—

'What's that black thing?' asked Brendan. On top of Big Jimmy's head was a puffy growth the size and colour of the plug in a kitchen sink.

'Don't mind that, just a lump of cancer,' said Big Jimmy. 'I'm on the waiting list to have it off.'

Leaning away from the growth, Brendan placed three fingertips on Jimmy's shoulder and said, 'May things not be too bad for you.'

Big Jimmy straightened up and stuck his cap back on. 'Good lad,' he said and he gave him a wink. He reached into his pocket, found a pound note and started to uncrumple it.

Brendan stepped away, saying, 'I don't do it for money.'

Big Jimmy looked to Christine but she wasn't able to respond, still astounded by the sight of Brendan in action, the ease with which he conducted himself. Her son didn't seem to enjoy or dislike his peculiar little duty; it was neither fulfilling nor draining. Brendan was asked to administer so he administered, that was it. Christine didn't know how she felt about it, although she certainly wasn't embarrassed the way her sister thought she ought to be. It was a moment of introduction, not the first and not the last, yet always surprising, not just for Christine but for all parents: the discovery that your child is their own person entirely.

'Take these then,' said Jimmy, thrusting the sausages towards him.

It was a few weeks later that Ambrose got his first exposure.

As a fisherman, Ambrose could tolerate all sorts of extremes, in weather, in working hours and in people. Brendan's activities didn't worry him, and any enquiries he made were driven by a warm curiosity and usually just for a bit of entertainment. Ambrose didn't pry, he'd just smile and shake his head, mystified but impressed by the niche his son had made for himself.

One evening Ambrose returned from sea and dropped onto a kitchen chair while the boys hovered about him, as they always did when he was back from a trip. Ambrose asked Brendan who he had blessed while he was away and Brendan, standing before him, offered some names, submitting them for approval like an employee called before the boss's desk. Ambrose grinned and said things like, 'That one could use it!' Declan, feeling outshone, got back to what he'd been doing in the kitchen area. After a few minutes he opened the oven and strong, strange aromas wafted across the room. Ambrose had assumed he was making cheese on toast but this was a different thing altogether, neither he nor Brendan recognized the smell of yeast. Declan put his creation on a plate and walked over, standing before his father and offering it forth. It had a baked dough base covered in some sort of tomato sauce, not ketchup, and about a dozen dark, glistening shapes.

'What are those?' asked Ambrose, a touch alarmed.

'Olives,' said Declan.

'Where'd you get them?' he asked, angling his head.

'They can be got in the North.'

'What's the smell?' asked Brendan. He leaned forwards, curious.

Declan pulled the plate away from under his nose. 'Garlic,' he said. 'You have to chop it fine.'

Just then there was a knock on the door and Ambrose quickly arose. 'Well, it looks highly interesting,' he said to Declan. 'I hope you enjoy it!'

Ambrose disappeared down the corridor leaving the boys side by side.

'I think it smells good,' said Brendan, looking up at his brother. 'I'd eat it.'

Declan ignored him.

Ambrose opened the door and there was Wilbur Kane, a sight so perturbing that Ambrose temporarily lost the ability to speak.

'You don't think I'd call here looking for a repayment?' said Wilbur, with a pained smile and a put-on voice, an attempt to be jokey that he then dropped, which was best for everyone. 'I'm not here on bank business, this is separate.'

Ambrose stepped aside, indicating that Wilbur could enter.

Wilbur didn't move. 'I'm sorry about this,' he said. 'It's my aunt, she's asking to see Brendan.'

Ambrose stepped into the middle of the door frame again.

'I haven't encouraged this,' said Wilbur, 'the very opposite. She's no longer sharp, she gets confused, but she says she wants to meet the boy from the sea. She's very insistent this week.'

Doris Kane lived inland in a grand but decaying old house near the top of a hill we called the Mount. Banks of holly and whin lined the driveway and out the back were a dozen apple trees in bad need of pruning. The windows were warped and the curtains, rarely opened, were grey. When Wilbur was ten his parents took notions and ran off to London to work in theatre and his aunt had raised him. He didn't live with her now, preferring to stay in a flat near the bank, and it was hard to blame him when you looked at the house, which could've been used in one of those horror films.

Now Ambrose felt unsure about the blessings, they were suddenly an obligation, tied up not just with the intricacies of community but the cruder ties of money. Yet, for that very reason, he knew he had to allow it. 'He's a good lad, I'll drive him up,' said Ambrose.

'I'll have to meet you up there and take him in,' said Wilbur, 'my aunt wouldn't react well to a strange man in the house.'

'Right,' said Ambrose, and he turned away to get Brendan.

'Not that you're strange,' said Wilbur quickly, 'just not known to her.'

'Yes, I got that,' said Ambrose.

In the living room Brendan was already standing in his coat. Declan was sunk into the two-seater, in an obvious sulk. The smell of garlic was now wafting from the bin. 'Let's go,' Ambrose said to Brendan.

Brendan got in the front passenger seat and Ambrose drove him through town. The streetlights were on but there was nobody about. Seagulls were walking around like they owned the place. 'Should we bring her milk or a sliced pan?' asked Brendan.

'She doesn't need for that sort of thing,' said Ambrose. 'Just go in there and do what you do.'

'What is it I do?' asked Brendan.

'Do you not know?' said Ambrose, and he laughed.

'I let them talk,' Brendan replied in a perplexed sort of way and with an exaggerated shrug. 'Then I say normal things like, don't worry, let's hope for the best, things will work out.'

Ambrose went quiet, he felt something quiver in him as he turned Brendan's phrases over in his mind. 'I can see that might help, actually,' he said.

They drove into the hills, Ambrose and Brendan following Wilbur's tail lights and the glow against the hedgerows. It was a narrow, winding route, the hedgerows channelling their head-lights and leaving the wider countryside pitch black; even as the land rose it felt like travelling down a tunnel.

'Do you tell them about yourself?' asked Ambrose.

He saw surprise in Brendan's face, like it had never occurred to him. 'They don't ask about me,' said Brendan.

'Don't wait for them to ask,' said Ambrose.

'What would I say?' asked Brendan.

'Tell them you're a Bonnar,' he said with passion. 'Tell them you're my son. Tell everyone you're Ambrose Bonnar's son.'

The house came into view, one ground-floor window was a burning orange, like a street light, the rest black. They passed through the gate and between dense hollies to where Wilbur was parking in front of the house. The two men got out of their cars and stood together on the driveway, its stone chips compacted into muck and coated in moss. Brendan got out of the car and walked away as if refusing to go in. Wilbur looked to Ambrose, who made a move of his head signalling no problem, Brendan was just being himself, prone to distraction. It turned out Brendan only wanted a better look at the house, he stopped a short distance away and gazed up at it.

'Hasn't he been here before?' asked Wilbur. 'Boys raid the orchard every year.'

'Brendan isn't that sort,' said Ambrose. 'Declan, on the other hand.'

'He's welcome to all the apples he can carry,' said Wilbur.

'How long has your aunty been asking to see Brendan?'

Embarrassed, Wilbur hesitated. 'About a year,' he said.

It seemed a long while to leave a person waiting. Ambrose rolled a cigarette so he wouldn't have to speak and didn't offer his tobacco to Wilbur.

Brendan returned to the two men and said, 'This house looks frightened.'

Ambrose looked up at the looming facade. It had been coated in ivy but Wilbur, concerned for the brickwork, had got J. J. Brown to sever the trunks and inject the stumps with poison, so now the walls were covered in the dead remains, looking like white capillaries. They were everywhere but for window cavities, dark panels of wavy glass. You couldn't help but be impressed by the boy's take on the world; Ambrose felt a fresh dose of love.

Wilbur looked up at the house. 'There've been some frights in it,' he conceded.

Ambrose waited in the car while Wilbur led Brendan inside. The front hall was wide and furnished, Brendan mistook it for a room. Wilbur opened a door and Brendan recoiled from a wave of hot air and fiery light. Three different bar heaters were all going full blast, casting an orange light on every surface as well as intense dry heat. Wilbur and Brendan crossed into the thick air, leaden with the smell of baked dust. Every couple of seconds there was a crackly thump from the speakers attached to a record player, an LP had finished but was still revolving. There were hundreds of other records in a glass-fronted cabinet; the walls were papered; there were real paintings; a coat stand behind the sofa and instead of a bucket for coal there was a brass scuttle on four curved legs. Doris Kane was seated in the middle of her big sofa, bed pillows propping her up, and she was gazing at the arrivals. Brendan got the feeling she had been sitting there for hours with nothing but the regular thump of the record player. Her eyes were bright and assertive and her cardigan was sensible, but when you saw she was wearing tracksuit bottoms you knew something in her had come undone. When he took his aunt on trips out Wilbur tied a scarf around her head and it was clear why, her grey hair had come away in clumps leaving several bald patches. Wilbur stood behind Brendan and placed a hand on each shoulder, a move some would've found oppressive but Brendan was used to that kind of thing, he had been getting handed about since birth.

'Here he is, Aunty Doris,' said Wilbur. 'The boy from the sea.'

She smiled, she had all her teeth but they were very brown. She extended a hand and said, 'Don't be afraid of me.'

* * *

The season turned. We didn't remark on the returning house martins or the interest rates, too busy talking about Brendan. We were pleased with him, our boy from the sea, and his blessings. He remained willing, the custom continued even after Brendan started at the vocational school and wore the uniform. Few in town raised concerns about the blessings any more, even Bella Power dropped the subject, defeated.

Perhaps the last to speak against Brendan's blessings was John Cotter, owner of the Ship Inn. He was an upright, controlled, headmasterly sort of man, about seventy years old. The wife, RIP, had run a bed and breakfast above the pub but he had closed that business since and made the rooms his living quarters. John could probably hear the burble of our voices each evening and would pity us for wanting drink and company while he sat alone watching documentaries and writing polite but firm letters to county councillors. You'd only see him at 9 a.m. taking his constitutional up and down the pier. We were talking about Brendan one evening when John Cotter made a rare appearance behind the counter, probably drawn down by the subject. John reminded us that Brendan was only twelve years of age and that we should mind him more, saying the boy wouldn't come out right if he continued this performance. 'There's danger he'll become hollow and get stuck that way,' said John. 'People will always use the hollowness as a place to put their angst, giving little attention to the bearer, and it'll ultimately leave him lonely.'

Manus McManus dared to argue, saying there was nothing wrong with a boy learning to serve his community. 'It's important to find a role for yourself,' he said, 'why not start early?' In those days Manus McManus's primary role seemed to be propping up the Ship Inn's bar. John could've easily mentioned this, but he wasn't one to waste words. He left us with a curt 'Good evening.'

But it didn't matter what anybody thought, Brendan wanted to play the boy from the sea. He felt the hollowness that John Cotter feared but misunderstood it, taking it for a lightness that made him buoyant, transcendental. He could rise above the ordinary, and as he hit adolescence, Brendan took on an aloof manner. Gradually the blessings became drawn out and ceremonial. When we asked him for one he'd stop and be silent for at least five seconds before responding, using a cultivated, unwavering voice that wasn't natural. Soon it was the only way he spoke, whatever the situation. In school he got brutally mocked for this fake voice, and the students weren't too nice about it either. Christine was driven crazy by his new personality and raised it with Ambrose. 'It's just a phase,' he said. 'It'll be grand.'

Mossy Shovlin made it worse the day he met Brendan on the shore road. Town was busy, lots of boats in. There was a stink of guts from the fishmeal factory and lorries going by every few minutes. 'It's the boy from the sea!' said Mossy cheerfully. There was always a spark of regard between the two of them, their encounter years ago was key in both their lives. Mossy had changed in ways you wouldn't have predicted, he now kept his hair neat and his shoes shined. Finding Brendan was surely when he began taking himself seriously. He was living away in Letterkenny, had full-time work in a warehouse and got everyone to call him Maurice. We still insisted on using Mossy when we saw him, but that wasn't often any more.

'I am touched by your use of my title,' said Brendan, 'but I am aware I did not truly float in from the ocean, at least not physically.'

Mossy made no remark on Brendan's pretensions, failing to notice, or perhaps just having an understanding of personal reinvention. 'Don't mind what the pricks here say to you,' said Mossy. 'They didn't have the power of mind to accept what I told them so they came up with a story about a girl, an easy story so as not to tax themselves. You came from the sea and I know because I'm the man who lifted you. I'll never forget that morning.'

That was it, Brendan became completely unbearable: going about exuding the belief that he didn't just have a gift, he was a gift. All his life Brendan had avoided the stony beach but now we'd see him there in the evenings communing with the bay and the stones. He'd take off his shoes and socks, roll up his jeans and stand in the water, which we wouldn't have advised as waste oil and chemicals flowed that way from the Ships' Graveyard. He seemed to fancy himself some sort of pagan druid.

In short, Brendan started making a show of himself.

We stopped asking for blessings, we'd nearly cross the street to avoid him. Brendan maintained his tranquil expression but we could tell our change of mood troubled him. He'd hang about the town giving us the chance to avail of his services, but we didn't. If Brendan had quickly reverted to his original manner the custom might've been saved but instead he became sneaky, blessing us without invitation. We'd be queuing in Hegarty's shop and he'd pat our arms as he went by, muttering. It was a bit much when we were only after eggs or a jar of Nescafé.

The last person in town to seek a blessing was Big Jimmy. He was sitting on the bench outside the hotel one day when Brendan went by so he gave him a big salute and called him over. Serenely, Brendan approached, hand extended, glad to soothe one of the common folk. Jimmy offered his shoulder, lowered his head and removed his cap respectfully. Brendan stopped – stopped moving and for a moment stopped breathing. 'You're cured,' he said.

The cancer had vanished, a shiny yellow indentation in its place.

Jimmy kept his head lowered but cast his eyes upwards to the boy, wondering why his fingers hadn't made contact. When Jimmy understood the situation he sat up to look at him properly. 'That wasn't you, son,' he said. 'I had it removed in hospital. Anaesthetic, overnight stay,' and he added, a touch breathily, 'fine-looking nurses.'

Brendan's hand fell.

'You're a good lad,' said Jimmy, 'but you're no saint. In my view you've a big advantage on the saints: you're local.' He offered his shoulder again. 'Go on then, give us a tap.'

Brendan calmed down after that encounter, you no longer went in fear of him into Hegarty's. His normal voice returned and the self-delight dropped from him. We felt sorry for Brendan sometimes, listless as he meandered along the main street, nobody paying him much heed any more. It was probably painful for him, although a learning experience too.

One day Christine drove Brendan to the dentist. They arrived early so were waiting in the car watching pellets of rain hit the windscreen while 'Everybody Wants to Rule the World' was playing on the radio. 'I'd hate to rule the world,' said Christine as she switched it off. 'I've enough to do.'

'Being responsible for something you never wanted,' said Brendan, gazing at the running droplets. 'Stuck with it. Being trapped.'

Christine looked at him curiously.

'That's one sort of trouble people told me about, if you're still wondering,' said Brendan. 'I'd give it one hundred degrees of the pie.' His homework lately had included drawing pie charts.

'That's an understandable worry,' said Christine quietly, not wanting to break the effect. She had noticed before that sitting side by side in the car, not facing each other, could draw thoughtful, revealing words from the men she lived with, all three of them.

'The past was another category,' said Brendan. 'Things they said or didn't say, did or didn't do, years and years ago, and they were still thinking about it. The past gets one hundred degrees.'

Christine just went *hmmm*, wanting him to continue.

'Worry for the future was the biggest category though,' said Brendan. 'One hundred and fifty degrees. How will I end up? They worried about their children too, even the grown-up ones. Will they settle? Will they ever be contented? That sort of thing.'

Christine gazed at Brendan and said nothing.

Brendan went quiet, it seemed he was done so eventually Christine said, 'You've ten degrees left.'

'Miscellaneous,' he replied.

9.

ALL THAT TIME THE BONNARS themselves had been immune to Brendan's blessings. They lived with him, knew his nose-picking and forgetting to flush the toilet, Ambrose and Christine couldn't have fallen for it even if they had wanted to. This was too bad as they had a whole miscellany of issues just themselves, but they'd have said their problems were rooted in one simple thing: want of money, and no kindly words or hand on the shoulder would fix that deficiency. Want of money was the last thing Ambrose and Christine thought of before sleep and the first thing hitting them in the morning. They could at least remember life without the menace of debt, but the boys had grown up with it and were shaped by it in ways hard to measure. Christine noticed that Brendan started picking up coins if he saw one on the street, even pennies. She had also seen a cynical, covetous look on Declan's face when people were chatting about holidays or having meals out.

Then the *Dawn* developed a rot problem, whole sections had to be replaced and she took on a patchwork look. Some owners would've finally given up at that point, but Ambrose needed the hope represented by the *Dawn*: there could be a strong season, prices might rise and costs might drop and they'd make good money again. If he sold up all possibility vanished, he'd be in another man's pocket for the rest of his life. Determined to keep the *Dawn*, Ambrose began an extra-strict economy drive at home. He only allowed the use of one panel of the Superser heater. 'A bit of cool air will keep us alert,' he said. He only allowed porridge at breakfast, banning the purchase of fancy cereals like cornflakes, even the cheap Homestead cornflakes that went soggy as soon as the milk went in. 'Porridge is a healthier breakfast,' he said, 'I was reared on it.' He started using teabags twice. 'There's a softness to the flavour the second time around, I prefer it.' Driving into town he'd save a teaspoon of petrol by switching off the engine and freewheeling the hill, remarking on the peace and quiet. 'When I was a boy we could go all week and not hear an engine, and you know what? We were happier.' He put a ten-watt bulb in the corridor fitting. 'Why use a strong light? You just pass through or stand there talking on the phone, neither justifies the burning of electricity.'

All this pretence seemed to cost Ambrose no effort at all, his ability to maintain a state of denial was extraordinary, we admired it, we really did. It's an underrated talent, denial. These days we're told it's a flaw, we're told we should be in touch with our feelings, be honest with ourselves. But try this: picture two people standing in barrels of steaming slurry, up to their necks in it, and made to stay there all day. Who'll have the better time of it? The one who's best at denial, that's who.

Despite the electricity it used Ambrose couldn't bring himself to ban telly, he was too fond of sports and the old cowboy films. One evening he was watching the news when what appeared only Rockall. The report was about a former British soldier who set himself up on the isolated rock. Ownership of Rockall is subject to international dispute and he was going to stay on it for forty days to claim it for Britain. It wasn't very long since they had won the Falklands War, which may've gotten the man over-excited about taking hold of small islands. There were few smaller than Rockall, for shelter he had to bring a wooden box and lash it to a ledge near the peak. The news report had footage of him screwing it together. He said he was enjoying himself and looking forward to the forty days.

Jealousy was a rare emotion for Ambrose so it was peculiar that he experienced it now. The convulsions of feeling jealous and then quickly denying it, driving it down, forced Ambrose physically to his feet but he kept his eyes on the screen. He had seen a few black-and-white photographs of Rockall but this was his first time to see footage close up, in colour, and he stood rapt before it. Rockall looked like a broken cone and was the super-hard remains of a volcano. It was about the size of our church and mostly sheer or near enough. Birds were wheeling above and despite the huge distance to any shore the sea was calm as a lake. 'Brendan!' Ambrose called down the corridor. 'Come here 'til you see this!'

Brendan appeared, stood with him and watched, although not all that interested. The report had just ended when Declan stepped into the room. He took in the odd arrangement, his father and Brendan for some reason standing before the telly. Ambrose told him what they had been watching.

'There was film of Rockall?' said Declan. 'Why didn't you call me?'

'I didn't think of it,' admitted Ambrose.

'But you shouted for him,' said Declan, becoming upset.

'Half the town calls him the boy from the sea so I suppose I just thought—'

Brendan was shaking his head, he could see a wrong direction was being taken. 'There was nothing to it,' he said quietly. Brendan was still a conciliatory kind of boy.

Declan disregarded his attempt. 'Why'd you call him and not me?' he said to Ambrose. 'I'm the one you told about Rockall. He just thought it was a bit of the forecast, he didn't even know it was an actual rock.'

'I think I did,' said Brendan, objecting mildly.

'I'm the one who'd want to see Rockall!' Declan shouted at his father.

Ambrose didn't like getting roared at over nothing, or rather he didn't like being forced to confront the fact that it wasn't nothing, he had slipped up. Declan was nearly as tall as him now, which made this childish outburst worse. He blamed the television for riling everyone up, dangling Rockall before them like that. 'I'll tell you what,' Ambrose snapped, 'let's have no more telly at all. It's nothing but rubbish anyway. Radio is better for the mind and uses less power. When I was young we only had radio, it develops the brain.'

He almost snapped off the telly's switch with the way he twisted it. The screen went black. When Ambrose turned around Declan was already gone.

The manager of our hotel respected Christine's work but there just weren't many hours to be had in the winter and next thing the *Dawn*'s drive shaft cracked and she had to be re-engined, missing half a season. A series of red-ink warning letters arrived and enough was enough: Christine went to war with Ambrose's denial, chasing it down with plain talk and hard numbers. Christine wasn't one for tearful pleading, she was a Lyons. 'It's just a bad spell,' Ambrose would say as he retreated, but you can't hide in a bungalow.

One morning after the boys left for school she finally said it. 'We need an income that's steady, and that exists. You have to quit fishing.'

Ambrose had no answer, but just then the phone rang and he grabbed the receiver like a life-ring. It was Phyllis, Eunan had fallen and she wanted Christine's help lifting him. 'I'll come sure,' said Ambrose. He put the phone down and hurried to get out the door. Christine walked up the lane with him but dropped the subject of quitting fishing, Ambrose having managed to change the atmosphere between them for a while at least. Wanting to keep the advantage he asked, 'Is she still being unkind to Eunan?'

'No,' said Christine. 'Declan gives her breaks and she can manage him without losing the run of herself.'

'*Manage him?*' said Ambrose. 'He's a thing to be managed, is he?'

'Yes, he is,' she said with some defiance.

When he and Christine arrived Eunan was on the floor before his armchair, like he'd simply slid off it, sitting up with one hand gripping the frame that concealed the fireplace. Any shock he felt at losing his seat was replaced by a refusal to acknowledge it. He was looking up to the ceiling and waiting for the ordeal to end like it was somebody else's. Phyllis was standing at the window kneading her hands together. 'He's not taking enough water so he gets dehydrated and confused,' she said. 'He tried to stand up for himself.'

Christine sat at the dining table across the room, more like the district nurse than a daughter. 'You should drink the glasses of water Phyl brings,' she said to her father, using the same loud, emphatic voice that Phyllis used with him.

Eunan's top lip curled, a look of revulsion.

'Thinks he's too good for tap water,' said Phyllis. 'He wants me to go fill containers from Marty Byrne's spring, as if I haven't enough to do.'

Ambrose crouched down before Eunan until their heads were level. 'Ah, you poor old buck,' said Ambrose, his voice contained a surprising amount of emotion.

Phyllis looked at her sister as if to say, *what's got into him?* Christine looked back but said nothing.

Ambrose assessed Eunan's position before taking him in a one-armed grasp. Eunan let his chin rest on Ambrose's shoulder, breathing drily across his ear. When he had the old man tightly held Ambrose gripped the chair with his other hand and arose, taking Eunan with him. Ambrose would've been in his mid-forties by then but still well able to arm-wrestle any man in the Pier Bar. He returned Eunan gently to his seat. Eunan didn't speak and gave no sign of appreciation, he sat upright, hands on his knees, minimizing the distance between where he was now and where he was a moment ago, trying to create the impression they hadn't actually seen him helpless on the floor.

Ambrose turned to the sisters. 'Every day he went out and worked that bay for you,' he said. 'You could at least get him some spring water.'

Ambrose looked from sister to sister and saw their resistance. 'Right,' he said. He returned to the bungalow, collected the ten-gallon plastic drum from the back press, got in the car and drove. On the road he felt his face become intensely hot and a sharp prickling rise behind his eyes. Gravel crunched as he hit the brakes outside Marty's house but Ambrose remained in the car a while. He made fists of his hands, placed them on the steering wheel then put his forehead against them, staying like that until he was ready to face the world again. Eventually Ambrose got out of the car and approached Marty's door, holding the ten-gallon drum aloft and calling a cheery 'Hello!'

One Sunday some weeks later, Christine picked up a thick envelope on the mat inside their front door. 'FROM A FRIEND' was written on the envelope with a shaky hand and inside there was money, a fair bit. She put the envelope on the table in front of Ambrose. 'Dropped through the letterbox last night,' she said.

Ambrose was startled and said nothing, trying to understand the implications. It was over three hundred pounds. 'Some drunk will've done it,' he said eventually. 'They'll soon have regrets and be up wanting it back.'

'Maybe,' said Christine, which meant she didn't agree.

'If no one appears you may take it up to the chapel and stick it in the poor box.'

'May I?' said Christine archly. Ambrose often dealt with difficult situations by turning skipper and issuing an order.

Ambrose suspected the money came from Wilbur. Brendan still called to the aunt sometimes, a bit of company for her. But a banker would surely have given an even total in twenties or tens, not this mix of notes, and he'd have better handwriting probably. Then Ambrose wondered if Wilbur might've deliberately thrown in those factors to avoid suspicion, causing Ambrose to suspect him even more. Ambrose decided he'd not share these thoughts with his wife, he'd keep them to himself.

Christine was looking at him. 'I doubt it was Wilbur,' she said.

'Who else would think we need this?' he asked, exasperated.

The boys' hand-me-down clothes were on the radiator and through the window Christine could see their car, rust on every rim and a headlight held on by cable ties. 'People are smart enough,' she said.

When Ambrose was out of the room Christine counted the money: three hundred and seventy-eight pounds stuffed in the envelope in a jumble. There were twenties but more tens, some crisp, some worn, a good few fivers and twenty-three individual pound notes. She could see the money came from many pockets. Before marrying, Christine worked in the Ship Inn a while and could guess what happened. The Ship Inn had two sections, a lounge and a bar. The lounge was where a married couple might go or a German backpacker with a book; it had carpet, soft seating and sometimes a fire going in the grate, while the bar side had nothing but stools on a lino floor. There was no rule saying the bar was for men, but the lack of a female toilet on that side sent a message and you'd only get the odd woman in there. Most evenings the men had quiet conversations in pairs or in threes and there'd be one or two silent individuals looking into their pints along the counter, but occasionally someone would hit on a topic that drew the others and the whole bar would get caught up in a single debate, stools repositioned inwards until the men were operating like a focus group. The state of the roads, the state of the North, quotas, the fastest route to Limerick; these discussions could become passionate. Christine could easily imagine a big talk rising around Ambrose and how he deserved help. Hadn't he lent Emmet Curran a net for two weeks when his gear was lost? Hadn't he helped Patsy John take in his turf and him a malignant sort of bastard few could stand? Above all, hadn't he and the wife taken in an abandoned child and raised him as their own, despite his quare ways?

That would've sealed it, Christine could picture one of the men suggesting an intervention and the contained urgency they'd have worked themselves into while discussing what form it might take. People in the town were always against meddling or interfering; doubts would've been raised, but then talked down. No need for a final vote, consensus was in the air, understood by men whose senses, when it came to such things, were as fine as you'd get in a whole warren of rabbits. 'Have you an envelope back there?' they would've asked whoever was working that night. One man saying something should be written on the envelope as leaving it unmarked would be perturbing, almost threatening, and everyone seeing the wisdom. The envelope was passed around, money placed inside, and one of them would slip up the lane on his way home to put it through their letterbox.

Christine told Ambrose the exact amount.

'We'll keep it aside and see if anyone comes looking,' he said.

Christine agreed this was the best idea.

In time they'd realize no one going to ask for the money back. Ambrose and Christine probably put it away for a week or two then decided to give the money to charity or spend it for themselves. What they did with the money was their business. We hoped they did spend it.

The season turned. The travelling funfair came and went. Philomena Burke had her appendix removed. During a trawl aboard the *Siobhán*, Francis O'Connell got his right arm caught in the cables and the whole thing was taken off him. A Spanish boat was arrested by the navy for fishing in restricted inshore waters and escorted to the harbour, we all went to look and agreed the crew were a dastardly-looking bunch. There was such a bad storm one night that the coastal road out by Muckross was smashed to pieces: great slabs of black rock thrown in from the churning sea until a thousand tonnes of hardfill foundation was shattered into boulder-sized chunks which were then further stirred by the beating waves and left sitting at all angles. Many of us went to look at the destruction. Ambrose was seen there with his sons standing quietly and looking up and down the shattered road.

Ambrose's power of denial could deal with his wife and even a donation of cash, but finally met its match: Joseph McBride quit the *Christine Dawn* to take a berth on a new supertrawler, the 140-foot *Girl Jacqueline*. Mackerel was only profitable in bulk but if you could get out as far as the big shoals and if your trawls and tanks were big enough you'd be on to a bonanza. No one blamed Joseph for quitting a small whitefish boat, least of all Ambrose. Joseph had stayed longer than might've been expected, friendship often meant helping a person maintain their denial, but ultimately the promise of better money took him away, and perhaps a few safety concerns about the *Dawn*. After their last trip Ambrose and Joseph sat in the Pier Bar discussing the wild times and close calls. The one pint would've done Joseph but Ambrose kept buying another round. 'I'm in no hurry to get back to the wife,' he admitted.

Ambrose was happy for Joseph, genuinely. He was happy for him all evening, and still happy for him when he eventually got home and lay down, uncomfortably, on the two-seater. He was happy for Joseph as he drifted off, but around 5 a.m. Ambrose awoke and wasn't happy. The unhappiness felt bound to his muscles, it actually squeezed, and he knew there'd be no getting back to sleep. He switched on the light but it was too bright, too exposing, so he switched it off and made a mug of tea by rote, taking the bag from the dish where they were laid for a second go. He found he couldn't sit so went down the corridor to look in at the boys, something that normally put him in good humour. The creak of the door made Declan grumble and his shape heave. He was as tall as Ambrose now and had broad shoulders, another man in the house essentially. The room smelled of his trainers. Declan was a sturdy lad, he'd do fine, but looking at Brendan made Ambrose's heart pinch. He was small for his age and set to become one of those compact men who'd always remind you of a child. Tonight, as always, Declan was sleeping in to the wall, his back to the room, to Brendan. It used to be that Brendan slept curled around a pillow and faced out towards Declan, but lately he'd started facing in to his wall too. So there they were, backs to each other. Ambrose leaned in the door looking at them both and waiting for the usual, uncomplicated pride to rise in him, but it didn't come.

He returned to the kitchen and sat in the dark.

Ambrose was in bad form for a long time then; weeks, months. At first Christine was delicate, asking him what was wrong and watching the battleground of his face while he sought the words, before giving up and saying he was grand. Ambrose had all the language required to define precisely the meaning of a cloud, the character of a sea, an attitude of rain, but to describe his own emotional weather he was limited to 'Been better', 'Been worse' and 'You know yourself.' When Christine first met Ambrose he seemed to have a great way with words but now she knew it was nothing but banter. He'd tell you about himself in a way that seemed spontaneous and open but he only began a story when he knew how it ended.

Whitefish prices were bad and there were difficulties getting a steady replacement for Joseph so Ambrose was ashore a lot. He would sit by the window for hours or pace back and forth, trying to work something out that Christine knew he never would. At times she felt her Lyons side revolt, insist on its turn to speak. She didn't want to sound like her father but it was difficult as she could think like him and, even when put differently, Eunan's sentiments slipped through. She'd say, 'I wish I'd the time to sit about,' or 'You'll wear a hole in the lino,' or the like. Ambrose would be unresponsive, and she'd get sharper. Eventually Ambrose might pull on his boots and march away off across the hills, not returning for hours. He wasn't the sort for fighting and roaring, although he was once seen kicking a fencepost.

One afternoon in town Ambrose saw something that came as another blow. The bay was still, a stony grey just like the sky. A Norwegian freighter was anchored a mile out, awaiting the outcome of some legal dispute. Ambrose was walking along the main street to where the car was parked when he saw Brendan sitting on the wall of the diamond with the not-working men. Brendan was approaching fourteen by then. He was leaning forward with his elbows on his knees, eyes cast down. There were no blessings going on or anything of that sort, Brendan was just there, among them, and he was in his school uniform, which made it worse. Many fathers would've gone over and plucked their son from the scene, bringing them home. That Ambrose didn't goes to show what bad form he was in those days. Instead he hurried to his car and escaped but at least he managed to put words on the issue, finding Christine in the kitchen and telling her about it as soon as he got home. 'He's easily led,' she said.

'He'll grow out of it, though,' said Ambrose. 'Do you think?' He was restraining his upset but Ambrose wanted looking after, wanted to be told that things would be all right. He'd have liked Christine to put her palm to his cheek, as she used to sometimes. He'd have taken a touch on the elbow.

But Christine was a Lyons today, her arms were folded. 'You should talk to him,' she said. 'He looks up to you, they both do. You know that, don't you?'

Ambrose didn't entirely. He had understood his sons' need for him when they were little, it had been physically demonstrated, home from a trip they'd dash to him, grab a hand each and pull him this way and that. But as they grew and ceased to be so obvious Ambrose had stopped recognizing his importance in their lives, he never was good at reading other people's motivations. The boys didn't have the contempt Ambrose had seen other teenagers aim at their fathers, but he didn't think they admired him either. Now that Christine had reminded Ambrose of his fatherly responsibilities he was suddenly gripped by them and determined to put in some great parenting. One interest he and his younger son shared was in assessing and predicting the weather, so he sat waiting at the window and when Brendan appeared on the lane he jumped up to meet him on the front step. 'Let's see what the weather's got planned for us!' Ambrose called brightly.

He left the front door open so Christine took the opportunity to step into the corridor and listen.

Ambrose and Brendan stood together looking west. The iron-grey cloud had so much texture and detail you'd think you could touch it just by reaching out. Meanwhile the slate of the sea seemed profoundly removed, like it belonged on another planet; it was hard to believe you needed only walk half an hour to dip your hand in.

'How'd you get on today?' Ambrose asked Brendan. He didn't mention seeing him on the diamond wall.

'Grand,' said Brendan.

'Did you stop off anywhere on the way back from school?'

'No.'

They looked west another while.

'That rain will hit us soon,' said Ambrose.

'Within an hour, I'd say,' said Brendan.

They were quiet a while.

'Good man,' said Ambrose.

They turned to go in for their dinner.

Christine backed into the kitchen, dismay bubbling inside her. She knew Ambrose would think he had done fine, tell himself those moments with his son were rich and companionable. Ambrose was passing on what he had himself inherited, placing Brendan in a lineage of quiet men, each contained to the point of self-repression, generation after generation of horizon-watchers, preferring to look out at a wordless immensity than have even a second of introspection. A terrible snare, Christine decided, to have set up a life with a man so inhibited. 'You can do your own chips,' she said as Ambrose and Brendan entered the kitchen. 'I need a lay-down.'

Christine's frustration simmered. One morning Ambrose was still in bed at nine. He said he was a man short and there was no demand for inshore fish that week anyway. No point going out, he said, looking at the ceiling. The sight of him laid there drove Christine from the house. Up at the Lyons's she sat at the dining table while Phyllis prepared tea and toast for them. Christine often visited her sister these days, Ambrose must've known it was mostly to give out about him, yet he never seemed to resent it. Christine would've preferred him to complain. She gazed out the window and across the lane. Taller than the house, the spruce trees made a formidable grey-green curtain. Amid the shadows a few fallen trees could be seen, their angles disrupting the impression of strong verticals. The trees reinforced Christine's sense of imprisonment and brought forth an anger. As Phyllis sat down Christine burst out with, 'Do you think they'll ever allow divorce in Ireland?'

'Divorce!' said Phyllis, horror-struck. She didn't like that sort of talk in her house.

'Yes,' said Christine. 'Divorce, will they allow it?'

'They might,' said Phyllis, when she had recovered, 'but it won't catch on in Donegal.'

Christine nodded towards their father and said, 'Don't you think Mammy would've divorced him if she was let?'

All the while Eunan had been snoring in his armchair, head thrown back and jaw fallen open. They could see the hard, grey roof of his mouth, shot through with vivid red veins. His hands were thrust forward and laid one over the other on the handle of his walking stick, which was upright and free-standing between his legs, the dead weight of his arms keeping the stick vertical even while he slept.

'She certainly wouldn't,' said Phyllis. 'Mammy wasn't crazy.'

Christine let it go.

When she returned home Ambrose was gone. The car hadn't moved and his boots weren't in their place, meaning he had likely headed off across the hills. He normally did this during a row but they hadn't had one in a week, Christine had been careful. She went out the back door and up the boggy slope and sure enough saw fresh boot prints in the muck. At a high spot, between clumps of rushes, Christine stood with her arms folded, gazing inland, the Atlantic breeze making her hair lift and wave.

Ambrose had reached a terrible conclusion and it set him off walking: the *Christine Dawn* was an unlucky boat. Most of us would've laughed at the idea of a boat being lucky or unlucky, laughed at getting moody over it, but Ambrose couldn't help himself. He regretted putting Christine's name on such a cursed vessel, he might apologize to her for it. Ambrose walked an hour then came off the headland to a ridge of rushy dunes near Fintra. We had seen him there a few times, pacing back and forth above the beach, the loaded sky beyond. The gusts were aggressive and showers were coming in off the sea but neither troubled him today, only his thoughts. He was thinking about past mistakes and if you were close enough you'd have seen his lips moving. To think *mistakes were made* wasn't enough. Ambrose slipped into self-recrimination as he walked the dunes, bad thoughts directed inwards. *I've made so many mistakes.*

After a time a car approached on the sandy track. It was Tommy. He was making money and you might've thought he'd drive something fancy and new but Tommy had more sense. He parked up on the verge and climbed the dune towards Ambrose, the wet rushes had him soaked to the knees by the time he reached the top. Tommy squinted into the wind, he'd have preferred to be out of the weather. His keys were in his hand, a lump the size of a tennis ball he held with his middle finger through the ring. Donegal men had strikingly big key fobs, we tended to have many padlocks in our lives. Tommy had gone grey but was yet younger-looking, he had gotten married and the wife talked him into having his teeth whitened and straightened. It was fierce expensive but he had submitted, that's love for you. 'How's it going?' said Tommy.

'You know yourself,' said Ambrose.

Tommy kept back. Ambrose was bristling, hunched, looking cornered despite the open and low horizon. Neither man would acknowledge it but Tommy's arrival was clearly no coincidence. 'There's a berth on the *Warrior II* for you,' Tommy said.

He was probably prepared for offence but Ambrose's reply was mostly tired. 'Have to take a course, would I?' he said.

'Not a bit of it,' said Tommy, 'not for general crew.'

General crew. Tommy had taken care not to say deckhand, and Ambrose knew it.

'There's a lot to get used to with this generation of vessel,' said Tommy. 'You'll pick it up though, if I could you can.' He smiled. 'You were always better at chess.'

'And you were always better at everything else,' said Ambrose.

Tommy laughed, letting on to think Ambrose had made a joke. 'I wish you'd do it, you and me again, eh?' he said. 'You might actually like the *Warrior*. I have her well-organized and all the latest kit.'

'Do you ever miss it though, the actual fishing?' he asked.

Tommy stopped smiling. 'There's a world to feed, Ambrose,' he said.

Ambrose looked away.

'Now, can I give you a lift home?' said Tommy.

'No thanks, you're all right.'

Tommy paused then said, 'Suit yourself.' He headed off.

Ambrose knew well what happened: Christine had rung Tommy and got him running around the country to find her husband and offer him a berth, anything to get him away from the *Dawn*. Ambrose headed home, and as he crossed the hills his stride became aggressive, chin forward and his arms swinging more and more until you'd have known he was in a rage from a quarter-mile away. Sheep scattered before him. Ambrose now felt sorry for any boat named after that woman, it was probably Christine who brought the bad luck, it certainly seemed to run in her family. He marched over the slopes to the house but the car was away and he was left pacing about the lane in frustration. Christine might've gone looking for him, or be demonstrating that she too could vanish. Either way no row was available so Ambrose decided to smash something instead. Inside the house he went for the telly, imagining the screen imploding around the toe of his boot, but he stopped short, the telly had cost fifty pounds. He blundered around the house, seeking an object that would shatter gratifyingly, but thoughts of money worked against him, everything was expensive: mirrors, the coffee table, the kettle, the toaster, everything cost a fortune. Finally he remembered their big Pyrex dish and lifted it from the cupboard. It was deep with two handles, a creamy colour, very slightly translucent and had an orange flower pattern. Christine would understand how wrong she had been when she saw this in pieces; it was a wedding present. She was always saying what a mighty dish it was, even her with no interest in cooking or its gear. Oven chips was all she ever used it for. Oven chips! That was her level. Ambrose's disgust was renewed. Phyllis borrowed the dish occasionally, and in a rare display of satisfaction she also called it mighty. Even Declan had remarked on it, saying it was great for shepherd's pie. Ambrose lifted the dish above his head, it was pleasingly heavy and ready to give him what he needed: a white-hot moment of irreversible violence. He didn't just drop it, he threw it down. The Pyrex resounded against the floor. The lino in the kitchen area was hardly soft, about as much give as pine board, but the dish didn't break, it bounced then sat unhurt. Ambrose stopped, his insides steadying for the first time since leaving the dunes. He contemplated the dish, crouched down and picked it up, revolving it between his palms and looking at it properly for the first time ever. Ambrose felt kinship with anything displaying qualities of hardy, uncomplaining servitude. He had to agree, this was a mighty dish.

10.

EVERY SIGNAL DECLAN RECEIVED SAID money was hard got and by the time he turned sixteen the lesson had gone deep, become buried in his spine. It would influence him all his life. Christine said it was important for Declan to stay in school and do his final exams if he was going to get well-paid work. In our vocational school students did the basic subjects, but boys were also trained to handle welders and lathes and girls learned how to keep accounts and roast a chicken, the idea being you'd get an occupation the minute you left, or at least be of use about the house. Declan was a bad student in every subject, seeing classrooms only as a place to assert himself among his peers, which wasn't done through good behaviour and homework. Recently he had come to understand his mammy's reasoning, but nothing on the blackboard was ever easy.

To be alone after dark Declan sometimes headed up to the bogland beyond the Lyons's house. The clingy smell of peat was stronger at night, holding up against the breeze from the sea. With the stretching spruces and round hilltop no lights from the town could be seen and if there were no boats on the bay then the world was completely black. He'd sit on a turf bank, not caring if the ground was damp. Fuel had been cut here by generations of his family, back beyond recorded history. His bloodline seemed represented, captured, in the stratifications of the peat itself, softly reverberating down through time. But Declan wasn't drawn here by the past, he came as it was the only place he'd get to have a good tug at himself. The bathroom at home had a sliding bolt, but Christine felt entitled to start speaking through any door in the house without warning, a lad could get no peace. The bogland may've still seemed a bizarre choice of location, given how open it was, but nobody walked that way, certainly not after dark. Declan would bring some toilet paper for the job, or he'd stand at an old turf cutting, support himself with the other hand, and masturbate away onto the layers of peat, where his forefathers had likely done the same, down through the centuries of that ancient landscape.

Afterwards he'd have a cigarette. Declan preferred proper cigarettes, but an advantage of rolling tobacco was that he could steal enough for four or five smokes from his father's tin undetected. One night Declan happened to be up on the bogland smoking a rollie as a trawler was returning up the bay. He knew her two miles out due to the arrangement of her floods, the *Dawn*. The sight of her toiling against the sea hit Declan with a slap. His prospects might be limited but he knew one thing for sure: he wasn't getting into fishing. Other boys in his class wanted nothing more than to head out the bay but hunting fish had never appealed to him. Add to that his parents' fear of losing their house and all was clear: fishing was grinding work and no reward, little better than slavery. A string of tobacco was annoying Declan's lip and the rolled cigarette suddenly tasted of old men and dirt. He spat it out, then stood up and dumped out his entire stash of tobacco, letting it scatter. Proper cigarettes from now on, he decided, or he'd go without.

Next morning the sky was the grey of old potato water and Declan was the first Bonnar awake. He took the fish slice and some elastic bands from the kitchen drawer and found a good straight stick, half his height, at the back of the bungalow, then headed down the road. The fish slice was stowed up his sleeve where it wouldn't be seen. He couldn't hide the stick but that was okay, no one was suspicious of a boy carrying a stick. Declan went to St Catherine's Well, which was outside of town, alone on a hill. The well was circular, lined in flat stones, three foot deep and five foot in diameter. In some parts of Ireland holy wells dripped with offerings: candles, toys, photos, rosary beads and the like, small objects of personal significance left behind by the faithful, and having accrued years of such offerings the wells seemed to hum with a gathered weight of feeling. Very nice of course, but we didn't go for that sort of thing. Our holy well was plain, ringed in concrete and unadorned. However, we did occa-sionally throw a coin in and, resting on the bottom's furry stones, they shone. After making sure no one was around, Declan knelt at the side of the well, used the elastic bands to attach the slice to the stick and dipped the device in the water. He lifted out all the fifties, the new twenties and a few tens before deciding he had enough and slipping away. Later Declan felt bad, but he still bought cigarettes with the money and the following month he returned to the well. This time, with great focus, he cleaned it out completely. Every single coin.

That wasn't the worst of his crime spree.

One day a few weeks later Brendan was walking up the Mount at his usual daydreamy pace, stripping ferns by running them through his fingers as he went by. It was a fine afternoon, birds were nipping about and there was only occasional soft rain. He passed through Doris Kane's gate and, to his alarm, Declan emerged from the hollies. He was wearing his military-looking jumper, with the patches on the shoulders. 'Are you going in to her?' asked Declan, indicating on up the driveway. 'The bank man's aunty?'

Brendan said nothing.

'I'll head in with you,' said Declan.

Declan's dominance was such a deep rut in Brendan's life that he slid into his role immediately. His submission wasn't comfortable but it was familiar and felt inevitable. They approached the house and although Brendan walked in front Declan was in charge. The door was unlocked but Brendan knocked anyway and called out as he entered, 'I've brought my brother.' Mrs Kane was sitting in the hall, in the built-in seat of the telephone table, wearing slippers and a red dressing gown of towelly material. She wasn't on the phone and seemed settled there for no reason, just letting the afternoon slip by, but she recognized Brendan quickly and stood, spritely enough. 'Who's this handsome lad?' she asked.

'Declan,' said Brendan.

Declan was alarmed by the old woman's dressing gown: her ankles were bare and he worried she was naked beneath. A lot, an awful lot, depended on the loose knot in the belt.

Brendan was untroubled, used to Mrs Kane's ways; he led everyone to the front room. As a concession to summer only one bar heater was going. She sat in the middle of the sofa, among her many pillows.

'Will you take tea?' Brendan asked her.

'Oh, yes please. And there are biscuits.'

Brendan went to the kitchen and left Declan standing. There were two empty armchairs, but Mrs Kane didn't invite him to sit, having lost the way of such niceties years ago. The dressing gown slipped off a leg, above the knee, revealing wispy hairs and blue veins. Declan was still standing there awkwardly when Brendan returned with a tea set on a tray. At the sight of Declan, uncomfortable and gawping about, a rebelliousness reared within Brendan. He placed the tray on the low table in front of Mrs Kane and gave Declan no attention, leaving him standing there. The Bonnars put teabags straight into mugs and their only tray was catching crumbs under the toaster but Brendan was confident with the china tea set. He approached the record player, lifted the lid and read the circular label on the record, making it clear he had done this many times as well, a record player was no bother to him. He skipped the names of the conductor and pianist as they were long and Russian and he didn't want to stumble on them, just reading out, 'Rachmaninov's Piano Concerto Number Two.'

Declan sniggered at 'number two'. Brendan looked at him witheringly. Declan stopped.

'A magnificent work,' said Mrs Kane.

Brendan lowered the needle and music rose.

Declan sat himself, taking the armchair nearest the door. From there, mercifully, Mrs Kane's pillows blocked the view of her legs but his taking a seat caused her to notice him again. 'Who's this handsome lad?' she asked.

'Declan,' said Declan.

Brendan poured Mrs Kane's tea then left and returned with a tin of USA biscuits, opened the lid and put the tin alongside the tray. There were no chocolate biscuits left on top, so Declan lifted the tray and took a few from the bottom layer. Heading into the bottom layer when biscuits were still available on top was an extraordinary break from decency. If you did that in any of our houses remarks would've been made, after you were gone.

'Don't eat them all on her,' said Brendan.

Mrs Kane didn't mind. 'A big lad like this needs to eat plenty,' she said, smiling over at him. 'What's your name?'

'Declan,' said Declan.

They all sat a while. Mrs Kane was made content and faraway by the record but Declan got fidgety. Did people really do this? Just sit and listen? Aunty Phyllis loved Daniel O'Donnell, but she'd only listen to him sing when cooking or doing housework. 'Daniel's just a bit of company,' she'd say. It would never occur to her to hold still and dedicate herself to the contemplation of 'My Donegal Shore'. The plonking piano rose and fell and stopped and started, both dull and impenetrable. 'Do you actually like this?' Declan said to Brendan. Mrs Kane's way of being made it possible to speak like she wasn't in the room.

'I think it sounds like the sea,' he said.

Declan looked at the record player accusingly, he had just discovered the music was hiding something from him.

'You can leave if you're not happy,' said Brendan, nodding towards the door.

Declan looked at him sharply, he had detected the new defiance in Brendan and didn't like it. 'I can do what I want, I know,' said Declan.

He stood and started walking around the room. Brendan followed him with his eyes but Mrs Kane didn't seem to register his movement, lost in the music, a placid smile on her. Declan examined the framed watercolours on the wall, hands behind his back in fake nonchalance. He stepped into the open area behind Mrs Kane's sofa and became silent and still, waiting for her to forget his presence. Half a minute was more than enough. During that time Declan listened to the music, it did indeed seem to swell and crash ashore.

Mrs Kane's handbag was hanging from the coat stand and he lifted it in the palm of one hand. Brendan gripped the arms of his chair, he looked like he might jump up but didn't, instead doing a kind of distressed jig in his seat. Declan didn't remove the handbag from its hook but used his other hand to flip it open and reach in, untoggling the purse he found, all the while keeping his eyes on Brendan, daring him to act. There were three twenty-pound notes in the purse, Declan knew he should take only one, making the theft less detectable, but he scooped the lot. Brendan hissed, 'No.' Eyes locked with Brendan's, Declan slid the money into his pocket, settled the handbag back into position and stepped away. The music clattered to a stop, the last chord disappeared into the vinyl static and somebody coughed. Declan dropped back into his armchair and Mrs Kane noticed him again. 'Who's this handsome lad?' she asked.

The season turned. Tank McHugh had to be admitted into St Conal's for a while. 'It's for his own good,' we said. There were high winds and trees came down along the roads. Justine O'Donnell's roof got blown off and she had to be put on tablets. Brendan was feeling alone and unhappy, an unsettled state that he didn't solely blame on Declan, he was also blaming himself. Brendan never told anyone what Declan did in Mrs Kane's house that day, he felt too included in the event. He had already started feeling uneasy about visiting the likes of Doris Kane and the theft seemed partly his own transgression. Deep inside he felt his activities were somehow suspect, born of shortcomings, not so different from Declan's thievery. He never visited Mrs Kane again and by now not even Big Jimmy was asking for blessings. Brendan had developed a spotty chin and greasy hair and a ritual that was potent from a young boy felt peculiar from a fourteen-year-old. The shyness that gave the smooth-faced child an otherworldly quality now made him seem shifty. Brendan understood this, he felt shifty to himself, perhaps he had washed up on the wrong shore. He'd look at others his age, the way they'd pal around on the road or in the chip shop and wonder why he couldn't get into their manner of talk. To Brendan they didn't seem to converse, they just made assertions, the girls too, barely responding to each other at all, just firing words back and forth, giving each other nothing but one vital thing: a sense of belonging.

The stolen money lasted Declan a while as there wasn't much to buy in our town, we weren't a shopping destination. Our shops stuck with essentials: tinned fruit, stewing steak, nails and the like. Once Declan saw a crowd gathered around the window of Gallagher's grocers and he approached to see what drove the scene. Sat in the window was our first ever pineapple. Nobody dared buy it, but it was something to remark on. Most of us were against 'luxury goods', if a woman wanted a knick-knack for the mantelpiece she went to Donegal Town where there was a shop with a display case containing animals represented in spheres of crystal, two spheres glued together and glittery eyes added to create cats, dogs or sheep. Gaze too long at these sculptures and you could be seduced by them and end up parting with £2.99.

Eventually Declan found a good use for a few pounds: Cindy.

Hers was a business establishment he hadn't registered as a young boy, he simply hadn't perceived it. If you had asked him what stood between the games arcade and the chemist he would've said nothing, the chemist and the arcade were right next to each other. But no, between them was Cindy's hair salon and shortly after it entered his consciousness Declan decided his mammy wasn't cutting his hair any more, he'd get Cindy to do it.

Although Cindy took anyone the atmosphere of the salon was female, with lots of posters of women with perms or their hair sprayed up, sometimes wearing big glasses and always heavy on the blusher. In letters shaped like lightning bolts a poster in the window said, 'New Sensations', an idea that both thrilled and intimidated us. Declan entered and stood inside the door, not sure what to do. Two women sat with their heads in big helmets suspended on shafts while Cindy went at another woman with a brush. 'Have a seat there,' said Cindy, with a dip of the head toward the waiting area. Declan did as directed.

Many considered Cindy a 'fine doll'. On the large side and tall with a high centre of gravity, she looked like she could've shouldered down a door if required, or just for the laugh. The hair was huge and from there her body tapered down to fine ankles that disappeared into leopard-print flats. Cindy knew what she was selling and it wasn't only hairdos, it was a bit of glamour.

Declan looked away from her and down at the glossy magazines arrayed on the waiting-area table. He flicked through one and was surprised to discover not just pictures of women, but men too: stubble on their faces, no shirt on their back and often holding a nice dry baby. These were 'new men' and there was talk of them on television and radio those days. New men were in touch with their feminine side, they were nurturing and sensitive. They weren't afraid to be 'vulnerable', they might talk about their feelings, cry and the like. We hadn't seen a new man in reality, they must've had them in England and certain parts of Dublin maybe. They weren't our sort of thing, but you may be assured if a new man had accidentally strayed into our town he would've been treated with respect.

'Up you get, love,' said Cindy, standing by the chair. Declan sat looking in the mirror while Cindy released a catch to drop him a few inches, her big loop earrings swinging. She was rumoured to have a tattoo. Cindy stood behind and gazed at him frankly in the mirror. 'Now,' she said, 'what are you after?'

'A haircut,' said Declan.

Cindy went at it, speaking only to get Declan to position his head this way and that but she soon stopped verbalizing and moved his head manually with her fingertips splayed to his temples, hard points of contact that sent charges along his body. To complete his fringe Cindy stood directly behind Declan and brought his head back until he felt it was resting, lightly, on her breasts. A weird exhaustion gripped him. In reality, his head wasn't resting on her breasts, the cushioning he experienced was just from the aura of her breasts, which was mostly his own projection, although her perfume did contribute. Anyway, whatever it was, it was well worth three pounds. He felt himself sinking—

The door to the street flew open and there was Mick Cannon. He stuck his head in, afraid of putting a foot over the threshold. 'The Africans have your brother!' he said to Declan.

All warmth evaporated and Cindy stepped away from the chair.

A Nigerian freighter had been moored that week, buying up mackerel. The vessel was British-built and probably forty years old but in good trim, every inch painted a sandy colour, like a desert tank from World War II. The crew had days ashore and made themselves part of the town scene. They all wore the same thick blue woollen pullovers and big black boots and were over six foot tall and very friendly. We enjoyed them. They'd speak to us in a formal, measured English, very polite, then turn around and use their own lingo with each other. They walked around arm in arm, apparently this was done in Nigeria so was acceptable. The Nigerians were industrious: during downtime at sea they constructed model boats, galleons with rigging and cloth sails, that they brought ashore to sell, walking around town with them. The models were big; when the hull was cradled in their arms the masts reached above their heads. Many of us bought one and for years afterwards you'd see the models on Killybegs sideboards.

Fully loaded, the freighter went under way that afternoon but had only gotten eight or nine times her own length when she powered down and dropped anchor. There was radio communication with the harbour master, who made a phone call and fifteen minutes later Ambrose arrived on the pier, cap on crooked and walking in a rapid way that didn't suit him. He found Declan by the auction house. He was feeling self-conscious in his new haircut, although Ambrose didn't even notice it. 'How did Brendan end up on that ship?' Ambrose asked.

'I don't know, what are you asking me for?' said Declan.

'You're going out with me,' said Ambrose.

They walked along the pier, Ambrose stretching his neck to look down at the clinkers. Con must've been out lately, a rod and landing net lay in the bow and the outboard was attached. 'We'll take a lend,' said Ambrose.

The outboard was in bad shape, needing thirteen pulls and seven expletives to get going. Ambrose took the tiller and he and Declan rattled towards the massive freighter. The bay was calm, no wind. A fair few lads observed their progress from the pier with their hands flat over their eyes, not as a shield from sunlight, it was a dull day, but as an aid to focus. The not-working men left the diamond wall and walked to the end of the pier to watch too, that'll give you an idea of how fascinating the scene was. It was a real reddener for Declan. 'You should've never taken him in,' he said.

'You're really still not over it?' said Ambrose, more sad than irritated.

When they got close to the freighter its hull was so enormous it seemed to fold around them. Seams and bolt heads had lost definition under layers and layers, decades and decades, of paint. With the softened details and the same sandy colour applied everywhere the vessel seemed not constructed of steel at all, but moulded from bright clay, only the dark portholes tending against the impression. Ambrose cut off the outboard and let the boat nudge against the steel. Declan gripped a ladder and held them alongside while Ambrose tied up. The ladder was composed of shaped bars jutting from the hull, every second rung cut away as if to make the climb to deck a greater challenge. It was a three-storey ascent; Declan went first and was terrified all the way but said nothing. Ambrose was panting by the time he flopped over the railing. 'Not as fit as I used to be,' he said to his son, laughing self-consciously.

Ambrose paused to take in the deck's features. It felt different from any boat he was on before: radiating a sense of warmth, as if its steel was permanently infused with equatorial sunlight.

Declan looked the other way, more interested in the town, the whole place visible at once: chapel, vocational school and the road up towards their own house; almost everything Declan ever did or had done to him happened within this single view.

So many overcoats hung along the superstructure corridor that Declan and Ambrose had to shuffle sideways to get by. The mess was large with a low ceiling and a steel shutter open to the kitchen. Booths had been stripped out years before but the tracks of the fittings were still visible in the panelling. The crew instead used wooden seats and stools and free-standing tables. Currently all the tables were pushed together to form a long one and about fifteen men were gathered along it. They all looked up as Ambrose and Declan stepped in, the nearside crew gazing over their shoulders. Ambrose removed his cap and held it in his two hands. Each crewman had before him a bowl of yellow rice and what looked like orange, stringy potatoes. Some also had glass bottles of Fanta with white paper straws. Only a few seats had backs and Brendan was in one of them, at the end of the table too, like an honoured guest. A bottle of Fanta had been placed in front of him and, uniquely, he had a sandwich in his hands. We were conservative eaters and Brendan had probably refused the rice and yams. He took a bite of his sandwich and chewed, gazing neutrally down the long table as if the new arrivals were nothing to do with him. One crewman arose to address the visitors, he could not stand quite straight as the ceiling was too low for him. 'Welcome,' he said, he must've been the captain.

'That's my son you've got there,' said Ambrose.

'Our stowaway! I am glad to know someone is responsible for him!' said the captain, smiling, you couldn't tell if he was being critical or not. 'Please, be seated.' He opened a palm and made a sweeping gesture down the table. Crewmen moved this way and that, freeing up two stools next to each other. Ambrose didn't want to stay but it was hard to refuse the gesture of a place at a table, he sat and so did Declan. Perhaps a crate of Fanta came out for special occasions, such as surprise guests, because two more bottles were fetched and set before them, uncapped with straws dropped in. No self-respecting man from Donegal would drink from a straw so Ambrose bent it aside and took a swig straight from the bottle. Declan did the same. The crew sipped then too, content with their straws. They looked to the native man with polite expectation and eventually Ambrose came out with, 'So, did you enjoy your stay?'

The captain nodded thoughtfully before saying, 'We appreciate your culture.'

'I'm sorry for the trouble my son caused,' said Ambrose. He wanted to throw Brendan a hard look but this wasn't the time, he'd give him hell later.

The captain made a magnanimous gesture.

'He wasn't a good stowaway,' said a crewman, smiling. 'We found him just after leaving.'

Declan was watching Brendan coldly. The boy loved slipping away, nobody knew where he was half the time, if Brendan had really tried he could certainly have found a hidden nook on a vessel this size. He decided Brendan had wanted to be caught, trying to get back some of the town's attention.

'It was I who saw him first,' said a crewman and he threw his arms back fast. 'I jumped!' He started laughing, smacking the shoulder of the man on the next stool until he'd gotten a few hoots out of him too. The Nigerians were eager for home but being indulgent. Their vessel hadn't gone far, if they'd gotten down the coast before finding the boy they'd be feeling differently. Every pair of eyes alighted on Brendan as he finished eating, still showing no sign of shame, or even that he was listening. He wiped his mouth with his sleeve.

'He told us he's from the sea,' said a crewman.

'Did he now?' said Ambrose, glancing at him.

Declan laughed and tapped his own skull, a gesture meant to indicate weak-mindedness, but the Nigerians didn't seem to understand it.

Ambrose got up and told Brendan to get to his feet as well. Brendan was sent walking ahead and the Bonnars left, the captain accompanying them to deck. The boys descended first, then Ambrose shook the captain's hand and got on the ladder. The captain remained watching them from the rail, he was only being polite, ensuring they got away safely, but Ambrose wished he'd go back inside. He kept watching even when the Bonnars were aboard the clinker. Ambrose had to pull the starter cord seven times, eight times then more. 'God bless!' the captain called to them at one point. When Ambrose finally got the motor started he took the tiller and aimed for the pier. Declan was on the bench nearest his father while Brendan sat leaning into the bow among Con's fishing gear, chin in his arms, and staring into the peeling water. Ambrose said nothing until they were a good distance from the freighter then roared, 'What in under fuck were you at?' His voice carried a mile on the bay, if not the exact words then the pitch – full of fury.

Brendan looked back and shouted, 'Nobody cares what I do anyway!' A shine appeared in his eyes, he turned back into the bow, focused on the water and ceased communicating.

'Suppose you'd ended up in Africa!' shouted Ambrose. 'What would your mammy say?'

There was no response from Brendan and Ambrose fumed silently, it was difficult to shout at the boy, he had an ability to remove himself and you'd just feel foolish.

After a minute went by Brendan made an unexpected move. He put one arm out, lifted himself from the bow and, without a sound, flopped over the gunwale and went head first into the bay, like a sack falling overboard.

Ambrose jumped, abandoned the tiller, pushed Declan aside and leapt forwards, plunging his arms into the water and grabbing for his son. The landing net had gone in with Brendan, a hoop very like a basketball net. Maybe Ambrose thought it was tangled with him but no, Brendan had grabbed it deliberately as he went in. Ambrose caught his son's ankle with one hand and the waist of his trousers with the other and, a young man's speed and strength revisiting him, pulled him from the wash and swung him inside. Just as he was dropped Brendan released the landing net and something was suddenly loose in the boat; a flexing, muscular mass, like a strong arm. It was a whiting and of rare size, over thirty inches long. It was amazing Brendan even got close to the fish, let alone netted it like that. Fins snapped frantically as the beast curved and leapt in the bottom. Brendan retreated, making room for Ambrose. 'Steer,' Ambrose ordered Declan and he fell upon the creature, pinning it between his knees. Knives were slotted behind the riser and Ambrose grabbed the shortest, drove the tip behind the fish's pectoral fin and sliced around the head. The body was still pumping, cold blood sprayed Brendan's face and ran over Ambrose's hands. He dropped the knife and there was a crack as he pulled head from body. The fish didn't accept death, a spasm shot from the rear fin to where its head ought to have been and only then did it give in.

Brendan watched from the bow, pushing his palms along his trousers to press out seawater, his hair clinging to his scalp, his face speckled with fish blood.

'I've never seen like of it,' said Ambrose as he threw the head overboard, 'you just dived in and caught it.' He was struggling to keep down his delight at what Brendan had done, remembering he was supposed to be angry.

Declan's hands were loose on the tiller, stunned too by Brendan's capture. His father was crouched in the bottom, his back blocking a proper view of the whiting but Declan could see it was huge. He looked past his father to Brendan seated in the bow and felt something icy run through him: Brendan was gazing at him. Their eyes locked. Over a few long seconds a smile spread across Brendan's face, until it was the biggest Declan had ever seen on him. It wasn't a friendly smile.

Ambrose picked up the knife, jagged the tip into the fish's anus and drew it all the way along its belly, opening it up. Using his bare hands he clawed the guts out, the liver and stomach, chucking them in the sea. The gas bladder, like half-set jelly, spilled out by itself and Ambrose used one hand to herd it into the other and tossed it overboard as well. Above, seagulls roved close, even seabirds were pathetic scavengers compared to Brendan Bonnar. 'That's the night's dinner arranged anyway, and tomorrow's,' said Ambrose, reaching over to clean his hands in the wash. He was nodding along to his own words, 'You just bagged it, bagged it like a natural-born fisherman!'

'I did,' said Brendan. 'I got it and you got me. Teamwork.'

'That's right!' said Ambrose, and he laughed so loudly it was heard on the pier. His delight was out now, anger forgotten, he beamed like the lighthouse on St John's Point. Ambrose lifted the fish in both hands to examine it, to experience its mighty weight. 'But you, son,' he said, 'maybe they were right all along, you're the boy from the sea.'

Declan had heard his father use that phrase before but only ever jokingly. This time was different, there had been real pride in the enunciation. Declan watched as his father lifted the fish above his head so everyone on the pier could admire it.

That night Ambrose called to the Ship Inn for a pint, his first visit in months. He barely discussed his time among the Nigerians, eager to get to the story of Brendan catching the whiting. 'He's some boy,' we said, indicating admiration with sideways tics of the head. It was great to see Ambrose in good form and we enjoyed the story, although the delivery was a touch overexcited, and we didn't need every single detail. Our town was full of sea stories, the Bonnar escapade was banked with the rest of them and we moved on. Ambrose would soon get over it and move on too.

Only one person didn't get over it. He played out the scene between Ambrose and Brendan again and again in his mind: the capture; the blood; the malicious smile. Declan stewed on the event until a new determination solidified within him and one evening he went into the kitchen to speak to his parents. The range was going, fuelled with scrap wood. The smell of blistering paint wasn't ideal but there was good heat. Outside it was raining, the view of the sea lost to murk. Ambrose was seated at the table, Christine had just put a mug of tea in front of him and Declan asked for one as well.

'Into the tea now, are we?' said Christine, but she did him a mug.

'I was thinking I could head out the bay,' Declan said to his father. 'I'll soon be seventeen. I'm ready.'

Ambrose's first reaction was curiosity. 'I thought you were against fishing. Misery, you called it.'

'I've changed my mind,' said Declan.

'A stupid waste of a person, you called it.'

'I was wrong,' said Declan.

Ambrose grinned. 'Only an idiot would get into it, you said, quite worked up—'

'I want to be a fisherman,' said Declan firmly.

Ambrose looked to Christine, who had taken her seat by the range. She returned his look steadily but wasn't getting involved yet. 'Right,' said Ambrose and he took a mouthful of tea, willing to entertain the idea at least. 'I could ask around,' he said. 'See if I can get you on the *Girl Jacqueline* or the *Far Horizon*. Good, steady money.'

'No,' said Declan, distressed by the misunderstanding. His face softened to a look of unhappiness, his eyes becoming big. 'I mean, I want to fish with *you*.'

Ambrose's face fell like he had just been diagnosed with something terminal. Declan hadn't expected this reaction, he turned to his mammy but she was just as surprised as Ambrose. 'It's not that your father doesn't want you on the *Dawn*,' she said, sitting up. 'He's just not sure there's much of a living in it.'

'But I want to work with him, not anyone else,' said Declan. He sounded broken-hearted.

Everyone pondered a while. Declan didn't touch his tea. Rain hit the window hard and bounced off the sill. Every now and then a gust pushed into the chimney and the range sent a puff of smoke into the room. Eventually Christine said, 'Take him out with you, Ambrose, let him at the fishing.'

'But school?' said Ambrose, surprised. 'You always said he should do his Leaving.'

'Declan was never one for school,' she said. 'His future is out the bay, why wait? And we need the money. Give Declan a berth and that way a bigger share comes home to us.'

'He'd be extra, not a replacement,' said Ambrose, 'and the crew won't accept a whole share going to a youngster they have to teach and keep an eye on. It'll be a fraction.'

'We need every penny,' said Christine.

Ambrose looked down into his tea, he realized what had happened: want of money had finally defeated his wife. When Ambrose was young, shortage still looked like it did in history books: poor people had no electricity, no bank account, no teeth, but they didn't have debt either; they lived outside money, in inherited cottages and supported by relatives and the community. But those people were gone, everyone had money now, just not enough. Shortage had become pernicious and harder to recognize. It crept into your brain and gave you no peace, keeping you at every moment aware of your home's easy crushability. And it was almost impossible to talk about. Many families were this way, but you still felt alone with it, so alone.

'All right, we'll go,' said Ambrose.

Everyone drank their tea.

11.

THERE WAS NO REASON FOR Declan to attend school next day but he thought he'd enjoy a final farewell. Ten minutes was enough to realize his mistake, at his desk Declan looked the same but inside he squirmed. He was a breadwinner now, a man more or less, and it felt wrong to be among schoolboys and girls, in their uniforms, in their rows of seats. When he told his classmates he was dropping out, the boys acted impressed, but the girls made him uneasy by looking like they felt sorry for him. Rose O'Driscoll was openly sad. They had a shift in the Limelight disco recently and he was up for another go but saw the likelihood vanish. He told her he'd be making good money but she turned away. At lunchtime Declan walked out of school, never to return.

At home he found his mammy in the kitchen. 'That's you then, is it?' she said.

'I suppose so,' said Declan and he sat heavily, dropping his arms on the tabletop like they were a tonne weight. His first trip on the *Dawn* was tomorrow.

Christine looked at him carefully. 'You'll be fine,' she said.

Her husband wasn't exactly right on what made Christine support Declan's bid to get fishing, there was more empowerment in it than he realized. Christine was no mere victim of the economy, although she had learned the need for close management, in day-to-day finances and in notions of what was possible. She had returned the Lingua-phone cassettes long ago. Christine thought she knew what Declan really needed and the sooner he got it the better: a role in life, a sense of purpose. She could see a fragility in him. His brother's ways, his very existence, had left him undermined; years of their penny-pinching had made him anxious; schoolwork gave him no pride. He may as well be learning skills and earning money, that would settle him. Christine reckoned she had a solid twenty-five years of matriarchy left in her and she'd always use it to direct Declan towards sources of self-esteem. If no good source was available she'd at least make sure he was occupied. As a fisherman, Declan would probably stay in Donegal and continue to live at home until he married and that would be fine, she'd keep an eye on him until then and maybe beyond if his wife was the meek sort.

And she'd take no ridiculousness. A couple of hours later she found Declan behind the house with a lighter, solemnly trying to set fire to his school shirt. She marched over and snatched it off him, saying it would do Brendan in a year or two. Phyllis stood at the back door and laughed heartily at Declan's end-of-school ceremony, now cancelled. The sisters bustled Declan to his room and put him sitting on the bed while they fussed around him.

'Get a steak into him tonight,' said Phyllis.

'I will,' said Christine. She tipped out his school bag, it would be fine for his gear.

'Pack plenty of socks and underpants for him,' said Phyllis. While Christine got on with it, Phyllis turned to Declan. 'Those boys from the town,' she said, meaning the crew of the *Dawn*, 'they'll talk awful nonsense to you. Don't mind them. Tell them to frig off if they annoy you.'

'I will,' said Declan.

'You will not,' she said.

Phyllis often laid traps like that, arranged words so you'd say one thing and then leap all over you.

Ambrose walked in. 'How about this?' he said to Declan. 'We head into town and I'll buy you your first pint.'

Phyllis made a cluck meaning, *Listen to that eejit.*

'Declan took his first drink ages ago,' said Christine.

Ambrose looked around at everyone, clueless.

'You could ride into the Ship Inn on a tricycle and they'd put a pint in front of you,' said Phyllis.

Christine snorted in agreement and Ambrose retreated from the room.

'You've been seen smoking too,' Phyllis said to Declan.

Christine didn't want to dwell on that one, she remained turned away, folding and stacking his clothes. 'It's an awful habit,' was all she said.

'Don't mope about when you're out there,' said Phyllis, 'especially not on deck.'

'I won't,' said Declan with an exaggerated, rebellious sigh.

Christine and Phyllis looked at each other and laughed at Declan's attempt at self-assertion. 'He's getting to be a big lad!' they said.

Declan saw they'd for ever regard him as a boy, his child's face always hovering within his adult one, it was the face they'd see first and the face they'd always speak to. Declan escaped to the kitchen. Brendan had pulled a chair to the counter and was listening to the radio on longwave, the shipping forecast was ending. He looked at Declan and made that smile again. 'Five occasionally six,' he said. 'Moderate or poor.'

'Bugger off,' said Declan, but it was he who left the room.

Having nowhere else to go, Declan went outside and stood in

the drizzle. He looked west but the bay was a grey haze, the horizon invisible. Smoke blew down from the chimney and the homely smell made him weak. After a while Phyllis emerged too, heading back up the lane. She seemed to understand it was time for a softer approach and walked over to him, taking something from her pocket. Phyllis placed the holy medal, on a leather cord, around Declan's neck. 'Your grandfather always wore this, it'll keep you safe,' she said.

It slid under Declan's vest and she patted his chest over it. The medal was charged with family and continuity; Declan felt these forces prickle against his skin.

Phyllis stepped away from him and gestured towards the Atlantic. 'Don't get infatuated with waves or clouds or the like,' she said. 'It's not poems you're after. Some men go wobbly out there.'

'I won't,' said Declan.

'I'm not so sure,' said Phyllis, studying him hard, one eyebrow raised. 'Remember that time you wet yourself during *Superman III*?'

On his first trip Declan was too seasick to be of use. He could only lean against boxes or over rails, sweating and salivating like a dog. Colours throbbed aggressively in his retinas: the pink in fish gills, the yellow in Tim's moustache, the orange of the floats. Sounds too were an assault: crate striking crate; his father's whistling and the squish from his own wellies. The vertigo that came with seasickness was a real danger, you could misread the arc of a swinging derrick, misjudge the distance to a rung. Declan was mostly left to deal with all this himself, even Ambrose didn't mind him much, just as Ambrose hadn't been minded when he was first out on a trawler. Becoming a fisherman meant completely remoulding yourself to a new environment and, ultimately, it was done alone. But even when vomiting over the side Declan was grimly pleased that he was fishing with his father; Brendan might be the boy from the sea but Declan was the one who'd belong out here.

Although he ate nothing but white bread Declan's stomach was on a gastric offensive for the entire first trip, and the second, his insides wanting outside and frequently succeeding. An acidic taste was permanently lodged behind his teeth. Tradition said the youngest always cooked but nobody wanted Declan at their food so Stevie Shine stuck with it.

Stevie never did go to England, he was married and settled and had a daughter. Tim had worked a few other boats but caused ructions and had returned to the *Christine Dawn*. We knew Ambrose would never again get the town's best, and he knew it too. He had recently taken on Big Jimmy, he wasn't bad with the ropes although the oldest deckhand in Killybegs. The *Dawn* was a small boat, twenty years old and not a great earner. These days they'd stay within Donegal Bay for an entire trip, never going beyond Inishmurray, while Ambrose leveraged the single advantage the *Dawn* had: a shallow draught. She was one of only a few trawlers able to go after fish schooling around the bay's sandy shores. Tim referred to it as retirement fishing.

'Suits me,' said Big Jimmy, 'I'm easing myself into retirement.'

By his fifth trip Declan was no longer vomiting every half-hour, was used to the exhaustion and developing initiative. They had a decent enough season and Declan spent hours below, putting fish under ice and ordering the boxes, his fingers aching with cold inside his gloves. He got fast with a needle and kept a short knife stowed in his woolly hat above the ear. 'You look the part,' said Ambrose.

One calm morning the *Dawn*'s crew were standing to stern eating soda bread and slices of cheese, about to begin the trip's first trawl. It was so clear they could've counted the cows on the hills. Far off there was a pleasing silver glimmer on the sea while close by the water was transparent to nearly two fathoms, they could see the bubble trails made by plunging gulls. Ambrose and the crew were after sole.

'Scad is what you want now,' complained Tim. 'The prices are much better.'

Declan couldn't see anything wrong in this subject but his father had busied himself studying the horizon as soon as Tim began speaking. Big Jimmy and Stevie acknowledged his words with sidelong dips of their heads but no verbal reply was forthcoming.

Tim didn't drop it. 'It's thick with scad out to sea,' he said.

Ambrose peeled the film off an EasiSingle, folded it over and slid it into his mouth.

'A lad like you needs to hit the Atlantic,' said Tim, speaking straight to Declan now. 'You're not really a fisherman until you're out there. You'd like to go further out, wouldn't you?'

Declan spoke slowly, feeling his way along: 'There's one fishing ground I'd love to try.'

Ambrose turned and looked at his son. Love was a strong word, everyone listened with interest.

'Rockall,' said Declan.

His father was first to laugh, that was the worst part. His laughter was his usual, good-humoured and inclusive, but Declan was hurt by it. Jimmy grinned too while Stevie giggled and said, 'If only we'd packed extra jumpers, we could've gone on into the Arctic Circle and done a bit of whaling.' Tim shook his head, saying, 'Imagine a crate like this on the seas around Rockall!' Ordinarily Ambrose would've come to the defence of the *Dawn* but he was smiling, enjoying the banter. Declan's best play would've been to laugh along at his own naivety, but he wasn't able for that. Feeling himself go red, he turned away to the rail.

Ambrose had forgotten that he was the one who had put the vision of Rockall in his son's head in the first place, and given it an air of legend, so he certainly didn't understand the next part: that his son's desire wasn't even much related to fishing. It was more that Rockall was something the two of them, just the two of them, not Brendan, might again share. But Declan didn't really understand that himself, the things we seek are often in fog.

Still missing the point, Ambrose did start to consider roving further again, not to Rockall of course, that would be madness, but offshore. Maybe Tim was on to something; it would be good for Declan to experience the open sea. Over the following weeks he talked with other skippers and was told about decent marks only fifty or sixty miles out. 'Let's give it a go then,' Ambrose announced one day to his crew. 'We'll get beyond.'

The first trips were successful, full shots, the nets coming up like balloons. Ambrose felt some of his old optimism return and only then realized how much he missed it. The Bonnars got a new second-hand car and Big Jimmy bought something he had wanted for years, a colour TV. Then the marks got busy. Mal Doran collided with a Spaniard, leaving big dents in both hulls and there was a great deal of aggro over the airwaves. With eighty boxes already in the hold Ambrose decided to go further out. He looked through his journal and found he had a great session of fish to the north-west exactly six years before. They'd try the area again, steaming overnight and getting there to shoot in the morning. He put the journal back in its slot and spun the *Dawn*'s wheel.

Two nights later the nine o'clock news was starting when Joe McGee of the Fishermen's Association knocked on the Bonnar door. The sky was black. There were smatters of rain and buffeting gusts. Christine stood in the doorway while Joe told her the *Dawn* hadn't made a prearranged contact and no one had seen or heard from her in over forty-eight hours. 'No one has seen or heard from her in over forty-eight hours,' she said. He told her a search would begin at first light, a dozen vessels, Irish and British getting involved, the lifeboat making box searches east to west. 'Box searches east to west,' she said. Joe paused after each phrase and Christine flatly repeated everything he said. When there was no more to say Christine looked seaward and didn't just see the darkness but felt it, a black hole moving in on them, eating up the land. Eventually it would reach their door, it was always going to.

Brendan was out somewhere so Christine was alone. She put on her coat and walked up to the Lyons's house, arms folded, rain stinging her cheeks. The plantation was creaking as the spruces filled with driven air. Inside, Eunan was in his armchair watching the news and Phyllis was at her book of crosswords. If only Christine had come up earlier, she wouldn't have been home to answer the door to Joe, though she knew it wouldn't have made any difference, he'd have tried the Lyons next. Phyllis was looking at her, probably noticing the dead way Christine's arms hung by her sides, her fallen expression. The curtains were drawn and the heat on high and with the yellow walls the room was like a cave, too stuffy, but a good place to curl up. Christine was tempted to curl up on the carpet right then, but she remained upright and said, 'The *Dawn* is missing.'

Phyllis switched off the television and left to put on the kettle. Eunan kept looking toward the darkening screen but didn't complain so he must've heard and understood Christine's words. She fetched the footstool from the corner, put it directly in front of her father and sat on it, her head a few inches lower than his. The footstool was once part of Eunan's seating arrangement but he now needed contact with the floor and seemed too fragile for the footstool anyway, raise his legs and he'd probably snap. He had continued to fade, losing words and developing a tremble in his lower jaw. Christine leaned forwards; her face upturned to his. 'No one's heard from them in days,' she said. 'I think they're lost.'

Eunan's mind had shed any bit of nuance it may've once had and life was purely mechanical to him, driven by thoughtless automation, and he assumed it was the same for everyone. We were preset to seek tolerable conditions and self-replicate and that was about it. Bad things happened but you shouldn't mope, moping stopped the machine from working. Eunan couldn't help but think it: fishermen often drown, they know the risks and so do their wives and what was Ambrose doing anyway, miles out on a boat like the *Dawn*? However, Eunan had just enough sense to know that it wouldn't be right to say such things. The best he could do was remain silent, so that's what he did.

Christine looked up and Phyllis was standing in the doorway, watching her sister trying to get a response out of him. Christine pressed her lips together until they disappeared, her eyes round and dejected.

'I'll get him down then we'll go to your place,' said Phyllis.

Walking back along the lane Christine and Phyllis saw every bulb in the Bonnar house was on, light from the windows pooling on the ground and several parked cars. The sisters looked at each other. The front door was open and three or four figures were moving in the living room. They met Noreen Coyle in the corridor with the sweeping brush in her hand, she let it fall to put her arms around Christine. 'We tidied up but haven't looked at anything,' she said. Inside, Sheila Gallagher was making tea with bags she brought herself. 'There's hope yet,' she said, squeezing Christine's hands. Mary Breslin was there, of the bus-hire Breslins, not the hardware people, although it doesn't matter as their Mary appeared soon after. Bella Power walked into the living room. 'Any news?' she asked and the others told her no. Christine didn't even need to speak for herself, the women would do that too; she sank in her armchair and was quiet. Bella looked at the front window. 'I'll close those blinds,' she said. Bella was never even in the house before and there she was claiming authority over the blinds, but Christine gladly submitted. 'Evil, that sea,' said Bella as she released the cord.

Certain women didn't appear, women who were bereaved to fishing, whose husbands or sons were lost at sea. Maybe they felt their arrival would've been too ominous for Christine, or they just didn't feel able, but other women came and went all night, some to sit meditatively with Christine, some to help about the house. They coordinated perfectly, like their husbands did out the bay, although organized in whispers and concessions rather than shouts and mockery. They tended to keep their eyes downcast, their purpose to be useful, to exude support without being excessively present. At one point the bathtub was being scrubbed and someone on the front step was beating out the doormat. There were similar scenes in Stevie's house and in Tim's. Big Jimmy had no family but in the pubs there was much fond talk of him among our town's committed drinkers. 'And him only after buying a colour television,' said Manus McManus.

Up in the Bonnars', Christine made just one request, 'Could Brendan be found for me?'

She wanted him close, inside the walls, even if only in his room. At times like these a house became a fort, everyone belonging to it was called in and once in they didn't stray. A family, together, had to allow themselves to be held in the wait. 'Where might he be?' asked Justine O'Donnell.

'He's been associating with those alternative lifestylers,' said Phyllis, the admission causing her discomfort. 'There's been talk.'

People rang around until Brendan was located and delivered back by an alternative lifestyler in one of their clapped-out cars. Brendan might've had drink in him or smoked something strong, he stood unsteadily in the middle of the room, not knowing where to put himself, his helplessness emphasized by the women, busy and focused around him. Phyllis looked at him with disapproval. 'You out gallivanting while your father and Declan, the earners, are missing,' she said.

'Phyl, stop,' said Christine.

Brendan spoke slowly, taking care over his enunciation. 'Conditions were fine since they left.'

Christine nodded in acknowledgement, no need to point out that two dozen things could go wrong at sea, weather was only one of them. They all knew that.

A decisiveness came over Brendan. 'We'll hope for the best,' he said and he approached Christine, hand extended to rest it on her shoulder, but the look on her face made him stop.

'Please don't,' she said.

So. Here's what happened to the *Dawn* and her crew, the whole story. The north-western grounds were rich but there was a problem on the second night. The *Dawn* had two fuel tanks and the connecting pipe ruptured, spilling fuel into the bilge. Ambrose and Jimmy were sharing night command and might've smelled the leak only for the automated bilge pump, which Ambrose had fitted recently thinking it a very clever yoke. The pump kicked in when its sensor detected liquid, not distinguishing between diesel and water. Merrily, it pumped all the fuel out from under the crew and at dawn the engine stopped dead. The silence awoke Stevie and Declan, they climbed from their bunks and found Tim raising himself from the bilge, having identified the problem. The sea was slight but without engine power the *Dawn* began to roll. They were too far out for their radio to reach a coastal station so Ambrose was scanning up and down the channels, calling for any vessels in the area. He was shy about saying 'Mayday' as it seemed a bit dramatic, but Joseph's voice appeared in his head saying use of Mayday would be reasonable given the situation. Ambrose used it but sounding flippant, like it was only half an emergency really. There was no reply, no boat in range. Declan made coffee for everyone.

'We'll sit tight, lads, until a vessel swings close enough,' said Ambrose. 'Might be a few hours.'

Ambrose stayed at the wheel for the little influence it had, and by the radio. Nobody wanted to sleep and there was nothing to do only smoke cigarettes so they went at that with abandon. The breeze was cold but light and the sea forgiving and the swells had a predictability that kept them from getting too aggravating. 'It's peaceful anyway,' said Ambrose, with a level of cheer that was strange. Crew regularly asked him what direction they were tending and the answer was west, a dozen times he was asked and the answer was always west but Ambrose displayed no irritation when asked again. 'I wouldn't mind visiting Canada,' he said.

Eight hours went by. Ambrose was pleased to see Declan coping well, he never asked about their direction. He was settled in the galley, not moving much, not speaking much, he was shaping up to be a fine man. Only Stevie got a touch emotional at one point in the evening. 'My nerves are shredded,' he said suddenly and loudly, dumping an extra spoon of sugar in his tea.

'It'll be something to tell your grandkids about,' Ambrose told him, laughing.

All night they drifted without radio contact. Conscious of the batteries, Ambrose transmitted for only thirty seconds every ten minutes, then every twenty. When no one was looking Ambrose pressed his hands together hard, a nervous tic normally reserved for waiting areas in banks and hospitals, never before used at sea. Christine's face rose up in his mind but he squeezed the vision away between his palms. 'Another day of rest and relaxation,' he announced as the eastern sky lightened.

Stevie was in bad form so Declan cooked, taking plenty of time over breakfast, cutting away the fat before grilling slices of bacon. He made toast and something never before experienced on the *Dawn*: poached eggs. However, no great appreciation was shown by the crew. Tim ate each of his in one swallow.

At one point later in the day Stevie went out on deck and was gripped by angst when he saw a jumbo jet passing seven miles up. He started twisting his fingers together, threatening to break down completely until an angry roar from Tim startled him out of it. 'They've no interest in us so take no interest in them!' Tim was now rolling his cigarettes as thin as knitting needles. Big Jimmy was running short on jokes. Declan remained stoic.

In the early afternoon troubling colours appeared, Ambrose first noticed them filtering through the spray; pinks and oranges with something of solid gold in them, sunset colours but heavier and too early. A few hours later they appeared overhead too, the weird hues of a loading sky. The sound of the sea, an undulating static, was getting louder and the barometer showed deepening pressure. Ambrose joined his crew in the galley, the gold light was filling it and bringing out every hair in their stubble. For a moment Ambrose was lost in the details of his crew's faces, especially Declan's. His son, Ambrose realized, was handsome, beautiful even. He leaned in the doorway. 'Well, lads,' he said brightly. 'Time for a bit of exercise. There's a small spot of low pressure, we're tending away but let's batten down. Then you'll be best off below for the evening.'

Big Jimmy looked from man to man, checking he had heard right, his ears weren't the best.

Tim huffed, like he knew all along things would get worse.

Declan said nothing.

Stevie rubbed his eyes with the heels of his hands. 'The wife doesn't know where I've hidden Jenny's birthday present,' he said.

'Get away out of that!' said Ambrose.

A high swell passed below the hull, the lift went on and on before they gently fell again. 'They'll build further and we can't manoeuvre,' said Tim plainly. 'We may die tonight.'

Ambrose made a splutter of annoyance and shook his head.

'The same as any other night then so,' he said, as if Tim's comment was nothing but bizarre.

Stevie folded his arms on the table and buried his face in them.

Declan stowed everything in the galley and helped lower the partitions into the hold so water crashing on deck would run off quick as possible. Spray was coming on stiffly already, in streams that waved in the air like whips. Crests snapped loudly as they broke and the golden light turned leaden. Despite the angry sea the wind speed was low, which was disconcerting. A dark knot of cloud formed north-east, they'd watch it until it was concealed by the stacking water, the horizon often rolling above their heads. Declan thought he could see three strata in the water. The top level was thin and loose, shifting and folding, webbed in foam. The next was maybe twenty feet deep and travelled west mostly, you could see the push in it, forming the waves. The third went down and down and heaved massively, the big sea would build from there and easily toss them over. Declan joined his father in the wheelhouse. They could hear Tim swearing on deck. 'He's out of tobacco,' said Declan.

'Tell him there's an emergency pouch in the first-aid box,' said Ambrose.

The *Dawn* wallowed in a trough, the deck was inundated and Ambrose and Declan gripped the walls. As the deck lifted, white water sloshed back and forth, looking for the fastest route off, and they heard Tim swear some more. Ambrose and Declan stood independently again, although close to each other. 'You've made a good fisherman,' said Ambrose.

'Wasn't the best career move though,' said Declan.

Ambrose waved towards the windows dismissively. 'I've been on seas much rougher than this,' he said.

'Yes, but you always had an engine,' said Declan.

This was undeniable. Ambrose sent Declan below.

There were only three lifeboat stations on Ireland's entire western seaboard, but one was on Arranmore. Ambrose had cousins on the crew and knew they'd be searching or on standby. A Nimrod might've come from the North to do an electronic sweep and they'd have sent a helicopter too. Ireland had a few helicopters but they were of limited range and for some reason stationed on the east coast. Ambrose had never felt angry about this until now and he decided that as soon as he got home he'd write a letter of complaint to the minister, strongly worded. Christine would help him, she was good at that sort of thing. Ambrose frowned, he had messed up, his mind had gone to her and he was too exhausted to push her away. How was he when she dropped him and Declan to the pier? No doubt he said, 'Mind yourself.' He always said that, a choice of words that pained him now. *Mind yourself.* How long since they had a decent ride? Months.

Shortly after Declan the others climbed down the hatch and got in their bunks too, Ambrose remaining in the wheelhouse by the radio and in control of the rudder. There was nothing for the crew to do but listen to the seething water and feel the knocks. The bunks were like coffins, built up from plywood to give each man his own alcove. The room was mostly below the waterline, salt water churning only inches from their faces. Declan imagined them submerged, drowning, kicking in cold water, it was easily pictured. Torches duct-taped to the ceiling in each bunk provided some light. Declan looked over at Tim and Jimmy, they were laid on their backs, knees up and eyes open. Directly above he could see Stevie's hand gripping the wood.

Each bunk had a curtain on stretchy string, Declan pulled his over and curled up around his pillow.

The *Dawn* took blows so violent that Declan and Stevie were sometimes lifted an inch from their mattresses. 'Another wallop,' said Big Jimmy every time although he wasn't lifted himself, too big for that. Tim was also fixed to his mattress, held by the iron nature of his resentment. There might be fifteen minutes of relative calm, when they'd exchange a few words, but eventually the hull would begin to shake and they'd quieten another while. They knew when the deck was swamped, feeling a squeeze on their eardrums and sensing the hard echo. Once they were under for so long it seemed sure they were done for. 'Finish the job then!' shouted Tim and the words resonated like in a cave.

In those moments Stevie thought of his daughter and how he had messed up fatherhood's first and most basic responsibility: remain alive. Big Jimmy was thinking of something very different; a poster he'd once seen. As a young man Jimmy had worked in New York a year and on weekends enjoyed walking the streets and having a beer in the afternoon. Once he went into a bar and was amazed by a poster of Katharine Hepburn taking up the entire back wall. It was enormous, like a billboard but indoors, pasted directly to the brickwork. He didn't have a particular fancy for the actress (although he wouldn't have said no, wouldn't have said, *No thanks, Katharine, you're grand where you are*), but the sight truly moved him. It was the shameless exuberance, the frank celebration of beauty and the sheer confidence of sticking up the huge poster, knowing everyone would agree. Katharine Hepburn, on the wall, ten times bigger than life. He never quite got over it. As water surged overhead Jimmy spoke. 'Don't worry about me anyway, lads, I've had a full life.'

Declan, fists tight and eyes squeezed shut, was going religious. He got through his First Communion and Confirmation without developing susceptibility but was now overcome. If I'm let live I'll do lots of good things, he told God, the sort of stuff you like. He felt around in his mind for an example, still able to avoid Brendan and instead thinking of Doris Kane. I'll return the money, he offered desperately, I'll return it!

Above, Ambrose watched the bow resurface. Water was seeping through the window seals and the wheelhouse walls ran wet. Ambrose had stripped off his sodden jumper but had to accept the water in his boots. The mix of exhaustion and adrenaline sometimes caused him to hop from foot to foot and his ears ached from the rage of the boiling sea: an earthy rumble with something sharp in there too; a crackle, like electricity dancing over the surface. The *Dawn* was tending to roll broadside in the troughs, that was keeping her right, but a fast rogue could get at her, like the one coming now. Ambrose sized up his opponent through the forward windows, the wave was brilliant white and rolling with a predatorial determination. The trawler shook like an aircraft going into take-off as the wave poured over the bow. Ambrose watched the wall of water coming at him. 'The deck's getting a good wash anyway,' he said aloud. Water hit the wheelhouse and the windows ran black, then green then clear again. Ambrose was up to his ankles in Atlantic but the *Dawn* held up; the bow lifted, water fluted off the deck and an upward force threw Ambrose to the floor. Then the radio blared and there was a voice.

Below, the crew were braced in their bunks when Ambrose raised the hatch in the ceiling, stuck his head down and shouted, 'Good news! The RAF have us spotted and a tow's on the way. It'll only be an hour or so.'

'An hour or so,' said Tim. 'Great.'

Ducking down to deliver the news had caused Ambrose to miss another vital matter: a second rogue wave had been hidden behind the last and that moment it hit. Smothered in tonnes of water, the *Dawn* was thrown flat against the sea. Two wheelhouse windows got punched from their frames, water crashed in, swamped the galley and went down the hatch, just opened by Ambrose, waterfalling into Declan's bunk. On its side, his alcove was now filled like a bathtub and he was underwater, unable to hear the others yelping and swearing. He thought the boat was pulled under, sunk. Numb with fear and the freezing sea Declan made his final offer: I'll be good to Brendan from now on, I'll be good to my brother.

For long seconds the boat wallowed on its side, then a rip and a suck was heard against the planks as the *Dawn* righted herself. Water poured from Declan's alcove and joined the pool on the floor, sloshing around with destroyed paperbacks and empty bottles of Lucozade. He sat up, struck his head off the top, spluttered, coughed.

Seawater continued to splash down the hatch until Ambrose kicked it shut. His kick seemed to ignite a strong white light and he had to concentrate to realize the kick and the light weren't related. He blinked salt water away, got to his feet and stuck his head out a window frame, immediately feeling a downdraught. A Royal Air Force helicopter, bright yellow, had its spotlight trained on them. The burning lights, the strangeness of it, Ambrose's brain struggled to accept what he was seeing. The helicopter's cargo door was open and the winchman was looking out, pulling the helmet strap tight under his chin. They gave each other the thumbs-up.

* * *

The *Dawn* got thrown about some more but the automatic pump redeemed itself a little by clearing the bilge of seawater and keeping the *Dawn* right. The lads in the helicopter decided that lifting the crew would be more dangerous than leaving them aboard so, in the end, no one got winched up. Two Greencastle trawlers joined the scene and got the *Dawn* under tow, bringing her to where the lifeboat took over. Phones started ringing all along the coast and news of the rescue reached us.

It was after dark the following night when the *Dawn* finally returned, six days since original departure and two since the alarm was raised. Only Joe McGee was on the pier to meet them, the rest of us being discreet. 'We were out beyond radio range when we lost all engine power,' Ambrose told Joe on the pier. 'There was a bad night with some waves but the *Dawn* held together well, no one got badly hurt. A helicopter picked up our signal and spotted us and a tow was arranged. Everyone's fine, but we had to dump the catch.'

Joe drove Ambrose home, stopping at the bottom of the lane as Christine and Brendan were standing there. They'd come out to wait at the corner, looking like ghosts when the headlights caught them. Even Joe, mere witness, felt emotion course through him at the sight and when Ambrose got out he turned and drove away quickly, stone chips shooting from under his tyres. Ambrose approached Christine and Brendan, his breath becoming laboured and something jagged, almost like panic, threatening to overwhelm him. He stopped a few feet back from Christine. It felt like meeting her for the first time, Ambrose wanted to reach out but it would've seemed too forward. He was surely permanently altered by all this. 'So, I survived anyway,' he said.

'Where's Declan?' said Christine.

'Gone into the Pier Bar with some of his pals.'

'You'd think after nearly dying he'd let his mother take a look at him first,' said Christine, but she knew that would be the way of him for ever probably: robust, unyielding but with certain limitations. At least he'd fit in.

'What happened?' asked Brendan.

'We were beyond radio range when we lost engine power,' said Ambrose. 'There was a bad night but the *Dawn* held, no one got hurt. We were spotted and towed. Everyone's fine.'

The next time Ambrose was asked he'd abbreviate the events further, and further again, until he'd distilled his description to looking off into the distance and saying, 'A bad night.'

On the kitchen table was a shepherd's pie in a ceramic dish brought by a woman from the town. Ambrose took it to the freezer but there was no space because five other shepherd's pies had gotten there faster. Christine sent Brendan up to Phyllis with it. She felt a want rise in her powerfully but made Ambrose wash first while she hovered outside the door, listening as he went at himself with the soap, feeling rebalanced by having the lump of him back in the house. She took off her clothes and when he emerged she steered him to the bed, laid him down, knelt over him and began to work him with her hands. She seemed in a desperate hurry. Ambrose submitted, he wanted no responsibility for anything tonight, he might never want responsibility for anything again. He managed a few sighs as she kissed his neck. She had let her hair down and the sensation of it on his chest, breath-like, almost made him ejaculate. Ambrose had a bit of flab now but, kneading his body, Christine met muscle and it got her going like it used to. She had gone soft about the hips herself but Ambrose got a good grip of her and found it agreeable. Christine positioned herself until Ambrose slid home.

Over the next while Christine and Ambrose had some great sessions, energized by their close calls; with death, with widowhood. Gusts on the slates might waken them at 4 a.m. and they'd get at it right then, without words, operating each other with their fingers, extracting shudders. Nothing fancy, they knew what they liked.

One dawn, after another good ride, Ambrose stretched out on his back across the bed and Christine lay on her side against him. They were delighted with themselves, naked and tingling like young ones. Christine raised herself and supported her head on one hand so to make a good study of her husband. The early light heightened contrast and brought out his old scars. One on his forearm was very clear, fatty and purple, the length and thickness of a crayon. She ran her finger along it. 'How'd you get this again?' she asked.

'Rope burn,' he said, 'on the *Ard Ciarán*, long time ago. We were going after haddock.'

Ambrose threw one elbow back so to support his head and get a better view of his wife. He used his free hand to take hold of her fingers, as if to kiss them, but instead angling them to the light to see the white scar over her knuckle. 'Remind me how you got this,' he said.

'Peeling knife,' she said. 'Going after carrots.'

Ambrose had an inch-long scar on one of his hands and he placed it alongside for comparison. 'This was the slip of a blade too, gutting whitefish,' he said. 'Tommy stuck a couple of stitches in it for me.'

Christine gazed at the scar for a few moments, then knelt up and swept her hair from her shoulder. 'This doesn't seem like a scar but it is,' she said, pointing to what looked like a cluster of freckles on her upper arm, brown and slightly risen. 'I was doing chips for the boys and got hit by a splash of oil from the deep-fat fryer. At the time I didn't even notice it happening.'

'It's amazing what you'll not notice when nerves are killed,' said Ambrose. He was still on his back and without apparent effort he raised a leg until it was nearly right-angled to the rest of him. They'd surprise you, these fishermen, with their middle-age spread, the way they'd lift their legs like ballet dancers. Years on rolling decks did it, and Ambrose had particularly fine legs; now that his hair was going Christine rated them his best feature. He took her finger so she'd feel the raised welt among the black hairs on his calf. 'I got that line fishing one time. Thought I'd lost the hook and was looking all about me for it. Wasn't it buried in my own leg!'

'I've a hidden one here,' said Christine, freeing her finger and taking a hold of one of his to guide it inside her hairline. 'Declan was falling from his chair, I grabbed him but banged my head off the table.'

Ambrose ran his finger twice over the hard nub then brought his hand down to stretch the skin on his shoulder, bringing a short pink scar forth to where she'd see it. 'Nasty one, this,' he said. 'I was lifting a crate on my shoulder and didn't see the shard sticking out of it.'

Christine took his fingers and steered them to her thigh, to a thin line, feeling like an inch of thread stuck to her skin. 'From a barbed-wire fence. Brendan, four or five years old, ran into Mack's field and refused to come out, I'd to get him. Ruined my skirt too.'

Ambrose clasped his fingers together behind his head and raised his other leg. They both looked at his ankle as he turned it this way and that, the light picking out a set of thin scars. They looked like month-old scratches but were in fact decade-old tooth marks from a porbeagle shark. The creature came up alive in a net and was flinging itself around deck while Ambrose danced about trying to kick it overboard. He succeeded, but only after it had bitten him right through his boot. 'It was some battle,' said Ambrose.

He gazed up at his leg longer than necessary, so Christine lowered it for him then pressed the fingers of both her hands into the flesh of her belly, stretching it up to reveal a thick dark scar. It was six inches long, waxy to the touch, raised crudely in some places and with spots above and below left by six staples. The scar was a reminder of hours of pain and fear. It was where a surgeon sliced through her abdomen and into her womb, opening her up to retrieve Declan, who refused to come out any other way.

'That was a real battle,' said Christine.

12.

THE SEASON TURNED AND THERE was a week of storms, keeping all but the largest vessels home. The rain was permanent and our children went about with their parka hoods zipped up until they'd only a small circle, like a porthole, to look through as they gathered rushes for their St Brigid's crosses. Our cinema had closed years previously but now, with the seats stripped out, the building reopened as a second-hand furniture shop. We all went in for a look and were surprised at how small the room was. Tank McHugh was discharged from St Conal's and placed in the care of his mother.

Finally there was no more avoiding it, Ambrose went to the pier to see the *Dawn*. She had a weary look about her, a window frame without a pane could do that, and she had two such voids. The towlines had cut runnels in the bow and the boom had come away from the derrick. Much of the damage was superficial yet Ambrose felt something fundamental had snapped in her, she was done. Ambrose was surprised at his lack of heartache. He put the *Dawn* up for sale, we saw an ad in the *Skipper* offering her as a working trawler needing overhaul. 'She really puts the concern in going-concern,' remarked Bella Power.

There were no offers and the mooring fee was a problem. This was how battered fifty-six-footers ended up abandoned in sheltered bays along our coast, the owner saying he'd just let her lay there until he had repair money or got her sold, but the money would never be found and no one would buy and the boat would lean into an easy angle and disintegrate. There were plenty such wrecks in sandy inlets around Donegal. Some considered them picturesque and a wreck might get photographed and put on a postcard. This made as much sense as putting a shut-down British coal mine on a postcard, but of course they probably did that too.

Ambrose didn't give up yet. He put an ad in the English listings, saying the *Dawn* was suitable for conversion into a pleasure craft. A lot of our old trawlers went that way, although we could never get comfortable with such conversions. We thought of our boats as noble labourers, each loaded with family history and stories. We didn't like to think of our trawlers deconsecrated and made frivolous, reduced to hosting crowds of London yuppies and their tawdry pleasures; drinking cocktails, snorting the 'coke', having orgies and the like.

Late into the evenings Ambrose and Christine discussed the future and what work he'd get into with his last decade or two of strength. He didn't want to work in a processing plant, saying the money was bad, but Christine knew he couldn't face a dull shore job in the fishing industry. If he couldn't skipper then he wanted nothing to do with fish. Lots of his brothers worked in construction in different parts of England, they were hard to keep track of, but he hoked out his address book and rang or wrote notes to them all. 'I'm thinking of going to England,' he told Christine.

Christine was surprised. 'The boys would miss you,' she said.

'They're raised,' said Ambrose.

'Brendan's still in school, for God's sake,' said Christine.

'He's well on his way,' said Ambrose.

Christine studied him, his oddly sunny demeanour.

'There's good money on the sites,' he said.

Ambrose wanted to be useful and had concluded that being a simple provider of money was the best role he could perform, maybe the only thing he was good for. Nearly drowning a crew was troubling, especially with your son among them, and some sad impulse had Ambrose feeling his family would be better off with him away for a while. He'd send every penny home, he'd provide. Brendan would be grand, Ambrose decided he wasn't as easily led as he had feared. Brendan's tendency to withdraw was in fact a kind of self-possession, it took a lot of courage to be so different and this would always serve him. It seemed Brendan was friendly with the alternative lifestylers, who were a peculiar bunch, but it was good he had found a tribe of some sort.

'And what about Declan?' said Christine.

Ambrose nodded, making plans in his head. 'He's got fine qualities,' he said. 'Declan just needs to be working. Leave it with me.'

The next day Ambrose drove into town, parked by the pier and walked through the doors of the big new auction house, not long built at that stage. It was a massive hall running up the middle of the pier. There was no catch in that day and it echoed like a cathedral, smelling of bleach and salt. One of the Hart boys was wearing a white coat and yellow gum boots, using a wide rubber brush to push puddles across the smooth concrete floor and down the drain holes. Tommy was chatting with a dealer and two Asian gentlemen in suits, but he left the conversation swiftly when he saw Ambrose approaching. They shook hands. Ambrose didn't need to ask Tommy to walk with him, he made a move of the chin and they went out the far doors. This side of the pier was dominated by the *Warrior III*, green, white, massive, well over two hundred foot long, the biggest trawler in Ireland at the time, just back from two days of sea trials. 'I'll be going after blue whiting and scad,' said Tommy. 'Brussels have no quota on those fish yet and my Japanese clients are mad for them.'

Clients. That was the kind of chat you'd get from Tommy.

'You have to keep ahead of the quotas,' agreed Ambrose.

'She's built to maximize catch quality, crew safety and comfort,' said Tommy. 'Would you like a tour?'

'Ah no, you're busy, I'm happy looking at her from here,' said Ambrose.

The trawler was like a single machine, every element interlocked, and mechanization was everywhere. The crew were mere assistants to the gear, a third of them were engineers. The winches were twice a man's height and at midship stood two towering fish pumps which would suck fish from the nets and straight below to be stored in chilled seawater tanks, no gutting or processing with this kind of fishing. The quarters were like a hotel. There was a lounge and you'd get fined if you wore your boots on the carpet, you had to change into slippers. The cook was an actual chef.

'Most men would give their— give almost anything to work her,' said Ambrose, running his eyes bow to stern. (We had stopped using the phrase 'give their right arm' since Francis O'Connell's accident on the *Siobhán*. It would've been deemed in bad taste.) 'You have men fighting for a berth, I suppose?'

Tommy paused before saying, 'I've room for one more surely.' A softness appeared in his eyes and he spread his feet to steady himself.

Quickly Ambrose explained. 'Not for me, it's Declan I'm thinking of,' he said.

Tommy breathed out heavily, shook his head. 'Will you not get over things?' he said, years of frustration coming through. 'It could be good, me and you again.'

Ambrose folded his arms. The engineers must've been testing the *Warrior*'s radar, the bars were revolving overhead and they could hear them swish. 'Declan's great out there,' Ambrose said, pushing on. 'He keeps the head down, keeps at it, nothing flusters him.'

Tommy nodded sadly. Of course he'd take on a son of Ambrose, he'd even risk Brendan if Ambrose asked. 'Glad to have Declan aboard,' he said.

Happy, Ambrose drove home and he was whistling as he came in the front door. Declan was peeling spuds at the sink and turned to the cheery sound. 'I've got you a spot on the new *Warrior*,' announced Ambrose. 'You're still a fisherman!'

Declan's arms dropped and the light in his eyes went out. If Ambrose noticed he pretended not to, but Christine walked in and saw her son's expression immediately. 'What's wrong?' she said.

'I've sorted him out!' said Ambrose, grinning. 'Work on the *Warrior*.'

Declan looked to his mammy, maybe she'd say something, suggest another possibility. He had wanted to fish with his father, not end up this way. Christine was making a careful study of her son. Then she said, 'It'll be something to be proud of.'

Declan turned to the sink again and carried on at the peeling.

Ambrose had now satisfied himself that his sons didn't need him any more. This was a grim way to think and we would've told him that had we been the types to meddle. It wasn't true either, those boys were still very young. More: even if they had been older, fully grown, so what? A parent remains the parent until they die and, sadly, a child remains the child even beyond that point.

Over the next week or two Ambrose's brothers got back to him with offers of work, he simply selected the one with the best rates and cheapest digs. He told Christine about it while they watched *The Late Late Show*, saying he may as well go soon, there was no point hanging around. She got up, switched off the telly and turned to look at him. Ambrose had hoped to avoid this.

'I'll be able to get back regularly enough,' he said, 'once we've gotten some money in the bank.'

Christine's face displayed disapproval.

'I'll put in a few months,' said Ambrose. 'We'll see where we are then.'

'So that's it?' she said.

'It's not a rare situation, ours,' said Ambrose.

True, but she would've preferred him to sound sad about it. With its return, Christine recognized Ambrose's fatalism. He seemed content to live within conditions that, he claimed, were out of his control. Years at sea had done it, a fisherman had to accept much was beyond his control or he'd go mad. Ambrose was now talking exactly as he used to before three days' fishing. He was already tending away from her and their home, there'd be no stopping him. Maybe it had become set in his brain, earning money meant travelling into a foreign environment, England was just another sort of fishing trip. 'Where exactly?' she asked.

'Huddersfield,' he said.

'Where's that?'

'I don't know, somewhere inland.'

Ambrose must've located it as that's where he went. We heard he was working in office-block construction: setting up moulds, pouring concrete, plain work. Sometimes a man couldn't cut it over there and would be back inside a fortnight, having discovered he needed his meals cooked for him or his family about him. Some of us predicted Ambrose would be one of those but we were wrong, he stuck at it and months went by. It was strange to imagine Ambrose in England, in a hard hat, among men all in hard hats, being told what to do. Decent money landed with Christine regularly, Ambrose kept his overheads low. He cooked each night on his single hob and never bought a takeaway sandwich, although he did allow himself a few pints on a Saturday night. He had a room in a place with a shared bathroom down the corridor and a payphone in the stairwell, its casing covered in stickers advertising curry houses and taxi firms. He rang home every ten days or so, it was expensive and besides Ambrose was never one for chatting over the phone. To Ambrose, phones were only for the brief transfer of essential information. Ambrose recalled the letters that arrived from America during his childhood. It always seemed a miracle the folded pages reached their island and they stirred great interest, the letters handed around a dozen people, every word measured and weighed, the stamps examined as artefacts. He wanted to join this tradition so spent money on writing paper and a Parker pen and wrote a letter home once a week, taking great care with his handwriting. He suspected he was creating heirlooms and was right, the letters would always be kept. Never, in any letter, or on the phone, did Ambrose hint at how unhappy he was over there.

* * *

Declan was also learning to work hard and not go on about things. He was now, as we put it, a *Warrior* man. Work on the *Warrior III* was more like a factory job than the fishing he was used to: arise with the bell, fuel up in the kitchen, get to your station. The rhythm of sleep, eat, work had nothing to do with the time, it was ordered entirely by trawls and he might go fifteen hours without stepping into open air. On his first trip Declan had to consult the deck plans, displayed in passageways here and there, to find his way around. He was issued with oilskins and a lifejacket but kept to sorting and net repair. It helped, Declan found, to think of the money he was earning.

Remembering past misdemeanours, Declan put a wad of cash in the chapel poor box, but only as a precaution, and he remained as distant from Brendan as ever. The *Dawn*'s last trip had become abstracted, dream-like, the intensity of experience simply couldn't be understood on dry land. It had been a night of heightened emotion, shrill and ludicrous. Any wild thoughts about Brendan that might've crossed his mind that night were forgotten.

It was his third trip on the *Warrior III*, the morning was a dark icy blue, the cold fierce and the rain steady when Declan was finally given deck duties, sent to stern with four other men to manage a haul. Half an inch of water chased back and forth across the steel deck, rippling around their boots. Gulls wheeled and cried overhead. The sea wasn't stacking but was breaking up in every direction, bands of grey and white. The *Warrior*'s speed was down to a few knots when the winch motors clunked into their first revolution. The stern gantry framed the horizon and Declan felt a kind of awe as the steel doors emerged and crashed against the sides, each the weight of a large car. He looked to the men beside him but they were unaffected. Their faces, creased against the rain, displayed only preparedness. Right and left the winch drums began drawing in a quarter-mile of steel cable. Over the ramps came dozens of orange spherical floats and black rubber discs, each disc the size of a wheelbarrow tyre, all locked in rows. Next metal struck metal and the shackles were pulled over the ramps, followed by chains, still running with water, clattering hard enough to ring through the entire vessel. Declan looked over his shoulder and up to the bridge, discerning Tommy through the reflections on the glass. He was at the stern-facing console, operating the gear, monitoring everything through the windows or CCTV. Days could go by without seeing Tommy any closer than this, he was more like a company director than a skipper. The winches were halted so the towing warps could be disengaged, Declan quickly slipping into the choreography of the operation. The net was attached to the knuckle-boom crane, which dragged the catch starboard, forward of midships. Declan followed with the rest of the crew, walking a zigzag on the rolling deck. He liked to get along the boat without needing the rail, one of the many little challenges he set himself to pass the minutes. Tall waves slapping the side sounded like gunshots. Tommy brought the *Warrior* around so portside faced the weather, creating some stability for the crew. The net was wound in, a few fish appearing, choked in the mesh, then tonnes more. Pulling fish from the pressure of midwater caused their eyes to bulge and their bellies to expand with gas. Scores of fish were jammed into the web, their mouths popping open and shut, sometimes their mouths stayed open and their stomachs oozed out. The first mate spotted some damage and told Declan he'd want his needle. Then came up the cod end, a huge sphere of fish that ran not just with seawater but blood and grey juices, like a removed brain. The stench of sea life was overwhelming. Declan helped get the pump mouth attached and the net was lowered again, the catch would be better preserved under the waves until the pump completed its work. Everyone stepped back, hoods went up against the teeming rain and cigarettes got lit as the pump began to beat, sucking out the fish and sending them below deck. At the belts, crew were busy throwing out unwelcome creatures, a large dead octopus causing a rumpus of laughter and surprise. It went out the waste chute along with a big number of slimeheads and long, half-mashed pieces of jelly-like matter that fell into putrid chunks when lifted. The stink was poisonous, in the contained spaces of below decks you could imagine it killing you. There was something of petrol in the smell, stirred up and activated in the abundance of oxygen. Most crabs survive coming out of high pressure and a few dozen scuttled about for hiding places; they were thrown down the chute too. All valued fish were shunted below into the tanks and Declan slid down a ladder to watch a tank fill and grab a few fish for sampling. He was glad of the cold at that level, it restrained the smell. The *Warrior* had eight tanks, each bigger than a high lane cottage, and they'd go home with more fish in a single trip than his father had caught in twenty years.

All hands worked to set up the next trawl, Tommy would be pleased if they got it running inside ninety minutes and everyone wanted Tommy pleased. Declan was to stern stitching a rip with Aloysius Concannon when the first mate came on the intercom and called him to the bridge. He looked to Aloysius apprehensively, but he said his deck work had been fine.

'Tommy's probably found an excuse to give out to you, though,' said Aloysius. 'Skippers like to show a new hand who's boss.'

It was Declan's first time on the bridge and it reminded him of the school science lab, pale wood and workstations. It was very clean and smelled of coffee. There were charts under Perspex sheets and chairs like in *Star Trek* but on taller shafts. Through the inwardly raked windows he could see rolling water for miles and was struck again by how steadily the *Warrior* ploughed its route. Sea and sky were similar cold greys but in here the light was warm and from many sources: lamps over the charts and sonar displays blinking with blobs of colour and data. Tommy was standing by a screen; he called Declan over and explained how to interpret the information, how a shoal's depth could be read and the species identified. Declan realized he wasn't in trouble.

'It's not easy with your father away, I'd say, is it?' said Tommy.

'We're doing fine,' said Declan, whose instinct was always to bat away anything requiring such introspection. Perhaps it wasn't easy, he hadn't really thought about it.

'You miss him, I'd say?' said Tommy.

Declan made a non-committal move of the head.

'Do you think you'll stick at the fishing?' asked Tommy.

'I suppose,' said Declan.

It wasn't the conviction Tommy would've liked but Declan had only just turned eighteen. Tommy put his arm around him in a half-pat half-squeeze and said, 'Come to me if you need anything, okay?'

'All right.'

Ambrose wasn't the most physically demonstrative and Declan found the arm jarring. It must've shown in his face as Tommy quickly withdrew it, but he didn't take offence, Declan was always self-contained. Tommy smiled. 'Anything at all,' he said again, 'here or ashore.'

Ashore was where Declan needed looking out for most, we'd have said he was safer at sea. He'd go crazy after every landing, straight to the pub and getting caught up with drinkers who spent every night roving the town. Declan had bought a car and any word of a get-together was excuse enough to go tearing miles around the country, this being before we got sensitive about drink-driving. He'd go for a pint in the Pier Bar or the Ship Inn and two days later, when Tommy was seeking his crew, he might be frying up black pudding for a bunch of strangers out on the peninsula, on the shift with a lass, or seeing in the dawn at a lock-in somewhere. 'Many's a lad goes wild without his father,' some of us said, with foreboding. 'He'll calm himself eventually,' said others. But we all knew some bucks never settle. We had among us permanently restless ones, and Declan reminded us of them, people who seemed weighed down yet could never stay still. Disliking their own company, they always had to be on the town. Much misery results when a person is unable to simply sit at home most evenings reasonably contented. Maybe these people had no idea why they couldn't, they'd never understand their own compulsions, or perhaps they knew exactly when their last chance for contentment had slipped by, lost for ever in a rejected proposal or inconsolable grief. So now they needed immediate experience, colour, laughter, impressions sharpened by alcohol, needs that kept them drinking and kept them moving, even if only about south Donegal and occasionally as far as Letterkenny.

Some alternative lifestylers were like this too and recognizing kinship both groups might mingle and go about together. Alternative lifestylers must've had even stronger compulsions; none were local and it would take a powerful force to get a person to our far corner. We were fond of Donegal but most of us would be willing to admit we were here mainly as we were born here. A few alternative lifestylers seemed to have brought awful worries with them, they were sad-eyed and found it hard to keep jobs. One man went into the sea in his clothes at Drumbeg and was drowned, his shoes and socks left tidy on a rock. We all thought it but nobody passed any remarks.

This wasn't the way of all alternative lifestylers though, most were relaxed enough, if rootless, or just youths wanting to see a bit of the world. They came from across Europe and the odd time America. Some went for hippy clothes but many dressed like us, normal, and you'd be talking to them like normal but then they'd say something peculiar and you'd know. They were never seen at mass. We tended to enjoy local politics while they were interested in the global. They were against nuclear weapons and of course we were too, we just didn't feel the need to go on about it. Many were against television and you'd end up feeling foolish if you asked what they thought of the goings-on in the soaps. The more forward among us might ask one of them, 'What brings you here?' They'd often say they wanted to live close to nature and it's true we had plenty. Some said they were attracted to our simpler lives but we'd soon set them right on that, we only made it look simple.

A Continental girl was among their number for a while with a bird tattooed on her hand and braids in her hair. Dutch or German or Danish, one of those. She was a free spirit and would appear in the Ship Inn and sit with us on the bar side but it was hard to assess the shape of her as she was always draped in loose woolly clothes. She caused a terrible disturbance one evening by pulling a tin whistle from her sleeve and playing it. No offence was meant, she probably thought we liked that sort of thing. It drove Manus McManus to go sit in the lounge and later he returned like an explorer, telling us that the lounge was actually quite pleasant. Despite the menace of the whistle, Declan took a shine to this girl and tried to get pally with her at the bar. His style was fine for locals; he had a car and steady work, projected solidity and, with the prospect of a shift, could fire up some acerbic wit. However, he might've come across too blunt or mainstream for an alternative type, who tended to favour long hair, socialism, guitar-playing and the like. Things weren't going his way and she said she had to get home, already slipping off the stool. Declan made one last move, offering to drive her. She accepted the lift but chatted all the way to keep his mind from any friskiness.

She lived with four or five other alternatives in a rented bungalow along Binroe, the former McGettigan place; they'd gone to England. It was almost surrounded by whin, the bushes out the back giving way to rocks and the shore. A greenhouse remained from when it was a respectable family home, several panes of glass now cracked. Declan was disappointed to see four cars and a van in the drive. A party was going on, he could see the shapes of people through the window. Declan had hoped for one-to-one time with the girl but he still invited himself in. There were nearly two dozen people in the big front room, they had obviously come together in a pub and returned here where they could smoke 'joints' and drink cheap tins. A few locals had been swept along, Derek Gill was standing by the door to the kitchen with a can in his hand and a grin on his face, looking delighted to be there yet afraid to move. He was a gormless, mumbling sort of fellow but tolerated. Looking at him Declan knew what impression he didn't want to make so he sat on the chair in the heart of the room, not asking if it was anyone else's. Four or five conversations were going on around him, there was a husky singer on the stereo, too loud, and a strong smell of hash. The Continental girl gave Declan a can of beer then slipped away, he wouldn't be seeing her again. He looked around, there was a full-size harp, a music stand, hundreds of books stacked on their sides, a fondness for drippy candles and an example of the most inane item of furniture ever smuggled into Donegal: a beanbag. Some lad was sitting in it and he looked like an eejit. To top it all, they had a pet ferret called Bullet, right then it was stretched across Sandra's lap enjoying a good stroking. Sandra was on the sofa opposite Declan, she had a Mediterranean look about her although she was in fact from Dublin. She was about twenty-seven years old and would've been considered attractive if it wasn't for the nose ring and the shaved head, very off-putting. She must've been under the influence of that singer O'Connor. Sandra wore political badges and was once seen being rude to a nun. Justin the Hippy was on the other end of the sofa. He had a long grey beard and was an American who originally came to Ireland to avoid getting drafted. Sitting between them was Brendan Bonnar. He looked comfortable and at home although zoned out, his pupils dilated. He was clearly smoking hash so Declan told himself he wouldn't, perhaps not ever, he'd stick with drink, and he cracked open his can decisively. He and Brendan looked at each other but said nothing.

Sandra smiled in welcome, she had lived in the house longest and had the mammy role. She must've recognized Declan from around the pier because she said, 'Much mackerel about these days?'

'Any mackerel around here are very lonely,' said Declan. 'The shoals are off Norway by now.' He was glad their first exchange was an opportunity to correct her, Declan felt sure everybody in the room needed correcting about something. Look at the cut of them, the men were tittering like girls and half of them were on the dole.

Sandra looked on, expecting more, but Declan said nothing so she put her hand on Brendan's wrist and said, 'This is the boy from the sea. Have you met him?'

Declan considered the possibility that he was getting tested but decided he wasn't. Most locals knew the Bonnars and their history but blow-ins like Sandra and Justin could easily be unaware. The music blasted and the other conversations continued, nobody else would enlighten her. Brendan's expression was blank, stoned, but Declan suspected he was paying attention, waiting for Declan to pretend not to know him, waiting to judge him for it. Declan didn't want to give him the satisfaction so evaded the question. 'That's not his real name,' he said.

Sandra smiled; these alternative types could be quite condescending. 'No, it would be a mouthful, wouldn't it? His name is Brendan.'

Declan drank from his can and didn't reply.

'He grew up here,' said Sandra, 'like you?'

She wasn't going to drop it. Sandra had two locals here of a similar age and was refusing to accept Declan's lack of recognition. 'He knows me,' said Declan.

Suddenly charmed, Sandra clasped her hands together. 'I love the way some of you flip it, *he knows me* instead of *I know him*. Why do you say it like that?'

It was a phrase Declan often used but he had no desire to

explain himself to this outsider. Besides, he didn't know the answer, it was just a way of speaking picked up from his father. His silence gave Justin the Hippy the chance to offer a theory. 'There's something deeply contrary in people here,' he said, 'it can put a twist in their way of talking.'

Declan didn't like that nonsense, and was sure he heard hostility in it, so much for hippies being easy-going, amiable sorts. Pressure to find a better answer led Declan to an insight: 'No, it's because we're not know-it-alls,' he said. 'People have private lives and they're entitled to them. We don't claim to have someone fully worked out, like they're transparent to us, that would be arrogant. We don't claim to *know* another person.'

'But you don't mind saying others know you?' said Sandra.

'We're prepared to say others might have more understanding than us,' said Declan, 'but that's not to lower ourselves, it's just being generous.'

'That is so fascinating,' said Sandra, like an anthropologist realizing she had a topic for a book. Hopefully she had the mind to realize the respectable suburbs of Dublin gave rise to tribes as well, with their ways of speaking, no less fascinating.

All this time Brendan's only move was an occasional slow blink. Sandra settled back in the sofa and resumed stroking the ferret, the beast stretched to its full length in a rapture of pleasure. Declan noticed Sandra's leg, knee to hip, was against Brendan's, more intimate than necessary, and her head and shoulder were also inclined his way. They hardly had a thing going on, did they? Declan's mind reeled at the possibility, would it even be legal? At that moment Sandra placed a hand on Brendan's arm and Declan was wild with trying to read the gesture while acting like he hadn't noticed. It didn't look like a girlfriend move exactly, more how you'd put your hand on your senile uncle in a retirement home, but it lingered. She brought her face close to Brendan's, and closer, then stopped, gazing into his half-comatose expression. 'He's gone to hidden waters,' she said, as if in diagnosis. 'When the boy from the sea has slipped away like this it means he's at the source. We are mostly made of water and if we embrace it we can draw directly from the sea, where life began and wisdom is found. Brendan is with the sea now, you can ask him about worries you may have. He'll try to channel that wisdom and help you.'

So, Brendan had found a new audience for his affirmations. His neediness, his desperation, Declan felt contemptuous, although a moment later he remembered that Brendan wasn't such a clown, he had the sense to stay in school. Declan's resentment, never too far below, resurfaced. He had just spent six days fighting boredom and nausea on the Porcupine Bank.

'I've gotten good steers from him a couple of times,' Justin the Hippy was saying, although smiling, not so reverential as Sandra. Other people in the room noticed something worth their attention was beginning and they quietened. They mightn't have taken it seriously either, but they were curious. The music was switched off and everyone present looked towards Declan.

This, Declan realized, was why the chair had been empty.

'Is there anything you'd like to ask the boy from the sea?' Sandra asked Declan and everybody waited for him to speak.

Declan looked at Brendan, he did have a question for him. He put his can down on the floor, placed a hand on one knee and leaned forward, a small change of position but enough to see Brendan's eyes follow him, and Declan was for the first time completely certain his presence was registered. He used his other hand to gesture breezily at Sandra and asked, 'Are you screwing this one?'

Brendan snapped out of his trance. Sandra's shock quickly turned prim and stony. 'Well, now,' she said, her hand frozen halfway up the ferret. The creature bent around to glare at Declan, baring its little teeth, and Justin the Hippy had a similar expression. Declan didn't care what anyone thought, he was pleased with himself. Brendan's face was active again, back from hidden waters apparently. 'Don't mind this lad, he's not worth it,' Brendan said to everyone. 'I know him, I know him better than anyone does.'

13.

LONG AFTER THAT NIGHT IN Sandra's house Brendan thought about what he had said about Declan. Yes, he was transparent to him but for enviable reasons: Declan was regular, uncomplicated, seemed to have a full grasp of himself; people found these likeable traits. We flowed with Declan comfortably but Brendan knew he came across differently: awkward and unsure; he was unpredictable even to himself. To Brendan, an encounter with a person felt like a complicated device, with hidden gears, unlabelled buttons and no clear product. You could see it in his eyes when speaking to him, he'd be wondering what you wanted from him, what he was supposed to do. We thought he could've done with his father about the place too, like Declan, for guidance, even if only by example, but Ambrose was still in England.

With no clue what else to do, Brendan began indulging in snobbery, deciding we were too stupid to understand an individuality such as his. The alternative lifestylers had a bit more imagination and Brendan was attracted to them, they too had broken from convention. But this attraction turned into a need, and Brendan could see he was beginning to frustrate them. He was just sixteen years old and under-formed. He'd see the disappointment in their faces when he showed up, unannounced, at their doors, needing a place to belong but with little or nothing to offer.

Late one evening Brendan went to Sandra's place and found the lights on but nobody in the front room. The back door was sitting open but there was no one in the kitchen either. He jolted at a loud straggled howl coming from the shore, beyond the whin bushes. Not an animal howl, human, followed by shouts of approval and laughter. Brendan tensed, not because of the howl but what had followed: there was no generosity in the approval, no community in the laughter. He approached the beaten route through the bushes, his way lit by the fluorescent light left on in the kitchen behind him. A figure came stumbling up from the shore, one arm up to protect his face from the whins. It was Derek Gill. He saw Brendan and said, 'Don't go down there, they've gone mental.' Then he ran off.

Brendan continued to the shore. The seaweed smelled rank, but mild compared to the stink of ground-up bones, heads and guts radiating from the fishmeal factory nearby. The night was still so the smell was settled and thick, the air full with it. Lights from the town made quivering streaks on the black water and red beacons out on the bay marked the booms of the salmon farm. Justin the Hippy was crouched on a tall rock and five other alternative lifestylers were below him, standing among clumps of congealed seaweed. Justin saw Brendan and roared, a domineering sort of greeting that reminded him of the school yard. Sandra was there too and Brendan stepped up beside her. She had brought a deckchair and was sitting in it with a cup of tea in her hand, like she wasn't really part of the scene, only observing.

Justin stood, hands on his waist, leaned back and howled into the air. It was impressive, sustained and wolf-like, with a touch of mourning, surely audible far across the water. Brendan was transfixed. The alternative lifestylers below raised their arms or made comments of approval as the howl faded. Afterwards, breathing hard, Justin pointed at him and said, 'Go on, let it out.'

Brendan smiled uncomfortably. 'Let what out?'

'Your pain, release it!' shouted Justin and he gestured westward, over the water. 'Howl like you did when you got born!'

Something in all this transported Brendan for the length of a blink. He had a vision of the stony beach so clear it made him step back. He was returned to reality when Sandra said to him, 'Justin gets like this sometimes.'

True, it wasn't the first night of such carry-on. We had heard howls occasionally for months, on calm nights they'd carry to the pier. We didn't know who or what produced them but we weren't thick, a visitor from Galway who suggested it was a banshee got roundly mocked. Eventually we discovered the alternative lifestylers were responsible. 'Those alternatives are at the howls again,' we'd say, as if remarking on the weather. We found this public display excessive and childish; by all means howl if it makes you feel better but do it at home with the windows closed. That's what we did.

'Come on, all of you,' shouted Justin, 'show the boy how!'

The others began to howl; horribly distended wails that raised the tendons in their necks. Some of their faces went so red you'd worry for their health. Sandra joined in although her howls were rather ladylike, limited by her seated position and refusal to set down her teacup. The others stretched from the balls of their feet to their contorting faces, their howls layering over one another. If you were awarding points Justin would've scored high on delivery, but his howls were too rehearsed, performed rather than lived, and you knew the ritual no longer helped him, which might've explained his frustration. The others weren't so skilled but their attempts would be impossible to forget. Their cries rattled, obviously causing them pain and even injury, but they burned with honesty. Their howls made sense.

Brendan didn't witness much of this. Frightened, he had already backed off and was gone.

At home Declan sometimes mentioned the alternative life-stylers. 'You should stay away from them,' he said to Brendan.

'They're my friends,' Brendan replied, although not convincingly.

'You're only a sort of pet to them,' said Declan, 'they think you're a fuckwit.'

'Boys, stop,' said Christine.

At least they were talking. There were times when Declan behaved like a brother: an argumentative, mean-spirited, sharp-tongued and capricious brother, but a brother nonetheless. Christine wondered if this was made possible due to their father's absence; without him to compete over the boys might find their way to acceptance eventually.

Declan even did Brendan his dinner one evening, or rather didn't complain when Christine directed him to. Declan had come home with a bottle of white wine and bag of monk tails, all given to him by the cook from a French boat. He laid two of the monk tails on the cutting board. 'Brendan's here too, in the bedroom at his homework,' Christine told him. 'If you're feeding me you're to feed him as well.' Declan slapped a third tail on the board, then got out a pan, a jug and a set of tongs he had bought himself.

'I'm heading out on the *Warrior* at midnight and will be gone a week,' he said. Declan was in the mood to complain but didn't want Brendan to hear how much he hated fishing, it would feel like handing him a victory. Declan closed the door before adding, 'And for every second of that week I'll be missing dry land.'

'No need for an extravagance,' said Christine, sitting at the table and looking at Declan's array of equipment. Many mammies would've enjoyed this turnaround, getting a meal made for them, but Christine was twitchy, annoyed by all the utensils Declan would use feeding just three people, knowing she'd be left to wash them. Nor did she want to hear Declan moan about work again, she was vacuuming carpets in the hotel all day and you didn't hear her complain.

'Being out there grinds you down,' said Declan as he ran a blade through the sharpener, 'the monotony, the exhaustion, the stink.'

He cut away the end of each bone, peeled back the skin, dark and silver, and snipped off the fins. Then he dropped the monk tails in the hot pan with butter, searing their sides before adding stock he had saved. The garlic press had yet to reach us but he took clove after clove against the grater, until a shocking amount of finely shredded garlic had gone in. He put the whole pan in the hot oven, put on plenty of rice then cut lengths of broccoli and dropped them in the smallest pot. The Bonnars didn't have a steamer but by putting just a splash of water in the bottom he'd get the same effect. 'The lads never stop their jibing,' he said. 'They stand at the belts, looking at you, grinning, waiting for you to mess up so they can have a great laugh about it.'

Declan reached into the fridge and dug out some parsley,

threw it on the board and chopped it at a ferocious rate, the blade a blur, as if machine-driven. When the fish was done he opened the wine and splashed some in the pan. He put a few plates in the oven to warm then scraped the parsley from the board into the pan and added a touch of cream. He seasoned the sauce. Christine didn't like this as she knew he'd complain when she added more salt, he'd say the food was already 'balanced'. There'd be even more trouble if she reached for the ketchup.

'I often think I'm going mad out there,' said Declan. 'I dreamed once we were sinking, when I woke up and we weren't I actually felt disappointed.'

Three times he loaded rice into a bowl and flipped it onto the serving plates so the rice was presented in a tidy dome. Some might've found this display enjoyable but Christine only saw a bowl that would need washing for no good reason. Declan laid out the broccoli and fish by the rice then poured the steaming sauce about the plates, the parsley bright within the muted tones. 'Tommy tells me to stick with it, saying it takes time to gain your legs,' he said as he stepped back to look at the presenta- tion, 'but, honestly, I'm just not sure I'm cut out for the life of a fisherman.' With his kitchen cloth still draped over his shoulder, Declan carried the plates one at a time to the table then sat down with his mammy.

'I just don't see what else you could do for a living,' she said.

After a minute Brendan arrived in and sat down. He had taken a notion and was letting his hair get long. They began to eat. Brendan seemed impressed, studying each forkload before savouring every bite and making appreciative noises. Christine, careworn, ate rather like her father used to, fast and joylessly, although without the noise. She finished first and went off to her room, attending to some chore, leaving the boys alone at the table. When Brendan was on his last piece of fish he held it up on his fork, looked at it thoughtfully and spoke. Declan was surprised by the way he referred to their parents, not using Dad or Mammy. 'Christine and Ambrose Bonnar,' said Brendan. 'They've got their own problems and will never understand what's best for you. If you're not cut out for the life of a fisherman you'd better find your own way.'

Declan was suddenly mad as hell. 'Fuck off,' he said although he was the one who jumped up. Shoulders tensed, he went to the window and turned to glare at Brendan from there. Brendan raised his hands in a peaceful, meant-no-harm gesture. The term 'passive aggressive' hadn't yet reached us but the thing itself had. Brendan had told no lie though, he had shared a truth, even Declan suspected that. After a few moments of silence Brendan got back to the meal, enjoying his last mouthfuls of dinner, indifferent to the hatred emanating from across the room.

The phone rang. Their father had already rung that week but this was his time of the evening and it was most likely him. Brendan stood to go answer but Declan bolted past him for the corridor, determined to be the first speaking to their father, he'd at least have this. Declan snatched up the receiver but the caller wasn't Ambrose, it was one of Ambrose's brothers and he asked for Christine. Declan and Brendan waited near their mammy, knowing something was wrong. The brother spoke at volume and both Declan and Brendan heard his words clearly when he said, 'Ambrose is gone.'

'Gone?' said Christine.

* * *

We knew death. The way we lived was poised for dying. Our young and old mingled, ageing and slipping away weren't hidden processes. You must also consider the dangerous roads, the sea work we did and the distance to casualty departments, we knew any of us could be taken and any time. Examine the tombstones in our graveyard and you'll see all ages recorded. Yet a death was still a shock at its point of contact, the families left behind. We knew Ambrose hadn't left his sons with much of a bond and, right then, they could've used it. For the rest of us a death was when we were most communal, and we became busy. Our first task was making sure everybody who'd need to know did know and the second was making sure everybody who'd want to know did as well. For Ambrose this added up to a lot of people, he was well known and liked, his family was extensive and he'd worked a lot of boats: scores of people had to be reached. Family networks activated, relaying the news to and through aunts, uncles and cousins. If you had no phone someone drove to your house, or rang your neighbour. If you were far away we put in extra effort, a chain of phone calls extended, probing each lead and possibility until you were got.

Everyone asked how Ambrose died. He was working on a construction site when the scaffold's decking buckled under a loaded drum and gave way. He didn't fall through the break, but jumped back which caused him to go off the side, down upon six bars of steel reinforcing set in concrete, set vertically. He might have survived the one in his side but the neck blow was too much, a lot of blood was lost and that was Ambrose, done. 'At least it was quick,' we said. Every conversation in town that week turned to Ambrose immediately and you'd hear the phrase on the street and in the shops, 'At least it was quick.'

Ambrose's body was flown to Dublin and Barney Lamb went to collect him while the Bonnar house was prepared. J. J. Brown was a great help, arriving with a tea urn and a set of perfect, crisp, white linen sheets. The bed was covered in the sheets, which were big enough to hang to the floor and cover the head-board too, making it like an altar; restful, still. Phyllis put away anything detracting from the effect; the slippers by the door and the lipstick that stood on the chest of drawers, secreting them away or removing them from the room entirely. Later Christine put the radio back by the bed, it seemed too terrible to take Ambrose's radio off him. The sisters stepped up to the front window as Barney parked the hearse in front of the house. He was training his son up at the time and had brought him along to help manoeuvre the coffin.

'I hope that young fellow is able for it,' said Christine, gazing at the box containing her husband.

'Those boys should be here to help,' said Phyllis coldly.

Christine didn't respond. It would've been okay if they were off somewhere together but she knew they weren't. Declan was likely in one of the pubs, though it was still early, while Brendan would be alone, along the shore or wandering the lanes.

The bungalow's narrow corners were no bother to Barney Lamb and he patiently talked his son through the navigations. We'd huge time for Barney's abilities as an undertaker but weren't sure if that son of his would ever develop the same fine judge-ment. They placed the coffin upon the linen and Barney asked, in this beautiful soft voice he could call up, if Christine wanted them to remove the lid. She said yes but backed out of the room. When the Lambs emerged Phyllis offered them tea. The son would've taken the tea and looked around for a biscuit but Barney knew exactly when to take tea and when not to and this was a time not to. He gave Christine an envelope containing the coroner's report and the Lambs withdrew. Then Christine approached the coffin. There he was, the lump of him, Ambrose Bonnar. His hair was pasted down, he had an unnatural sheen to his skin and make-up couldn't entirely conceal the bruising under one eye. Christine placed her hand to her face, not covering her mouth in shock, but against her cheek as if presented with a problem.

Phyllis stood by her. 'They did a fine job fixing him up,' she said, her warmest words were always reserved for good craftsmanship.

'But the handsomeness has left him,' said Christine.

Ambrose was in a suit and tie, the first time since Brendan's confirmation, the shirt collar pinched high to conceal the neck. Phyllis adjusted his sleeves so white cuff showed each side equally.

'I suppose it was never really in the shape of his face,' said Christine thoughtfully. 'It was more in the way you'd be wondering what he was thinking.'

They gazed at him another while.

'I'd like the lid back on,' said Christine, 'but his people will want an open cask the minute they arrive.'

'They're not here yet,' said Phyllis.

Taking an end each they lifted the lid, feeling a connection through the lacquer. 'They're the sorts to want coins on his eyes too,' said Christine, 'but I wouldn't like that, it's creepy.'

Phyllis looked at her steadily. 'Don't worry, I won't allow it,' she said.

They replaced the lid and stepped back to look at the set-up. Phyllis took a breath and with deep finality said, 'Now.'

For three evenings the house filled up, all of us calling at least once. At any point there'd be one or two people up the corridor taking a last look at Ambrose and a dozen people in the living room. We preferred to stand but took tea from the urn and ate a sandwich. We told stories expressing Ambrose's character: Stevie Shine talked about the day he made the crew hold him by the ankles and lower him into the water so he could untangle gear caught around the prop. Big Jimmy talked about his love of drinking raw eggs straight from the shell. Tim O'Boyce remarked on his fair dealings. Joseph McBride talked about their journey to Arranmore to save his grandfather's range, that very range over there. Many wanted to tell this story, but Joseph was actually present so was always given the floor. Christine only listened in a distracted way; she kept busy, reciting a list of tasks under her breath, refilling the urn or washing cups. Women hugged her and she'd pat their backs briskly and move away. We didn't see Declan at all on the first or second night while Brendan only appeared on the second, and then just for half an hour before ducking away again. Treating it as another chore, Christine bustled around looking for Brendan and found him sitting in the back seat of the car. 'It's all the people, is it?' she said to him. 'Here, get out and I'll show you the way of it.'

Obediently, Brendan got out and stood by the car. He shivered in the cold.

'Your father couldn't take to a man with a watery handshake,' said Christine, putting out her hand. 'Here. And look them in the eye. After me. *Thank you for coming, how are you?*'

'Thank you for coming, how are you?' said Brendan, applying only middling pressure.

'*I'm grand, how are you?*' said Christine, squeezing on his hand and levering it up and down in demonstration until Brendan matched her force. 'That's right,' she said.

Phyllis was keeping the Bonnar house drink-free but naturally some showed up with pints in them. Tommy appeared late on the second evening with a face that showed he had been drinking, although he moved across the room without a wobble to go at the sandwiches. We greeted him but got in return a dismissive shake of his shoulders. He was in bad form and beyond chat, just standing and brooding, tense in the face, speaking only to correct us sharply when we misremembered the name of a boat or applied a little innocent exaggeration to a story. 'No harm done,' we'd say to him carefully. When Christine appeared Tommy strode over to her, his expression seemed desperate and she was afraid of him until she saw he was crying. 'I always thought of him as my brother,' he said to her. 'Do you think he knew?'

'I think he did, Tommy, I think he did.'

On the third night Declan made an appearance and, on top of that, all Ambrose's brothers and sisters had arrived, the living room was crowded just with them. We never quite established the number of Bonnar siblings but at least a dozen, all with similar faces and sturdy bodies. Ambrose always seemed unique to us, so it was strange to dis'cover that all along these variants of Ambrose had been alive in the world, talking and walking about, including female versions. They lived in England: the men all builders or factory staff and the sisters all nurses or other sorts of health workers, the NHS was badly short-staffed that weekend. You could tell the sisters lived in England as they had unusual shoes, coats of fine bright colours and plenty of the accent, but the brothers could've just stepped off the Arranmore ferry, England had made no impact whatsoever on their pronunciation, dress sense or deportment. The oldest sibling, a sister, arrived last and took position at the table. She was a big woman and you got the impression she didn't like to get up once she was down. From her chair she alternated between phases of benign silence, listening to everyone's conversations, and sudden fearsome bouts of loud dictatorship – directed mostly at her siblings but some of us got a feel of it too. We imagined she took little nonsense from sick ones in England, you'd need both legs lopped off before she'd offer you a chair. When Brendan drifted by she grabbed him by the wrist. 'Are you the one who came out of the barrel?' she asked.

'Yes,' said Brendan.

She seized him tight to her, forcing his knees to buckle, and locking his head under her chin for a three-second squeeze. Then she ejected him but kept a hold of his wrist. 'I remember Ambrose as a child bringing home a seagull he'd found. It had a broken wing and he tried to fix it. He fed the creature, talked to it.'

'Did he mend it?' Brendan asked eagerly. 'Was it saved?'

'He couldn't save it, of course not,' she said, annoyed by the boy's attempt to take her story down a bizarre tangent about healing; she had only wanted to illustrate young Ambrose's kindness and naivety. 'A gull would be too big, too wild,' she said. 'Our father put it out of its misery.' She pulled a face, made a claw of her hand and mimed hitting it with a rock.

'That wasn't Ambrose,' said a brother. He was sitting in Christine's chair by the range. 'It was me who brought home the seagull with the broken wing.'

'Will you stop!' said the sister angrily. 'Wasn't I only trying to tell the lad a nice story?'

'I'd a notion to make a pet of it,' said the brother in reminiscence. 'I named it Bob. Our father was right though, there was no fixing it. He did the kindest thing possible.'

The sister tightened her grip on Brendan's wrist and called Declan over too, who was sitting alone on the windowsill. Declan obeyed but didn't get too close. 'Look after your mother, the both of you,' she said. 'You're the men of the house now.'

Brendan and Declan looked at each other. They said nothing.

Some of us couldn't help but think it would've been better if Ambrose had died at sea, we didn't say it in the wake house but did later in the Ship Inn. We hated to think of his life slipping away as he lay under a thin layer of concrete dust, among columns and right angles, so far from his element. Drowning would've been more fitting, even if it meant the high price of no body to bury. This opinion caused some bad feeling, stirring men who were rarely stirred and voices were raised. John Cotter appeared behind the bar. Mr Cotter didn't need to say anything, we went quiet the moment we saw him. 'A man's dead, it's not about the look of the thing,' he said. 'It's not about what's *fitting*.'

Yet, privately, many continued to relate to the death that way, feeling its tragic sweep even more forcefully for it. Don't judge, it was a way of coping. The brutal fact of Ambrose dying on a building site, in a country that considered him 'unskilled', intensified the loss into something powerful and complete. We were gripped.

We all turned out for the funeral, it got a bigger crowd than Tom Hunt's in 1979, dispute that and you were soon shouted down. There were so many the chapel got too warm and there wasn't an echo. Ambrose's coffin was on a trolley before the altar and a decent sun made the stained-glass windows above glow nicely. Immediate family and the brothers and sisters took up the front pew. Declan parked Eunan, in his wheelchair, at the aisle end and tucked a blanket around his legs. We hadn't seen Eunan in a long while. Wisps of hair from his chin and ears caught the light as he looked around, disturbed by the vaulted ceiling and the crowd. He wasn't wearing his glasses. His face was pale but the sagging bags beneath his eyes were large and pink.

The priest went to his pulpit and talked up a good portrait of Ambrose, highlighting his love of friends and family and alluding to Brendan's adoption: 'Taking in a poor cub left on the rocks,' was how he put it. He didn't gesture about too much with his arms, as he sometimes tended to do, and his speech was well judged, we were pleased with him. After mass we filed by the family's pew to shake their hands, it took a full thirty minutes for them to get through us. Ambrose's brothers and sisters had a friendly style, clasping our hands in both of theirs. Eunan couldn't shake hands any more, he'd just raise and drop one arm in acknowledgement, like someone getting tired halfway through a salute. Brendan was a great hand-shaker by now, although a touch machine-like, while Declan was as solid as you'd expect. It was noticed that the boys were sat at opposite ends of the pew. Too alone, as we'd feared, and we weren't sure their mammy could help them right now. Christine's grip was firm but you would've thought from her face that she didn't recognize any of us.

Ambrose's coffin was pushed down the aisle on its trolley and we walked out after it and stood around in front of the chapel as he was slid into the hearse. Our graveyard was nearly a mile from the chapel and normally we'd get in our cars to reconvene there for a burial, but some spontaneous urge took hold and, with hardly a word, we set off walking after the hearse. You could trust Barney to notice everything and read a situation correctly; he was at the top of the road when he saw the crowd in his wing mirror, so he stopped and let us catch up before continuing at our pace. It was a fine, dry morning and we couldn't help but smile as we looked right and left at each other, impressed by our procession and the sheer number of us.

At the graveyard, Barney reversed through the gate and opened the back of the hearse. Ambrose's brothers approached and gathered to the coffin. They were all wearing black jackets and their broad backs made walls, one parting to admit Declan and, on the opposite side of the coffin, Brendan. We all felt our hearts tighten as we were struck again by the loss. No need for a command, the coffin rose smoothly between all the Bonnar men. Then something happened and there was no excuse for it. With the coffin overhead between them, Declan glared across at Brendan and snarled like an animal. Brendan looked back, bewildered. Declan had both hands to a coffin handle but released one and used it to shove Brendan away. Brendan stumbled; he didn't fall but he lost his grip. His contribution to keeping the coffin aloft was small, it was more likely the withdrawal of Declan's strength that caused the coffin to dip. Each of us in the crowd produced whatever noise we favoured when seeing a thing teeter; gasps, curses, whimpers, and our arms shot out. Ambrose's brothers rapidly adjusted their holds, emitting grunts of concentration, the moment too urgent for words. The coffin stayed up and Declan took hold of it again. Brendan was bent over and no one saw he had made a fist until he straightened himself, stepped under the coffin, drew back his elbow and punched Declan. The punch contacted Declan's upper chest and sent him back a step. Ambrose's brothers over-adjusted to the danger, the coffin lurched the other way and we produced our desperate noises again.

A few of Ambrose's sisters marched straight in, seized both Bonnar boys by their upper arms and delivered sharp words into their ears. 'You've a job to be doing,' one was heard to say. The coffin remained up and the ruction settled but the day had taken a bad turn and wouldn't be fixed. Declan and Brendan were not removed as bearers, but they were watched. They turned and stared ahead, faces like knots while the coffin was lowered onto everyone's shoulders, Brendan limited to putting his hands to the underside as he was the shortest. They walked to the grave, the rites were completed and Ambrose got buried. Extensive analysis was conducted in the Ship Inn that evening, especially around the graveside behaviour. It was a long while before we'd forgive those lads for ruining what could've been the most powerful funeral in years.

14.

POOR CHRISTINE COULD SAY NOTHING to either of them. She couldn't cope with her sons that day, or during the days after, they'd have to sort themselves out. Christine had another preoccupation: she was unable to stop thinking about the coroner's report. She hadn't actually read it, the report was still sealed in its envelope, but she was obsessed by the question of whether or not she should read it. She feared the details of Ambrose's death but also felt reading the report would be as close as she'd get to being there, to taking Ambrose's hand as he lay under the scaffolding, and she longed to do that. Christine left the envelope in a kitchen drawer, sometimes lifting it and putting it back again unopened.

A week after the funeral Christine noticed normal thoughts slipping into her mind: there was no bread, the car needed insuring, her roots were showing; and with the encroachment of such thoughts she felt a severe emptiness that seemed to expand in her until it was painful. Christine went to the drawer, ripped open the envelope, stood in the window and read the report. The first sentence described Ambrose as a 'Caucasian male', which made Christine smile, he would've argued Donegal Man was his ethnic identity. She read on. The print was faint so required extra concentration, causing certain terms to hit extra hard: 'blunt insertions', 'destruction of jugular vein', 'severing of muscle', 'internal trauma'. The report was only a few paragraphs but it put pictures in Christine's head, the facts of getting impaled. Reading the report was a mistake.

Christine got no sleep and the next day she wondered if reading the report again might purge the pictures from her mind. She'd read it slowly this time; a full, fearless exposure that would hopefully desensitize her. She sat down for it, with a cup of tea, steadied herself, went in. But the reread didn't help, it did the opposite, driving the pictures further inside. She got out of her chair and stood at the window. Several hours vanished.

Steel objects began to upset Christine. Steel, she had learned, wanted in you, wanted to invade you, it had to be watched. The knives and forks in the drawer raised her heart rate. Even spoons were a worry, they had gouging potential and weren't to be trusted either. In more collected moments Christine knew she couldn't fear cutlery all her life, if she couldn't reduce her anxiety she'd have to reconfigure it, give it a different point of focus. So, late one night, to shake things up, she read the report again. Sure enough, it jolted her hypersensitivity away from cutlery, but now she was afraid of everything. Our whole town was a deathtrap: unguarded drops, ten-tonne lorries, freak waves and bad bends. Late one night she remembered the twisted and broken steel gate that was entwined with a roadside hedgerow on the way into town. The gate was off its brackets but standing as it was enmeshed in the growth, the gap behind it long since sealed by the expansion of thorn bushes and bramble. For Christine's entire life the gate had been there and she hardly noticed it, but she now couldn't bear the thought of that gate; the protruding bars had so much dangerous potential, serrations, stabbings, lockjaw. Fall on it from a particular angle and it might kill you outright. She went into the boys' room and woke Brendan. Sitting on the edge of his bed, she started talking about the gate without blinking, like she was recounting an intense dream. The clock read 2 a.m. but Brendan didn't complain, he sat up and watched her cautiously.

'Will you come with me?' she asked. 'I want to get rid of it.'

Brendan nodded slowly.

'Where's Declan?' she asked, looking at his empty bed.

'He hasn't been here in a few days,' said Brendan.

'Working?'

'Or out on the town,' said Brendan.

They were an odd little procession, mammy and son on the empty road. Christine was speaking with an inveigling tone, as if trying to sell something, while Brendan tried to convince her that she could stop with the justifications, he was glad to do the job. They stopped at the gate, the sight of it making Christine go quiet. She had brought two pairs of rubber gloves from the kitchen; they put them on as protection, and, side by side, leaned in, gripped the gate and tugged. Dew on the bramble was shaken off and fell like rain inside the hedgerow. They pulled until the tangle conceded and the gate came away. There was an empty skip by the electronics workshop and they threw the gate in there. It clanged against the bottom. 'At least that nasty thing is away,' she said, satisfied with their night's work, tugging at her rust-stained gloves until they came off with a slap.

'Do you think you'll sleep now?' asked Brendan.

'I think I will,' she said, and she did.

By the time a mass was said for her husband, about three weeks later, the details in the coroner's report had burned through Christine. The pictures stayed away and she could think about the report, even talk about it, without too much distress. She raised it with Ambrose's eldest brother early one morning as she drove him to Donegal Town to meet the bus for the airport. He had stayed around for a long stretch after the funeral as it was his first visit in eleven years and, with realism, he said it was probably his last. From the front passenger seat he commented approvingly on every stretch of widened road and the fine signage. The national economy was in tatters but mass-tonnage pelagic fishing continued to inject liquidity into our area, big houses still getting built by those making money or with their money made. The brother was surprised and amused by them. 'Another monster of a house,' he'd say at every bend. This brother had worked with Ambrose and was the last to see him alive. Christine asked him about the bruise under Ambrose's eye, visible when he was returned. 'There's no mention of it in the coroner's report,' she said.

'Because he had it already,' the brother told her, 'nothing to do with the fall, he picked it up on the weekend.'

He offered no more so she asked him to explain.

'Just a scrap, nothing major,' he said.

Again, he offered no more so, again, she asked for more and he told her Ambrose got into a fight on the street the previous Saturday evening. 'Defending himself surely?' said Christine.

The brother tightened his lips and made a move of the head, *not necessarily.*

'But he never hit anyone in his life!' said Christine.

'He was making up for it then so,' said the brother.

Christine didn't notice she was letting their speed drop until she got a beep from the car behind. She was silent, the kind of silence that marks internal struggle and rarely lasts long. 'You mean he was in more than one fight over there?' she said.

'I'd say Ambrose was looking for trouble the odd time,' he said. 'We kept an eye on him, but he got riled very easy and would start up on any man who happened to be near. It was never too serious. Well, no charges were brought.'

At the bus stop Christine parked behind the waiting coach. The air freshener, shaped like a pine tree, that dangled from the rear-view mirror became still. Rain was falling, the drops on the windscreen fuzzing and refracting the morning, all blues and greys but for bright red splatters from the coach's rear lights. To Christine everything seemed terribly real and assertive: the texture of the dashboard, the butts in the drawer ashtray, her own pale fingers around the steering wheel. They watched the bus driver open the luggage compartment doors and men and women, in their twenties mostly, sliding in their bags, heading off for a few months or years.

'It's an adventure at their age,' said the brother. 'It's harder for older ones, nobody hitting fifty really wants to start again in a new country. I've seen a fair number of men like that on sites over the years. They come over, they try their best, but their minds are taken up with whatever trouble drove them from home, and England is always there reminding them that things didn't work out. They can't get loose of it, they get frustrated.'

He went to get his suitcase from the boot. After they had said their goodbyes and the coach pulled away Christine turned for home. Halfway back she felt a peculiar numbness in her face and pulled into a lay-by. The numbness went away but she stayed parked there five minutes. The feeling, she slowly realized, was rage, a rage so pure she hadn't recognized it. From what the brother said Ambrose had felt this sometimes too during his final months and so, after she'd given up on the possibility, she at last experienced a final moment of togetherness with her husband. She took his hand. The feeling between them was of being entirely against everything.

Christine decided she deserved some time to herself. She turned the car around and drove, no clue where she was going.

15.

DECLAN WAS BELOW THE WATERLINE. Knowing the ocean reached above his head felt profoundly lonely, yet also right. His grief was something very solitary. He didn't speak much to the *Warrior*'s other crewmen, at the chutes he stayed at the far end of the line and was slowly excluded from jokes and chat. He focused on his tasks, let himself feel like nothing but an append-age to the machinery, just some muscle and bone attached to a brain, fuelled on stew and a weekly envelope of cash. This too felt lonely, this too felt right.

Conditions were fair and they had four high-yield days. Declan was scrubbing down the gangways between the tanks when Tommy appeared. He was mostly ensconced in the bridge but descended occasionally, on the prowl for slacking and flawed procedure. Another big haul was settling and they looked across the tanks, the top layers of fish like woven mats of silver and blue. Declan knew Tommy was preparing to say something about his father and he didn't want to hear it so he said, 'Do you think we've overdone it on the mackerel?'

Tommy made a dip of the head, acknowledging the remark while not engaging. He withdrew to the bridge.

Nineteen hours later, some miles off Tiree, a small vessel came alongside and two inspectors boarded the *Warrior*. They wore hard hats, lifejackets and one was carrying a lined back-pack containing pink, green and white forms. The men were Scottish but representing European law. They said no thanks to tea, checked the logs and walked between the tanks. Kevin Beattie, the first mate, was already stowing his apron and changing into his downtime socks. Everybody knew they had broken quota and there'd be no letting on otherwise.

While the inspectors completed their report the crew were sent to wait in the dining area. Everyone was at the large oval table but no one wanted to play cards, gambling had lost its appeal as the arrest might hit their earnings. The television had no reception, Tommy spent a fortune on the *Warrior*'s electronics but hadn't installed a video player in case the crew tried to watch blue movies. The rolls were annoying, the *Warrior* down to just a couple of knots. There was nothing to do but sit, look at each other, drink tea and smoke, everyone tapping the ash from their cigarettes with unnecessary force. Rory Murrin had sat himself next to Declan and, much to Declan's discomfort, he started asking about Brendan. He didn't mean any harm, he obviously hadn't heard about the scene at the burial. Rory was five years old when Brendan arrived and was touched profoundly by the town's excitement, his clearest childhood memories were the candles in the windows and the packed chapel. Rory had gotten blessings off Brendan a few times and was now nostalgic for the ritual. 'Too bad your brother's not here,' said Rory. He didn't notice the way Declan wasn't looking at him, instead staring towards the centre of the table and flexing his fingers, Rory Murrin wasn't the most observant. 'The boy from the sea would get us feeling better,' he said.

Declan arose sharply from the table and, against orders, went below. Earlier he had seen a few small squid in a crate of by-catch and he went to find them. He picked up the squid, their flesh feeling like cold jelly, and took them to the galley. He gutted and cleaned the squid, washing the ink down the sink, then used a serrated knife to cut up the tentacles and slice the bodies into rings. He switched on the fryer and the smell of hot oil bloomed. A single bottle of beer was allowed aboard each trip to make batter and the chef was sure to go mad but Declan felt he had no option but to use it, he wasn't just preparing this feast to calm himself down, he needed to make a statement about who he truly was. It wasn't something we were usually given to, but Declan wished to express himself. He made the batter, coated and fried the squid pieces, tossed them in paper towels to remove excess oil then arranged them on the biggest platter, sprinkled the lot with rock salt and threw on a few lemon slices. Holding the platter aloft like a posh waiter, Declan returned to the table and set it in the middle.

The crew looked at the mound of battered cephalopods. Lips curled, faces became pinched, Aloysius Concannon made the sort of exhale you'd produce if you looked out the window and saw someone urinating in your garden. 'You'll never see me eating one of those creatures,' he said. This view was general. Onion rings might've been acceptable but this was another thing entirely. Kevin Beattie pushed the platter down the table so it wasn't near him but it was shoved up again and it went back and forth a few times before settling in a mostly tolerable location. Humiliated, Declan felt his insides constrict. Had he been older he might've mocked the crew but he didn't have the status or confidence.

Only Rory Murrin took a piece of squid and nibbled at it,

obviously being polite. 'I'd say your brother likes seafood, does he?' he said.

'He's not my brother!' shouted Declan so that Rory recoiled in his seat and everyone looked over. Declan expected embarrassment, maybe an apology, but instead Rory straightened up and took on an indulgent expression, close to smiling. 'Yeah, all right,' he said.

Declan looked around but the crew glanced away, none wanting to involve themselves.

The intercom crackled and Tommy's voice emerged. 'Gentlemen, let's go home.' The crew stood to go scrub and stow the gear, glad to have something to do. The inspectors returned to their own vessel and the going steadied as the *Warrior*'s speed increased. Declan thought about that look on Rory's face, but when he asked Aloysius about it, he only got a 'Don't mind him.'

But Declan did mind him, enough that he was slow and brooding over his work. Too slow, although no one gave out to him. The *Warrior* powered home and when everyone took the chance to sleep Declan lay awake in his bunk, listening to the snores, fixated on that look of Rory's.

After dinner the following night the rest of the crew were in better humour, getting tea for each other and chatting agreeably, it was always good to be heading home whatever the reason. Beyond the windows was nothing but blackness and the dining area, with every light glowing, had a charmed, enclosed atmosphere. This was the only bright spot for fifty miles in any direction. While bowls of vanilla ice cream were passed down the table Declan left his seat and went to sit next to Rory. It didn't look like a sociable move, everyone registered it with sidelong glances. 'So, do you have anything to say about Brendan?' said Declan.

Rory would've clearly preferred peace. He took a mouthful of ice cream and shook his head, looking like a big child.

The crew fell silent, they couldn't pretend not to have noticed Declan's aggression, though neither would they meet Rory's eye when he sought support. Declan realized something: he was making Rory afraid. He felt a weighty adjustment within himself, a slab lifted to reveal new possibilities. Declan hadn't noticed gaining enough physical presence to be able to threaten, he hadn't understood how a hard look on his face could intimidate. But he knew now, and he'd remember. His pulse went up a notch but his voice went lower. 'It's just I've a feeling you're holding back on me,' he said.

Rory was looking down into his bowl and his face was turning red and Kevin Beattie decided it was his duty to stop the painful spectacle. 'Listen sure, Declan, nobody is judging your father. He was a sound man, good as they come.'

There was much muttered agreement. 'A fine example of a man,' said several.

Declan looked around, confused.

'No one is saying a word against him really,' said Aloysius, 'except the holy Joes.'

'And nobody heeds a holy Joe,' said Kevin.

'What are yous going on about?' demanded Declan, looking from face to face.

'Everyone knows a man can get tempted,' said Aloysius, deciding the news should be delivered with some psychological analysis, 'he can, you know, get ideas.'

Declan scanned their faces, seeking understanding, slowly finding it.

'Ambrose was Brendan's real father,' said Aloysius.

'That's why he adopted him,' said Rory, leaning away, afraid Declan would hit him a blow.

'Who's claiming that?' said Declan.

'Everyone,' said Kevin.

'He's not my brother!' said Declan but his voice had gone high, pre-adolescent, any power gone.

'Everyone says he is,' said Aloysius.

A low moan emerged from Declan without his permission or encouragement. *My brother.* He cut the moan off by getting to his feet and he took one last frantic look at the crew before escaping the room. He almost fell down the steps then stumbled about below; the lights stung, the floor lurched and the handrails were greasy to the touch. The ice plant in the bow was the coldest and loneliest spot on the boat; Declan went in, clamped the door shut behind him and immediately the freezing air stung. Ice flakes were piled high into the forward tip of the V-shaped room and Declan could sense, through the steel, the waters parting overhead. He breathed in and let the freeze hurt his insides. Could his father have been that devious?

Nobody could take minus five for long and the only other place to go was his bunk, so Declan went to the shared cabin, climbed in and pulled down his blind. Yes, his father could've been that devious. Everyone had sneakiness in them, Ambrose was the very man who'd planted this mistrust in Declan, pressing it deep the day he arrived home holding another child. Declan lay with his back out to the cabin, boots on, and decided he'd refuse to move if called for duties.

That wouldn't be necessary, none of the crew said anything, relieved to be free of him. Declan was left alone the entire distance to Donegal Bay.

As the *Warrior* manoeuvred to the pier Declan emerged from his bunk and looked out a porthole. It was a rainy night but there was a crowd of us waiting, our faces wet and full of energy. An RTÉ news van was parked among us, their camera was set on a tripod and protected by a sheet of plastic while their spotlight illuminated the boat and the streaks of rain cutting through the beam, silver shooting across black. Declan's condition was so brittle he thought the camera crew was there for him, planning to film one of those jokey *wait 'til you hear* news items slipped in before the weather, one about a man who adopted a boy so as to raise him without having to admit being the actual father. It looked like the whole town was in on it. But then Declan saw our cardboard signs, they said, 'Bigger Quota Needed', 'Plenty of Fish in the Sea' and the like. TV people in Dublin had decided the *Warrior*'s arrest was worthy of a news report and when we heard a camera crew was on the pier we formed a protest so the viewers would know our opinion.

Tommy lowered a bridge window, leaned out and smiled and we all cheered and shouted, 'Good man!' We got the feeling Tommy found all the attention proper, as if he thought there should be a camera crew and cheering fans here every time he rolled home with a full hold; our town relied on the likes of him, after all. He disappeared from the window, reappeared on deck and climbed up onto the pier. Tommy looked well under the spotlight, shy around the eyes but with teeth like you'd see in a movie actor, probably not the main star but the friend who sorts things out at an important moment. He looked over at the television crew and we saw him decide he had a duty to perform. When Tommy walked straight for the camera we got excited, thinking he was going to speak directly into the lens, address the nation. But no, that would've been a bit much, he stopped by the reporter. A load of us stood behind Tommy so our placards and solemn faces would be his backdrop on TV, although a couple of younger lads worked against the effect by gurning and acting up. They got a talking-to after.

The reporter asked what happened and Tommy said, 'We were working men on a working vessel and we were out there working. The country was happy with us doing that for years, decades, on wooden tubs, getting a few barrel-loads. From that, through our own graft, we've built a profitable and safe industry. Now we're told we're too big, you liked us better before. European scientists tell us there's not enough fish, stocks are dwindling, and they're allowed to take our tonnage off us. Well, I invite them to come on a trip and have a look at what our scanners say and what our trawls say. Until then everyone should leave us at it, leave us to the work we're best at.' He gestured at the *Warrior* and there were shouts of approval. 'Now if you'll excuse me,' said Tommy, finishing up, 'I've fish to offload and there's many in need of the protein.'

That was Tommy's speech, he turned, raised a kingly hand to us and we all cheered.

Apart from Declan, he was already gone.

Declan had climbed to the pier, walked through town and towards home without speaking to anyone. Approaching the bad bend there was a cold wind at his back and squalls were hitting twice a minute, loud and further amplified in his ears as the rain struck his hood. Outside the Bonnar house, Declan could see a glow from a new lamp stood near the window. Inside, even in his current state of mind, Declan noticed a plush new cushion on the chair his mammy was sitting in, the china teapot within her reach and, at her feet, a new sheepskin rug. The rug made no sense, sparks from the range were sure to speckle it with burns, but it would be out of place anywhere in the house, ridiculously soft and bright. Christine didn't arise, which was unusual when a man returns from sea, and was looking at him with a certain insolence, expecting negative comments about her fancy goods. 'Was Dad Brendan's real father?' said Declan.

Christine blinked. 'No, he wasn't.'

Declan still had his hood up and the water dripping from him was making a dark circle on the floor. 'People in the town claim he was,' he said.

'Well, he wasn't.'

'They're saying that's why he took him in.'

'I'd have known,' said Christine. She didn't panic like Declan, she simply weighed the suggestion for the time it deserved, a tenth of a second, then dismissed it. Ambrose was no mystery, certainly not to her. The idea that he went off with another woman, even briefly, was laughable. She could always account for him.

Declan dropped into the two-seater, arms flopping to his sides.

'You're getting the seat wet,' said Christine.

He stood, took his coat off then dropped into the two-seater again. 'That's what people are saying,' he said.

'Some people maybe,' said Christine, 'the sort with nothing better to do, the sort with no sense. Do you think something like that could've stayed hidden so many years? Of course not. It's only that your father's gone, so there's an opportunity for mischief, but a story like that won't last. Everybody knew Ambrose and knew he wasn't the sort for secrets, even the stupidest of them will cop on soon enough.'

She was right, it was obvious. Tears of relief welled in Declan's eyes. Christine observed them a moment. 'No need for that,' she said.

Declan awoke the next day in great humour, and he stretched out in his bed. He had discovered his father wasn't a liar and Brendan wasn't a blood relative, but Declan wasn't simply going back to how he was before getting misled. Having fully believed the story for twenty-four hours the sense of escape was mighty enough to change him, he was suddenly smarter and more compassionate. Declan could see how badly they were dealing with Ambrose's death, all three of them spiralling away in wild directions. The night before, his mammy had confessed that feeling angry at Ambrose she had driven to the posh shop across the border in Strabane and spent a heap of money, knowing how much he would've hated it. Declan now decided he was going to fix the Bonnars, starting with himself. He saw that he should be thankful: he was the natural son of the household, no one could ever take that off him, and he could choose to be generous towards the family adoptee. He got out of bed and went looking for his brother, finding him at the kitchen table copying figures from a school textbook. Declan sat down across from him and, friendly like, said, 'What are you at there?'

Brendan looked up at him warily, he glanced down at his textbook warily and at Declan again, warily. 'Accountancy,' he said.

Traditionally this was a girl's subject and Declan would've been expected to mock him, or at least snort, but instead he said, 'Good man, it's no harm knowing about that sort of thing.'

Brendan's studiousness was a new development, he had only

ever been a middling student and after Ambrose's death had neglected schoolwork entirely. His mocks had been bad and Christine said she'd talk to a few skippers for him, find him a berth. That had given Brendan a fit of initiative and he had drawn up a study schedule. 'I've applied to do a course in it when I finish school,' Brendan said to Declan, still holding his pencil to a column of numbers in his notepad. 'Three months, then I'm put on a work placement.'

'Brilliant,' said Declan.

Once such a display would've gotten Brendan smiling and reciprocating, but too many years had gone by. Brendan gazed at Declan neutrally, noting his slack, foolish expression and said nothing. He wanted to see Declan humble himself more.

'Listen, I'm sorry about the funeral,' said Declan. 'Pushing you over and all, I don't know what got into me.'

Brendan continued saying nothing, still holding pencil to paper. He could've matched the apology, but felt no obligation, it was Declan's accounts that were in the red. He waited.

'I'm sorry about lots of things,' said Declan and he gestured about with one hand, implying a long history but failing to make words. This was the most self-exposure he ever attempted, and his inhibition was manifesting physically: a rigidity in his upper body and a dry throat. Leaning forwards helped and when Declan next spoke it was in a rush. 'Sorry for never hanging about with you. Sorry for being a prick. Sorry for recording over your cassettes and smashing your Astro Wars. Sorry . . . it was me wrote that love note, letting on to be Irene Tully.' He stopped there.

'I figured that was you probably,' said Brendan.

It wasn't much but Declan seized it, determined to believe

they had a conversation. 'Good man,' he said and before anything happened to ruin the moment he jumped up and dashed from the room.

Declan's good humour only lasted a day, there was still something rattling about in him. He had ended the battle with his brother but Declan still held an entire infrastructure for conflict that he couldn't simply dismantle, his personality was built on it. The thought of us talking nonsense about his family was the next source of aggravation. Family, for Declan, now included Brendan and his anger was directed at us.

The idea that Ambrose was Brendan's true father was already being rejected by everybody. Brendan's look alone proved it, his distinct narrow nose and dark, thick wavy hair were nothing like a Bonnar. Brendan tanned well too, while Ambrose and Declan both burned red during a five-minute break in the clouds. But our wisdom had come too late, Declan was already on the warpath. He wanted to find out who'd started the rumour, the original author, and then, who could tell what might happen.

Lorries were going back and forth along the main street and about five hundred gulls were wheeling overhead, crying and shrieking, when Declan approached Cindy. She was leaning in the doorway of her salon, having a smoke. 'There was a story going around about my father,' he said to her. 'You heard?'

'I did,' she said.

'It started here, I bet.'

'Why would you think that?' asked Cindy and she contemplated him, as if genuinely curious about his answer and willing to wait for it.

Declan wasn't prepared for the counter-attack; he had probably expected Cindy to immediately concede that women love gossiping and stirring up trouble, that was just the way of them. He looked past her inside the salon, where women incessantly nattered and the kettle relentlessly steamed, surely an incubator for wild stories, but he didn't know how to word his accusation.

Cindy didn't leave him suffering long. 'Maybe you presumed too much,' she said and she took a drag on her cigarette. Declan was about to back away when Cindy pursed her lips and blew a stream of smoke so fine that Declan followed it with his eyes. She was drawing his attention to the not-working men sitting on their wall.

Declan crossed the road, his righteous anger returned and at its height. He stood staring at them, breathing in the exhaust fumes from passing lorries, and said, 'So, you're the people who started saying Ambrose was Brendan's real father.'

The men squinted up at him guiltily, picking at their nails and scratching their noses. 'We weren't the very first,' said one.

'Then who?' asked Declan.

'He told us to keep him out of it,' said another.

'Who?'

'Him,' said the third. He was looking towards a boy on the pavement outside Hegarty's, walking home from his final school exam. Brendan Bonnar must've sensed the attention because he stopped and looked around. He froze.

Declan and Brendan looked at each other.

Brendan started away and Declan watched him jog from sight before understanding what he was doing; Brendan wanted to talk to their mammy before he did. Declan wouldn't allow that and had a strong advantage, a car. He pulled out of the diamond but got delayed by a jam of lorries and forklifts. Brendan must've run faster than ever in his life, halfway home Declan still hadn't over-taken him, although he passed his school bag dumped by the road. He saw Brendan himself up ahead at the bad bend, dark against the sky, a pained-looking figure, hunched over, gripping his abdomen and still trying to run. Declan swerved sharply, get-ting satisfaction from scaring Brendan into the fence. He stopped the car in the middle of the lane, crunched on the handbrake and stepped out. Brendan was already loping across the heather and he got to their door first. Calmly Declan followed as Brendan staggered down the corridor and collapsed before Christine. She was standing by the kitchen counter, looking at him in concern, the washing machine banging away at the end of its cycle. Brendan couldn't speak, only heave for breath. Declan walked in and said, 'It was him, he tried to get the town believing Dad got another woman pregnant.'

Christine looked at Brendan. Her face, over five seconds, became angular and severe. 'Ambrose took you in, he raised you,' she said.

Brendan said nothing, all he could do was lean on the counter and try to stand upright. His face uncrumpled and as he opened his mouth to speak his mammy pointed to the door, like you'd command a dog. 'Out of my sight,' she said.

Brendan did as he was told, they heard him leaving the house as the washing machine clicked off.

'We should throw him out permanently,' said Declan.

Christine didn't hear, still looking at the door Brendan exited through. Declan had to repeat himself before she registered his words and she turned to him in disbelief. 'He's not getting thrown out,' she said. 'Don't be thick.'

She knelt to unload the washing machine, shaking out towels

with sharp thwacks and tossing them in the laundry basket. Her lips were tight with frustration.

'That bastard brought shame on our family!' said Declan.

'Shame?' she said. She looked up at him sharply, then stood. 'Shame! That's the kind of thing you think about? You're unbearable, both of you are unbearable.' Christine made a boyish move and it caused Declan to jolt; she kicked over the laundry basket and the towels flopped onto the lino. 'There,' she said, 'do something useful, will you? For once?'

She left, throwing open the back door and marching towards the hills. Her shoes weren't best suited but she didn't care. She kicked her way through the rushes and didn't stop until the house was distant and small under the grey sky. With foresight, Christine had grabbed her cigarettes from the counter as she left and she sat on a rock and lit one. Christine had been smoking more since Ambrose died, the yellow of her fingers had taken on a richness and she could feel oil as she rolled the filter between her fingertips. She watched the house. Smoke from the chimney was slowly thinning; Declan was obviously letting the fire die and he hadn't hung the towels on the line either. After a while his car pulled away but Christine still didn't return to the house, she stayed in her vantage point as evening drew in.

Christine wondered what role was she supposed to have in Brendan's fiction: foolish woman, bringing up her husband's child without noticing, or, just as bad, was she supposed to know Ambrose got a girl pregnant and, of her own free will, gone along with a mad plan to raise the child while keeping the fling secret? Those were the roles available to her: blind fool or spineless sap. You raise a child to manhood, then he turns around and offers you that menu.

Christine lit another cigarette.

In time, sitting out under the darkening sky, she concluded the truth was something else and it might've been worse: Brendan just hadn't thought about her feelings at all, not for a second did he consider what effect the story might have on her. This was a mammy's position: inspiring devotion from her children, yet from the same children, and at the same time, existing out of frame and unconsidered, like the world before they were born, or their large intestine. It wasn't hard to figure why Brendan put the story about; it was a desperate claim on Ambrose. Declan too was handling everything badly, mistaking intransigence for strength. The boys were at the age when a person's traits are becoming permanent, decided, so unless they smartened up soon they wouldn't have good lives. The answer, clearly, wouldn't be found with her, Christine couldn't deal with them at all. I want to be home, thought Christine and she got a shock when she realized she was no longer looking at her own house. Her eyes had drifted along the slope to where the tops of the spruce plantation jagged into the sky. The house was out of sight, but she could see smoke rising from the Lyons's chimney.

Brendan didn't return that night, probably kipping with alternative lifestylers, and in the morning Declan left for a six-day trip on the *Warrior III*. Christine walked up the lane to the Lyons's house and followed the smell of polish to the kitchen. 'All them ones in the town are going on about Brendan's conniving,' said Phyllis without preamble. 'For years I've tried to warn you about that child, haven't I? Haven't I?'

Christine didn't want to get caught up in that discussion, or any discussion. 'Why don't you head out a while, I'll take care of himself,' she said.

Christine waited until her sister had driven away before stepping into the front room. Eunan was in his armchair, delicate as a pile of autumn leaves. His seat had a new plastic covering, easy wiped, hospital blue. The same colour had slipped into every room: stacks of pads in his bedroom, packages of wipes by the toilet and plastic cutlery in the kitchen drawer. Eunan was small in his clothes and wearing slippers. The walking stick laid across the chair's arms seemed to imprison him. His knuckles were pronounced, much wider than his fingers and darker, his sluggish blood pooling in them. He looked up when Christine stepped between him and the glow from the television and he made a sound in his throat. Months before, when he initially stopped speaking, Christine and Phyllis thought he was just in a bad mood, it took a week to realize he had lost the ability. Christine folded her arms and studied him. Coming to terms with the house actually meant coming to terms with her father.

Eunan made another throat sound, it had no meaning, yet Christine considered him a while, as if he had offered an opinion. When she went to put on the kettle he gazed after her exiting shape.

With or without glasses, Eunan couldn't see much any more. The television was often on, but just for the company of low voices and shimmering light, anything across the room was lost in a haze, an impression with two main tones: pale in the daytime and dark yellow at night. The haze began about an arm's reach away and was slowly getting closer. Figures would solidify as they crossed into his zone, his daughters, his grandsons, their hands and fingers making contact. To others in Eunan's state their touches would've been understood as love, insistent but helpful, but Eunan felt no warmth from his family's hands. They seemed sharp, brittle, like lengths of dead coral, reaching for him through water thick with sediment.

At eleven Christine helped her father up and kept him steady on the trek to the toilet. He had developed a hunch, his head was slung forwards like a prow. At the toilet he slowly revolved, until his back was to it, then waited. It was hard to know if he thought about these moves or if they happened by rote. Christine undid his trousers and slipped them down to his ankles then took down his underpants. He was sagging, like a flag in no breeze. Using the bars, Eunan was able to lower himself down but she stayed close, ready to grab him if need be. He settled and became still, at some point a turd would slip loose.

Christine stepped into the hallway and waited, leaning against the wall with her palms flat against it. It was many years since she had call to settle here, she looked at the framed photo of herself and Phyllis in their pigtails, Christine with a goofy grin but worried eyes and Phyllis the same only more so. After a while she tapped twice on the bathroom door then looked in. He was attempting to raise himself and she went to help. To clean him she first used wet wipes through his crevice, then kitchen towel to dry. While she did this Eunan stood, gripping the support bars, gazing towards the door, trembling slightly, his face exactly as it would be if she was reading to him or buttoning his cuffs. Christine flushed the toilet then hoisted up Eunan's underpants, his trousers, redid his front button and accompanied him on the journey back.

Over the following days Christine spent a lot of time up the lane. Phyllis was delighted, she'd make soda bread every morning and they'd have lunch together. Phyllis's good form was noted, she was very chatty in Hegarty's as she bought flour, sugar, jam and extra milk. Assistance with their father didn't even matter, she was just pleased having her sister for company. For her part, Christine felt more comfortable than she would've thought possible. It was certainly better than being in her own bungalow, there she could feel a pressure building. Declan would soon be back.

'I've been trying to mediate between them for years and it's never worked,' Christine said to Phyllis. They were in the Lyons's kitchen drinking tea and eating thick slices from a Swiss roll that Phyllis had made. 'Yet, in the latest drama, they both ran to me again.'

'Maybe they'll only grow up when you're not there to run to,' said Phyllis. She looked at her sister with significance, then poured more tea.

The next morning, while Phyllis went to buy up all the baking soda in town, Christine stepped into her former bedroom. It was kept well, not let go to storage. She sat on the edge of the bed and her body remembered the next motion, compelling her to reach to the wardrobe and pull open the door. The oval mirror inside caught the light. She looked at herself. Christine was still sitting on her bed when she heard Phyllis return and go into her own room. Christine repositioned herself on the mattress, causing the springs to squeak, and Phyllis stopped whatever she was doing. Christine could imagine her sister staring at the wall, not sure if she had heard a sound or not.

'You're home?' said Phyllis, through the wall.

'Yes,' said Christine tentatively.

During those same days, Brendan was either out of the house or in his room. The Bonnar place was cold but neither he nor Christine lit the range, neither resisting the grey mood that had taken over. Christine knew Brendan was waiting for her to talk about his lie, she could see him watching her, but she stuck with basic exchanges about meals, chores, going to the post office and the like. She had decided to wait for him to raise it first, but it wasn't until she was packing her bag that he gave in.

It was the afternoon after Christine revisited her room up the lane; Brendan arrived in and found her at the table in the kitchen area packing her clothes into a big holdall. 'I'm going to stay with Daddy and Phyl a while,' she said to him. She could feel Brendan standing and staring but Christine concentrated on the job, eyes cast down. She was afraid that Brendan would be hurt and she didn't want her resolve to falter. 'I want you and your brother to work on getting along,' she continued. 'He's due back tonight or tomorrow. You should be on the pier to meet him when he steps off the boat.'

'He'll probably throw me in the bay,' said Brendan.

'Not if you apologize, quickly.'

'But I'm not sorry,' he said, 'I'd the right to a father.'

Christine looked up at that. Brendan's expression was flat, he didn't seem upset, although it was never easy to tell with him. 'You had a father,' said Christine.

'I wanted to make it complete, and he's gone so I did him no harm.'

'And me?'

Brendan was silent.

'Everyone knows Ambrose couldn't have kept a secret like that,' Christine continued, 'you ought to have known it too.'

'Some may think so,' said Brendan, 'but they're very innocent. You forget that I've heard a lot. There's plenty of shame in this town, and shame makes people keep secrets.'

'There's that word again, first from Declan and now you,' said Christine. 'Shame wasn't a big issue for your father. Shame is more your brother's problem, and yours.'

Brendan said nothing.

'Ambrose was more touched by pride, too much, and he would've been too proud to hide a thing like that,' said Christine. 'He'd have risked excommunication or whatever they call it, he'd have risked our marriage, he couldn't have resisted telling people, telling the world, you were his true son. Don't you know how much he loved you?'

Christine needn't have worried about Brendan's face, it was her own words that distressed her. A sudden imbalance, born of pain, affected her coordination. She pulled at the bag's zip too sharply and it came off the teeth, Ambrose would've fixed it but Christine could only slap the broken thing away. 'I'm just a few minutes up the lane, not far,' she said, lifting the holdall and heading for the door. Brendan went out after her and they stood together in front of the house. The clouds over Crownarad were slate grey and massive, their undersides shredded with rain. Pine needles were matted thickly on the lane, carved through with channels of water. There was a wobble to her voice as Christine said, 'I've stocked the fridge for you, don't just be eating spaghetti hoops.'

With that she walked up the lane.

16.

DECLAN HAD BEEN SET TO refuse his berth on the *Warrior III*, let them go without him. He had wanted to stay ashore and have it out with Brendan once and for all. Declan's hands made fists when he thought of him. Then Aloysius said that they were going to work in the vicinity of Rockall and this information had drawn Declan back to the pier and up the *Warrior*'s gangway. He'd corner Brendan when he returned. Declan would have this, he decided, he'd be the one to see Rockall for real.

They pressed north-west, trawling as they went, each trawl bringing them closer to Rockall. In Declan's mind it was waiting for them. Checking the *Warrior*'s progress, Declan would go to the bridge where Rockall was a point of light on the digital chart. He'd just stand and gaze at it until chased back to work by Tommy. Below, working the haul or by the tanks, Declan was constantly imagining Rockall: its stone face forever battered by the sea yet impossible to disturb.

Forced off mackerel for the season, Tommy had decided to investigate the peculiar and unfamiliar creatures inhabiting the hidden valleys leading to Rockall. It took a while for Declan and the crew to learn what to toss and what to keep; argentines had bizarrely big eyes; scabbards were wicked-looking, like demons; while orange roughy were indeed very orange and had undignified faces. So far we didn't eat these fish but Tommy reckoned markets could be found. He was wise to chase new possibilities, the fishing industry was expanding so fast an entire species could suddenly fall from circulation. No one yet admitted it but the North Atlantic cod fishery was collapsing and there'd soon be next to none. Declan worked fast at the chutes, picturing Brendan as he pulled out dead slimeheads. He liked the smack they'd make against the side of a chute when he threw them hard enough. A smack then gone.

By day four they were in Rockall's vicinity and Declan took every opportunity to get on deck or to a window and scan the horizon for it. But something was always against him; the light, the conditions or the *Warrior*'s bearing was a little too removed.

During the trip's final trawl, when the latest catch was sorted, everyone went to their bunks but for Declan who climbed to the galley. Darkness had fallen while he was below. He rounded his palms each side of his face and leaned to a window, blocking out the cabin lights to look into the black. He had seen the *Warrior*'s course plotted on the bridge's display and knew they were making an arc south of Rockall, but there was nothing to see, no stars, no horizon, no rock; just a few shimmering crests revealed by the *Warrior*'s spots. Declan's frustration was intense, early tomorrow they'd turn for home and he had not yet seen the rock. He went to his bunk but set his own alarm so he'd be first to wake and some hours later he was back in the galley. Declan leaned to the window again. Light was bleaching the heavy sky but now conditions were against him. It was hitting six on the Beaufort, spray was lashing down on the decks and visibility was poor. He could see high bands of white water but only for a mile through the saturated atmosphere. The bell went and other crew appeared, no one saying much, respecting the mood of dawn, Kevin Beattie whistling a soft, slow version of the *Dallas* theme tune. The chef sparked up the grill but even the smell of crisping bacon didn't persuade Declan from the window, he remained gazing north. Then a mile and a half away he saw a crash, water slamming up a hundred feet, perhaps against a massive, immovable force. Without turning, Declan said, 'I think I almost saw it.'

The rest of the men arose and approached the windows. They all stood together, each face pale in the soft light, searching for Rockall.

'You'd think Tommy would swing closer and give us a chance,' said Rory Murrin.

'Tommy's not going to burn fuel for sightseeing,' said Aloysius.

'My father would have,' said Declan and he felt a stab of grief.

'Aye,' said Aloysius before slipping into silence. Other men nodded and said nothing.

No one else saw any sign and soon doubts were expressed about Declan's claim, the sea was crashing everywhere, hard to read. Their chatter was annoying to Declan and he was glad when they all drifted back to the table. Not interested in breakfast, Declan leaned on the window's casing, focusing on the distance and trying not to blink. The view was disturbed by pulsing droplets racing down the glass and Declan decided he'd have a better chance outside. He went to the external door and pulled on his boots. 'Is he gone mad?' he heard the chef say, but nobody intervened. When Declan had opened the door just an inch air rushed in and the sea noise was already tremendous, an immense creaking and crashing within a wall of white noise, like every tree in a forest getting shattered, re-formed and shattered again. Declan stepped out into the weather, shut the door and climbed to the bridge deck, face clenched against spindrift. The high sea required both hands to the railing and weightlessness overtook him during the boat's downswings. Two dozen fulmars were gliding along the troughs, which were deep and continuous enough that Declan saw no bird with a backdrop of sky. At the top, he clung to the railing and watched north. There was a crash again, he saw only white water but it told him where to focus. He stared at the point, experiencing the strange sensation you get when, among fierce noise and commotion, you focus completely on a far-off movement made tiny and silent by distance. When it happened it happened perfectly: the water fell, rolling apart in all directions and Declan saw the dark mass revealed. Rockall, certainly, the size and shape of his fingernail, there for a full twelve seconds. The boat dipped and for an instant his feet left the deck, this moment of flight would for ever remain part of Declan's memory of Rockall.

From the bridge Tommy spotted Declan, lowered a window and ordered him below. 'You're not required there,' he shouted, voice raised to the wind, confused by Declan's presence on the bridge deck. He didn't want a crew member exposed without operational purpose, especially in such conditions. Declan knew Tommy wouldn't understand so he did as he was told, going down the steps and back into the galley. He stood in the middle of the room, an air of shell shock about him, the exposure had left his skin glowing, he was breathing hard and had forgotten to remove his boots. Everyone was looking at him. 'Did you sight it?' asked Kevin.

Declan didn't hesitate. 'No,' he said.

A few hours later the *Warrior* turned for port. Seeing Rockall hadn't placated Declan; on the contrary, it fuelled his rage. He wouldn't just kick Brendan out of the house, he'd kick him out of town.

It was ten at night when offloading was completed, most of the crew headed for pints, but Declan strode home, his mood darkening further on the road. Brendan wasn't in the house and Declan was left pacing about the rooms, insides twisting with frustration. The range was cold, the air was settled and touched by damp. Two official-looking letters were lying on the mat, there were unwashed cups on the table and in the sink he found a pot with a layer of spaghetti hoops stuck to the bottom. Might the rat have gone up the lane? Without even showering or changing Declan marched up to the Lyons's, letting himself in. Brendan wasn't there either but Christine and Phyllis were in the front room, having got their father down for the night. They stood to greet him and Phyllis went to stick on the kettle. Smelling of fish and with a wound-up expression, Declan stood in contrast to the pleasant atmosphere; a freshly baked sponge cake sat on the table, the television was off and a coal fire was burning in the grate, Declan felt the heat on his face. He had never seen a fire there before, never seen the grate, it had been concealed for years. Eunan's chair had been moved near the far wall and the television reorientated to face it. This was done so two armchairs could be placed facing each other before the mantelpiece, where his mammy and aunty had been seated.

Christine saw Declan come to understand the new arrangement, realize that she was staying here. 'I need you and your brother to get along, please try,' said Christine. 'I know you have it in you.'

Without a word Declan turned and left. Phyllis was in the

hallway, before speaking she shooed him to the front door, not wanting to be overheard. 'Make things nice with Brendan, okay?' she said, a pleading in her voice. 'That way your mammy will be content to stay here. She's better off with me, she's not long widowed and I'm well used to taking care of people.'

Getting her sister back was the best thing to happen to Phyllis in twenty years, she almost wept when Christine suggested staying. She warned her that it was only for a short while but Phyllis didn't seem to register that part. The baking had continued non-stop, getting the place homely. The two of them up here and Declan and Brendan below, it would be a pleasing arrangement. Phyllis wasn't one for daydreaming but a few times, while kneading dough for example, she lapsed into fantasies of Christine staying for ever. Their father would die eventually surely and then the two of them could grow old together.

Phyllis was looking at Declan, seeking a clue to how he was minded. 'I'll do what I need to do,' he said and Phyllis stepped back, frightened by his expression. She'd have to get more bread in the oven straight away.

Declan returned to the Bonnar bungalow and stood several minutes in the living room, taking in the implications. The only sound was from the fridge, a hum he had never noticed before. His mammy was gone and the house was effectively his now, he decided, and he wasn't going to share it, not even for a single night. Declan retrieved the suitcase from the loft, it had belonged to Ambrose and was full of paperwork for the *Dawn*. He dumped it all out. The deck plan, records of catches, a chart of the bay, Declan let none of it bother him. He packed the suitcase with two blankets, Brendan's clothes, his cassette player and seven tapes, music copied from the collections of the alternatives. That was everything, not even enough to fill the case; these few items were Brendan's entire grip on the world. Declan didn't let that bother him either but he did add a can opener and a carton of plasters and one of the letters on the mat was addressed to Brendan so he stuck that in too. Finally, he opened his wallet and put two hundred pounds in banknotes on top. He closed the suitcase and left it out on the front step. What Declan felt wasn't satisfaction, but there was a sense of completion: a piece of cold iron sliding into a correctly sized slot. No need for a note, the suitcase was statement enough.

Declan went to bed and lay looking at the ceiling for an hour.

Brendan had been in Sandra's place all evening. The empty Bonnar house troubled him, his mammy gone, the quiet, but he wasn't comfortable with the alternatives either. Sandra loved playing psychologist and kept asking him how and why his family was so messed up. Brendan couldn't look at the issue steadily enough to be able to explain, he'd evade the question all his life if he could. So he finally returned to the lane, arriving after midnight. He wasn't surprised by the suitcase although he gazed at it a while before picking it up. The action gave Brendan a sense of completion too, he accepted his destiny. It felt better to think of it as a destiny rather than a sad state of brokenness. Holding the suitcase, Brendan stood with his back to the bungalow, tasted the Atlantic air, and experienced a stirring sense of being special. He had no family, not really. Maybe all along, he told himself, he was only passing through this town. He had floated in from the sea and tomorrow he'd leave, head for another town where another set of people might need his help. He would help them, but he wouldn't get too close, knowing he'd eventually have to move on again, this would be the life of the boy from the sea.

For now, Brendan knew a dry place to pass the night, somewhere he'd be alone and have peace. He hummed the title song to *The Littlest Hobo* as he walked around the bad bend and away. 'I'll just keep moving on,' he said aloud, the only sound on the black road.

The Ships' Graveyard was a shallow inlet of broken stones where our decommissioned trawlers, stripped of engines, lights, props and winches, were dumped. The whole place smelled of stagnant salt water and puffed-up woodwork. Timber vessels decayed in stages; pine decking went first, then a decade or so later the hull, often of larch, would peel apart until only the oak frames remained, sitting starkly like a ribcage for years more. Eleven vessels lay there at the time. Dead seaweed clogged the breached hulls, decomposing into a grey paste where millions of tiny soft eggs squirmed open daily, releasing greasy, hopping fleas. The wrecks weren't set in rows or ordered in any way, just dropped from a crane, some angled across each other. The *Ard Barra*'s stern sat high in the air, her entire wheelhouse removed, leaving a black hole in the deck.

Brendan made his way no bother over the uneven ground until he merged with the shadow of the newest wreck. The *Shining Light* still had Plexiglas in the windows and a complete mast, horizontal to the stones as she was on her side. She was furthest from the water, where even a spring tide couldn't reach. Brendan crawled under the wheelhouse, pushing the suitcase before him, stood up through a vacant window and stepped inside. Rainwater had warped the wheelhouse's plywood but the hold, entered through a slot cut in the boards, was dry. He sparked his lighter and held it up, finding everything as it was on his last visit, the crates he sat on and the candles he stuck in jars. The abandoned tackle was still ordered: a mismatched pair of wellingtons, three floats, a large bent spanner and a coil of rope. Grand, he thought, as he lit a candle. The light didn't reach the corners but threw patterns up the sides of the hold, Brendan sat and watched them for a long time. Years listening to our problems had given Brendan an ability, he could shut down parts of himself; maintain basic functions while largely absent, only half-listening. Tonight he shut off his superfluous parts, until he was only ticking over. Brendan's self-esteem wasn't reduced by doing this, in fact he was gaining some. He was proud to be a survivor, of being able to lose everything and start again.

He wrapped himself in blankets, lay down on the crates and fell asleep straight away.

In the morning Brendan was woken by the sound of engines, two engines of massive horsepower and not far away. Was it better to lie still or make a bolt for it? He didn't want to be seen and gambled he was safe in the *Shining Light* so remained laid across the crates, looking up at the hold wall, listening. The engines stopped and there was the sound of compressed air shooting from a braking system. There were men's voices, a burst of laughter uniting them all for a few seconds. Time passed. A drone of hydraulics. Creaking. More time passed. Voices again. Then the crash, something massive, the floor lifted and the jars fell over as the *Shining Light* shook and resettled. It was a fright, but no harm was done that Brendan could see. He heard the wash of disturbed water. Voices again, the words couldn't be made out but Brendan detected satisfaction, a tone of job-done. Vehicle doors slammed shut and the two engines pulled away.

Brendan planned on taking the first bus out of town but it didn't leave for another hour so he waited to be certain no one was near before stepping from the hold and lowering himself out of the wheelhouse. Cold stones under his palms awoke him fully. He crawled out, noticing the view to the horizon was blocked by a new wreck standing in three feet of water. The keel had shattered in the drop, so the hull hugged the stones and kept her upright, some boards broken with clean snaps and others turned to mash. She was the *Christine Dawn*. Brendan sank to the floor, gaze fixed on the vessel, and a feeling of brokenness overwhelmed him at last. It couldn't be denied; it was a physical sensation. Brendan didn't make it to the bus. He stayed in the Ships' Graveyard all day and into the night.

17.

WE WERE TALKING AGAIN ABOUT Brendan, talking as much as when he first arrived, but without generosity or wonder. We were against tricks and dishonesty and many of us were disgusted with his lie, especially those who had fallen for it. We had a keen sense of proper conduct, principles handed down to us wordlessly by our parents, taught to us by example. Brendan had mocked them and in addition broken a special rule that had existed only for him, a rule that we only discovered upon his breaking it: Brendan should've been more grateful. Not just to Ambrose and Christine but to all of us, the whole town. Hadn't we all offered him sanctuary? 'Sure, we all adopted him really,' said Manus McManus at the counter of the Ship Inn.

But in a while our attitude began to change and the clean-up in the chapel's graveyard played an important role. This was a traditional summer occasion and it happened to land the day after the *Warrior III* returned from Rockall and Brendan left the Bonnar house for ever. Many of us drove to the graveyard with detergent, buckets, cloths and garden equipment in the boot. We greeted each other and remarked gladly on the decent weather then got to work, washing down our family's tombstones, scraping away any moss and weeding the beds: a general dose of cleaning and maintenance. We raked the blue stone chips and Hughie Devlin arrived with a sack of new chips, carrying it from his car on his shoulder, to renew his parents' plot entirely. Broken or faded ornaments were replaced, plastic spheres containing artificial flowers were popular at the time. Many of us brought a flask of tea and ham sandwiches and made an afternoon of it. Our youngest children might tumble about in the grass or wander together among the graves, their lips moving as they read the inscriptions. There was chat about this and that as we worked but the mood was subdued overall, we felt this was the best way to go about such things. No grave was left out, if somebody had nobody then the people attending the nearest plots would take care of theirs too. Biddy Donoghue's neighbours from the high lanes plucked the weeds that had rooted above her. Ambrose was at the top of the slope. Still new, his grave needed no work but perhaps the sight of his chiselled name inspired reflection among us. It can't have been easy for Brendan. Despite our wakes, open coffins and big funerals we weren't necessarily great at dealing with grief. Life was a sort of procession and we all marched in it together, you had to keep up. The truth was we didn't give each other much time, we didn't give ourselves much time, we didn't like to go on about things. If you were struggling your immediate family would be the ones to pick you up and get you along but not all families functioned well enough for that. Over the day in the graveyard, while we raked and pulled weeds, we began to forgive Brendan.

As the light faded the priest appeared and led prayers at the top of the slope, we gathered around and said our lines. We'd never step on a plot of course, but didn't mind standing on the graves' low concrete surrounds for a better view. Christine appeared, which made us more attentive. Our shoulders went back, we lifted our voices and held our hands together prayerfully. She had a faraway look about her but accepted our condolences and asked after our families. She shook our hands just like Ambrose used to and we admired that. After the session of prayer she went and stood by her husband's grave for a time.

The priest walked down between the tombstones blessing them as he went, casting holy water just like the bishop did with the fleet. We all followed after, in procession along the path or moving between the graves, stepping among our parents, sisters, brothers and children.

Afterwards Christine returned to the lane and headed into the Lyons's. In the front room her father was gazing towards the flickering screen with a blanket over him, up to his neck like a huge bib. He seemed to be basking in the television's light. Christine patted him on the shoulder then went to the kitchen. There was a strong sweet smell of baked oats and syrup, flapjacks cooling on the rack. Phyllis was at it again.

'I need to make sure you're eating properly,' said Phyllis, with forced cheer. She was standing by the table and could tell already something had happened, Christine seemed altered.

'I'm sorry, I better go back to my own house tomorrow,' said Christine. 'I was foolish to leave the boys like that.'

'Sure, we're just up the lane,' said Phyllis, smiling desperately.

'And I'll just be down the lane for you,' replied Christine.

'Why don't you have a think about it?' said Phyllis.

'I have thought about it.'

Phyllis knew anger wouldn't help but couldn't stop a little getting in her voice. 'They'll be fine!' she said.

Christine knew Brendan was out of the house but assumed

he was staying with the alternative lifestylers again. 'If I'm there Brendan will come home,' she said.

Phyllis turned back to the oven, her heart breaking.

Meanwhile, down the lane, Declan was hitting the drink.

He got through a load of cans then on to the cream liqueur he found at the back of a cupboard. It was ancient, crust under the top crunched audibly as he unscrewed it but that didn't put him off, he took a big gulp. He looked around, needing distraction, and decided to light the range, more for the sense of inheritance than the warmth. First, he crumpled newspaper into balls then put them on the range's grate, stuck sticks on top, added turf and then put a match to the paper, footering with the grille on the door and adjusting the air flow until a fire took. A realization crept over Declan as the flames grew: all his big life decisions were made. Occasionally he had the notion of becoming a chef but he could see no easy route to that and what he needed now was simplicity, seeing a clear path ahead came as a relief: he'd be a fisherman. He'd pay off the mortgage and finally get the extension done. Declan felt no desire for youngsters or a wife but knew they were standard procedure around here and didn't kid himself that he was special, eventually some woman would talk him into it. Then he'd grow old here, by this range. Yes, the big decisions were made, now he just had to live them out. He celebrated with another slug from the bottle.

Early the next morning, before Christine had awoken, Phyllis arrived in the back door. She looked with disapproval at the empty cans on the floor. 'Why didn't you go to the pub?' she asked.

Declan was laid across the two-seater, legs hanging over one end and the ashtray resting on his stomach. His face seemed bloodless and he had yellow rings around his eyes. 'I was happy here,' he said.

Phyllis stepped close, having uncomfortable thoughts and hoping Declan would coax them from her, therefore becoming partly responsible, but Declan wasn't fit to notice her needs. He closed his eyes again, placed his thumb and forefinger to the lids and kept them there. When Phyllis next spoke it was with a low voice, as if fearing the house was bugged. 'If you want Brendan out of your life you'll have to find somewhere for him to go,' she said, 'somewhere he'll be able to situate himself.'

Declan removed his hand and looked at her, confused.

'If he's contented Christine will be too, and she'll let me look after her,' said Phyllis, 'which'll be best for everyone.'

Declan waited for her to go on.

'I might know a place for Brendan, it could work out well for him, for everyone, but to arrange it we'd have to take a drive. Just you and me. Right now.'

Laboriously, her nephew removed the ashtray, put his feet on the floor and stood. Phyllis watched him, afraid he was judging her harshly. It would've been understandable, she wasn't happy to be sneaking about either, but surely Declan knew her heart was in the right place? Taking care of family could require some tough moves.

Declan was looking at her, saying nothing. Then he stepped across the room and lifted his car keys from the table.

He drove while Phyllis explained that when the Bonnars first took in the baby she had made enquiries, seeking the mother. Despite all the apparent mystery getting a few facts wasn't hard, the girl had worked a month or two in a processing plant and anyone who cared to could've got her name, Christabel

McGilloway. She left no address but Phyllis rang some women who worked the belts near her, discovering Christabel had told them where she was from, not exactly, but roughly. Looking through the phone book, Phyllis got the names of businesses in the area and rang them all, shops, pubs, garages, trying to get the McGilloway phone number. This was difficult, people were cagey, but in the end Phyllis was convinced the girl's house had no phone. She wasn't able to get a full address either although she got the name of a townland, which was probably enough to find her if anyone went and looked. Phyllis never told anyone she had this information, by then Christine and Ambrose were determined to adopt and she hadn't the strength to follow through. The townland was in north-east Donegal, on the border, a couple of hours away. 'I drove there once,' said Phyllis, 'when Brendan was going about blessing people and developing a high opinion of himself, but I thought of Christine and couldn't finish the journey. I was only a few miles away when I turned back.'

'But you want to find the mammy now?' said Declan.

Phyllis adjusted her seat belt. 'It'll be the best thing for everyone,' she said.

They left the sea behind, the roads narrowed and the markings disappeared as they drove into higher country; a landscape of open bogland, monotonous and scoured by wind. It reminded Declan of the Atlantic, the horizon low and the sky overwhelming. Every couple of miles they'd meet a bungalow with a stack of turf against the wall and maybe a few children in mucky trainers out front. After they passed the children stepped out onto the road to stare after them. Black-faced sheep stood in the breeze and even with the windows rolled up Declan and Phyllis could hear their bleats. The sheep were sometimes loose on the road and Declan would slow to squeeze by as they always refused to step aside. They seemed too big; Phyllis was certain a sheep with four hooves on the ground shouldn't be able to look you in the eye through a car window, but these ones could.

A dark band appeared at the sky's edge: a spruce plantation, like the one along their lane but vastly bigger, about ten miles across. Above it, like an insect from here, hovered a British military helicopter. The road before them led straight into the trees. As they got closer the trees remained dark and just before crossing into the plantation Declan halted in the middle of the road. No need to pull in, they hadn't seen another car in twenty minutes.

'What'll we say to this woman, if she's here?' asked Declan.

'Tell her we know the whereabouts of her son and can put them in touch,' said Phyllis. 'Maybe he'd like to stay with her a while.'

Declan shut down the engine and clasped his knees. The car made little clicks and ticks as it cooled. They were too close to the plantation to see it but the helicopter could be heard somewhere a couple of miles away.

'You're not going to lose the run of yourself, are you?' said Phyllis.

Declan was squeezing his knees hard. 'No,' he said.

'I'm not so sure,' said Phyllis. 'Remember the time you wet yourself during *Superman III*?'

Declan breathed out heavily, reached for the key and started the engine. They went into the plantation.

There were no signposts but several junctions and they were soon combing the woods rather than driving with direction. The light was low and the bends meant that even in front and behind they could see nothing but trees. All the spruces were grey-green and some appeared diseased, duller and covered in hanging weeds. Either they or the pilot must've roved across the border as the helicopter was directly above them at one point and they felt its scrutiny upon them. 'Act natural,' said Phyllis.

At one point they saw an old woman leaning on a fence post by the road, wearing a dirty jacket and jeans. Her glasses were held together with duct tape and the lenses were very thick. Declan stopped, rolled down his window and asked the way to Christabel McGilloway's house. She gestured onwards, reeling off a list of rights and lefts. They went on their way, driving another ten minutes before meeting the woman again, leaning on the same fence post. This time she looked at them in disgust, turned around and disappeared into the trees.

On a second run they got a different result, a road they hadn't travelled before.

Rows of spruces gave way to a patch of open ground and, not far from the road, a bungalow. It was just like the Bonnars', complete with crazy-paving detail up the side. They were apprehensive looking at it and stopped on the road, by the track to the house but not fully committed to pulling in. The ground about the bungalow was riven with thistles, dock leaves and nettles. There was no smoke from the chimney and the lank net curtains gave it a dead look. A red and white Honda motorcycle stood half-covered by a tarp and beside it something almost traditional in certain corners of Donegal at the time: a wheelless car up on breezeblocks. A dog started barking somewhere and ten seconds later a man burst out the front door and strode towards them. He was about sixty, thin, unshaven and wearing an old black suit jacket over a jumper. A few feet from the car he stopped in a poise of assertive enquiry.

Phyllis looked to Declan but the man was on her side of the car, meaning it had to be her to roll down her window. 'We're very sorry to disturb you,' said Phyllis, doing something peculiar with her voice, making it high so to sound formal or sophisticated. 'Is this Christabel McGilloway's residence, perchance?'

'You've come to the right place.'

'Wonderful,' she said, unconvincingly, and looked to Declan again.

The man bent into a right angle, looking past Phyllis and instead addressing Declan. 'What's wrong with her?' he said.

'Could be your lack of trousers,' said Declan.

Surprised, the man looked down at himself. He had no trousers on but didn't seem concerned once he had established his Y-fronts were in place. 'Christabel is the love of my life!' he said, straightening up. 'Come in!' He turned and walked back to the house.

Phyllis and Declan looked at each other. Both had noted the man's distinct narrow nose, the well-taken tan and the hair, grey but full and wavy. They got out of the car and walked to the house. The front door lay open and inside was a sparse household, lived-in, yet barren. Marks on the walls showed where pictures once hung and the musty carpets seemed to have shrunk, not quite reaching to the walls. The living room smelled of dog and was bare but for a big television on a stand, switched off, a brown three-piece suite and a coffee table. On the table were a few stained mugs and a bottle of rum. The sofa was covered in crumbs and dog hairs but the man waved them that way so Declan and Phyllis sat on it, each taking an end of the sofa as most hairs were in the middle. The man had put on a pair of trousers, which was a relief, but they weren't offered tea.

'Might Christabel be in?' said Phyllis, looking towards the door to the kitchen.

'She might,' he said, and sat forwards in his chair, his face active with expressions that appeared curious or hopeful. 'What led you here?'

'Christabel worked in a processing plant in Killybegs many years ago,' said Phyllis.

'So, you're Killybegs,' he said, and he looked at Declan. 'I'd say you're a fisherman, are you?'

'I am, aye,' said Declan.

The man sank back in his chair and became still, all his attention on Declan. It was in the angle of the man's forehead too, his slight frame, even in his stillness: this was certainly Brendan's father.

'One of those big trawlers?' he asked him.

'The biggest,' said Declan.

'Have you been up around Rockall?' the man asked.

Declan, already spooked by the familiar face, couldn't hide his surprise at hearing that word here, from this man. It was like he had reeled off Declan's date of birth and middle names. But the man showed no sign of knowing he had asked a probing question. 'I have,' said Declan.

'I've seen it on here,' he said, directing a nod at the television. 'It's a fine thing, Rockall.'

'So, is Christabel your wife?' asked Phyllis.

He looked to Phyllis again, like he had forgotten her presence. 'I should've married her of course, made it official,' he said, addressing Phyllis. 'But I took her in, fed and clothed her and allowed no one trouble her. Some did try! We had her brother here a few times, wanting to fight me.' He gritted his teeth and looked away.

A mouse ran along the skirting board behind him. Phyllis and Declan saw it but said nothing.

The man faced Declan again. 'I've been thinking,' he said. 'For years I've been thinking this: I'd like to go and live on Rockall for a spell. I'd only need help organizing a hut and supplies.'

The mention of Rockall jarred Declan again, although he didn't show it. 'Why would you want to do that?' he said.

'I'd be claiming it for us,' said the man, reasonably.

'You want to claim Rockall for Ireland?' said Declan.

This agitated him, the man's shoulders sprang aggressively and he sat forwards in his chair again. 'Fuck the Brits and fuck Dublin too,' he said. 'I'll claim it for Donegal. We should have it, not any other crowd. Rockall is a north-western isle, just like Arranmore or Tory. Further off the coast I admit, but it's part of Donegal certainly, you can tell by the look of it.' He was glaring at Declan, face hung in a way that expected a response.

'I see your point,' said Declan.

The man settled again. 'It's a magnificent thing, Rockall,' he said.

'Do you think we could speak to Christabel?' asked Phyllis.

He looked at her and opened his palms, there was admission in the gesture. 'Is this the only address you have for her?' he asked. 'Nothing more recent?'

Phyllis and Declan glanced at each other. 'Just this one,' said Phyllis.

'She ran out on me,' he said, raising both hands and letting them slowly fall. 'She's in England most likely. Her brother doesn't know where either, he still hassles me about her. It's what I get for taking up with a younger woman, no gratitude for all the things I did for her.' He looked at Phyllis. 'We wouldn't get that with our generation, would we?'

There was a significant pause before Phyllis responded, 'No, we wouldn't.'

'She's run out on me before,' he said. 'I just wait, she always comes back in the end. She's not the sharpest, if you know what I mean, she can't cope with the world by herself. Once, long ago, she was gone a year, but even then she returned to me.'

'How long is she gone this time?' asked Phyllis.

The man looked towards the window. 'Oh, I'd say ... I couldn't say exactly. A touch longer.'

'She left last year?' asked Phyllis.

'Further back than that,' he said.

'The year before?'

'Ah, longer,' he said, 'but definitely no more than ... Well, definitely not much more than ... ten years.'

Everyone was quiet.

'Now, will you take a drink?' he said, his fingers actually wiggling towards the rum.

'No! No thank you,' said Phyllis.

'It's a bit early for us,' said Declan.

He grunted and sat back, they had annoyed him. 'It's not easy being sociable these days,' he said.

'We need to make a move, don't we, Phyllis?' said Declan.

Phyllis ignored him and spoke instead to the man. 'I don't like to pry,' she said, 'but might you and Christabel have any children?'

Declan looked at her sharply.

'No, no,' he said, 'there was something wrong with her innards, I'd say. It pains me greatly, I often think on it. I'd be a great father.'

Phyllis was about to speak—

'You know what!' said Declan. 'I will have a drink.'

The man sprang forth in his seat and lined up two mugs.

'I don't suppose you'd have a glass handy?' said Declan. 'It's not often I drink before noon. I want to do it right.'

'Certainly!' he said, nodding rapidly. He almost skipped to the kitchen. They heard the gush of a tap.

Declan turned to Phyllis and said, 'Don't you dare.'

'I'll say nothing, of course,' she replied, looking away, acting offended, pursing her lips and raising her eyebrows. 'I only wanted a full understanding of the situation.'

The man returned with two almost clean glasses and poured a measure each. Both he and Declan sipped, the host smacking his lips as if it was pure spring water. Then he addressed Declan. 'So, do you think fishermen would be willing to get together and sponsor me?'

'To do what?' asked Declan.

'To live on Rockall!' he said. 'My presence would secure your fishing rights to the area. There I'd be sitting contented, doing something good for Donegal. I wouldn't take a penny for it, not a penny. I'd just ask to be kept supplied with food and other basic essentials.'

Declan responded carefully, 'I could mention your offer at the next Fishermen's Association meeting.'

'Please do,' he said and he looked towards the television screen, remembering the mighty image of Rockall. His expression melted into pure longing. 'I'm sure I could be happy there.'

It must've been the drop of drink, the man got very chatty then and was desperate for his visitors to stay. It took a while for Phyllis and Declan to get as far as the door and still he kept talking at Declan, holding him with an onslaught of questions.

Phyllis went ahead, although it was Declan's car she got behind the wheel, started the engine and sat like a getaway driver. Declan had to give the man a pack of cigarettes and a tenner before being allowed to go.

They drove in silence until they escaped the plantation, then Phyllis said, 'Let's not tell anyone what we did today. Nobody, ever.'

Declan nodded. 'We'll say nothing.'

They drove home. Phyllis went to make dinner for her father. At Declan's request, she dropped him off before town, at the turn for Binroe. Declan started walking.

He realized something as he walked; despite his years of antagonism he had often searched for Brendan, following him to Kathleen Cunningham's; to the Nigerian ship; to Doris Kane's, and then on that recent chase through town to their mother. Each time he was driven by a mission that seemed important, but anyone charting their courses over the years would see a basic truth that Declan had missed: Brendan moved and Declan trailed after him, his route always following. Once this realization would've maddened Declan but now it caused him amusement as right then he was at it again, walking to the alternatives' house hoping to find Brendan. Approaching, he saw Sandra working in the greenhouse. A couple of sections were replaced with cardboard, but there was plenty of glass too, with the season's greenery pressed against the panes. She saw him and stepped out, wearing her army surplus coat with the German flag on the shoulder and holding a bunch of coriander. He asked after Brendan and she said she hadn't seen him in two days. He turned to leave. 'Do you want this?' she asked, offering the coriander. 'I hear you're a good cook.'

'Who told you that?' he asked.

'Who do you think?'

Declan took the coriander in a brown paper bag and walked all the way to town. He passed the bank, the chapel, the clinic. Outside the Ship Inn he met John Cotter and asked him if he had seen his brother. John hadn't but he held Declan in conversation, he didn't often get a chance to speak with him. John offered to put the coriander in a fridge for Declan to collect later and they went inside. At the back of the lounge a door led into a store-room. Or rather it was being used for storage, under crates of beer and boxes of crisps Declan could see a steel worktop and an industrial hob. 'This was all fitted when we ran a bed and break-fast,' said John. He looked at Declan and patted the steel. 'It's sad seeing something wasted, isn't it?'

A little while later they both appeared behind the bar. It seemed a particular honour to be behind John Cotter's counter, and with John himself, and we all sat up at the sight, none of us would ever be allowed back there. Declan enquired after Brendan's whereabouts; he knew we were very observant, but all we could do was look at each other and shake our heads. Except Manus McManus, from the far end of the bar, without raising his eyes from his newspaper, he said, 'I may have seen him about the Ships' Graveyard.'

'Ah, Jesus,' someone said. We were all thinking it: the Ships' Graveyard was dangerous.

'What?' said Manus. 'I didn't want to interfere.'

Declan set off along the shore road. The sky was reddening for evening and the smell of fungal rot was hanging over the Ships' Graveyard. The tide was out leaving streams of hairy weed, like wet green bunting, hanging along ropes and chains. Declan looked at the most recent wrecks and had a cold moment of knowing something, still unclear, was going to hit, then he experienced the blow. There was the *Christine Dawn*. Declan felt his insides crumple, it was so strange and wrong to see her out of the water. He knew that he should've been warned the *Dawn* was there, not left to discover her like this. He shook his head; nobody had wanted to interfere.

Declan approached the *Dawn*, listening hard, but the only sound was the breath of the bay. He put a palm to the hull and he stood there until he heard a howl, an animal-like cry rising with power then petering away. For half a second Declan thought the howl emerged from himself, but he soon realized it came from along the shore. It would've been safer, drier and maybe faster to go out to the path and follow it round but Declan went directly for the howl, clambering over the boulders along the water. Blankets of seaweed shifted under his feet, sliding loosely over the rocks, only half bound to them. One of his feet went into a pool of mud, black with pollution, and came up saturated, each further step causing the oily paste to squelch between his toes. He pressed on. There were no more howls but when Declan arrived on the stony beach Brendan was there, wearing a pair of mismatched wellingtons and standing in the water.

'Get away to hell,' said Brendan.

Declan stayed, but didn't get any closer.

Brendan turned his back to him and looked out to sea.

Declan couldn't have begun to describe these moments. It wasn't love or hate; it was a complete entanglement. It was suitable that he was among the rocks while his brother stood in the water, they were like sea and shore.

'Was that you at the howling?' asked Declan.

'Maybe,' said Brendan.

'Did it do any good?' asked Declan.

Brendan was silent, feeling around inside himself for any change, still looking out across the bay. The sun was setting and lights were coming on along the far shore. 'No,' he said.

Declan settled down on his haunches, balanced on a boulder. 'I got talking with John Cotter in the Ship Inn,' he said. 'There's a little kitchen out the back and he's invited me to have a go at serving meals for people in the lounge, making it into a sort of restaurant. He doesn't even want a cut, he reckons he'll make money from the bar. I've a mind to give it a shot.' Brendan said nothing so Declan pushed on. 'I was thinking we could go in together, you and me. You can take care of accounts and the like.'

Brendan still said nothing, gazing at the points of light across the bay. 'You'll want to serve fancy stuff nobody'll touch,' he said eventually. 'People here have no need of soufflé.'

'I'll not be foolish,' said Declan. 'It'll be solid grub, like lasagne.'

With a sound of stirred water, Brendan turned to face him. 'You'll have to serve it with chips,' he said.

There was a short silence but Declan eventually conceded. 'Aye, with chips,' he said, 'nothing wrong with that.' When Declan next spoke he did so slowly, not wanting to push too hard. 'Maybe, the occasional evening,' he said, 'if we can get them fresh, we'll put crab toes on the menu.'

Brendan thought some more.

Declan got to his feet.

Brendan said, 'No.'

'No?' said Declan, surprised.

'I've been offered a place in university,' said Brendan. 'I'm going to take it. I'm leaving.'

Declan remembered the letter he had put in the suitcase,

printed with a three-letter acronym he hadn't recognized. 'Where?' he asked.

'Galway,' said Brendan, turning and gesturing south over the bay, away.

'How can you afford it?' asked Declan.

'There are grants these days, from Europe.'

'You're going to do accountancy?' asked Declan.

Brendan shook his head. 'History,' he said.

Good man, thought Declan, although he couldn't quite bring himself to say it.

The season turned. There were clear days and we could read the hills and mountains far south of Donegal Bay. We'd point out the peaks and name them for our children, whether they were inter- ested or not. Johnny the Matchbox took cancer and was admitted to the hospice. Tommy O'Gara was making regular visits to a shipyard in Norway where the *Warrior IV* was under construc- tion. Phyllis Lyons took a job in the library. It was good to get out of the house but, she reminded us, it was only for a few hours a week, she had plenty to be doing at home. We remarked on the annual cycles: the travelling funfair set up for a few weeks then departed; house martins went south and mackerel went north; the children went back to school and the hotel emptied. We might remark on the town's slower rhythms too: alternative life- stylers came and went, and whenever a not-working man passed on or came to prefer staying indoors another not-working man would appear to take his place on the wall of the diamond. Meanwhile our youngsters grew and got jobs, went out the bay or perhaps left us entirely.

The Bonnars would sometimes have their lunch in Melly's,

Declan and Brendan sitting side by side and Christine opposite creating a pleasing balance that we all noticed. Of course we'd have preferred a different shape to the triangle they made, this new shape was formed in loss, but triangles are sturdy, used to form hulls and supports, ask the lads in the boatyard. Christine would do most of the talking, looking from one son to the other, cajoling and advising, but she knew better than to chase every concern, like Brendan's lying in until lunchtime and Declan's drinking. She'd leave it go, better to avoid pointless aggro. They'd grow out of it. 'So,' she'd say, looking across at her sons. 'How are yous coping?'

Brendan would say, 'Been worse.'

Declan would say, 'You know yourself.'

The sight of a scar or a powerful forearm and Christine might close her eyes and be swamped by grief. Hearing somebody making a ridiculous denial had the same effect, as did the smell of fried liver. There were times that Christine got in a rage with Ambrose again and she'd go and spend more of his life insurance on things he would've hated, like a video recorder and packets of Crunchy Nut Cornflakes. She did see sense about the sheepskin rug and returned it but came out of the shop with a duck feather pillow that cost nearly as much. The pillow was weighty and rather than rest her head on it at night she'd lie against it. She let on to no one but she bought the pillow to fill the bed space left by Ambrose, to represent the lump of him, having it there helped her sleep. Sometimes in the night she dreamed him up, Ambrose would be stretched against her, she'd feel his breath on her cheek and hear him whisper, 'Have you left the kitchen light on?'

Brendan helped Declan set up his new venture in the Ship Inn and it was good to see them working together. We made occasional expeditions to the lounge and sampled the food, it was a sensible menu. 'Will you not stay among us?' we said to Brendan one evening. He leaned on the counter and looked around the walls like he was considering it, although he was perhaps just being polite. He promised to visit.

'There'll always be a spot for you here,' we said.

Declan was in his apron and standing in the door to the kitchen. 'You never get free of a place like this,' he said. 'If you don't come back, it comes to find you.'

One afternoon in autumn we saw the Bonnars parked in the diamond, facing the street, the boys in the front and herself in the middle of the back seat. Something stately had developed in Christine's character and she never drove if Declan was available, she expected to be driven. Brendan's hair had gotten long and was tied back while Declan's was clipped short as always. Much of the fleet was in, our supertrawlers sitting stern to pier so there'd be enough room for all. The boats made a mass of steel so tall and wide it seemed the town was in fact moored to them. It was the day of Brendan's departure for university, his bag was laid on his lap and they were waiting for the bus. Christine was talking at Brendan and he'd nod or shake his head at intervals. 'Work hard,' she was saying. We didn't need to lip-read to know that.

When the bus arrived they all got out of the car and crossed the street. Declan carried the bag and stowed it in the luggage compartment. Brendan wasn't bringing much, he travelled light and we imagined he always would. 'You've most need of this right now,' said Declan, and he handed his brother a holy medal on a leather cord, the one their aunty had passed to him. Brendan smiled and slipped it over his neck. 'I'll visit and make sure you're eating properly,' said Declan.

Brendan stepped over to the bus's door where Christine was waiting for him. She adjusted Brendan's collar and ran her hand down his arm once, from shoulder to elbow. Brendan gave her an easy smile and said, 'Mind yourself.'

Christine closed her eyes and when she opened them again Brendan had climbed aboard. The bus pulled away and she remained watching. Only when Brendan had left her sight did she return to the car to be driven home.

Acknowledgements

I'm very grateful to Pat Conaghan and Pat Nolan for information about boats and the fishing industry in Killybegs. Pat Nolan's books of interviews with fishermen were also invaluable. Any errors are my own. Thank you to Paddy Roche and Cian Brosnan for the photographs. Thanks also to Michael O'Boyle for trawler deck plans and Claire Timoney for sending them.

Thank you to Irene Baldoni for sticking with the Bonnars and the Lyons, and everyone else at my agency: Georgina Capel, Rachel Conway, Polly Halladay and Simon Shaps. The brilliant team at Picador also put a lot of work into this book. Much gratitude to Sophie Jonathan, Mary Mount, Camilla Elworthy, Daisy Dickeson, Mary Chamberlain, Laura Carr, Siobhan Hooper, as well as Reagan Arthur and the team at Knopf: Jordan Pavlin, Maris Dyer, Izzy Meyers, Samantha Bryant and Kathryn Zuckerman.

Further thanks to Aisling Reid, Orla Fitzpatrick, Eve Patten, Laura Sheary, Emma Devlin, Rebecca Hunter, Emily Byers-Ferrian, Louise Kennedy, Ian Sansom and Glenn Patterson, as well as my other colleagues, students and our fellows at the Seamus Heaney Centre at Queen's, Belfast. I'm grateful to Damian Smyth of the Arts Council of Northern Ireland. A shout-out for my neighbours: the Yardies.

A big thank-you to all the translators getting *The Boy from the Sea* into other languages.

Thanks to all the Carrs and all the Sumpters. Love and gratitude to my two boys, Lorcan Patrick Carr and Fabian John Carr. It started with you. And thanks as ever to Caroline, you made it possible.

A NOTE ABOUT THE AUTHOR

Garrett Carr was born in Donegal in 1975. He teaches creative writing at the Seamus Heaney Centre, Queen's University Belfast. He has previously published novels for young adults and a work of non-fiction, *The Rule of the Land: Walking Ireland's Border*. He lives in Belfast.